the LAST SESSION

ALSO BY JULIA BARTZ

The Writing Retreat

the LAST SESSION

A NOVEL

JULIA BARTZ

EMILY BESTLER BOOKS

ATRIA

NEW YORK   AMSTERDAM/ANTWERP   LONDON
TORONTO   SYDNEY/MELBOURNE   NEW DELHI

EMILY
BESTLER
BOOKS

ATRIA

An Imprint of Simon & Schuster, LLC
1230 Avenue of the Americas
New York, NY 10020

First Emily Bestler Books/Atria Books hardcover edition April 2025

EMILY BESTLER BOOKS/ATRIA BOOKS and colophon are trademarks of Simon & Schuster, LLC

Simon & Schuster strongly believes in freedom of expression and stands against censorship in all its forms. For more information, visit BooksBelong.com.

For information about special discounts for bulk purchases, please contact Simon & Schuster Special Sales at 1-866-506-1949 or business@simonandschuster.com.

The Simon & Schuster Speakers Bureau can bring authors to your live event. For more information or to book an event, contact the Simon & Schuster Speakers Bureau at 1-866-248-3049 or visit our website at www.simonspeakers.com.

Manufactured in the United States of America

1   3   5   7   9   10   8   6   4   2

Library of Congress Control Number: 2024950879

ISBN 978-1-9821-9949-4
ISBN 978-1-9821-9951-7 (ebook)

Content warning: Alcohol use disorder, religious abuse, child abuse, sexual harassment and assault, physical violence, murder, cults, psychosis, suicide attempt (off-page).

To those harmed by the communities tasked with protecting them.
May you find healing and a newer, truer home.

Prologue

This is a womb.

That's the image I cling to now, the only one that keeps me from screaming.

My voice has long since gone. My throat is raw and burning and I keep bending over the ledge, cupping the cold water to my mouth to soothe it. I drink until my belly distends and I vomit most of it back up. There's no comfortable position, but it feels best to squeeze myself into a ball, listening to the rushing water thundering through the tiny chamber.

Right over there, much too close, is the body. Normally, it remains underneath the water, waterlogged, but every so often the current pushes it back up. The water's cold, so it's decomposing slowly, but there's still a stench.

Since I first explored this place by touch, I was confused when my fingers met the rancid, jelly-like mass. Then I realized what was in here with me. At that moment sheer horror overtook me and I tried to force myself back through the tunnel I'd come out of, almost drowning myself in the process. Sputtering, swallowing, coughing. The current was superhuman, pushing me back like a hand. I knew even as I struggled that it was pointless. I was trapped.

How long have I been down here? There's no way to know, but it feels like days, weeks. After the initial shock and terror, anger started buzzing through my body, battling with the cold that numbed my fingers and toes. I replayed the scene over and over: standing at the lip of the hole with the others, my chest squeezing in sadness and fear. I hadn't wanted her to go in. But it was what she'd decided. Only: she tricked me. They all did. As she walked up behind me, I didn't even turn. And then: two warm palms on my lower back, shoving me into the swirling void.

Eventually, hunger overtook the anger, steak knives stabbing into my belly. But that receded too. I think you can survive a long time on just water, and I have all the water in the world. I drink where it comes out, away from the corpse.

Now, the cold: that's what will probably kill me. I knew it was important to dry off on the ledge, but even now, I continue to shiver. Sometimes it stops, starts again, like I'm a faulty machine.

The darkness is the worst part, even more than the cold, but I've gotten used to it too. Now it feels like a velvety sleep mask, helping me to drift in and out of consciousness. There's no night or day. Just slow seconds that tick by whenever I happen to be awake.

My mind has become very still, empty, like a flat pond. Every so often the claustrophobic reality breaks the surface: the awareness of the tons of solid rock surrounding me, that immense weight pressing in from all sides. When this happens, all I can do is shriek and keen into my hands. My fingers, scraped and bloody, burn from the salty tears.

New thoughts arise: *This isn't a cave. This is a womb. I am not yet born. I do not yet exist. All I have to do is wait.*

They're soothing and help me drift back to sleep.

At some point, something new happens. Under the rush of water, I hear a voice. At first it's a whisper, a hiss by my ear that sounds so real I sit up and hit my head on the rock ceiling.

But no—of course there's no one else here. There isn't room.

It's just me. My own mind, turning on me.

But it's weird—isn't it?—that I can't quite make out the words. A phrase repeated, either: *Are you the savior?* or *Will you save her?* The whispers are sibilant, snakelike.

Savior/save her?

Save what? Save who? I dwell on the question, lazily, like a stoned person pausing in a stream to pick up an interesting rock. The whispers multiply, meld. Eventually, they become a symphonic kind of lullaby. I drop the interesting rock and lie down in the stream. It's warm, and the sun shines overhead. Something slips against my calf, smooth and scaly. I shiver, wishing it away.

You're not done yet.

The same voice, this time warning in a clear tone. But I *am* done. My mind is shunting inward, slipping out of my grasp, like a phone dropped down a deep well. Right before I turn off completely, I wonder if it's the next life, tapping on my knee, waiting for me to be reborn.

Part One

1

"Why don't we draw our greatest fears?" Ace cocked his head as he handed me back the stack of computer paper. "Or is that too dark?"

"That's an idea." Uncertain, I took my own sheet and set the stack neatly to the side. *Was* it too dark? I'd been thinking of asking the art therapy group to draw their favorite meal, but knew Ace and Lydia would reject it immediately. I was running out of ideas. There was only so much you could do with crayons, the sole approved materials: blunt, soft, safe.

"Don't ask me about those, honey." Lydia swept back her gray-streaked mane. She looked like a well-kempt Upper East Sider, incongruous with the sights and sounds of a public hospital's inpatient psychiatric unit. "That's a door you really don't want to open."

"Why not? Come on! You need to face your fears head-on." Ace spun a red crayon in his fingers. "Right, Dr. Thea? Aren't you always saying that?"

"Ace, you know I'm not a doctor." I'd told him this multiple times to no avail. My coworker Amani had warned me during his first hospitalization, but being a naïve newbie, just off my two-year social work program, I hadn't listened. Ace had seemed so friendly, so *pleasant*. But in addition to manic episodes that caused him to think he had to save the world from human-presenting aliens, he also had a sixth sense for messing with you.

"*Miss* Thea," he corrected amiably, scratching the back of his shaved head.

"And when do I say that?" A bead of sweat rolled down my chest. Outside, the March sky was frigid, gray, and rain-speckled, but in this wing it was always so *hot*.

He stared at me. "Maybe you don't."

"All right." Lydia plucked a black crayon. "Biggest fear. I'm in."

"Great." I jumped up and went to the window, struggling until it burst open — it stopped at two inches, so no one could slide through. Damp, cool air washed over me and I sucked it in greedily. My head ached from last night, when my roommate, Dom, had again canceled our reality-dating-show-and-takeout night and I'd unwisely opened and finished a bottle of sauvignon blanc. The fluorescent lighting did not help with hangovers.

When I came back to the table, everyone was admiring a drawing Lonnie proudly held aloft. He was the best artist of the small group, but didn't follow instructions and always produced something just like this: a naked woman with flowing locks and enormous breasts. I'd tried to fight it, first stern, then cajoling, but it hadn't made a difference. Now I just let it go.

It now seemed strange that I'd made the efforts to start this group in the first place. Past me of only a year ago had been a different person: a second-career thirty-two-year-old who had high hopes, who really thought she could make a difference. Current me, frankly, found her embarrassing.

"A woman," I said evenly to Lonnie. "You're scared of women?"

"Oh, deeply." Lonnie set down the paper and shaded in his subject's hair — orange, just like mine. I'd been shocked to find out Lonnie had been a college professor decades before. He'd gone on medication after his first psychotic break in his thirties, but had stopped taking it, devolved into psychosis, and subsequently lost his job and home. Recently he'd been taken into police custody after threatening people on a subway platform, and we were in the process of transferring him to a longer-term care facility.

"Are you fucking kidding me?" Lydia paused in her scribbling. "You think *women* are the scary ones?" She caught my eye, colluding with me.

"Maybe what you're afraid of is intimacy, Lonnie?" I tried to sound open, curious. "That would make sense. A lot of people fear — "

"Nope." He pointed the orange crayon at me. "*You.* All of you."

"I think Lon has a point." Ace sat back, folding his arms. "Because men are physically stronger, y'all have come up with your own weapons. Mental ones."

"Mind control?" Lydia looked skeptical, but Lonnie nodded vigorously.

"Exactly!" He stabbed the figure's right boob with the crayon. "My ex-wife was so good at manipulating me, I would've done anything for her. And you know how she repaid me? Stole all my money and ran off with our goddamn dog walker."

Lonnie's stories about his ex-wife changed daily. It was actually interesting how he mythologized her. I didn't know if she'd even really existed. Lonnie was mostly stabilized by meds at this point but occasionally seemed to lose his grip on reality.

"They know *just* what to say." Ace nodded sagely.

Lydia scoffed. "That's ridiculous. You want to talk about what *we* have to put up with? Fear of men attacking us, raping us, *killing* us."

"Here we go." Ace rolled his eyes.

"Oh, so it's not true? So I'm just making it up? You hearing this, Red?" She turned to me, but I concentrated on dumping out more crayons. There were incredibly disturbing stats on women and domestic violence, of course—but I also knew jumping into the fray would just make it worse.

"Calm down." Lonnie waved a dismissive hand.

"You're just going to sit there and let them talk shit about us?" she asked me, her volume increasing.

"Why don't we focus on the prompt. What are you drawing?" Hopefully, I could head off one of her rages, which were rare but legendary. Before she could answer, Ben, the fourth and mostly silent member of our group, let out a prolonged groan. He held the sides of his head and stared down at his paper as if he'd made an unforgiveable artistic mistake.

"Shut up, Ben," Lydia spat. For some reason, she treated him like a bratty teen instead of the half-catatonic sixty-year-old he was. He was on a powerful dose of meds for schizophrenia and was also in the process of being moved to another care facility. He'd spent most of his time in the TV room, but had shown up for art therapy the previous week, where he'd peacefully doodled cartoon characters.

"Hey." Ace straightened. "Don't talk to him that way."

"Or what?" Lydia faced him. "You'll use one of your trusty male weapons? Kill me? Rape me?"

"Don't worry, honey." Ace smirked at Lonnie, who smirked back. "No chance of that."

"Oh, I'm too old and gross, huh?" Lydia stood so fast her chair fell over. "Is that what you're saying, you piece of shit?"

"Hey." I set down a crayon. "Everyone, let's just—"

"You got it!" Ace chuckled, unbothered. "No one wants to see your ugly ass."

Lydia's pale face flushed tomato-soup red.

"Watch out!" Lonnie called, gleeful. "The old hag will slit your throat."

"Stop." I said it loudly, but no one paid attention.

"Maybe I *will* slit your goddamn throat," Lydia yelled, her shout bouncing around the small room.

"*What* is going on in here?"

We all turned. My boss, Diane, stood in the doorway, eyebrows near her hairline.

"Nothing." As if a switch had been flipped, Lydia calmly plopped back in her seat. Ace and Lonnie went back to coloring, docile as schoolboys.

"Well, it doesn't sound like nothing." Diane strode in, her trademark block-heeled pumps clicking on the floor. Diane was only a little over five foot two, but the power she held here was incredible. I'd brought it up once with Amani. *Transference.* She'd shrugged. *Everyone sees Diane as Mommy.*

"Hi, Diane." Guilt and embarrassment flooded my system. I felt like my teacher had asked me to monitor the classroom and returned to find that I'd completely lost control.

Diane stood behind Ben's chair, peering down at the scribbles. Lonnie had deftly flipped his paper over and was now drawing a large tree.

Lydia offered Diane a rare grin. Several of her lower teeth were stubs, melted by meth use. She'd been brought in after having a psychotic break at her inpatient rehab program, where she'd punched her roommate. We were hoping the program would take her back.

"We're just talking about our greatest fears." Lydia tapped her paper. "I was going to draw a clown. They freak me out."

"Mine is intimacy," Ace jumped in smoothly. He pointed to his paper, where he'd quickly drawn two stick people next to each other.

"Oh yeah?" Diane peered down. She'd been unsure about the art group to begin with.

"Ben's fear is failure," Ace went on, unable to keep an amused smile off his face.

"That's a pretty . . . intense prompt." Diane looked over at me.

"Our idea," Lydia said quickly. "Not hers. She wanted us to draw our favorite animal."

Now they were protecting me. The hangover headache resurged.

"Sorry if we were getting loud," I said. "People were feeling real passion for the topic."

"Okay. Well." Diane stepped back. *Clack.* "Thea, can you come to my office when you're done here? There's something we need to talk about."

"Ooh," Ace murmured under his breath, like I was getting called to the principal's office.

"Sure," I said breezily.

Diane left and the rest of the hour passed slowly. Ace, Lydia, and Lonnie continued to quibble, but the dangerous tension of earlier had dissipated. At the end I gathered up the crayons as the others threw their papers away.

"What's that?" Lydia pointed to the paper I'd mindlessly scribbled at. Before I could look down, she snatched it and held it aloft.

"Is this a *cunt*?" Her voice was gleeful.

And I guess you could see it that way: a scribbled space, becoming darker in the center.

"Something on your mind?" Ace winked. "You know, I could give you some tips."

"Caves." I said it quickly, willing the incoming blush down. If I blushed in front of them, I was done for. "I have a fear of caves."

"Scary," Lonnie agreed in a rare moment of solidarity. Maybe he was just glad I'd let him draw breasts the whole time. They walked out together, chattering, Lydia taking Ben's arm to lead him back to the TV room. I was reminded ridiculously of *The Breakfast Club*.

I stared at my paper for a moment. I hadn't really been thinking of it—I'd mostly been pondering what Diane wanted to talk to me about, and where to get lunch—but I *had* dreamed about a cave last night. I'd been trapped in a tiny space. I didn't remember the dream, just the setting: cold, damp, wet.

The memory triggered a curl of terror in my chest. I crumpled the paper up and tossed it in the trash with the others.

2

I stayed in the conference room a minute longer, breathing in the still-ness before opening the door. Thudding music and piercing basic cable news blasted from the nearby TV room. Halfway down the hall, a patient shouted at full volume, but as I approached he went back to muttering. Several other patients paced the hall, two of them silent, one laughing to himself. While the art therapy patients were pretty lucid, many others—because of medications or difficult diagnoses—were not.

At Diane's office I knocked, pausing in the open doorway. She motioned me in, setting down her phone. A Black woman in her fifties, Diane was consistently poised, her raspberry lipstick always perfectly in place. Her ability to stay regulated sometimes amazed me.

"Thea. You have time for a new patient?" She watched me expectantly.

I cleared my throat. "Yes, of course."

"Good. I have a new admission; she just came from observation." Diane handed me a folder. "Jane Doe. Found wandering the Brooklyn–Queens Expressway three days ago; police brought her to CPEP for eval. No drugs or alcohol in her system. But really no other info."

"What did she say?"

"Nothing." Diane paused. "She's mute."

"Selectively?"

"We don't know. But so far, she hasn't said a word." Diane smoothed her braids, which were twisted into a low bun. "That might change; we'll see. She's a 9.39 for now; we set her up in Block D. One milligram of Ativan TID. I want you to keep an eye on her."

9.39 meant that we could involuntarily hold Jane Doe for up to fifteen days. Diane often asked us to watch out for the younger female patients, though for the most part they were able to hold their own against any SAO (sexually acting out) by other patients.

"Of course," I said crisply. I often felt like I had to prove myself to

Diane, though I suspected that tendency came more from my own insecurities than her expectations.

"Bring some paper." Diane shrugged. "Maybe she'll write something down for us."

I glanced through the intake form and psychiatric evaluation notes as I headed to Block D, one of the female-only rooms. The notes were carefully handwritten and more descriptive than usual.

White female
Age unknown (20s/30s?)
No drugs/alc in system according to tox report
Arrived wearing new clothes—sweatshirt still had Target tag
Fingers scraped and scabbed—one fingernail half torn off
Scratches and bruises along arms + legs
PT refuses to make eye contact or speak
PT can do basic functions (eat, urinate) when prompted
Working diagnosis: Psychosis Not Otherwise Specified
Differential diagnosis/Rule out: substances not showing up in tox
    report, organic etiologies, schizophrenia vs bipolar/MDD with
    psychotic features, acute stress disorder

The back of my neck prickled. The unit was always full of a variety of patients cycling in and out, but the root causes of their issues were normally pretty straightforward: untreated disorders, lack of housing and resources, drug use, often connected and exacerbated by a societal lack of support.

This case seemed less obvious. What had happened to this woman?

Lonnie stood motionless in the entrance to Block D, hands pressed to the sides of the doorway.

"Lonnie. You know you're not allowed here."

He turned slowly, then smiled. "Hello, Thea."

"Time to go." I tried to say the words with authority, like Diane would. But he just watched me, eyes narrowed. "I'm serious."

"I know her." He nodded with his chin. "I think we dated."

"I think that's probably unlikely. But whatever the case, you can't be here."

Femi, one of the nurses, strode by, watching us openly. Lonnie pushed off the door, gliding in the opposite direction. I exhaled, relieved he hadn't dug his heels in.

It smelled ripe in here: stale sheets tinged with metallic sweat. Three of the beds were filled with sleeping women, their bedding gently rising and falling. The meds and boredom meant many people were sleeping at any given time, despite the noise pouring in from the hallway.

At the back of the room, Jane Doe was on her side facing the wall. When I skirted the bed, I found her eyes wide open and staring. It made my stomach dip with eerie unreality, like I was looking at a doll or mannequin.

Her pale face was bare of makeup, her hair greasy, but she was conventionally attractive: big green eyes, sharp cheekbones, full mouth. I found my hand going automatically to the back of my head. She had the same thick copper hair as me.

That was weird. Had Diane assigned her to me because we looked kind of similar?

Of course not. It was just a coincidence. I wasn't the only redhead in the world.

But it was more than that. Beyond the similar features, she looked— she *felt*—familiar. Crouching down, I studied her. Where had I seen her before? Maybe a party?

Her eyes stayed trained on the wall behind me. I followed her gaze to the scribbled-over wall, where bubble letters spelled out EAT SHIT. One hand was curled by her side, bandages covering several fingers, which jarred me back into my role.

"Hi there," I said in a soft voice. "My name's Thea. I'm the social worker who will be working with you. Diane told me you just got here today. If you need anything, you can let me know."

No response.

"In the meantime, if there's anything you want to tell me, I'll leave this . . . shit." The word popped out, unbidden, as I realized I hadn't brought paper *or* a pen. "I'll come back with some writing supplies."

"Be careful." The sharp words came from the next bed. Another patient, Shana, propped herself up on one elbow. "I don't trust that bitch one bit. And you're giving her a pen? She might stab me in my sleep."

"No one's going to stab you," I said.

Her forehead creased, but then she just rolled her eyes. Her head dropped to her pillow. "Whatever. Maybe she'll get you first."

3

"She looks like me." I dropped the take-out bag on the glass coffee table, the rich, spicy scent of pad see ew and fried rice making my stomach growl. "People are calling her Hot Thea."

"Seriously?" Dom was half in the fridge, rummaging for IPAs. "They said that in front of you?"

"Well, not to my face." I settled on the couch, unboxing the spring rolls. It felt like a relief to spill to Dom, whom I'd barely seen over the last few weeks. She'd texted that afternoon, asking if I was down to reschedule takeout-and-TV for that night. *Last Chance Love*, a reality show where undateables went through a dating boot camp before being paired with their "perfect match," had been our favorite show all through grad school.

"I overheard this patient say it to someone." I dug into my noodles. "Lydia. To her credit, I don't think she knew I was right behind her."

"Was Lydia the one who asked when you last got laid?" Dom settled next to me.

"Yes! Same person." That had been an interesting art therapy session. She and Ace had proceeded to discuss how old they thought I was, and whether or not I'd want dinner first. My chest warmed that Dom remembered. Early in the job, she'd convinced me to stay when I'd felt completely overwhelmed.

"You know more than you think," Dom had said then. "And you're naturally caring. You listen. You want to help."

It had been encouraging, even though it was also easy for her to say. Dom's wealthy parents had connected her to the sex therapist she now worked for. An inpatient unit was laughably different from chatting with clients about their love lives.

"Well, I think *you're* the Hot Thea." She opened her beer and took a deep gulp. "But maybe you can have some kind of gladiator-style competition to see who comes out on top."

"I'm down."

"Of course you're down. You'd *win*. It's always the nice ones who're the most vicious."

I chuckled. I'd missed this, our easy banter. Dom and I had connected over a group project early in grad school. She was a second-career therapist, like me, but she'd come from the fashion world and was herself model-like: tall, long-limbed, with a pushed-back crop of short blond hair and a dazzling smile. When she found out I was new to the city, she'd planned various nearby outings in between classes: getting classic New York–style pizza, visiting a hole-in-the-wall bookstore, downing a pickleback at a dim-lit pub. For a short time, I'd had a crush on her. While I'd always identified as straight, it had made me giddy to wonder if her attention went beyond friendliness. But I'd soon realized that many people felt this way—Dom was charismatic and flirty, and had quickly started dating several women and a nonbinary student in our program.

To my surprise, Dom had continued our friendship even after the semester ended. Our second year, she'd asked if I wanted to move into a two-bedroom she'd found. I'd jumped at the chance, even though the rent was more than I could afford.

"Anyway." I speared a shrimp. "It's still driving me nuts. I could swear I know her from somewhere."

"The mirror?"

"It's not just that," I protested. "I've seen her before. Her specifically."

"Hmm. Long-lost twin? Alternate reality Thea?" Dom scooped up a forkful of rice. "The possibilities are endless."

"Truly." I grabbed the remote. "Okay. Ready to see Hunter meet Tiff's family?"

"Uh, yeah. One sec." She leaned forward, unfurling like a spider, and set her container on the coffee table. "There's something I wanted to talk to you about."

"Sure." I felt a flash of unease.

"So . . ." She fixed her slate-gray eyes on me. "Amelia and I have been getting more serious. And we've decided to move in together."

I froze, shocked. *Amelia?* Dom was nonmonogamous and often dating multiple people. Had I heard the name Amelia before? I definitely hadn't met her.

"Sorry, who?" I asked.

"I met her at the sex toy expo last summer. We were casual through the fall, but then this winter . . . I don't know, something just clicked. You probably noticed I'm, like, never here."

"I have noticed that."

"I'm always at Amelia's." Dom shrugged. "She has a rad apartment, but unfortunately her building got bought and everyone's getting kicked out. So . . . since our lease is up, too, I thought it seemed like perfect timing."

"Oh. I see." Panic surged up through my chest. Was I going to have to find a new roommate? Share a bathroom with a complete stranger? The other option was living in a tiny studio far away, which I'd done throughout grad school. I couldn't go back to that. Especially not when I was still recovering from my breakup with Ryan two months before.

Dom took a long sip, studying me.

"Are you still dating other people?" I asked.

"We decided to just focus on each other for now. But we may open up again down the road." A cute smile pulled at her lips. "It's just . . . God, I don't know. I'm in love! I haven't felt this way in so long. Not since Mara."

"That's great." I tried to smile. "I'm so happy for you."

"I'm sorry to spring it on you like this."

"No, I get it." I kept my interested expression fixed. "Are you finding a new place?"

"No, she'll move in here." Dom looked around, considering. "She's at a private practice, too, but all of her sessions are virtual, so we figured we'd turn the second bedroom into an office."

Oh. So I was getting kicked out. Okay. Tears formed behind my eyes, but I held them at bay.

"I hope that's cool." She touched my forearm. "I'm going to miss living with you."

"Me too," I managed. "But it's fine. I totally understand."

"Good." She leaned back, relieved. "I'm sure you can find something nearby. Oh, and Amelia's cousin works at a moving company; she can totally get you a deal."

"Great." I shoved a spring roll in my mouth so I wouldn't have to speak.

"Thanks for being so chill about this." She picked up her rice. "I know things have been tough for you after the breakup."

So she did remember. It felt too vulnerable to agree, so I downplayed it. "I'd barely call it that. We dated for like four months."

Her brow wrinkled. "Yeah, but it sounded pretty serious. Weren't you calling him your boyfriend?"

"For like a week." I tried to laugh, but it sounded more like a honk.

"Commitment-phobe." She shook her head.

Maybe that had been part of it. But it wasn't the main reason. I envisioned Ryan staring at me, his mouth twisted in disgust.

I hadn't told Dom the full story. I knew she'd be more open-minded— she was training to be a sex therapist, after all—but if there was even a flicker of judgment in her eyes, I wouldn't be able to handle it.

Instead, I'd broken down and texted my former therapist, Cynthia. She hadn't responded.

"Any dates on the horizon?" Dom dug cheerfully into her food. "Are you on the apps?"

"I was, but it's just . . ." What was the best term: Depressing? Exhausting? Demoralizing?

During grad school, I'd widened my search to include women and nonbinary people after my brief infatuation with Dom. It had felt weirdly anticlimactic, maybe because I was in a progressive program and there were lots of queer people around me. Of course, I struggled with impostor syndrome, and I also knew my parents would have major issues if I dated someone who wasn't a man. But I hadn't yet had to worry about it—getting people to message back on the apps, much less plan to meet in person, often seemed near-impossible.

That's why Ryan, who I'd met in person at a social worker happy hour, had seemed like such a godsend.

"Probably not a great time of year to date. Everyone's depressed." Dom tapped her beer can. "I'm sure things will pick up soon."

I forced a smile. "I'm sure."

4

For the rest of the week, I kept an eye on Jane Doe, increasingly certain I knew her. Every time I stopped in her room to study her blank, frozen face, the feeling grew.

If only I could talk to her. If only I could find out what had happened to her—something so presumably horrific that it had caused her conscious mind to shut down.

On Monday morning, I came into a flurry in the break room: joyful voices ringing out, growing louder as I approached.

"Gorgeous!" Rachel was gushing to Amani. The twentysomething new hire was nice enough, but I disliked how she constantly used the royal "we," bringing her boyfriend into every conversation. I'd always been vaguely annoyed by people who did this, shoving the reality of their relationship—the fact that they'd been somehow *chosen*—into my usually single face.

Now, she hoisted Amani's wrist. "Thea, look! Our girl's enga-a-aged!"

"Oh, wow. Congratulations!" I took Amani's hand, exclaiming over it like a courtier, the way you were supposed to. "It's beautiful! Derek did a great job." I let go and Rachel snatched her hand back, examining the ring like a jeweler.

"Thanks." Amani smiled demurely. "He let me pick it out, thank God. Otherwise I don't know what you'd be looking at."

"Tell her how he did it." Rachel nudged her.

I kept my face ecstatic as Amani shared the proposal, which involved their first-date restaurant and the ring dropped in a glass of champagne.

While Dom was my aspirationally nontraditional friend, Amani was the opposite. A stunningly pretty biracial woman, she'd been with her boyfriend for years and wanted to get married and have kids soon, even though she was only twenty-six. At thirty-three, I didn't know what I wanted. Admittedly, I'd fantasized about a more traditional life with Ryan. After all, that was the way I'd been raised: in a conservative town, to Christian parents, where the path to partners and parenthood was so straightforward. But there was a reason I'd left.

Still, a weight sat in my stomach as I did my morning rounds. Why did it seem so easy for certain people to find their person?

Maybe because they don't have disgusting, shameful secrets like you. The insidious thoughts rose like smoke. *Ones that cause people to dump you instantly.*

I tried to push them away as I approached Block D. Lonnie was again in the doorway. But this time he clearly had an erection.

"Lonnie, you can't be here." This wasn't the first time I'd seen someone masturbating at work, but something about it being Lonnie disturbed me.

He pulled his eyes away and focused on me. "What?"

"You. Cannot. Be. Here." I pointed to his groin. "Do I need to call someone?" I knew he hated being put on observation, which we did for patients acting sexual or aggressive.

He scoffed, straightening his glasses. The ghostly air of his past professorship came through. "No need for dramatics."

"Then you need to leave."

He raised both hands. "It's not my fault. Look at what she's wearing."

I peered in the door. Jane Doe was sitting on her bed, facing the back of the room, wearing one of the standard-issue sports bras given to female clients. Her shirt was laid out neatly beside her like a nurse had been called away in the midst of dressing her. The nurses had to do everything for her: walk her into the shower and soap her up and rinse her. Sit her on the toilet every few hours so she wouldn't soil her pants like she had the second day. Feed her with a spoon.

"She's doing it on purpose, you know." Lonnie spit the words out, his face now rigid with anger. "She's fooling us all. She's a spy; can't you see that?"

Before I could respond, he strode off, muttering to himself.

I took a deep breath and went into the room. One of the other patients' gentle snores sounded like purrs.

"Hi there," I said in a soothing singsong as I approached Jane Doe. Diane had encouraged me to talk to her, even if she didn't show any signs of hearing. "It's me, Thea. Looks like you need a little help getting dressed today."

She sat hunched over, her hands curled in her lap. A strand of drool wet her chin. I watched her for a moment, considering Lonnie's words. He was stretching it with the spy thing, but it wouldn't have been the first time someone had faked mutism or catatonia. According to Amani, one patient had done just that two years ago. It had ended when he'd been caught making calls in the bathroom. He'd owed dangerous people money and thought the locked doors, security cameras, and security guards would protect him. I'd wondered what had happened to him after he'd been kicked out.

But Jane Doe . . . It was clear to me, at least, that she truly wasn't here. That she'd retreated to some back corner of her brain.

I picked up the shirt, noticing a tattoo on her pale, sunken chest, over her heart. It looked like a symbol or hieroglyph about two inches high. I didn't remember reading about a tattoo in her chart.

I leaned closer. The symbol was a spiral inside a triangle, with dots at different intervals along the curve of the spiral.

I'd seen it before. The small tug of recognition ignited a spark of excitement.

But where? I couldn't remember. If I could look it up, though . . . it had to be online.

I looked to the bedside table for the pad and pen before remembering another patient had presumably taken them. I pulled my phone out of my back pocket, and before I could even pause and question it, I took a photo. The sound was on and the loud click in the quiet room made me flinch.

"Okay." I slipped the phone back and stood. "Let's get you dressed." It was surprisingly hard to wrangle an item of clothing onto someone who did nothing to help you. But as I pushed her cold hands through the sleeves, I also shoved away the remorse and fear rearing up.

Taking a picture of a shirtless female patient—I could get fired for that.

But another part argued back.

You did it for a reason.

It's a clue to who she is, what she went through.

You're just trying to help.

5

As soon as I got home that night, I grabbed my laptop to research Jane Doe's tattoo. I'd felt vaguely guilty the entire day with the shirtless photo on my phone. But now my unease switched to anticipation. With a quick Google search I found a free, ads-laden site called Shapefinder. As directed by the site, I drew the symbol on a piece of paper, then took a picture and uploaded it. I clicked *FIND SHAPE*, as weirdly excited as a kid holding a wrapped present. What—of everything in the world—was within it?

But the top result was a letdown: *NO HITS*.

I let out my breath. Really? Nowhere in the vast universe of the internet?

Below the result were the words: *DID YOU MEAN?* and a row of symbols. I clicked on the first one, which showed a spiral within a box.

Symbol for Nehebkau, one of the original Egyptian gods who took the form of a snake. Nehebkau's name means "to unite." He was thought to yoke the ka (double or spirit) with the physical body. Before creation he lived in the waters of Nun with other primordial gods.

Okay. So Jane Doe's tattoo was somewhat similar to a hieroglyph. Which made sense. I'd seen various hipsters in Brooklyn with ankh necklaces; at a yoga class I'd listened to a teacher explain the goddess Isis. Maybe this was the new wave in (cue eye roll) white girl spiritual chic?

Jane Doe's blank eyes shone like headlights, cutting a path through my mind. The feeling returned, more strongly than ever, that I knew her. And that the answer was right there, if only I could unlock it. The symbol hadn't shaken anything loose, specifically, but a surety spread through my chest. For some reason, it felt *right* for Jane Doe to have this tattoo. But why?

My phone pinged. **Hey!** Dom had written cheerfully, as if we hadn't been avoiding each other. **Here's a 10% code for Amelia's cuz's moving co!**

"Wow," I said out loud. "Thanks *so* much." But there was no point in sharing my hurt. And to be fair, Dom *had* found the apartment originally. I opened Facebook Marketplace to keep searching. I had new message notifications; a few were apartment-related, but my eyes went immediately to the message from Melissa Bellmont, paired with a friend request.

My body went still, my breath waiting in my lungs, as I clicked.

> Hi Thea! I'm co-heading the committee for the 20-year OSLS 8th grade reunion. Can you believe it's been 20 years???? I know we've fallen out of touch, and you live in New Yawk now, but if you're interested in being on the mailing list, LMK, I don't think I have your current email. Here's the <u>FB page for the reunion</u>. If you can't make it, I'd still love to see you sometime, LMK if you're ever back here in town. XOXO M

With a sick, sliding feeling in my gut, I clicked on the link. The Facebook page featured a scanned photo of twenty-three eighth graders in front of a playground. Some of the boys were casually hanging out on top of the monkey bars. My eyes went immediately to Adam, his dark curls tousled by the breeze. He was flanked by Scott and Mike, who were always there to laugh hysterically at his insults. Then I scanned for the blurry, unsmiling girl standing next to the slide. There she was: her shoulders curved in, her frizzy red bangs covering her face. My younger self. Melissa's arm slung around her shoulders. This must've been taken before Melissa had moved into the cool group. At least in the beginning, she'd protected me. She'd had no idea what had happened, or rather—at the time this picture was taken—would happen.

> 20 YEAR REUNION!!!!! We can't believe it's been 2 decades either!!! If you missed the 5, 10, or 15th year reunion, NOW is the time to return to the community that made you who you are today!!!! Tickets include a full night of swanky fun: dinner, drinks, and dancing. Contact Pam Felcher or Melissa Bellmont with any questions.

Special guests include: Mrs. Hobbs, Principal Duffy, and Pastor John—

I slammed the screen down.

I sat there for a moment, mind swirling, then threw the computer on the couch and went to the bathroom. I washed my hands, staring at myself in the mirror.

"You're fine," I told my reflection. I looked dazed, my freckles standing out more than usual against my pale skin. My eyes were ringed by blue circles, despite the concealer I'd spackled on. I hadn't been sleeping well since the breakup.

In the kitchen, I pulled out the vodka. This called for a drink. Multiple drinks. The message from Melissa had opened the floodgates, and even as I took my giant gimlet back to the couch and turned on the TV, I couldn't help but feel like I was back there, where I'd been frozen in time, at thirteen.

A year ago, Mom had gone on a Marie Kondo binge and had mailed me my old papers, drawings, and diaries. I'd tossed most of the assignments and art, but hadn't been able to get rid of the diaries. Especially the one from eighth grade, with the grinning cartoon cat face on the front. Instead, I'd shoved them as far back in the closet as they'd go.

But it wasn't that simple. Even though I could keep the memories locked away most of the time, there was one situation where they'd undoubtedly resurface:

If I wanted to have an orgasm.

It felt particularly cruel that everything that had happened with Pastor John and Adam that year would become what my sexuality would grow around, like a pearl forming around a rough grain of sand. Last year on a Reddit deep dive, I'd found the term "trauma-informed kink," which seemed related, but not totally accurate. After all, it wasn't like I *enjoyed* what I had to do, to revisit, in my mind. It was just necessary for me to get off.

I'd never told anyone, imagining the horror that would spread over their face. I hadn't even told my previous therapist Cynthia, the shame just too sharp. But with Ryan, I thought it'd be different. After all, he was a social worker, too, and the most understanding and sensitive man I'd ever dated. I'd felt at first a tug and then an urgent need to open up to him, to show him this part of me that felt so embarrassing and ugly.

After he asked me to be exclusive, I couldn't hold it in any longer. I spilled one night while we were cuddling in sweaty sheets postsex. Ryan was the first man I'd been able to have sex with completely sober, something that would've blown my mind in my twenties. I'd never felt this safe and loved before.

"Can I tell you something?" I asked. "Something I've never told anyone?"

"Of course." His eyes widened with anticipation.

So I told him. I watched his eyes go from sleepy to alert to, finally, pissed off.

And then, when I finished, he slipped out of bed and started putting his clothes on.

"What are you doing?" I asked, my voice caught in my throat.

He paused to look at me, his lips pressed in a line behind his beard. "I'm not sure what to say, Thea. Other than that makes me feel extremely uncomfortable. I'm not cool with it."

"Well, I'm not either." I wanted to melt quietly into the bed but forced myself to sit up. "I thought . . . I wanted to tell you because it's something I struggle with. I don't *enjoy* it. I hate it, actually."

"Okay. Well, what are you doing about it? Are you working on it in therapy?"

"I told you—Cynthia moved away."

"That was like a year ago. Why haven't you gotten another therapist?"

"I've just been busy." I looked down. "With work." The truth was that when Cynthia had left so quickly—announcing her two-week departure after years of working together, years in which she'd helped me survive COVID alone in a tiny studio in Queens—I'd felt completely blindsided and burned. I couldn't even imagine starting all over again, trying to trust someone who might end up dropping me in the same way.

And I knew it was hopeless, anyway. I'd tried many times to have an orgasm without dipping back into the memory—but it just didn't work. It was like trying to unlock a door without the key.

Ryan clapped the back of his jeans to check for his wallet, and I forced myself to continue. "Maybe I'm not explaining it right. I didn't mean to offend you."

"I mean, what do you expect? You're using my body like a sex doll."

He raised his hands. "Not that there's anything wrong with sex dolls. But I'm not okay being used in that way."

"That's not what it's like," I protested, but Ryan was already striding out of the room.

I sat there stunned, listening to him gathering his things. By the time I pulled my discarded dress over my head and went out into the living room, the door was slamming shut behind him.

If only Dom had been there that night. Maybe I would've told her what had happened. Maybe she would've responded more kindly than Ryan had.

But instead I drank a bottle of wine, cried, and passed out in bed.

The next head-splitting morning I was still mortified but trying to figure out what to text him to make this okay. Maybe I could pretend it had been a joke? But then my phone dinged.

I'm sorry. I can't do this.

I wrote back immediately: Can we talk?

No response.

Ever.

I'd texted Cynthia that night, saying I know she'd moved away but I really needed to talk to her. She, too, had failed to respond. I'd waited for a day, two days. I couldn't believe that this woman I'd spilled my guts to, someone whose kindness and wisdom had made me want to become a social worker myself, would just ignore me.

But she did.

And so finally, I decided there was only one way forward. I might be irrevocably sexually broken, yes, but other people didn't need to know.

I would just not make the mistake of telling anyone ever again.

6

The next day, I figured out who Jane Doe was.

It happened in the morning. I'd gotten in earlier than usual and was taking the time to stalk Dom and Amelia on Instagram. Dom rarely ever posted—until now, when she'd put up a ton of lovey-dovey photos with Amelia: kissing in a red-lit lounge, grinning lazily over brunch, driving somewhere in hip sunglasses—where were they even? It looked rural . . .

Amelia had a luxurious mane and a cute gap in her front teeth. She and Dom together looked like actor/models who'd met on a movie set.

"Morning!" Amani sailed towards the coffee machine. "How're you?"

"Hi! I'm fine." And I *was* fine. Dom had originally found the apartment, and she was now allowed to bring in Amelia. I couldn't have expected us to live together forever anyway.

"How are *you*?" I turned to Amani. "Any wedding planning happening yet?"

She rolled her eyes as she poured a mug. "We had an argument about it last night. Derek has no concept of how much work is going to be involved. I think I'm going to demand a wedding planner." She settled at the table next to me. "What's been going on? Hey, weren't you supposed to go on that date . . ."

"They canceled." I rubbed my eyes. "It's just so much freaking work. Sometimes I wish I lived in a small village and had only two viable options to choose from."

"But that's the cool part," she protested. "I never would've met Derek in person—we moved here at different times, lived in different neighborhoods, and worked in different industries." She smirked. "And he's so different from the guys I used to date."

"In . . ."

"College. High school."

"What about junior high?" The question triggered that anxious, edgy feeling I'd had seeing the reunion Facebook page. "Did you date then?"

"I had a boyfriend." Amani stared into space. It made sense, her being one of those girls who aways had someone holding her hand, carrying her books. "Jared."

"Was he nice?"

"Nope. He cheated on me with my friend." She chuckled. "Kissed her at our eighth-grade graduation party at Dave & Buster's. Total shit show."

"Yikes. I'm sorry."

"Yeah. I decided: only nice guys from now on. Though I had to learn the lesson a few more times." She shrugged. "What about you?"

This was the great thing about social worker colleagues: everyone always asked questions back.

"I didn't date at all back then. I was way too shy and nerdy." The words felt slightly hollow. That was true, of course. But in some ways, I had felt like I'd been in a relationship.

Suddenly, I felt like I needed to tell someone what had happened the night before. "Speaking of junior high, I got a random Facebook message from my former BFF." I filled Amani in, watching her eyes widen.

"You have to go!" She sprayed granola particles in her enthusiasm.

"No way. I'd never want to see any of them again." At her consternation, I continued. "It was a Christian school — just twenty-three of us in the grade. There was bullying, that kind of stuff."

"Oh." Amani became more subdued. "I see."

"I wonder if it was easier or harder being a thirteen-year-old in — what year was that?"

She chuckled. "We're only a few years apart."

"But that can make such a difference!" I cried. "You're — what, twenty-six? I'm thirty-three. So that's . . . wow, seven years. What was popular back then, do you remember?" This felt weirdly compelling, connecting our thirteen-year-old selves across space and time.

"Well, we loved the movie *Ricky's Room*." Amani laughed. "We'd get high on candy and drool over Charlie Becker."

"He was after my time. But I had some major crushes too. Do you remember Sebastian Smith?"

She stared blankly.

"You don't know Sebastian Smith?" I asked.

"Maybe it sounds familiar?"

"Oh my god. He was gorgeous. And talented. It was actually really tragic; he died young, in his twenties." I pulled out my phone, googled, and showed her a moody black-and-white portrait.

"Oh, he's cute." She considered. "He kind of looks like Leonardo DiCaprio in *Titanic*."

At least she'd seen *that*. "Yeah, he had the same floppy early 2000s hair." Warm nostalgia spread through my ribs. "Melissa and I really thought we were in love with him. He was in this bizarre movie that we loved: *Stargirl*." Something twitched in the back of my brain.

"*Stargirl*," Amani echoed.

"Have you seen it?" I asked eagerly.

"No. But if you saw it at thirteen I was only—what. Six?"

I clicked back to the images of Sebastian. Many were from his heyday as a young teen: middle-parted blond hair, large blue eyes, freckled snub nose. He looked so young, delicate, even feminine. Maybe that's why Melissa and I had liked him. Compared to older men with muscular arms and bulges in their pants, Sebastian was pretty and safe.

"What was *Stargirl* about?" Amani asked. Clearly, she didn't want to start work today either.

"It was kind of bizarre. It was about this Egyptian priestess." I typed it in. The Rotten Tomatoes ratings showed a 22 percent critical score and 31 percent audience score. The still images from the film reminded me of the other reason I'd liked the movie so much: the actress who'd played the titular *Stargirl*, a thirteen-year-old redhead and Sebastian's love interest, had looked a little like me. I googled the cast. The picture of Sebastian was from when he was older—still acting but swiftly moving towards his death by heroin overdose. His feminine features had morphed, his large eyes alien-seeming in his gaunt face.

"Egyptian priestess?" Amani echoed.

"Yeah. She was in love with this guard, played by Sebastian. But . . . yeah, I think she was also having an affair with the king?" The actress was Catherine O'Brien. Of course.

"Scandalous." Amani yawned and stood, grabbing her purse and walking to the lockers.

And it *had* been scandalous. Melissa and I had snuck into the R-rated film after buying tickets for a PG movie. We'd both been shocked and titillated by how someone our age could be so tantalizing that adult men couldn't stop themselves from seducing her. Thinking back now, it was quite horrifying that a thirteen-year-old could be sexualized to that degree. But at the time, at least in my memory, most people hadn't questioned it. Maybe because it had been set in "ancient" times?

I clicked on Catherine O'Brien's headshot. I remembered that she'd dated Sebastian IRL after the movie—which had caused it to seem even more romantic. The pictures that popped up mostly showed her as a teen, her red tresses blow-dried into the chunky layers people had back then. Wow. She really *had* looked a lot like me, more than I remembered. I scrolled down and paused on one of the few pictures of her as an adult.

My stomach dropped.

"Amani." I waved her over and showed her the screen.

She squinted. "This is . . . the actress?"

My mouth was suddenly dry. I licked my lips. "Who does that look like?"

"What do you mean?"

The photo showed twentysomething Catherine on a white leather couch in a chambray shirt, smiling serenely into the camera.

All the pieces locked into place.

"It's Jane Doe." An immense relief settled over me. I *had* known her.

"What?" Amani grabbed my phone. "Oh my god." She went on, her speech rapid, but I didn't hear. It was like scratching an itch I'd had for days; I luxuriated in it, the answer to all the persistent questions.

"*Thea.*" Amani handed my phone back. "We need to tell Diane. I mean, this is her, right? It looks exactly like her!"

"Yeah." I stood, taking a swig of my cooled coffee, feeling tranquil. "We do."

On the way to Diane's office, a memory popped up. At thirteen, I'd been so fascinated by Catherine—and by how she'd mesmerized Sebastian—that when I'd read she favored Clinique Happy perfume, I'd stolen a twenty from Mom's purse to buy it at JCPenney at the mall. I'd never done anything like that before; I was always the good girl, but I couldn't figure out how to explain to Mom why I needed it so badly without revealing that I'd seen an R-rated movie.

I hadn't regretted it either. I'd kept the sweet, citrus scent in my backpack and only put it on in the bathroom at school. It was like a magic potion, giving me some of *her* confidence, so that the cruel barbs from Adam and the gleeful smirks of the cool girls didn't hurt quite so much. The scent would fade by the time I got home, but often I'd put it on before I went to bed, hoping for a rare but delicious dream that I was Catherine, holding Sebastian's hand and kissing his soft lips and basking in his adoring gaze.

7

When Amani and I burst into Diane's office, talking over each other and waving our phones, she was reapplying her lipstick. She nodded, remaining composed as we explained our findings.

The only crack came when she muttered, "Good Lord" under her breath, studying the pictures of Catherine. There were just a few photos of her as an adult—from announcements that she'd been cast in a TV show before it had been canceled, as well as from a red-carpet event where she'd worn a shimmering silver dress. But even with her makeup, blown-out hair, and bright grin, you could tell. Jane Doe was Catherine O'Brien.

"We have to call the police, right?" I asked. Seeing Catherine all dolled up, her features rendered obscenely large by makeup, felt like I was looking at an Instagram-filtered version of myself. It also made her current state—blank, pale, unable to meet her basic needs—even more alarming. "Or her parents?"

"No." Diane handed back my phone. "We talk to her."

"But she *won't* talk," I protested. "Because of whatever horrific thing she's been through."

"Lots of our patients have been through horrific things." Diane stood, smoothing down the front of her blouse. "We don't breach their confidentiality or treat them differently just because they're actors."

So Diane thought I was asking for special treatment because Catherine was a celebrity.

But Catherine wasn't just *any* celebrity. I wouldn't feel this buzz of excitement coursing through my veins for just any famous person, would I? Catherine had unknowingly been a huge part of my life at thirteen, when everything had felt so intense, so momentous, so stormy. Of course her arrival in my workplace would give me a thrill.

Still, I had to act calm. Diane sent Amani off to her daily duties and we headed to Block D. The room was unexpectedly empty apart from the prone figure of Jane/Catherine in the last bed on the right. I wish I'd come here first, before telling Diane, so that I could fully take her in, watching her expressionless face meld into my memories of the beautiful, brash teenage Catherine.

Her glass-green eyes were wide open, staring at the wall. Diane leaned over and put a hand on her shoulder. As if mechanized, she pulled herself up to sit, her bare feet dangling over the side of the bed. I'd seen this a few days before; it was like the nurses had trained her — to sit up for food and medications. The blue socks with rubber treads on the bottom were set neatly on the tiny nightstand, to be slipped on before walking her to the bathroom.

I remembered suddenly that in *Stargirl*, her priestess character had been named Thuya—another cause for connection, the name so close to mine. It now seemed obvious that she was an actress, her features so sharp and defined. Sure, her eyebrows were overgrown and she had a smattering of acne on her chin. But I should've known immediately who she was.

Diane crouched in front of her. "So, we just received information that your name is Catherine O'Brien. You're an actress from Los Angeles. Your parents are Killian and"—she checked her phone—"Lisette. Does any of that sound familiar?"

Catherine remained motionless. But she swallowed, her throat jumping. The movement made me clench the pen and paper I carried.

"You're over eighteen, so we don't have authority to call your parents or the police without your permission. But"—Diane motioned and I handed the items to her—"we want you to think about it and let us know how you'd like us to proceed. Okay?" Diane set the paper and pen in Catherine's lap.

What now? Diane stood, her knees popping. "Why don't you stay with her for a little bit." I nodded, but Diane was already clack-clacking to the door. "Talk to her," she threw over her shoulder.

It had always felt awkward to me, conversing one-sidedly with Catherine. But now, in the empty room, just the two of us, I couldn't *not* talk.

"I—I hope this isn't ridiculous to say, but I was a *huge* fan." I perched on the bed next to her, the mattress shifting under my weight. "My best friend and I watched *Stargirl* so many times—she got the DVD at the mall and we would secretly watch it in her basement late at night during sleepovers. We had a such a big crush on—" It hit me that Catherine—catatonic or not—probably wouldn't want to be reminded of her deceased costar and ex-boyfriend.

"Anyway," I went on. "Some people thought I looked a little like you." One person in particular. Catherine's bottom lip dropped open; she was breathing through her mouth. Her shoulders were slightly slumped, her whole body, as usual, slack.

"That's why you have the tattoo," I said as it clicked into place. The symbol had looked familiar because it had been in the movie! I tried to remember what it had stood for, exactly. I wished I could pull out my phone and scan the red-carpet photos of her, see if I could spot the mark. But I'd refrain until later.

"I wonder what happened to you," I went on. "I wish I could help you." Catherine hadn't moved, and maybe it was my own imagination, but it felt like there was something—some new awareness—in the room.

I could almost hear her responding words: *Help me what?*

"To wake up," I said softly.

A rustling: Catherine's hand was moving against the paper. My body went rigid as I watched her fingers close around the pen.

But she was holding it wrong—grasping it like a baton, the tip facing up.

I moved to correct the pen's placement, my mouth forming words— *Wait, let me*—when the pen flew upwards at my throat.

8

I scrambled back, leaping off the bed and pressing myself against the wall. Catherine's face was suddenly a blotchy red, her teeth bared, and she wielded the pen like a knife.

"You tricked me!" she cried. "How could you do that to me?"

Even in the rush of shock and fear, I marveled at the familiar throaty voice.

"Catherine, wait." I held up my hands. "I didn't do anything—"

"You tricked me!" She took a step forward, and I darted towards the door, shouting: "Security!"

"It should've been you! It should've been *you*!" She lowered her head and ran at me. I raced into the hallway, where a small crowd of patients was already gathering. I had a split second of unreality— *Catherine O'Brien is chasing me, seriously?*—before she jumped on my back. We both hit the ground, and I managed to wrench the pen from her grip and shove her off. She sprang back onto me, pinning my shoulders to the ground. Tears poured down her cheeks as she shrieked, the words unintelligible. Then she looked up, jumped to her feet, and took off down the hallway.

"Run, bitch, run!" one of the watching patients called out.

Catherine was nearly at the doorway when her bare feet slipped. Her head connected with the metal doorframe, and she sank to the ground with a moan.

Security guards Frank and Caleb appeared and bent over her. Catherine reanimated—punching, kicking, and screaming—until Nurse Femi managed to stick a needle in her arm to sedate her. In the sudden silence, the ghosts of Catherine's shrieks still rang in the air.

"Thea." Amani kneeled next to me and pointed at the front of my button-down shirt. Somehow in the struggle it had ripped open and my nude bra was visible.

"Oh." I closed it, aware of the patients surrounding us.

"I have an extra T-shirt in my locker."

"Thanks." I was shaking. I got up and strode to the group around Catherine. A small trail of blood streamed from her head onto the gray tile.

Femi turned to me. "We paged the medical rapid-response team. They should be here in a minute."

"You all right?" Frank asked.

"I'm fine." The fear and adrenaline pumping through my system would say otherwise. I stared down at the now-unconscious Catherine, who looked like she was peacefully sleeping.

What the fuck had just happened?

"Okay, show's over!" Amani clapped. "Let's clear the hall, everyone."

"Damn, Dr. Thea." There was Ace, chewing gum and smiling. "Was it something you said?"

The rapid-response team took Catherine to the medical unit for testing, including a CT scan, when she awoke. For the rest of the day, staff and patients alike kept asking me to rehash what had happened, and I responded that I really didn't know (staff) or that I couldn't talk about it (patients). But any psych unit is filled with constant activity, and though shaken and bruised, I slipped back into work mode surprisingly easily.

It wasn't until I was on the subway home that the feelings of disquiet and disbelief rushed back. I watched myself in the reflection of the subway car's window. It was blurry and smeared, enough that I could imagine myself looking at Catherine.

Somehow Diane and I confronting Catherine with her name and identity had 1) snapped her back into reality and 2) caused her to attack me. I couldn't get her eyes, shining with a mixture of anguish and fury, out of my mind. She'd thought I was someone else—but who? What did she think I'd done?

You tricked me!

It should've been you!

I pulled out my phone at the next subway stop and googled Catherine when the cell service kicked in. Her Wikipedia page shared the basics: that Catherine was the only child of writer and director Killian O'Brien and actress/model Lisette O'Brien. That she'd grown up in LA and had been acting since she was a baby, first in commercials, then in a two-season sitcom. She'd been in various movies throughout her childhood, and at eleven was still acting in ensemble casts; her first lead role was in her father's movie *Stargirl*, which came out when she was thirteen.

I clicked on the Wikipedia page for the movie, pausing at the paragraph labeled *Development*:

Catherine's father, Killian (who she became estranged from in her twenties), has widely stated that he got the idea for Stargirl from a dream Catherine told him about. He claimed in interviews that he believed Catherine may have been dreaming about a past life experience—both Killian and Lisette are self-proclaimed Buddhists and believe in reincarnation. Killian shared that Catherine helped him write the script, answering his questions easily about life as a "living goddess" or a temple priestess.

The movie had grossed more than $198 million and had been generally favorably reviewed at the time. There was a section on *Controversy*; apparently feminist and religious groups had rightly blasted the film for its sexualization of a child. Catherine had been thirteen during the filming, and though a body double had been used for nude scenes, her implied sexual relationship with both Sebastian Smith, as the temple guard, and thirty-six-year-old David Cunningham, who'd played the pharaoh, had raised at least some eyebrows. Killian had defended the movie by stating that girls in ancient Egypt were considered marriable adults after their first period.

Whoa. Well, that's gross.

Feeling unsettled, I went back to the plot summary:

In ancient Egypt, thirteen-year-old Thuya is a living goddess who resides in the city temple. During a ceremony, she passes out from heat exhaustion and wakes up to hear the pharaoh's aide questioning her fitness for the job. Back in the temple, Thuya argues with a guard named Hapi. She calls him disrespectful and rude, but softens towards him after he teaches her how to play a logic game. Thuya finds it stimulating in her otherwise tedious life. The pharaoh calls Thuya to his chamber and complains that his wife can't give him a child. He points to Thuya's birthmark, which looks like a dotted spiral within a triangle, and says that it shows she has been marked for greatness and that he would like to take her as his wife.

That's what the symbol was—Thuya's birthmark.

Thuya tells Hapi about the pharaoh's plan and Hapi threatens to kill him with his prized possession: his deceased father's dagger. During preparations for a festival on the spring equinox, Hapi convinces Thuya to use the confusion of the day to run away with him to a neighboring town. Conflicted because of feelings for the pharaoh, Thuya finally agrees.

Shortly before the festival, a newcomer arrives at the palace, claiming to be a sorcerer. He tells the queen of the affair between Thuya and the pharaoh and advises her to kill Thuya. The sorcerer promises to put a spell on Hapi to get him to fall in love with the queen so that he'll reveal their escape plans.

Thuya's mother has a dream of Thuya dying in the desert. She comes to the palace with her husband and demands to see her daughter. But Thuya refuses, angry that her parents gave her up at a young age to the royal court because of her birthmark and red hair.

As Thuya and Hapi escape, the queen's soldiers stop them. At first Thuya believes Hapi has betrayed her and refuses to follow him. Guards spear him, and he dies in Thuya's arms while slipping her his knife. The pharaoh appears, confessing he overheard her and Hapi and decided to put an end to their plans. Guards subdue Thuya, take her knife, and leave her in the desert, where she dies.

In the last scene, Thuya opens her eyes to find she's on a spaceship. She enters a kitchen to see the queen, who smiles and says, "Good morning, Theta." The camera pans down, showing that Thuya/Theta is clutching Hapi's dagger behind her back. Then the camera pans out the window and into space, zooming out until the entire galaxy is visible—which matches the birthmark on Thuya's/Theta's chest.

Reading the description was bringing the whole melodramatic and problematic movie back. And it also made me remember the real reason I'd become so fixated on it, a reason I hadn't shared with anyone, even Melissa.

The truth was that the movie had echoed my own life. Pastor John couldn't have looked more different from the brooding, muscular pharaoh, but the dynamic had reminded me of us. We'd never had sex, never done anything physical, but in our numerous closed-door meetings in his office, he'd told me things about his wife and marriage. Even, in a roundabout way, their sex life. Things I now knew that no adult man should be telling a thirteen-year-old girl.

The wildest part was that just like the pharaoh, Pastor John would end up abandoning me.

We were between subway stops and the screen froze. I glanced up, noticing the man standing right in front of me was wearing sweatpants with a *Jaws*-like mouth, lined with teeth, on the crotch. Yikes. He noticed me looking, so I went back to the frozen Wikipedia page. Beneath Catherine's image—her on the red carpet, smoky eyes glittering—it showed her birthday.

October 24, 1991.

Seeing the date made another memory slide into place.

She had the same birthday as me.

9

We're twins!

On the walk home, I automatically skirted trash and a fighting couple while my mind remained twenty years in the past. I had known this factoid at thirteen, and I now remembered fantasizing about Catherine being my long-lost twin sister. Some of the actual fantasies resurfaced: going to LA for a class trip and passing Catherine on the street, where we'd recognize each other immediately. Or writing her a letter and enclosing my picture—somehow I'd have one of me solemn and gazing off into the distance, like an author photo—and her sending me a plane ticket to LA to come hang out with her and her celebrity friends.

At home, still in the trance, I poured a huge glass of sauvignon blanc and kept digging. First, I searched the more current pictures of Catherine—and found that, no, she didn't appear to have the *Stargirl* tattoo on her upper chest. So she must've gotten that within the last few years.

Then I googled older photos. Apparently, I wasn't the only millennial still thinking about Catherine and Sebastian, because I was able to easily find the *Stargirl* premiere. He wore an oversized gray suit; she wore a sparkly purple dress and platform shoes. Searching Instagram tags led me to accounts with scanned images of old articles from *Tiger Beat* and *YM*. Some I'd actually read. Many of the fluffy interviews focused on Catherine's relationship with "bad boy" Sebastian Smith.

> "He's definitely more adventurous than me!" Catherine said, giggling. "But I love it; he gets me out of my comfort zone. And I do the same for him!"

Oh yes—he'd been the bad boy to her quirky cool girl. She'd worn velvet bell-bottoms and neon sunglasses and chunky stacks of bracelets.

I remembered going to thrift stores and trying to put together similar outfits that were woeful imitations at best. But I'd thought that if I could just look the part, my Sebastian would come.

Their relationship had been relatively short-lived, though maybe that was to be expected at such a young age. A few years later, she was linked to a pop-punk singer, twenty-two years old to her fifteen. Three years with him, then on to another actor, ten years her senior, who she was with for two years.

In her early twenties, she'd started getting DUIs and falling out of limos. Her Wikipedia page had a whole section on her trips to rehab. As well as her estrangement with her father, who'd been her manager until they parted ways.

In her late twenties she'd filmed the pilot for a show. It was supposed to be her comeback role, playing a former child star who'd become a high school teacher. It hadn't been picked up. Another rehab stint at thirty. And then . . . no further info. No Wikipedia section on why she'd been wandering the expressway in new clothes, her fingertips bloody, her brain turned off like a lamp.

I paused to get more wine, my mind spinning. Would Catherine now remember what had happened to her? And would she tell us?

When I sat back down, one of the browser tabs started blinking. Facebook. Maybe it was someone responding to a roommate-related inquiry . . .

But no—another message from Melissa.

> Hi! I'm not sure if you got my message before but I just wanted to check in. I've been thinking about how nice it'd be to catch up. Maybe we could plan a Zoom? LMK!!

Why was she so insistent on talking to me, a friend she'd dumped decades ago? Maybe she felt guilty? Her profile photo showed her with a toddler and baby. All were dressed in identical white T-shirts and jeans. *Oh good god.*

It was fun, this bitchy distraction, and I accepted the friend request so I could see her mostly private profile. I was a little surprised we weren't following each other—a few random people from Our Savior had added me in high school, right when Facebook had opened to the public. I clicked on the Photos section: more pix from the photo shoot that included her husband. He smiled calmly at the camera while she laughed like he'd just said something hilarious.

I had the quick thought, *Okay, he's attractive*, before realizing who he was.

It couldn't be. But even as I hovered the arrow to see the tagged name, I knew.

Adam.

Melissa had married Adam? The class bully? The one who had tortured us, particularly me, at least until . . . until . . .

I felt a wave of nausea but couldn't stop clicking. More photos, just the two of them, gazing at each other with cheesy grins. Someone had written a comment:

You two are SO CUTE. Has it been 10 years already???

How on earth had this happened?

After junior high, I'd begged my parents to let me go to public high school instead of the Lutheran one our school funneled into. I'd been shocked when they'd agreed. Thinking back now, it made sense. They were religious, but they weren't stupid. They knew their daughter was depressed, even though they didn't know how to talk to her about it, or offer her support.

So I'd gone and made new friends, mainly emo kids from my art classes. Apart from those few former classmates finding me on Facebook, I'd cut all ties to my past.

I clicked on an album titled WEDDING. They'd married right after college. The photos made me scoff in disbelief as I saw familiar face after familiar face: our whole grade had been there. Here were the speeches: Melissa's father, bald and gentle, who'd always been kind to me. Melissa's older brother.

Then Pastor John.

I forced myself to study the picture even as my chest tightened. He was still handsome, especially in a suit. Still had that sandy beard and private-joke grin.

I clicked on his profile, which was completely open to the public. Add on ten more years since Melissa's wedding—he must be mid-forties now?—and he still looked much the same. He was still with his wife, and I couldn't decide if that was surprising or not. His voice arose in my mind: *It's been a hard year. With Jamie. We're not even . . . you know. She always says she's too tired. It's been* months. *I don't know what to do.* A tilt of his head, a glance to see if I *did* know. His expression was a strange mixture of embarrassment and curiosity.

The moment was crystallized in time; I'd never forget it. I'd nodded, thrilled and desperate to seem knowing and adult, to be worthy of this confidence. A tiny part of me had even wondered, in a vague and murky way, if this was his way of telling me things were ending with Jamie. Because . . . well, clearly there was some type of energy between us, wasn't there? Not that we could be together now, but maybe in a few years?

It felt shocking to see him now—and Jamie, and their two kids, who were fully grown adults. A recent family picture showed them hiking somewhere, grinning in front of a waterfall, the son and daughter now with partners who looked a little too much like their parents. I became lost in their family life—football games, cookouts, fishing trips—until . . .

Blast from the past!! read the caption. This was from the Our Savior era. Pastor John sat on the edge of the auditorium stage with his guitar, which he sometimes played for our youth group meetings. Melissa stared up at him reverently. Next to her was a cut-off arm with a charm bracelet.

That was me.

Rage surged up through my stomach. He'd used me. He'd used me and he'd fucked me up forever. No wonder I felt broken, unable to be in a normal relationship.

I clicked the *Message* button and typed, You fucked up my life. I sent the message, then stared at the blue bubble. I expected mortification to seep in, but I just felt numb.

I went back to Melissa's profile. How could you marry Adam?????

This time the sent message made me panic. For a moment I considered deleting my profile altogether.

But why should I? Who gave a shit what they thought? They were the ones who'd burrowed deep into the folds of my soul and had stayed there, festering wounds that would never heal. If they got even a tiny bit of shock, of shame, from my messages, then they deserved that.

They deserved much more than that, actually.

10

The next day, walking from the subway to the hospital under yet another gray-swirled sky, I received a link from Amani: *Missing Actress Catherine O'Brien in a NY Loony Bin!*

The subtitle: *Has the former child star flown over the cuckoo's nest?*

With a sinking feeling in my gut, I scrolled down the neon-lettered gossip site. *Catherine O'Brien, best known for her role in* My New Family, *is currently being held in the observation unit, according to an unnamed source. Catherine disappeared from the public eye three years ago.*

I rubbed my forehead, willing away the headache from last night's wine. Well, that hadn't taken long to come out. I felt a lump of guilt, as if I'd unmasked her to the public myself.

In the lobby, our receptionist Hazel was arguing with someone.

"But I'm her therapist," he was saying, his vowels rounded by an Australian accent. "All I ask is that you give her my new number. I need her to be able to reach me." His hand extended over the desk.

"Sir, I cannot divulge any information about our patients." Hazel spoke slowly and loudly. She'd worked on the unit for many years, and I'd always been impressed by her unwillingness to bend to those demanding to talk to patients—including, a few times, the police.

"I'm not asking you to." He noticed me pulling my key card out of my purse.

"Miss, do you work here?" He took a step towards me, his dark eyes pleading underneath a knit cap. He was my height, athletic-looking, his chin clefted like a Disney prince's. "Would you be able to pass along my number to Catherine O'Brien? I'm her former therapist; I just want to make sure she has my information."

"Can't she look you up if she needs to?" I asked, feeling a zing of uncertainty.

He shook his head. "I stopped seeing clients last year."

For all I knew, this guy could be a TMZ reporter, trying to talk his way in.

"We stopped therapy a year ago," he went on. "I was living in LA at the time. I'm here doing research now." He held out a slip of paper. "Can I just give this to you?"

Hazel was watching us, but then the phone rang and she picked it up. In that moment, I took the paper.

His eyes flashed with gratitude. "Thank you."

As I entered the ward, I considered the exchange. Typically, therapists weren't allowed to breach confidentiality, which meant they couldn't tell anyone who their clients were. But not all therapists followed the rules, and maybe he'd thought this emergency situation merited it.

The small, boxlike letters spelled out DR. CLINT. The phone number had a 323 area code.

I paused in the hall and googled it. Okay. Downtown LA.

Catherine was still in the med unit, but news about her celebrity had gotten out. When I started my rounds I passed by the security guard Frank telling a nurse about it. Lydia hovered nearby, clearly straining to hear every word.

I stopped in front of her. "Ready for art therapy today?"

Lydia rolled her eyes. "Your twinsie started to self-destruct, huh? Maybe she's a—what are those called—fembot."

"Those are just in the movies." I tried to sound kind. Diane always encouraged us to reality-test with patients.

"Lighten up, Red." Lydia stared at me. "It's a joke."

"Gotcha. I'll see you later." Frank and the nurse had already moved away.

"You know," Lydia called after me, "maybe you fucked up. Maybe you blew up her spot."

I slowed to respond, annoyed, but Diane called from down the hall, beckoning me.

"She's awake and talking," Diane said when I reached her. She started striding down the hall, towards the medical wing, and I hurried to keep up.

"Oh my god," I couldn't help but blurt out. "Is she okay?"

"Well, she's lucid. And no longer psychotic. She was still agitated and aggressive when she woke up yesterday; the nurses had to restrain her. They finally did the CT scan; no cranial bleeding, thank God. We're bringing her back to the unit today, but I thought you could connect with her now if you have time." Diane gave me one of her dissection-level stares. "Are you comfortable with that? I know she . . ."

"Oh yeah, totally." I nodded frantically, even though my knees were still sore with bruising. "It's fine. As you said, she was in a psychotic state."

"Try to see if you can get more information from her." Diane checked her phone. "So far she's refused to call anyone. But she'll probably want to be moved somewhere else."

"Somewhere else?" I echoed.

"Unless she wants to stay here." Diane raised an eyebrow and the implication was clear. It was unlikely that a celebrity would choose to stay in our public psychiatric unit, not when there were private, spa-like treatment centers to recuperate in.

A heavy sadness filled my stomach. After having been reunited with my thirteen-year-old celebrity twin, I felt a bit despondent that she'd now exit my life so swiftly.

We entered the wing and approached a hallway filled with beds cordoned off by teal curtains. My pulse quickened.

Diane pointed to the last bed on the left. "I have a call. You good?"

"Yep." I steeled myself as I approached, a patient to my right coughing while another to the left hissed angry words into her phone. There: a flash of Catherine's russet hair through the gap in the curtains. Time to put on my competent social worker face.

"Knock, knock." I stepped inside. Was that too corny? "Hi, Catherine."

She was awake in all senses of the word: sitting up in her green hospital gown, eyes wide and clear. A bandage encircled her forehead, and her face was slightly swollen.

She looked me up and down. "Hi." That familiar husky voice again.

"How are you feeling?" I stood there awkwardly.

"Fine."

"I'm glad to hear it." I sat on the plastic chair next to the bed. "How's your head?"

"It's . . ." She touched the side of her head and flinched. "The nurse said that I fell?"

"Yes."

She rubbed a wrist. "I was, like, tied up when I woke up."

Four-point restraints were sometimes necessary for agitated patients—psychiatric or otherwise.

"That must've been confusing," I said.

Her leaf-green eyes flicked back to me. "Sorry . . . who are you?"

"Oh! I'm sorry." I chuckled. "I'm Thea. I'm a social worker. I've been working with you in the psychiatric unit."

"Oh." She squinted. "Were you the one I pushed?"

"Push": now, that was a nice euphemism. "Yes."

"Oh." She swallowed. "I'm sorry about that."

"It's okay. You were . . ."

"Acting insane." She dropped her head back against the pillows.

"Upset," I supplied.

She was quiet for a minute, staring at the ceiling. I felt a flash of unreality: Was this truly happening? Was I really here, sitting across from Catherine O'Brien?

"How long can I stay here?" she asked.

The question surprised me. "You mean . . . in this unit? Or . . ."

"Anywhere. People can't see me unless I agree to it, right?"

"Right." I thought of Diane's words. "Are there people you'd like us to contact?"

"No." She said it stonily.

"All right." I took a beat. "Do you remember coming here?"

"I don't remember anything." Now she looked anguished, her eyes turning glassy with tears.

"That's okay," I said. "You were in a catatonic state."

"They told me. I didn't know that actually happened to people."

I took a breath. "What's the last thing you remember?"

She closed her eyes. "I'm not sure. It all feels blurry."

"Okay." Better not to push. Even though Catherine had to remember *something* to make her not want anyone to visit her here.

We were quiet for a minute.

"Can you talk to me?" she asked in a small voice. "Like, I don't know . . . maybe tell me about yourself?" Her eyes were still closed.

"Sure." The request jolted me. "What would you like to know?"

"Anything." She lifted a hand. "Where are you from?"

Casual dinner party convo. I hid a smile. "I'm from upstate New York. A town you've probably never heard of."

"Are you Irish?" Her eyes opened into slits.

"Oh, the red hair?" I tucked a strand behind my ear. "Yeah, my mom's side. What about you?"

"Dad's side." Her lips curled. "So it's real. You don't dye it."

"Nope." There were fewer of us than you'd think.

"Me either." She studied me, her gaze so intense it felt like a touch. "We look alike."

"Oh yeah?" My chest swelled. My thirteen-year-old self would *die*.

"How old are you?" she asked.

I paused at the unexpected question. You were only supposed to disclose personal information if you could make a case for it being beneficial for the patient.

But wasn't this a clear example? Catherine was alone and afraid. She was trying to connect with me.

"Thirty-three," I said evenly.

She blinked. "Me too. What's your birthday?"

"Um . . ." Giving the exact date—even if it matched hers—felt like going too far.

"Late October?" she asked.

I didn't answer, just stared at her dumbly, but her creased forehead smoothed out. She nodded, a satisfied smile spreading across her face.

Why was she assuming that just because we looked similar and were the same age, we'd have the same birthday? I didn't quite understand what was going on, but I was sure Diane wouldn't find any of this professional. I cleared my throat, aware that other patients could be overhearing our conversation.

"Is there anything else I can help you with?" I asked to change the subject.

"When will I see you again?"

"You've been through testing and observation, so you'll probably come back to our unit soon." I cleared my throat. "We can help you figure out next steps. Like where you'd like to be transferred." I hated bringing it up, but Catherine clearly needed support.

"Great."

I slipped my hand in my pocket for my phone and my fingers brushed crinkled paper. "Hey, did you have a therapist in LA?"

Her eyes remained blank.

"Dr. . . ." I pulled out the note. ". . . Clint?"

Her eyes widened in recognition. "Clint. Yeah."

"Great." I couldn't read her expression. "I can give you his number if you'd like to coordinate with him."

"Sure."

I handed her the paper, suddenly certain this man hadn't been her therapist. Her fingers were cold and they closed tight around the scrap. I'd taken a picture of the number before coming upstairs. I wasn't sure why, but I'd wanted to have it.

"Anything else you'd like to talk about?" I asked.

"No. See you later, Thea." She closed her eyes, and I left the space feeling strangely giddy. Catherine O'Brien knew my name.

And more than that—she'd commented on our likeness and our birthdays. It felt strangely validating to my thirteen-year-old self. Even if she'd soon be whisked out of here, back to California. Even if I never saw her again.

11

The next morning, Lydia accosted me by the break room. "She's back. Your friend."

My friend? Before I could say anything, she went on. "Why is she still here?"

"Catherine? It's because she needs help." I said the words gently.

"This place isn't for fucking rich girls." Lydia's blue eyes narrowed.

I sighed; I hadn't even had coffee yet. "She's having a hard time, too, Lydia."

"Oh, I get it." Lydia sneered. "You rich girls stick together, huh?"

"You think *I'm* rich?" I scoffed, unable to keep the irritation from rising. "So I just work here for fun, right?"

"You won't be here long." Lydia crossed her arms. "You'll get your practice hours or whatever and then you'll jump ship. I know how you see us. You look down on us."

The words stung. I put a lot of effort into making it clear that I respected the clients here, even the ones who sometimes challenged me. I understood how dehumanizing it could be to survive here, when you had no other choice.

And yet. There was something to her words, a truth deep down that I could only catch a glimpse of. Maybe I didn't look down on patients, but in some ways, I did distance myself. Because of my role, I got to stay on the side of helper versus helpee. And in the process of helping those with mental health challenges, I was able to plant myself firmly in the category of: sane.

Lydia grinned, as if she could see my discomfort. "Guess what, Red. You're just as crazy as any of us. You just hide it well."

The words caused a sliding sensation, like I'd been standing on a cliff and the ground was dissolving under my feet. My heart pounded as panic spread through my chest. Squaring my shoulders, I pushed past her into the break room. I sucked in a deep breath. My hands were shaking.

What was happening? I hadn't had a panic attack since college. This wasn't a full-blown one—it was more like hovering on the edge, but still. I took deep breaths as I poured a cup of coffee, relieved when the distress started to abate.

It was just stress, that's all. I'd been attacked two days ago, for god's sake. Plus all the Adam and Pastor John stuff had gotten kicked up by Melissa's messages and the twenty-year reunion. Throw in this confrontation with Lydia, and of course I was a little on edge.

I'd never been good at conflict. Growing up, my parents never fought in front of me; in fact, the angrier they got, the more polite they became. But I wasn't an idiot. I could always sense it, bubbling just below the surface. Mom had been a fiery-haired small-town beauty queen who'd wanted a full household of kids. But they'd run into fertility issues after having me, and my dad had declared that it was God's will for them to stop trying. Her postpartum depression had never really gone away, and she spent her years as a homemaker cleaning the house to what I now knew was an obsessive degree. Dad seemed not to notice; he was often traveling for his pharmaceutical managerial job anyway.

When fighting, they'd retreat to different parts of the house—Mom to their bedroom, Dad to the living room. Sometimes I'd hear Mom crying behind her closed door, on the phone with her sister. But Dad, relaxing on the couch with a newspaper, was always stoic. After all, he was the man, and in our Christian family, that meant that he automatically won.

On my rounds, I stopped at the conference room. Inside, Catherine sat across from Amani, listening to her large headphones. Seeing her gave me a burst of energy. Catherine had stayed! It wasn't because of me. That would be ridiculous. But maybe it had a tiny something to do with it?

Amani was scribbling on a piece of paper, looking bored. She looked up and spotted me, then motioned me inside.

"Hey." She smiled as I approached. "You just get here?"

"Yup."

Catherine acknowledged me with a nod but kept the headphones on. Her face was less swollen, back to sharp lines and planes. She still had a fragile air to her, but appeared worlds different from the dead-eyed Jane Doe of the last two weeks.

Amani noticed my stare. "She said podcasts calm her down. Diane told us to draw, but we're not six, so . . ."

"Is she—does she need to call anyone, or—"

"Her parents are picking her up tomorrow morning. Ten o'clock."

"Oh." Disappointment flooded my chest. Which was absurd—it was a good thing, a *great* thing, that Catherine was going home.

"They're in Hawaii, so it's taking them a day to get here." Amani cleared her throat.

With a sigh, Catherine pulled off the headphones and handed them back to Amani.

"What were you listening to?" I asked.

She grinned, the full beam of her perfect smile startling me.

"Just a podcast," she said. "They really chill me out."

"Hey." Amani got to her feet. "Thea, would you mind staying here while I do my morning rounds?"

"Of course." The prospect thrilled me—one last private conversation with Catherine. Though it also made me a little nervous. At thirteen, despite my grand fantasies, I'd known that if I ever met Catherine in person, I'd go speechless with overwhelm.

Catherine studied me as Amani left. It gave me the same prickly feeling as the day before, as if she were searching for something specific on my face.

"So." She grinned again, but this time it felt like an offering, vaguely pleading. "Someone in my room told me about how I attacked you." The smile dropped. "I'm really sorry."

"It's okay." I picked at a crayon wrapper. "Do you remember . . . what you were thinking?"

"No. Nothing." She stared into space. "All I remember is waking up yesterday tied to a hospital bed." She rubbed at her right wrist. "I thought I was dreaming."

"I can imagine." I didn't want to push, but I couldn't help it. This was my one chance. "Do you remember what happened before coming here? Why you were walking on the expressway?"

She glanced down. "The last few months . . . I guess I have amnesia or something? Is that what it's called?"

"It is." *She's lying.* She was a good actress, of course, but somehow I could tell. She remembered *something*—whether it was part or all of it. She just wasn't going to say.

"Yeah, I was in LA, everything normal, and just . . ." She trailed off, looking down at the table. The silence stretched out.

"You know . . ." I tapped the crayon against a sheet of paper. "I do art therapy here." That was innocuous enough.

She looked up. "You do?"

"I do. Every week." I pulled Amani's paper towards me; it was full of childish flowers and plants. "Sometimes people like to draw things, even if they don't want to talk about it."

"Are you an artist?" she asked.

I paused, unsure how to answer. "Well, I used to be."

"What kind of art?"

"Drawing and painting, mostly."

"What did you draw and paint?"

I smiled at her questions. "Mostly people. Portraits, nudes. It was fun, but . . . I couldn't really make a living at it." Catherine wouldn't be able to relate—her family was loaded. "I went into arts nonprofits, and then the art stuff just kind of dropped off."

She nodded, picking up a blue crayon that had rolled out of the box. "I get that. Wanting to make art but people not appreciating it."

"Oh yeah?"

"I was an actress." Her hand went to her chest, as if to play with a necklace that wasn't there. It dropped again. "When I was younger. But I was typecast."

"How so?" I had to play it cool, though my chest tightened with excitement. I was literally sitting across from Catherine O'Brien, talking about her acting career.

"Oh, they had me playing these kind of sexy roles from a young age. And then when I actually grew up, I guess everyone found me too old?" Her lips pressed together. "It's a brutal industry."

"Sounds like it," I said.

She stared at me, her gaze calculating. "I don't want to sound like an asshole, but . . . do you know who I am?"

I nodded, feeling a small rush of relief. "I do."

"You recognized me?"

"Well, not at first. When you came in, you looked familiar, but I couldn't figure out how I knew you. And then I just happened to talk about *Stargirl* with Amani and . . ." I stopped. Lydia's words came back to me: *Maybe you blew up her spot.*

"So you figured it out." Catherine nodded.

"Yeah. I mean, I can't believe I didn't figure it out sooner. I watched that movie so many times." Suddenly, I wanted, *needed*, Catherine to know my connection to it. "I think it helped me because I was going through something similar in my own life. You know how Thuya was connected to the pharaoh and the guard? Well, I was going through this weird thing with my pastor and religious studies teacher. And there was also this guy my age, Adam, that I . . ." My mouth snapped shut. What the fuck was I doing? Even if Catherine was a famous actress, she was also a patient. Not someone I should be spilling to about my trauma.

But Catherine just nodded, casually, like she'd been expecting to hear this. "That totally makes sense. Can I tell you something kind of strange?"

"Of course."

"I think we're connected." She held my eyes, as if expecting me to agree.

"In what way?" I was connected to her, certainly, but why would she feel connected to me?

"Our birthdays . . . You're October 24, right?"

After a moment, I nodded.

"We look alike. I met you here randomly." Her hands were folded on the table, almost professional.

"So what are you saying? We're long-lost twins?" That had been my fantasy. But I'd always known it wasn't real.

She considered. "Do you think that's a possibility?"

"No way." I barked out a laugh. "I look just like my parents. Who would not have given away their child. And also—I was born in upstate New York. You were born in California, right? It's just not possible."

She tapped a finger against her lips. "Do you believe in reincarnation?"

"Um . . ." I blanked. How to describe the cloud of confusion that had replaced my once-fervent Christian faith? It was something I'd managed to successfully avoid for many years. Since eighth grade, really. I wish I'd been able to slide neatly into atheism, the other end of the confident belief scale. But that had never felt quite right to me either. How did atheists *know*? Or Christians? How could anyone know?

"Your parents are Buddhists," I said finally. "Right?"

She looked down, like I'd given the wrong answer. But then she glanced up and her stare again felt physical, like tiny hands pulling me towards her.

"Don't you feel like we've met before?" she asked.

"You're saying we met in a past life or something?" I tried to follow the thread, but it was starting to dawn on me: Maybe this was a delusion breaking through her assured, sparkly surface. Maybe she really did need to be institutionalized. She opened her mouth to respond, but then the door creaked opened and we both turned.

"Catherine, ready to fill out the discharge paperwork?" Diane stood in the doorway.

Please, *no*, not at this moment, not when Catherine was going to tell me more about our past life connection, which was obviously a fantasy but also incredibly interesting.

Catherine reached out and squeezed my hand. Hers was bony and cold. "Can we talk more later?"

"Of course." She looked nervous enough that I squeezed her hand back.

12

"I love you, Thuya." Sebastian softly touched Catherine's cheek, ardent even in the throes of death. "If I have to search every cavern of the underworld, I will find you. I will never let you go."

Watching *Stargirl* for the first time in two decades seemed the only reasonable thing to do after the exceeding strangeness of the week. After our conversation that morning, I'd waited for another chance to talk to Catherine. But after filling out paperwork, Catherine had been approached by Shana, who took her to the TV room and questioned her about her "Hollywood affairs." Whenever I peeked in, a small crowd of patients surrounded her. I'd considered bringing her back to the conference room, but my own day had gotten busy, and I'd completely lost my chance to find out more about this mystical link between us. I'd have to catch her the next morning before she left.

A part of me had wondered: Could my thirteen-year-old self be right? *Had* my feelings of connection and closeness with Catherine been more than just a parasocial delusion? She'd been such a big part of my life then. It was like praying to a deity and then running into her in a grocery store. It just felt so *weird*.

But it was all ending soon, and maybe that was a good thing. Catherine would soon be flying back to her world, leaving me to mine. Since the public knew she'd been at the hospital, I no longer had to bite my tongue. If I kept the details vague, it could even become a juicy story, maybe one I'd tell at parties: how my teen-era celebrity twin showed up in my psych unit.

Watching the movie felt like an appropriate bookend to the experience, though I had no idea how I would react to it.

Oh boy. It did not age well. Beyond the hokey sets and wooden dialogue, thirteen-year-old Catherine's affair with the adult pharaoh now felt incredibly disturbing. In spite of the heavy makeup, it was clear she was still just a kid. This movie would never be made today. I considered turning it off more than once, but the eerie nostalgia it provoked caused me to keep going.

At the tail end of Sebastian's death scene, there came the scrape of a key in the lock. Dom and the mysterious Amelia tumbled in, mid-laugh.

"Hi!" Dom ran over and hugged me. "How are you?" Her breath smelled like whiskey.

"I'm okay." I smiled at Amelia. "Hey there."

"Hi. I'm Amelia." She stuck out her hand. Her fingers were filled with silver rings, her nails neon pink.

"What are you up to?" Dom flopped next to me on the couch. "Wait. Is this . . ."

"*Stargirl*," I supplied.

"With that actress." Dom snapped her fingers. "The one who showed up at the hospital, right?"

"Right." At some point, Dom had texted me about it, sending one of the cat-outta-the-bag gossip site articles. I'd written back: See? I DID know her!!!

Dom jumped up and went to the fridge. "You kept saying you recognized her—I should've believed you."

"What's she like?" Amelia asked, flipping the part in her hair.

"She's . . . you know. Nice." It hadn't gotten out that Catherine had attacked a social worker, thankfully.

"I think we should all discuss this at the show." Dom came back balancing three glasses of whiskey. "Amelia's friend is performing."

"Oh, you know what? I *just* put these on." I pointed to my sweatpants.

Dom smirked. "What if I told you our cute friend Matt is going to be there?"

"Do I know him?" I asked.

"Not yet!" she cried, almost spilling her drink. I had to laugh; tipsy Dom was enthused and accident-prone. "Hey, when's the last time you chatted up someone?"

"Chatted up someone? What, are you Bri-ish?" I teased with an accent. Seeing Dom in party mode reminded me of grad school nights when a group of us would hit a nearby dive bar for karaoke.

"Trust me, gov'na!" Dom clinked my glass. "You won't regret it."

Two hours later, I'd managed to snag a stool at the bar. Live music blasted from the back room, where Dom and Amelia camped out. I'd felt dizzy in the hot, cramped space. But even out here it was packed, mostly with twentysomething hipsters with shaggy haircuts and ugly-cool glasses. I felt old, out of place. And the much-touted Matt hadn't yet materialized.

"Just thirty more minutes," Dom had shouted when I'd tried to leave. "He's on his way!"

After a few drinks, I was yearning for human touch. But it was near midnight—way past my bedtime. I ordered one last IPA and opened my phone. I'd posted on Instagram during the first set, a video of the band. The bartender set down the glass, but when I picked it up, the guy to my left bumped me, jostling my arm. Amber liquid sloshed over the rim.

"Oh, shit, I'm sorry," he said.

I turned, slightly annoyed, and found myself staring into warm, brown eyes. They were buttressed by under-eye circles that gave up-all-night-writing-poetry vibes. I zoomed out: heavy, concerned brows, a full lower lip, slight stubble, a mop of curly dark hair.

This guy was gorgeous.

"No problem." I flashed him a grin.

"It's crazy here tonight." He was so close I could smell him: a mixture of laundry detergent and a woodsy, smoky cologne.

"I know." *Be cool be cool be cool.* But I couldn't help but glance down at his left hand resting on the bar. No ring.

"I'm Jonah." He held out his hand. "Let me buy you a fresh one."

"Oh, it's fine. And I'm Thea."

"Great name." His mouth quirked in a cute smile.

"Thanks." What was happening? Was this overly hot man flirting with me? True, I'd been told that I underplayed my own attractiveness—seeing my skin as pasty, not ivory; my green eyes as muddy instead of catlike; etc. Still, Jonah might really be out of my league.

But who knew? Some guys really, really liked red hair.

"It's not like this on weekdays normally." He took a sip.

"Come here often?" I cringed at the clichéd pickup line.

But he just nodded. "All the time."

We chatted through one round, then another, which he insisted on paying for. The rest of the loud bar receded into the background. We leaned in, and it felt like we'd entered into a cozy sonic cocoon.

At one point, Dom brought up a wan, blond boy. We shook hands before I turned back to Jonah. She gave a subtle wink as they left.

"My friend was trying to set me up with that guy." I rolled my eyes, secretly thrilled that Jonah had witnessed it.

"Ah yes." He nodded wearily. "The ol' setup. I get that sometimes too."

So he was—confirmed—single. I rejoiced inwardly. The next round I somehow forced myself to order a water, knowing I was ready to tip over into too-drunk at any moment. I'd learned Jonah was a software engineer, he was teaching himself piano, and he was dad to two cats his ex had left behind. And then, somehow, he was saying those magical words:

"Do you want to get out of here?"

We took a cab to my apartment; I texted Dom to let her know I'd left the bar—with him.

GET IT, she responded.

By the time we walked up the four flights of stairs to my apartment, I was giddy with anticipation. After the stress of the past few weeks— hell, months—maybe years?—the universe seemed to be throwing me a literal bone.

But when I ushered Jonah into the apartment, he kept his black coat on and beelined for the couch. That was fine. We had all night. I grabbed two beers—I would just have a sip or two, no more—and sank alluringly beside him.

"Nice place." Jonah slung his arm over the back of the couch.

"Thanks." I had the sense, suddenly, that Jonah was a bit skittish. I couldn't make any sudden moves or I might scare him away.

"So." He fixed me with those soulful eyes. "Tell me more about your job. It sounds fascinating."

"Oh." The last thing I wanted to talk about was work. "It's interesting, that's for sure."

"You work at that place on the East Side? Isn't that where that actress was?"

"What?" I'd mentioned my job early on—I knew working at a psych ward would catch his attention—but I didn't know he'd heard about Catherine. A defensive wall began to rise.

"I saw it on social media." He shook his head, his expression serious. "I can't imagine what happened to her. To make her end up there."

"Yeah." I shrugged. "It's a mystery."

"Is it?" He pulled out his phone. A text lit up the screen.

Fuck. I didn't want him to get distracted. So what was the harm in sharing a tidbit? "She has amnesia."

He eased his phone back into his pocket. "Oh, wow. Really?"

"Yeah."

"Has it been a media circus there? Like, reporters hanging out and stuff?"

"Not really, actually. I think they know they can't get in." How could I push this conversation into flirtier territory?

"So when did she leave?" Jonah asked.

"Why are you so interested?" I tilted my head.

He smiled. "I'm not allowed to ask about my teen crush?"

"Teen crush?" I echoed.

"Oh yeah." He chuckled. "I remember taping this *Stargirl* newspaper review to my wall. My parents actually didn't have a computer at home until I was seventeen, so . . ."

"She was your Pornhub?"

He grimaced. "It felt a lot more innocent than that."

"I get it." I scooted forward. "I had a huge crush on Sebastian Smith, her costar. And for the record, I never looked at porn either. Our computer was in my dad's office, and I was *sure* he was going to walk in on me."

"Porn-free adolescences." He smiled. "We have so much in common."

"I know, right?"

"You know, you kind of look like her." He studied me.

"The less attractive version." *Jesus. Don't neg yourself.*

He shook his head. "Not at all."

"Well, thanks." I set down my beer. "To answer your question, she's leaving the hospital tomorrow morning. So, in about . . ." I checked my phone; it was almost two. "Eight hours, this will all be over."

I was going to be wrecked at work the next day, but it'd be worth it. We gazed at each other, and I started leaning forward.

He pointed behind me. "That your bathroom?"

"Yeah."

He disappeared, and I took the opportunity to run into my room and chuck a pile of dirty clothes into the laundry basket. Thank God I'd made the bed this morning. When the bathroom door opened, I hurried out and perched expectantly on the couch's arm.

"Hey." He winced. "I'm really sorry to do this. But there's a family thing I have to deal with. My dad's been blowing up my phone. I need to head out."

"Are you sure?" I jumped up. "You can call him here."

"Yeah, no, this is going to be a whole thing. He's got some addiction issues." He zipped his coat and something in my chest wilted. I wanted to wail, to force him to stay. We didn't even have to have sex; couldn't he just hold me for a few minutes?

"Do you want my number?" I asked when he reached the door.

"Oh. Sure." He typed it in, but I knew he wasn't going to call. I'd just been a distraction, someone to waste time with.

"Night." He waved. "Thanks for the beer."

After he was gone, I downed both of them, one after the other, in defiance of something. As if it would hurt him instead of me.

13

"Thea?"

Someone was shaking me. I opened my eyes to see Dom.

"You didn't make it to bed, huh?" She glanced at the two empty beer cans.

"No." My head pounded like I was slamming it against the wall. I pulled myself up into a seated position. The movement activated my stomach, which started to churn.

"Ho-ly shit." Dom straightened. "You got crunk last night, huh?" She chuckled and went to the kitchen.

"You could say that." I watched her through slitted eyes. She was wearing the same clothes as the night before but seemed clean and chipper. "You seem . . . not hungover."

"Oh, I am." She handed me a large glass of water. "Amelia and I went back to her place and drank tequila, for some reason. What happened with that guy?"

I took a tiny sip and leaned back against the cushions. "He claimed to have a family emergency and left." Memories of the night poured in, and I remembered with a twist of guilt how I'd spilled information about Catherine to try to get him to stay. Sure, the public knew she was at the hospital, but I shouldn't have shared details. I never would have, sober.

"That's too bad." She stood. "I'm going to bed. Thank God my first client isn't until four."

"What time is it?" I jolted up.

"Nine thirty."

"*What?*" I grabbed my phone off the coffee table; it was dead, so the alarm hadn't gone off. I stood, groaned, and sat down again. "Oh my god, I feel like shit."

"Take it easy." Dom paused in her doorway. "Can't you just call in sick?"

"Catherine's parents are coming this morning. I have to see her before she leaves." Staggering to the bathroom, I turned on the shower and stepped into the hot, stinging water.

I got ready in record time and hurried to the subway. On the way I convinced myself that she'd still be there, that surely Catherine and her parents would have to spend time coordinating with Diane before they left.

A police car waited outside the entrance, which sent a cold chill over my shoulders.

Something bad had happened.

I raced into the lobby, wincing at my throbbing headache. No police here, which meant they must be inside.

"What's going on?" I called to Hazel.

She paused in her texting. "You'd better talk to Diane."

Diane's door was closed, but through the window I could see her leaning forward, intent on the couple across from her. From his bright red hair and her blond, it was clear who they were.

Killian and Lissette O'Brien. Catherine's parents.

Two officers stood next to them. One was talking to Diane, whose lips pressed together.

Oh *no*.

I rushed to the break room. Amani and Rachel talked in low tones by the coffeepot.

"What happened?" I cried. "Is she okay?"

"Where were you this morning?" Rachel asked, her face drawn.

"I overslept. Where's Catherine?"

"We don't know." Amani shook her head. "She left with her parents. Well . . . we thought they were her parents."

"What?" The words weren't computing. "But her parents are in Diane's office."

"Her *real* parents," Rachel said. "Yeah."

At my confused expression, Amani held up a hand. "So this couple showed up early, like at eight, and said they were Catherine's parents. And she went with them. Her real parents came at ten, and Diane had to tell them that she'd already left. It took a minute to figure out what was going on."

"Who were the first couple?" I asked.

"No one knows." Amani shrugged. "Except Catherine, I guess."

I thought suddenly of Clint, the "therapist" whose number I'd given to Catherine. But he'd looked to be younger, in his thirties. It couldn't have been him.

"No one knows what her parents look like?" I couldn't keep the exasperation from my voice. "They're famous."

"Thea, I didn't even know who *Catherine* was. Not until you showed me pictures." Amani shook her head. "They said they were her parents, and they had IDs."

"It is weird, though," Rachel mused. "If she didn't want to leave with her parents, why didn't she just check herself out?"

"So she knew the—the impersonators," I said.

Rachel nodded. "Seemed like it."

Catherine had gone through something, some ordeal that had triggered psychosis, mutism, and amnesia. Had the people who'd shown up been somehow involved?

The shock was beginning to shift into something else, something darker. I shivered despite the warm, stuffy room.

"She asked for you." Rachel's expression was curious, maybe even a little sad. "She said she wanted to tell you something. I told her you weren't in yet."

Dread filled my chest. Had she wanted me to help her? Had she known these people were coming for her?

If I'd come into work this morning as usual, would I have been able to save her?

14

A half hour later, Diane called me in to talk to Catherine's parents.

I'd seen pictures, but experiencing them face-to-face was startling. They had that same celebrity aura as Catherine, wealth and fame surrounding them like a cloud of perfume. Killian—creepy director dad—was compact and rugged-looking, his thinning copper hair tousled, his tan face etched with lines. Lisette had reached the age where her upkeep work made her look uncanny: eyes too wide, lips too puffy. Her smooth face was shiny with tears that continued to fall as I told them and the two police officers everything I knew, which wasn't much.

Officer Rivera, who had a baby face despite his beard, asked me where I'd been that morning. His questions threw me: Did they think I was somehow involved? Officer Kim, a fortysomething woman, watched silently as I confessed to having fallen asleep on the couch.

"Do you recognize these people?" Officer Kim turned Diane's computer screen to show video footage of a man and woman walking in the front entryway and stopping at reception. He wore a baseball cap, she a wide-brimmed felt hat. Had they been trying to shield themselves from the cameras?

"I don't think so." The man was tall, slightly stooped, and had a noticeable paunch. The much smaller woman leaned on the front desk, using one booted foot to scratch the back of her left ankle. Her light hair flowed in soft waves over her back.

"One more." Officer Kim nodded and Diane clicked on another clip. Rachel and Catherine sat at the conference room table, papers and crayons strewn around them. Despite the graininess of the black-and-white footage, I could see Catherine stiffen when the couple arrived. My shoulders tightened as the woman ran to give her a hug. The man swooped in to embrace her. Catherine had recovered and even looked like she was smiling as they broke apart. Diane appeared on-screen, her back to the camera. The woman remained by Catherine's side, one arm possessively clutching her shoulders.

"I don't recognize them. I mean, from what I can see." I shook my head. "But it looks like she knew them. Right?"

"Thanks for your cooperation." Officer Kim gave me a tight smile.

"But—"

"Thanks, Thea." Diane nodded at the door.

My stomach growled; after the intensity and strangeness of the meeting, and of seeing Catherine's famous parents, I was suddenly ravenous. As I grabbed my coat and wallet from my locker, Rachel's words circled in my head. *What* had Catherine wanted to tell me?

Outside, the icy wind snatched at my hair, and I squinted into pale, lemony sunlight. It took me a second to register the dark-haired man sitting on a bench outside the building.

"Jonah?" I stopped short. For a brief moment, wild, tentative hope blossomed in my chest. Was he here to surprise me? I had told him where I worked.

But when he looked up from his phone, his smile was too casual, verging on patronizing. "Oh, hey. How's it going, Thea?"

"What are you doing here?" If he wasn't here for me, why was he looking at me like that? Like I was an elderly aunt he had to make nice with so she'd go away?

He stood and ran a hand through his curls. "I thought I might run into you."

"Yeah. I *work* here." This still wasn't computing.

Jonah slipped his phone into his back pocket. "I can explain."

"Okay . . ."

"I'm a private investigator. Catherine's parents hired me."

"*What?*" Staggered, I took a step back.

"They contacted me yesterday." He crossed his arms. "I'm not sure if you're aware of this, but Catherine disappeared four years ago. Her parents hired me—they hired a couple of us, actually, in different cities she had connections in—but we weren't able to track her. So when she resurfaced here, they wanted me to check on her before they arrived. Of course, I couldn't get inside. So I looked up employees on LinkedIn."

"But how did you . . ." My stomach abruptly heaved, and I placed a hand on my belly. *Do not throw up. Do not.* "You knew I'd be at that bar last night?"

"You posted about it on Instagram."

"So you don't live in that neighborhood."

His gaze was steady. "No."

I sputtered. "But that's illegal, isn't it? To pretend to be someone else? To pretend to be . . ." I didn't finish the thought, because it was too pitiful: *Interested in me?*

"It's not, actually." There was that gleam of amusement in his eyes that I remembered, but now it looked hard, cruel. "People lie about themselves all the time."

"But you came *home* with me. You were in my apartment. When I was drunk."

"Well, maybe don't invite strange men over when you're wasted."

The words shocked me enough that I was, for a moment, speechless. Then rage began swirling up through my chest. "Are you fucking serious? Did you actually just say that out loud to me?"

"Look." He raised his hands, conciliatory. "I'm sorry. I'm honestly just trying to help her parents. They wanted her to be safe. Which . . . clearly, we failed in that."

I shoved my shaking hands in my pockets.

"What happened to her?" Even in the midst of my shock and outrage, I wanted answers. "Why did she disappear?"

"We don't know." He stepped closer, his voice low and urgent. "If you have any information, it might help us find her."

I laughed. "Oh! Now you're expecting the drunken slut to help you? Is that what's happening?"

"Thea, please. This is about Catherine, okay? Not you. And not me."

"You don't know shit about Catherine," I spit out. The words surprised us both.

Mildly, he asked: "Did you recognize the people who picked her up?"

I turned and stormed past him.

"The-a." He drew my name out, as if I were being unreasonable. I hurried on, holding my breath until I rounded the block and was out of sight.

15

She asked for you.

That night, I cranked open my laptop as if I had some kind of spy technology that would help me track Catherine down. According to Google, the day's events hadn't hit the wider world. Wouldn't her parents want the public to know? And why had her disappearance four years ago been kept a secret? I looked up "Jonah" and "PI" and "NYC": no relevant hits. But who was to say his name was even Jonah?

I glanced at the spot where he'd sat just the night before, my chest filling with unease.

Ding. Another Facebook message from Melissa, my junior high Judas.

Omg, so good to hear from you! About Adam: I KNOW, isn't it nuts?? But don't worry, he's totally different now. We became friends in HS and started dating in college. Are you coming to the reunion? We'd love to see you!

I jumped up and hurried into my bedroom, throwing open the closet door. I methodically pulled out shoes and plastic tubs until I reached the cardboard box. I opened it slowly, reverently.

There were more journals than I remembered. Some were completely covered in stickers; others had their covers untouched. At the bottom was the diary from eighth grade, with that bright patchwork pattern and grinning cat face. I opened to a random page.

OMG!!!!! Pastor John told me he liked Stargirl too!!!! :) :) :) He watched it after I told him about it. And . . . HE TOLD ME I LOOK LIKE THE GIRL IN IT!!!! I was somehow able not to blush!! Because . . . well, she's naked in parts of it! Including a scene where she's lying in bed with the pharaoh—which is very UN-Christian for a pastor to watch! He said I *was less innocent than I looked if I was going around watching movies like that hahaha.*

The memory of his office reared up in full color: the heavy wooden desk, the bookshelves full of dusty religious texts, the framed photo of his wife, toddler, and baby that I'd study when he left to get us sodas. He'd been in his mid- to late twenties, which seemed young now but had felt so old back then. It had all started when he'd asked me to stop by to talk about an essay I'd written for his religious studies class; he'd complimented it and acted like my thoughts about a particular Bible verse were incredibly interesting. No adult had ever given me this kind of attention before. Initially, the conversations had centered on Christianity but then shifted to personal: we spilled about our lives in a way that had felt decidedly equal. At some point, a subtle flirtiness had entered the room, proven by this entry, where he was teasing me about my innocence. I also remembered him grinning as he questioned why I didn't have a boyfriend—and hinting that Adam must like me if he was messing with me.

Those many hours in his office had been a respite from the rest of school, from Adam's taunts and Melissa's growing absence. But now I could see them for what they were: an incredibly inappropriate relationship that he should never have started or cultivated. By the time he'd started complaining about his sex life with Jamie, it had felt natural, because he'd already stepped over the line.

I flipped through more pages, stopping on one with a list I vaguely remembered.

THINGS I'VE HEARD ADAM SAY TO GIRLS IN OUR GRADE (MOSTLY POPULAR ONES BUT NOT ALWAYS)
- Nice t*ts
- I'd like to f*ck you in the a$$
- You give great bl*wjobs don't you?

THINGS I'VE SEEN ADAM DO
- stand behind Mrs. Iona and pretend to have s*x with her
- "accidentally" grab girls' butts and boobs
- pretend he's m*sturbating under his desk (with moans)
- pretend he's unzipping his pants and is going to pull out his you-know-what

THINGS ADAM HAS SAID TO OR ABOUT ME
1. BEFORE PASTOR JOHN:
- The quiet ones are such freaks, right? (looking at me)
- Damn, Thea! You left claw marks on my back again
- Oh-oh-oh (pretending to be me having s*x)

2. AFTER PJ:
- He f*cks you over his desk in his office, doesn't he?
- He f*cked you in the a$$ with a cross, didn't he?
- He came (?) in your mouth and said it was the blood of Christ, didn't he?

Okay. I softly closed the diary. So I hadn't been overreacting: Adam really had sexually harassed me and others. I felt it now, a familiar swirl of shame in my chest, mixed with fear, mixed with—the most mortifying of all—an activation low in my belly.

I threw the diary in the box and went back to the living room, plopping on the couch and feeling restless. I again pictured Jonah next to me, his infuriatingly gorgeous face. How dare he try to slut-shame me? But my anger shifted into something else as I imagined leaning forward and kissing him. Getting on top of him. Him kissing me back, grabbing my hips, grinding against me.

I unzipped my pants and closed my eyes. I imagined us making out, unable to control ourselves. It didn't matter that I was a "job"—he wanted me. Even if he hadn't known he was attracted to me until that very moment. Or maybe he *still* wasn't attracted to me—maybe I disgusted him. But he still wanted to fuck the shit out of me.

I went to my room and pulled a vibrator out of my bedside table. On top of my comforter, I kept envisioning us on the couch: Jonah pushing me off him so that I was facing away on all fours, pulling down my pants, touching me, his erection hard against me. He'd never felt this turned on before, even by his hot girlfriend—no, his wife—who was at that very moment at home, sleeping innocently in their shared bed. Their newborn in the next room.

He gripped my breast over my shirt, then pulled my hair, snapping my head back.

"You're so fucking ugly," he whispered.

Suddenly, I was on a blanket in a dark shed. Cold air rose through the slats, through the thin rough blanket *he*—no longer Jonah—had thrown down in a rare moment of thoughtfulness.

"Don't you think you are?" Adam was behind me, thrusting furiously. He grasped a chunk of my hip. "Fat too. You're fat and ugly. You liked being fucked by me, don't you?"

"Yes," I gasped. Because it was true, I *did* like it, and something about being shamed at the same time was making the power build up in my groin.

"You're such a slut. An ugly fucking slut. You think he would ever like you? Stupid slut." The words came in short bursts. He slapped my ass, and the sound seemed to echo in the silent space. Crickets chirped outside, their calls mixing with the burps of frogs. The shed smelled of dank, rotting wood.

"You're my bitch." He leaned forward, his breath in my ear. "Say it. Say you're my bitch."

"I'm your bitch."

"Touch yourself, bitch."

I obediently brought my fingers between my legs, unsure what to do. He grabbed my hand, moving it in a circle.

"Slut," he muttered. "I knew you wanted this. I knew the whole time."

I wanted to flee my body, but I also wanted to stay here, riding this wave that was coming from far off, causing my abdominals to clench and quiver.

"Say his name," he ordered in my ear.

"What?" I gasped. But I knew who Adam was talking about. He hadn't known, though, what I'd just seen Pastor John do. What had shocked and horrified me. What would change things between us forever.

Adam didn't relent: "Pretend I'm him. *Say it.*"

So I did. And almost immediately, I came, crying out, shocked and scared by the waves crashing over me. It was my first orgasm.

Adam collapsed on me. His thin body felt so much heavier than I would've expected. He pulled out and I felt liquid wetting my thighs.

"Fuck." He said it thoughtfully.

I sat on the blanket, raising my knees, clutching my legs, suddenly embarrassed by my nakedness. His eyes ran over me.

"You *are* a freak." He said it neutrally.

Now, I lay back, heaving and spent. I tossed the vibrator away.

That was it: my first sexual experience. With a boy who'd called me names and invoked our pastor—a man who'd also used me. I'd heard from pastors and teachers for years just how sinful it was to be sexual— to even *think* about sex was a reason to beg God for forgiveness. And what had I done that night? Gone all the fucking way. True, I'd been wandering around in a state of shock, not even aware of my body, at least at first. Maybe—probably—Adam had sensed that. But hey, according to my community, boys would be boys. As a girl, you were the guardian of your own virtue. And at that age, it felt like I'd crumpled it up and thrown it in a gutter.

Adam and I had mostly avoided each other afterwards, though he'd stopped with the remarks about Pastor John. All he had to do was smirk at me, and my stomach would drop. He could tell anyone at any time what had happened between us. It was surprising he'd kept it a secret, but I think he liked holding that power over me.

I'd also held it in, but the shame had been unreal. Especially when, afterwards, I'd gotten a UTI that necessitated my mom taking me to her gynecologist. Another awful experience. My big sin continued to reside deep in my belly, causing frequent stomachaches that, when I complained, irritated my mom. Though I prayed frequently, I wasn't sure that something so sinful could be forgiven.

It was only when I had Mr. Russo for ninth-grade social studies that the scales began to fall from my eyes. I couldn't square that my favorite teacher, who was gay, was headed straight for hell. As soon as I had one doubt, others surfaced. By the time I went to college, I was still going to church with Mom and Dad but no longer believed in the God that had judged me all those years.

Unfortunately, I would still be forced to carry Adam and Pastor John around with me for the rest of my life. And this burden would cause the rare interested person like Ryan to gaze at me with horror when I shared the truth: In order to have an orgasm, I needed to imagine being back in that shed, losing my virginity to my bully, *while* he was bullying me. Using that cruel aggression that seemingly informed all of his lust. (The social worker part of me faintly wondered: *What had happened to* him *to make him this way?* while the rest of me didn't give a shit.)

There was absolutely nothing wrong with kink; I knew a lot of people were into BDSM, being dominated, being called names. But this was not that. I hadn't known what kinks even were back then. I hadn't made an informed choice.

And I didn't get pleasure or excitement from the memory now. It was pure utilization, a mental tool I had to grab to get over the finish line.

After Ryan ghosted, when the loss was still whole and torturous and tinged with faint hope, I came across a post on Instagram. One of the therapists I followed had posted about "rights" in sexuality. One of them was: *You have the right to <u>privacy</u>. You're allowed to fantasize when you're having sex and you're not required to tell anyone, including your partner.*

The comments were brutal. Pretty much everyone agreed that if you were fantasizing while having sex with your partner, whether or not your partner was in that fantasy, you were cheating. Not just that, though, you were a malicious monster. You were, as Ryan had called it, using your partner as a sex doll without consent, an unforgiveable offense.

I was amazed I'd told Ryan in the first place. If only I'd seen this post just a week before, I never would've dared.

Twenty years later, I was still tied psychically to my eighth-grade bully. It felt like my sexuality was warped, like a small plant that contorted itself to reach sunlight. It meant that I would never be sexually "normal." That I just had to live with this forever.

All while Melissa and Adam were clowning around and taking cute professional photos.

I went back to the living room and grabbed my computer, rage radiating in my solar plexus. This would be the end of it. All of it.

Here's some fun dinnertime convo for you, I wrote back to Melissa. Maybe ask your amazing husband how he took advantage of me on our eighth-grade trip while calling me horrible things (fat, ugly, etc). Unless you knew already?

I pressed *Send*, then blocked her.

16

On Monday, Catherine reached out to me.

I was in the conference room, unlocking the cabinet with the art supplies. Lydia and Ace walked in, howling uproariously while Lonnie and Ben shuffled behind them.

The laughter made me flinch. I'd laid low that weekend, managing not to drink any alcohol, feeling uneasy about how much I'd been consuming lately. But at night, I'd tossed and turned in bed for hours.

"Isn't that right, Dr. Thea?" Ace asked as I approached the table with papers and crayons.

"Isn't what right?" I asked, not bothering to correct the designation.

"That that actress chick was hiding out here." He sniffed. "Probably from the mob."

I felt a grateful warmth that not everyone had moved on from Catherine. Talking about her made it seem like the past few weeks hadn't just been a strange, vivid dream.

"I think she was leading some sex ring." Lydia looked around like someone might overhear. "And pocketing all the money. She knew her boss would kill her, so she jumped out of the car and pretended to be crazy. But they tracked her down here anyway."

"For the love of god." Lonnie scoffed. "Can't we stop talking about that goddamned floozy?"

"Hey," I warned, and all four looked at me.

"Shut up," Lydia told Lonnie. "Dr. Thea misses her."

"Oh my god." I let my forehead sink into my palms. Maybe it was worse to talk about her.

"It's okay." Lydia patted my shoulder. "You were probably related, third cousins or something." She raised an eyebrow at Ace. "You see the dad? The real one? Whole head of thick red hair."

"What should we draw today?" I asked in a faux-cheerful voice.

"Madam Catherine's sex den," Ace said grandly.

"Ace," I warned.

"Sorry." He held up his hands. "We can draw whatever you want, Dr. Thea."

"Death." Lonnie's chin rested on his fist. "We avoid it, but it's always there."

"Death?" I echoed uncertainly. This didn't feel like something Diane would approve of.

"How we think we'll die?" Lydia blinked, waiting.

Then inspiration struck. "How about we draw what we think happens *after* death? You know, heaven or . . ." I made myself say it. "Some people believe in reincarnation."

"Yes." Ace wagged a crayon towards me. "That one makes the most sense. Heaven and hell, they're kind of silly, you know?"

"Speak for yourself." Lydia bristled.

"Oh, what, you're religious now?" Ace smirked.

"I've *always* been religious. Well, Catholic."

"It's a cult." Lonnie scoffed. "They all are."

"Whatever." Lydia rolled her eyes. "It makes a lot more sense than reincarnation. What, every blond girl thinks she was Cleopatra? Come on."

I rolled a crayon in my fingers as they continued to chatter. Lydia had a good point; it did seem like people who believed in reincarnation often claimed they'd been someone famous. It psychologically made sense too: to escape the finality of death, you could just return, over and over.

I'd had a brief period in college when I'd actively looked for spiritual answers. I'd taken a Religions of the World class, and though it had been interesting, I hadn't felt any need to know more. Maybe religions really were just there to make us feel better about death. And, of course, for the authority figures to amass power and money.

When Catherine had brought up reincarnation, though, something had pulled at me. Some curiosity that she knew something I didn't. Of course, it could've just been my ego, thrilled that she thought we were connected, however esoterically.

Lydia dumped out another box of crayons. "What the hell?" She held up a folded piece of paper. On the front, written in red crayon, it said THEA.

"Message for you." Lydia started opening it.

I snatched it out of her hands.

"It's from her, isn't it?" Lydia's eyes widened. Lonnie shook his head in disgust, while Ben and Ace watched with interest.

I backed away from the table, as if one of them might jump up and grab it. I should shove it in my pocket right now, but I couldn't. I had to read it. Because I knew they were right; it was from her.

The thick crayon letters took up the whole page.

HI THEA, SORRY I DIDN'T GET TO SEE YOU BEFORE I LEFT. I MADE A MISTAKE AND NOW I HAVE TO DEAL WITH THE CONSEQUENCES. THANK YOU FOR LISTENING TO ME. AND THANK YOU FOR LETTING ME BORROW YOUR PHONE TO LISTEN TO PODCASTS.

CATHERINE

"What does it say?" Ace asked.

"Nothing." I refolded it and shoved it into my jeans.

"Hey!" Lydia cried. "You can't do that!"

"It just said goodbye. Really. That's it." I forced a smile. "How's everyone's drawing going? Lonnie?"

Lonnie held up a picture of another naked woman.

"She's dead," he said helpfully.

The rest of the afternoon, all I could think about was the note. Had Catherine really written it? Or was it some kind of prank? The art therapy group had seemed genuinely surprised. Besides, the supplies cabinet was kept locked.

When had Catherine written it? I vaguely remembered paper and crayons being on the conference table as she waited for her parents. If that was the case, she might've had the chance to write the note and slip it into the crayon box.

But why hadn't she just given it to Rachel or Diane to give to me?

Granted, the message was strange. What mistake had she made? The word was so ominous. Was this her explanation for leaving with the impostors? If so, why was she telling me?

And thanking me for using my phone—that was weird too. She'd used Amani's phone; did she not remember? It also seemed like a random thing to mention.

At the end of the day, I knocked on Diane's door. Her expression remained placid as I showed her the note and explained the situation. I was relieved when she pulled Catherine's file so we could compare the handwriting in her discharge form. A match! Diane then opened the video footage of Catherine meeting the impostors.

"Yes!" I cried triumphantly at the sight of the supplies scattered on the table. "Can we rewind? To see when she wrote it?"

"We just saved this portion; the videos are taped over every twenty-four hours."

"Oh." I bit at my lower lip. "Well, should we call the police?"

"Why?" Diane frowned.

"Because . . ." I spread my hands. "It sounds fishy, right? Catherine having to deal with consequences? Maybe that's something the police should know."

Diane folded her hands on her desk. "Thea, I'm going to share something with you that Catherine's parents shared with me."

"Okay." I didn't like her pained expression.

"This isn't the first time Catherine has run off like this. She disappeared right after COVID started. Turned off her phone. Stopped paying rent on her apartment. Her friends and family had no idea where she'd gone."

This matched what Jonah the PI had told me.

"So she went missing?" I asked.

"Well, not exactly. Her bank account was still open, and they could see she was withdrawing large sums. Or maybe it was a trust. Anyway, they could somehow tell it was being drained. But not where she was withdrawing it from."

"So what does that mean?" My brain whirred, trying to make sense of this new information.

"It means that whatever *all this* has been"—Diane gestured in a circle—"it's a pattern. But it's not our job to figure it out."

"Okay . . ." What was she saying?

"Look," Diane went on. "Even the police coming here yesterday— that wasn't actually necessary. Catherine is over eighteen and checked herself out. But her parents are powerful people, so . . ." She shrugged.

"But Diane." I cleared my throat, attempting to sound reasonable. "You saw the state she was in when she came here. And we both saw what happened when she woke up. She went through something *bad*. What if she went back to that same situation?"

"She could. But that happens all the time. Think of women who return to their abusive partners. Of course, they're caught up in a cycle of coercion. But we can't physically stop them."

I paused, at a loss. "So that's it? We just forget about her?"

"There're plenty of other patients who need your attention." Diane sat back, her perceptive gaze holding me in place. "And that might be something to consider, Thea. Why you feel so invested in *this* woman, who just happens to be a movie star."

"It's not just because of that." Indignance and embarrassment circled my chest.

"Look, I get it," Diane went on in a softer tone. "Catherine might have characterological traits. And people with personality disorders can be very seductive in a clinical sense. They know how to read us, how to tap into our desires. They can make us want to save them. But that's not your job. And regardless, Catherine is no longer under your care."

"Fine." I cleared my throat. "I get it."

And intellectually, I did. I left Diane's office feeling foolish, like Catherine had pulled one over on me. I'd worked with plenty of clients at my grad internships and at the hospital, those who ran the gamut from neurotic to borderline to psychotic. The neurotic ones were grounded in reality, the psychotic in unreality. And the borderline clients moved back and forth, setting foot in one world and then the other. They did a similar dance in their relationships: swinging back and forth between idealizing and devaluing. Young parts of their psyche craved connecting, but then, when others inevitably disappointed them, that urge might shift into an unconscious desire to destroy.

Of course, these borderline traits weren't chosen; they usually came from intensive early trauma. A lack of solid connection to one's caretakers, often due to the caretakers' *own* trauma. That thread of agony and anguish unspooled through generations.

I hadn't even considered Catherine in this realm, but maybe I'd been blinded by her celebrity and our—well, my—history with her. Maybe this was why I couldn't stop thinking about her, wanting to help her.

Diane was right: this was classic borderline countertransference.

That night, from the comfort of my couch, I pulled up a photo of the phone number "Dr. Clint" had pressed into my hand. True, I didn't have a signed HIPAA form, but maybe he'd be willing to share something about Catherine. Maybe he could confirm some of these new inklings, so that I could finally put this all to bed.

But when I dialed, the first ring switched to an electronic voice: "This phone number is no longer in service."

I hung up, feeling disturbed. Why would his number no longer be in service? Who was he? Could he be a part of whatever Catherine had gotten involved in five years ago?

I took a sip of wine, setting down my phone. This was a sign. Diane was right. I needed to move on from Catherine, from all this. After all, there was nothing else I could do.

But when I woke the next morning, ears filled with the soft trills of pigeons on the fire escape, I understood the secret message that Catherine had left for me.

17

"Amani, hey." I approached her in the break room, where she was scrolling on her phone. "I was looking for you this morning."

"Doctor's appointment." She set down her soda, engagement ring glittering in the fluorescent lights. "What's up?"

"This is going to sound a little weird." Better to give her fair warning. "But I think Catherine left something for me on your phone."

Amani cocked her head. "Huh?"

"Yeah." I knew how it sounded, so I tried to explain the note as calmly as possible.

"Okaaay." She drew out the word. "Well, let's see if we can find anything. Where should we look?"

"Maybe the notes app?" That seemed like the most obvious place. I peered over her shoulder as she glanced through the notes. "Maybe that one?" I pointed.

"Nope. This is all me."

"Hmm. Maybe she took a picture of something?" I mused.

"Here's the thing." Amani tapped one white-painted nail against the screen. "I was sitting next to her the entire time. I would've noticed if she wrote anything, or took a picture of anything."

"Yeah." A pull of disappointment in my belly. "So all she did . . ."

"Was listen to podcasts."

"Which one?"

"Which podcast?"

"Yeah." A new hope emerged. "What was she listening to?"

Amani opened the podcasts app, which showed a row of recent listens.

"Okay, this one." She clicked on a square. The podcast picture showed a tall blond man and a shorter dark-haired woman smiling warmly into the camera. The background was bright turquoise, the title splashed in bold capital letters: *THIS IS WHY YOU'RE SINGLE: A PODCAST ABOUT DATING AND RELATIONSHIPS.*

Amani clicked and a quick-voiced ad filled the room. She fast-forwarded and stopped.

"I swear to god!" a male voice cried.

"That's ridiculous," the woman responded, her voice low and sardonic. She had an accent I couldn't immediately place. "Listeners, I apologize on behalf of my partner. He knows not what he does."

I pulled the podcast up on my own phone. "That's the most recent episode?" I asked.

"Yup."

I scanned the episode notes. *Episode 102: Ghost Lover: Why We Date Who We Date. Moon and Sol take a deeper dive into the term "ghost lover." Integrating research and philosophy, they explain how our intrinsic longing to merge with another causes us to project our needs and desires. Moon and Sol explain how to find our own ghost lovers so we can banish them and see others as they truly are.*

Below this, linked text said: *Learn more about our offerings at the Center for Relational Healing.* I clicked and a new website popped up, showing a group of people smiling and laughing in front of a mosaic-covered wall. I scanned their faces, half expecting to see Catherine. Nope.

"The Center for Relational Healing?" Amani looked over my shoulder. "I've never heard of it."

"Me either." The About Us tab showed a full-length picture of the podcast couple. The guy was in his forties, windblown and confident, with a sleeve tattoo that gave him an aging rocker vibe. The woman gazed out from underneath his arm with an impish smile, her nose ring glinting. She looked to be in her thirties or forties, with large eyes and a lot of dark hair tumbling over her shoulders. They were both tan.

Moon and Sol met in Los Angeles ten years ago and knew their partnership would have a lasting effect on the world . . .

"Isn't 'Sol' the Spanish word for 'sun'?" Amani asked.

"Yeah," I said. "So they're calling themselves Sun and Moon."

"Now that's cheesy."

I clicked on the Photos tab, stopping on a picture of a swimming pool surrounded by swaying palms and colorful lounge chairs.

"Look." Amani showed me a picture of a group in front of a huge firepit. One woman was crying, while Moon crushed her in a hug, also crying.

"That's intense." I clicked on the Retreat tab.

The Center is typically closed to everyone but full-time students. However, once a month we offer a weekend three-day intensive for those who would like to get a taste of our philosophy. People often come out of this weekend with their entire lives changed. In fact, we offer a money-back guarantee to those who don't believe the CRH Method caused their relationships to blossom.

There was a sign-up tab below with monthly dates—the next was this coming weekend.

I scrolled down to the Details section, which included pricing. I blew out a breath. Damn. Four thousand dollars for two nights? Plus airfare to . . . I scrolled to the bottom of the page for the address. New Mexico?

"It looks kind of cult-y, right?" Amani said, just as I noticed the symbol at the bottom of the page. Holding my breath, I zoomed in, blowing it up until it covered the screen.

A dotted spiral trapped in a triangle.

"This is the symbol!" I cried. "Catherine's tattoo! It's also the birthmark from *Stargirl*." I slumped back in my chair as wonder and relief filtered through me. This was the message I'd been searching for.

Amani looked confused. "Why would the retreat center use a symbol from an old movie?"

"No idea. But Catherine is clearly connected to this place. She might be there now."

"But what if it's a coincidence?" Amani asked. "Or what if Catherine did go there, and liked that they used the same symbol and decided to get a tattoo? Or—who knows, maybe she just likes the podcast."

"The bio says that Moon and Sol met in LA," I said. "Where Catherine lived. She *must've* met them there."

"Maybe." Amani looked unconvinced, but it didn't matter. I was certain this was what Catherine had wanted me to find.

The rest of the day flew by, but I pulled out my phone and started googling on the subway home. There were several articles about the Center for Relational Healing on second- or third-tier women's sites, all with titles that were variations on "THIS RETREAT PROMISES YOU A PARTNER." I was surprised to read that the group basically guaranteed that you'd find "your person or persons" within three months.

One article, titled "Healership Stories: A Conversation with Moon and Sol," called them a "spiritual power couple." The short and clearly paid-for interview showed pictures of Moon and Sol in meditation poses and laughing in each other's arms. My eyes lingered on one paragraph.

> Moon: We think it's possible to meet a highly compatible partner or partners. But you have to be willing to do the work first. If you don't, your own ghost lover will get in the way. That's the image you have of the perfect partner, which is made of parts of yourself that you've disowned. For example, if a woman has cut herself off from her power—something requested of women all the time—then she might long for a powerful partner. But if she's able to reconnect with her power, then she can find someone who does or doesn't have that trait; it's no longer a need stemming from lack.

That was actually interesting. I remembered "imago theory" from one of my clinical classes; it seemed like the same thing. Could I apply that to Ryan? Had he had traits that I longed for? With his confidence and ease, maybe so. I felt a sudden stab of loss and pushed him out of my mind.

I clicked on a *Medium* article from a woman who'd gone to the retreat. She coyly stated that she couldn't say too much about the methods—apparently people were sworn to secrecy—but that she'd been deeply affected and had in fact met her "life partner" just three weeks later. I tracked her down on Instagram—and indeed, there was her dude, smiling across various restaurant tables at her.

I also found an article about the Center on an art site, with pictures of the mosaicked building and pool. It named the artist as Steven Leister and said the building was a "communal living space in the desert."

Nothing overtly negative or cult-y yet. But it felt strange that the articles only referred to Moon and Sol by their first names. And there was very little about their backgrounds—just one piece that referred to Moon as a "yoga and wellness instructor from Mexico" and Sol as a "former musician and entertainer."

A hit came up on Reddit in a thread for empowerment workshops. A Redditor had responded to someone who'd recommended the Center for Relational Healing:

STAY FAR, FAR AWAY FROM THIS PLACE

Well, that was ominous. Several Redditors wrote back, asking for more info, but the person never responded.

The Redditor—User40458312—had only posted this one comment about two weeks ago. I clicked on *Start Chat*.

> Hi there, I just saw your post about the Center for Relational Healing. I am actually looking for Catherine O'Brien, who has ties to CRH. Do you know her? I'm a friend—close enough—and am worried about her. Thanks.

The CRH didn't have a social media presence at all. But overall, the lack of info deflated me. Sure, there was one strange comment. But they hadn't shared any explanation; maybe they'd just had a bad time. If shady things were going on, wouldn't more people be talking about it?

Maybe Amani was right—maybe it was just a coincidence that the Center used the *Stargirl* image. And even if Catherine was somehow involved in the Center, it didn't necessarily mean she was back there now. Could I be reading too much into her note? It was possible she'd truly forgotten that she'd been using Amani's phone and not mine. She probably had other things on her mind.

Still, I continued to scroll through the Center's site over dinner. A Resources page showed dozens if not hundreds of photos. There were quite a few with groups, ranging from six people to more than twenty. The vast majority of them were white people—maybe not uncommon in certain types of New Agey circles? I zoomed in, studying the faces.

Wait. A smiling male face popped out at me.

Shaved head, dark eyes, a cleft chin.

It was Dr. Clint, the so-called therapist who had pressed his number into my hand. A number that was no longer in service.

I studied the picture, searching every face. No Catherine.

Moon and Sol stood at the center of the group, grinning widely.

18

It was easier than I'd expected to reach Officer Kim. I'd found her and Officer Rivera's full names in the visitor log, and decided to try her first. Though she'd said less than him, something about her energy had made her seem in charge. Standing just outside the hospital, I found her precinct and the operator transferred me immediately.

Officer Kim listened as I explained who I was. I told her about the note, the podcast, the tattoo connection, and Clint the faux therapist. After I finished, there was a long pause.

"Hello?" I pressed the phone harder to my ear, trying to ignore the biting cold; the temperature had just plunged back into wintry depths. "Are you still there?"

"I'm here." She cleared her throat. "Thanks for sharing this info. I'm not sure what you'd like us to do with it."

"I mean, you could call this retreat center at the very least. Maybe it's too much to expect someone to actually go *out* there —"

"We're no longer investigating this case," she interrupted.

"Why not?" I pressed.

"Catherine has a history of disconnecting with her family. And she's an adult, so it's her prerogative to do so."

This was what Diane had said. I felt a flash of annoyance. "But what if she's in trouble?"

"I really can't speculate on that."

"All right." I tried to regroup. "So basically you're saying that if I want anyone to check this out, I'll have to do it myself?"

"I strongly suggest you do *not* do that." Officer Kim coughed and spoke quietly to someone else, her voice muffled like she was pressing the phone to her chest.

"And why is that?" I felt defiant, and enjoyed the feeling. It gave me energy.

She came back. "I'm going to be very honest with you . . ."

"Thea."

"Thea. You seem like a caring person. But in these types of cases, the person in question is often caught up in some sort of illegal activity. So I would not recommend getting further involved."

I paused. "Do you think I could talk to her parents?"

"They don't know anything. Really."

"How do you know?"

"I've been doing this awhile. I can tell." Her voice changed, became faux polite. "Is there anything else?"

After we hung up I stood there for another minute, chilled and staring at the slate-gray sky until it started to rain.

On the subway home, a presumably unhoused woman curled up on the two-seater at the end and moaned, "No," over and over again. By unspoken decree, the rest of us pretended we didn't see or hear her. I changed cars, feeling a heavy dread in my gut.

The apartment was empty. I lay down on the couch. My conversations with Officer Kim, Diane, and even Amani had led to questioning looks: *Why are you still thinking about this?* The implied message: *What's wrong with you?*

Maybe I just *gave* a shit. Was that so bad? Maybe there was a reason I'd crossed paths with this looming figure from my past. Because I couldn't deny the unsettling feeling that she was in danger, even if no one else seemed to think so or care.

So what was I going to do? Spend $4K I didn't have, adding to my sizeable debt from grad school, to investigate in New Mexico? It was ridiculous.

I looked again at the website, at the money-back guarantee. The idea that you could meet someone based on a weekend retreat seemed bonkers. Maybe it was a self-fulfilling prophecy: attendees believed they'd meet someone, so they upped their efforts until they did.

But what if I went and tried to get info about Catherine . . . and then asked for my money back? It was possible they'd make it difficult. But I could threaten to write bad reviews and tip off journalists or influencers in that world. It looked like they were just getting started, and they wouldn't want negative press.

Wait, was this happening? Was I actually considering going?

I pulled up the podcast episode and started it from the beginning. If there was anything fishy, then maybe . . . but if not, then I needed to listen to everyone and let this Catherine thing go. It could just be lingering countertransference, after all.

After the peppy intro music, Moon and Sol introduced themselves and bantered about their week, how they'd found a new hot spring a few towns over, and how an older man at a gas station en route had slipped Moon his number.

Then: "Let's get into it." Moon's accented voice was smooth and low. "Today we're going to get back to the basics, yes? We're going to talk about ghost lovers."

"Yeah, we are!" Sol's voice was medium pitch but crackling with energy. "You want to start, babe?"

Oh, that smug "babe" that couples used, that *I'd* used, briefly, with Ryan.

"Sure." A pause. "So I want to talk about my first crush. I was still in Ciudad Juárez with my mother. My father had already disappeared— presumably kidnapped, as I've talked about here before. So it was just the two of us. We lived in a small trailer park just outside of town. I was ten. The summers were sweltering. Our air conditioner always broke. My mom would go to work, and I'd be alone during the day. I was bored; no other kids around. But then, one day, there was this boy." She chuckled. "A beautiful boy."

"*The* most beautiful boy?" Sol asked, smiling.

"I thought so at the time. He'd come to stay with his uncle who lived next door. And my god . . . I was in love!" She laughed, a hearty sound. "I'd watch him out of the windows like a spy. Finally, I got up the nerve to go outside. But I didn't talk to him. No, I just acted very casual. I'd bring my biggest book and sit in the shade. I wanted him to think I was an intellectual. But he hung out with his uncle's dog and just ignored me. I daydreamed about him. What he'd be like, what he'd say. Even what his voice sounded like! My mom told me his name was Carlos. It was the most enchanting name in the world."

"I sense this is not going to turn out well," Sol said.

"Just wait. I decided to talk to him on my birthday—I figured this was big enough news to share. So I dressed up and put on some of my mom's lipstick. I found him in a field nearby.

"When he saw me, I suddenly realized how stupid I'd sound. But I said it anyway. *Hi. It's my birthday.*"

"We've made contact!" Sol cried. "How did he respond?"

"He was just like, 'Okay. Hi. Happy birthday.' And you know what—his voice shocked me. In my fantasies he'd always had this deep, rich voice. But his voice was high and kind of screechy. So I stared at him and thought, *Oh no.*" She laughed. "Luckily, he was very nice and we became friends. But it amazed me how different he was from my daydreams. I'd thought he would be suave, smart, maybe even a little mysterious. But he was actually pretty nerdy. He didn't even really *look* the same as I'd been picturing in my mind."

"And you took that to mean . . ."

"Well, it was a difficult time in my life. I felt very alone. And I think a lot of young girls in particular are told that all we need is our prince to feel better. So I focused all this energy on my crush. And when I spoke to him—poof! It disappeared, just like that."

"So you'd call Carlos a ghost lover, right?"

"Yes. My first ghost lover. But not my last."

"Should we define the term?" Sol asked. "For anyone who hasn't heard us talk about it before?"

"Yes, of course. Your ghost lover is your inner vision of a perfect partner. They're a ghost because they don't really exist. You can only see them when you project them onto another person. It could be a crush, like I had, but it also often happens in the beginning of relationships."

"Exactly," Sol said. "And to make it even more complicated, your ghost lover holds parts of you that you're not able to access, so that you look for them in another person. For example, for a lot of men, their ghost lover might be nurturing, emotional, and supportive. Traditionally feminine traits that men and boys are often conditioned out of. Of course, that's a super-generalized example; many women may also long for a nurturing partner if they don't take care of themselves. But to keep it simple, this type of man would see his ghost lover in other women. He may even be attracted *because* he can overlay his ghost lover on them."

"Right. And when we date someone, we start to merge with them," Moon added. "So we feel like we're able to take on those disowned traits *through* the other person."

"Yes! An anxious person feels comforted. A stick-in-the-mud wants to party all night. It's like a drug. On top of all those other love chemicals we get high on."

"But at some point, it ends." Moon sounded mournful. "You can't stay merged forever. And when you separate and see the real person, with all of their flaws, it can feel disappointing or even scary. *Who is this person?* People may fall out of love fast."

"But there's a solution," Sol said.

"There is!" Moon cried. "It's possible to deconstruct your ghost lover by integrating their traits back into your own life. For example, before I met you, I started boxing. It helped me feel more powerful, and I started protecting myself more, setting boundaries and telling people what I needed. Then I didn't feel like I needed someone else to give me those things."

"But that's just a part of it, right?" Sol asked. "With regards to what we help people do?"

"Oh, of course. There's a whole other piece of the ghost lover that's connected to your caretakers, and what you did or didn't get from them when you were young. We can help with that too." She paused. "Do you want to talk about Catherine?"

I sat up straight on the couch, my heartbeat kicking up a notch.

"Absolutely." He was smiling. "Catherine is a member of our community who gave us permission to tell her story. That's not her real name, of course. But she thought it was important for us to share her breakthrough with you all."

"Catherine actually had two ghost lovers," Moon went on. "They were based on two different males from her childhood. One of them was abusive to her. So she really struggled with dating and relationships."

"Until . . ." Sol prompted.

"Until she came here." Moon sounded quietly pleased. "We did some of the deepest work possible to excavate those ghost lovers. And at the end of our sessions, she was able to let them both go."

"And best of all," Sol went on, "she was able to connect with partners who she didn't have to project on. She's now living here full-time, pursuing her art, helping us spread these teachings. And she has not only a real-life partner, but many connections and friendships to rely on."

"And this all started with a weekend retreat, yes?" Moon asked.

"It sure did." Sol grinned. "Speaking of, we have a retreat coming up this month. All of us are really looking forward to it. If you come, you'll even be able to meet Catherine." A beat. "What did she want us to say again?"

"She wanted us to say: 'If you feel a tug, a longing, listening to this, then take it as a sign.'" Moon's voice became urgent. "I'll add to that: Even if you've never met us, this place is your home. Here, you'll feel a sense of belonging that I can promise you've never experienced before."

"Totally agree. I love that." Sol gave a contented sigh. "So take our words as an invitation from the universe: It's a beautiful time to come home."

Part Two

19

As the plane neared Albuquerque, I started having second thoughts.

Dom had appeared the night before as I was packing. I could see it in her eyes as I explained Jonah the PI and the fake therapist and the podcast episode and the weekend retreat. A sort of *uh-oh* look, though she didn't actually question my decision.

"Just be safe, okay?" She'd perched on the edge of my bed. "Maybe check in and let me know how it's going?"

"Sure." I'd still been in a daze. After feeling so much uncertainty about so many things in my life, it had felt like a relief to sign up for the retreat and book a flight. It wasn't a coincidence that Catherine had directed me to the podcast. This couple—cult leaders?—had sent her a secret message, calling her by name, directing her to "come home." By leaving the note, she was clearly asking for help.

I was her last chance. If I didn't help her, no one else would.

But now, the certainty was wearing off. The adrenaline too. I'd gotten up at 4:00 a.m., and the lack of sleep was hitting me. I'd never been able to doze on planes.

A sigh emanated from my seatmate, a Black woman around my age who was nestled against a faux-fur coat pressed to the window. She smelled like expensive sandalwood perfume and had an alternative vibe: a section of her hair shaved, the rest in delicate locs, silver jewelry twinkling from her ears and nose. She wore patent high-heeled boots, patchwork jeans, and a button-down black suede shirt.

I envied people who wore chic outfits on planes. In my leggings and a sweatshirt, my hair twisted in a messy topknot, I looked like a college student flying home for break.

One of the flight attendants roamed the aisle with a garbage bag, intoning, "Trash," in a solemn tone, as if pronouncing judgment on each of us. I opened my backpack, catching a flash of feline side-eye from my eighth-grade journal. I'd grabbed it at the last minute. I wasn't exactly sure why, beyond the fact that it brought me back to that point in my life when I'd felt so connected to Catherine. Maybe it would act as a talisman, pulling her towards me.

I opened the confirmation email for the tenth time.

We're so excited to meet you! Based on the flight info you all sent us, we're providing two shuttles from the airport, one at 10:00 a.m., the other at 3:00 p.m. Our driver will be waiting for you outside of baggage claim with a sign. It's about a 2.5-hour drive to the Center.

According to the website, the Center was built on a half-completed resort that had languished when the owners ran out of money in the sixties. The Center had bought it in 2020 and had remodeled it under the guidance of mosaic artist Steven Leister—which had been detailed in the art site article. All the pictures made it look impressive: a huge, colorful structure in the middle of the desert.

It also looked quite remote.

I felt a flicker of unease. Which would be worse—that I'd spent close to $5K I didn't have on a ridiculous wild-goose chase? Or that my questionable suspicions would turn out to be right?

I'd done everything I could to conceal my identity: I'd hidden my LinkedIn and changed my social media handles. Of course, they still had my name from my credit card. But nothing online linked me to the hospital, which was the bare minimum of deception I needed to find out anything useful on this retreat.

I texted Dom with the in-flight Wi-Fi. On my second flight. I'll send some pix when I get there! I also texted a link to the CRH site. It didn't hurt for her to know where I was. Just in case.

As we walked off the plane, the airport decor made it clear we were in the Southwest. The carpets were lined with jagged hunter-green and mauve stripes, the chairs were wrapped in studded brown faux leather, and paintings of horses and buffalo dotted the walls. I pulled my carry-on past a man facing away whose T-shirt read: *I DON'T RUN. I RE-LOAD.*

Guess we're not in Kansas anymore. I passed a kiosk of silver jewelry, then another selling hot sauce and jars of green and red chile. Out the windows, beyond the runway, clay-red mountains clashed against the bright cornflower blue of the cloudless sky. I was trailing my hip seatmate, and a white-haired man in a teal shirt and name tag grinned and motioned at us. "Baggage claim's down the escalator, ladies. Watch out for rattlesnakes!"

The baggage claim was lined with neon blue and green lights, clashing with the tan and orange tiles. I followed Silver Jewelry Girl to carousel five—could she be coming for the retreat too? Would it be weird to ask? Besides those who'd been on our plane, there weren't many people around.

I walked outside, breathing in the fresh, sweet breeze. My shoulders loosened. I hadn't even thought about how it'd feel to be in New Mexico. To get out of the gray, depressive chill of New York's early spring.

No one out here with a sign. I walked back through the doors and a sixtysomething white woman sitting on a nearby bench leaned forward. "You looking for something, hon?"

Another airport helper? But no, she had a suitcase next to her, a paperback splayed on her thigh.

I gestured vaguely. "Oh, I'm supposed to get a ride . . ."

"Are you here for the retreat? Center for Relational Healing?"

"Yes." I approached her, relieved.

"Have a seat." She patted the bench next to her. "The driver's not here yet." The book resting on her leg showed the pink outline of a woman, overlaid with the words: *CRACKING THE CONFIDENCE CODE: Getting Back in the Dating Game After Divorce!*

When signing up for this retreat, I hadn't considered who the other attendees might be.

"I'm Karen." She had a kind face, tan and crisscrossed with laugh lines. A large mole punctuated the bottom left corner of her mouth. I offered my name, and we shook hands. Then she picked up the book. "I probably shouldn't be reading this in public, should I?"

Had I embarrassed her by looking? "Oh, I wouldn't worry about it."

She chuckled. "That's the best part about getting older—you give less and less of a shit. Although it's a little late to read it. I've been divorced ten years this week." Her turquoise-blue eyes narrowed, mischievous.

"Oh, wow." I hesitated; should I add a *Congratulations*?

"It's a good thing." She waved a hand. "We were together for two decades. And a lot of the time it felt like taking care of another one of my patients. I was a nurse back then. One day I told him, *Art, it's over. It's time for me.* And . . ." She grinned. "It's been me ever since."

"That's great," I said.

"Not that I don't date." She sniffed. "I just haven't had much luck. But that's why we're here, right?"

"Right," I echoed.

Silver Jewelry Girl appeared in front of us, lugging a shiny black suitcase. "Hey, I couldn't help but overhear. You're going to the Center too?"

"We are!" Karen pumped her fist. "I'm so glad you ladies are here."

"How long have you been waiting?" Silver asked.

"Not long. An hour or so. I got some chips, read my book. And now I'm ready to rock!"

"Great." Silver caught eyes with me for a second, amused. I tried to smile neutrally. Karen seemed like kind of a lot, but I needed all the allies I could possibly get this weekend.

"What's your name?" Karen asked her. "I'm Karen, and this is Thea."

"I'm Mikki."

Karen and Mikki: two such incredibly different people coming to this retreat. What would the others be like?

"So no driver?" Mikki looked around, playing with her necklaces. "Should we call them? It's after three thirty."

"Ladies, you came from New York, right?" Karen nodded at the electronic sign over the baggage claim. "This land has its own rhythms. I'd suggest going with the flow this weekend. It'll all turn out fine."

"I'm sure it will." Mikki settled next to me, smirking. "I'm just starving."

Karen opened her large leather purse. "You want some almonds?"

Fifteen minutes later, after Mikki had eaten the rest of Karen's reserves and was wondering aloud about heading to a nearby restaurant and having them pick us up there, a girl with bright orange hair ran into the baggage claim. She grasped a faded posterboard sign that said THE CENTER in thick Sharpied letters. "Hi! You're here for the retreat, right?"

"Yep!" Mikki jumped to her feet.

"Great." The woman—twentysomething and cute, with the ability to pull off highlighter-bright hair dye—grinned at us. "I'm Grace. Come with me."

20

"How's everyone today?" Grace threw over her shoulder as she hurried us into a parking lot. She was tan, although white lines crisscrossed her upper back. She wore a tight camisole and baggy green pants. With her freckles and wide smile, she looked like a friendly and popular girl you might see at a liberal arts college.

"Great!" Karen cried.

"Awesome. What's everyone's name?" As we introduced ourselves, she led us towards a shiny white SUV. The license plate said LAND OF ENCHANTMENT, which I somehow recognized as the state motto. The sun landed on my neck like a warm hand, and I held my face up to the light. God, it felt nice here.

Grace opened the side door but tapped obliviously at her phone while Karen struggled to heft her bag inside. I rushed forward to help.

"Thanks, hon." She climbed in carefully. Mikki hauled her bag in after.

"You want to sit up front?" Grace asked.

"Sure." I sank into the leather seat, inhaling the too-sweet vanilla air freshener hanging from the rearview mirror. Grace turned the car on and pop music blasted. She turned it down and pulled out.

"So you and Mikki flew in from New York, right?" She slipped on a pair of aviators. I was momentarily distracted by the landscape—even as we drove by big-box stores, those mountains beyond planted us firmly in a new land. And that sky! The blue was so vivid it glowed.

"Yup." I turned to her. "The weather here's way better. What is it—seventies?"

"Yeah, it's been warm this week." Grace chuckled. "Spring is nice, but it gets cold at night." She drummed her fingers on the wheel; the silver nail polish had mostly flaked off.

"How long have you been at the Center?" Might as well start to dig now. We passed a bench with a sign on the back: WANNA GET TO KNOW GOD BETTER?

"It's been a while." She drove surprisingly aggressively, cutting off a car that didn't even honk. "A couple years."

That was vague. "How did you come to work there? Did you know— Moon and Sol?" My tongue faltered over the names, which felt slightly ridiculous to say out loud.

"Nope, I came for a retreat, just like you." She grinned. "And I never left."

Well, that was cult-y. "That's great."

"Trust me." She shook her head. "You're not going to want to leave either."

Mikki leaned forward. "What are you guys talking about?" Beside her, Karen was scrolling on her phone.

"Just how incredible the Center is." Grace beamed back at Mikki a few seconds too long for my comfort. I clutched the sides of my seat, and she finally turned to the road. "First time for both of you—all of you—right?"

"Right." Mikki tucked back a loc that had slipped in front of her face. "Is it just women coming?"

"Oh no." Grace shook her head. "We have two guys. They flew in this morning."

"How many altogether?" Mikki asked.

"There are . . ." She squinted. "Six."

"That's the usual number?"

"Well, sometimes it's a little higher. But usually we keep it small. So there's a lot of personal attention, you know?"

We crossed a street called Gun Club Road, then passed a building with a cracked sign: HEALING HERB DISPENSARY. We were on the outskirts now, and on our left was what looked like a junkyard.

"Where are you from?" I asked Grace.

"Santa Fe. Not too far away." She flew through a light that had just turned red.

"You heard about it . . . how, through the podcast?" I asked.

"Oh no. This was before the podcast." Grace glanced at me. "Every-one heard about it when they started building. It's the largest mosaicked structure in the world. Wait till we get there." She grinned. "I promise you've never seen anything like it."

Outside of Albuquerque, we entered the desert: flat and then rolling golden hills dotted with shrubs and sprouts of grass. Beyond, majestic mesas rose up from the dirt, some of them dotted with metal crosses. On the horizon were those ubiquitous mountains. The landscape was beautiful, otherworldly, seemingly filtered through a washed-out seventies color scheme.

"Wow," I said during a lull in Grace's easy chatter. "There's so much empty land. It's just . . . the opposite of New York."

We'd been driving more than an hour with little to break up the landscape. I hadn't even seen a gas station. Good thing I'd peed on the plane.

"Yeah, I love living down here." Grace nodded. "My brain felt so cluttered when I was in a city. It's great to have space, you know? And there are some cool places we can drive to." She started telling us about a town called Truth or Consequences, which had renamed itself to win a radio contest in the fifties.

Eventually, we turned onto a gravel road. Here the land rolled gently, and far off something winked in the sun.

"Is that it?" I pointed. "The Center?"

Grace smiled. "You'll see."

"This is, like, the driveway?" Mikki asked. "How long is it?"

"Oh, about three miles."

"Damn." Mikki gazed ahead. "You guys are isolated."

"Just the way we like it." Grace chuckled.

The closer we got, the less real our destination became. It was like a mirage: the sparkling, jewel-toned castle of a kids' show. I'd seen photos, but they hadn't done the place justice. The building was an enormous adobe structure at least five or six stories high, with turrets and small balconies and one especially tall tower thrusting towards the sky. All surfaces were covered with mosaics: glittering pieces of glass and mirror and ceramics. It was too bright to look at without squinting, even with my sunglasses. I glanced back; Karen's jaw hung open in awe.

"Nice, huh?" Grace sounded smug. The closer we got, the more intricate the mosaics became. There were numerous patterns and pictures in the walls, mostly from nature: animals, flowers, plants, ocean waves. Ranging from small—some were too delicate to make out from this distance—to enormous, like an imposing elk that was at least twenty feet tall.

"It's amazing." I meant it, and Grace gave a satisfied nod. There was one other car—a red sedan—parked in front of the building, on an unceremonious patch of dirt outside the double doors.

I wondered for a moment if Moon and Sol would be waiting for us, parental and waving. But no one emerged from the miraculous kaleidoscopic chateau.

"Welcome to the castle," Grace cried as she stopped the car with a jolt. She cranked open the door and hopped out, kicking up dust. "That's what we like to call it."

"It's really something." Karen shook her head.

"What was that place in *Mister Rogers' Neighborhood?*" Mikki stepped onto the dusty ground. "The Neighborhood of Make-Believe?"

"I was just thinking it looked like something out of a kids' show." I slammed the door shut.

Mikki pulled her large suitcase to the ground. Grace was already at the doors. "Let's see if the inside is just as nutty."

Karen had paused, and I held out a hand.

"Thanks, hon." She carefully stepped down. "Sometimes flying makes my knee act up."

"Sure." We headed to the double glass doors, held by the rounded edges of the adobe walls. They were covered in large black lettering: CENTER FOR RELATIONAL HEALING. WELCOME HOME.

Inside, it took a few seconds for my eyes to adjust to the dim light. The walls of the entryway and lobby were similarly covered in mosaics, though they were partially hidden by couches and paintings. Antiques covered every surface—a stack of old books here, a stuffed owl on that cabinet there. For some reason it felt vaguely postapocalyptic, like a group of survivors had moved into an art exhibit, dragging in anything they could find.

"All right!" Grace bounded behind a check-in desk. It was scattered with papers, pens, paper clips, markers, and a beat-up paperback of bell hooks's *All About Love.* Grace pulled out three folders and handed them to us. Peeking inside, I saw a map and a printed-out Word doc.

"Self-reflection packet." Grace pulled a pack of gum from her tote bag. "And map."

"Map?" Mikki echoed. "How big is this place?"

"You'll get the hang of it fast. But sometimes when people first come here, they feel . . ." She waved her hands. "Disoriented."

Karen looked around. "It *is* a little busy."

"We're maximalists." Grace shrugged. "A lot of our members are artists. But everything has its place."

"No cell service?" Mikki held up her phone.

"Nope. We have Wi-Fi, though." Grace snapped her fingers. "We *just* changed the password, so let me get back to you on that. Also . . ." She pulled a stack of papers from under the desk. "One thing to sign."

"Nondisclosure agreement," Karen read.

I scanned the many-paragraphed packet. *Both parties agree to keep confidential training materials, attendees' stories, and other proprietary information ("Confidential Information").*

"Yup." Grace snapped her gum. "We get really personal here, even on just weekend retreats." She glanced at me. "Thea, you're a therapist. You get it."

I felt taken slightly aback that she knew my profession. I'd written in the sign-up form that I was a therapist, figuring "social worker" might be suspicious, but I wouldn't have expected Grace to have read it. Maybe she had more power here than I'd assumed?

"I get it." I forced myself to smile, wondering exactly how binding this was. I knew that cults often used legal action to punish people. If I found out information about Catherine and shared it, would they come after me?

Mikki and Karen were signing the packet; I clicked my pen and scribbled something that looked nothing like my signature. Maybe that would protect me.

"Thanks." Grace took the forms back. "Ready for the tour?"

"Yeah!" Karen cried, causing us all to crack up.

"Good! Leave your bags here, we'll help get them to your rooms." Grace marched through a door, and we followed. An energy crackled in the air, and whether it was the stunning reality of this place, or the zinging possibility of getting closer to finding Catherine, I breathed it deep into my chest.

The hall, filled with framed photographs, opened up into a courtyard filled with plants, sculptures, and a large, burbling fountain. Enormous, spiky aloes reached up to my chest level, and several cacti in the corners towered over us. I slowed to take a closer look at the sculptures: two life-sized heads peeking out from underneath the plants. The effect was unsettling, like they were people who'd been buried up to their necks. One looked like an older woman, another like a boy or · teen. Both had dark holes where their eyes should've been. Even more creepy.

But there was so much else to take in: oil paintings propped on side tables, a row of closed doors, and a mosaicked staircase curving up to the second story. It was at least twelve feet above us, with a wraparound landing.

Someone was watching me.

I paused. Grace, Karen, and Mikki were up ahead, their voices melding with the gurgles of the fountain. I turned and scanned. No one was here, but my eyes landed on a door to the right. While the other doors were mosaicked, blending into the walls, this one was a wooden door painted purple. There was a small window towards the top of it, covered by a lace curtain. Was someone watching from inside?

"Coming?" Grace called from the edge of the courtyard.

"Yes!" I pulled my gaze away and hurried over.

"You okay?" she asked.

"Yeah! I've just never seen a place like this before. It's . . . a work of art."

"It is." She seemed pleased by my choice of words. "You should've seen it before." She motioned us into the next hallway and pointed to a framed black-and-white photograph. It showed what looked like a half-built mansion, flanked by the surrounding hills and mountains.

"This is the old resort?" Mikki leaned in to study it.

"Yep. They were able to use some of the old structure, but most of it's new."

"It must've cost a fortune," Mikki said.

"Oh!" Grace paused. "Let's stop here. These are the bathrooms." She waved us through an open doorway, and we filed into a yellow-tiled space. The color reminded me of a middle school locker room. There was a row of aluminum bathroom stalls and a row of sinks.

"The bathrooms are . . . communal?" Karen looked bemused.

"They are!" Grace nodded enthusiastically. "We don't break things down by gender. The showers are through here." She led us through another doorway. Showerheads dotted one of the walls. At the end of the room, a lone set of curtains surrounded one showerhead.

"For those who want privacy." Grace gestured.

Mikki and Karen nodded, seemingly unfazed, but I couldn't help but feel a pinch of discomfort. I hadn't showered in front of other people since gym class decades ago. That had been bad enough. If I used the "privacy" shower, would everyone else judge me?

"Where do Moon and Sol record the podcasts?" Mikki asked as we continued down the hall.

"Oh, they do that in a studio in Las Cruces."

"Is that far?"

"Everything's pretty far around here." Grace led us out a back door. "Okay, here's one of my favorite places. The pool!"

"Now we're talking," Karen cried. Mikki grinned as she slipped on her round sunglasses.

The pool area was gorgeous—lush and colorful, like the background of a funky *Vogue* magazine spread. The kidney-shaped pool itself was patterned with mosaics, which were all sea-themed: tropical fish, seahorses, anemones, even a large octopus with far-reaching tentacles. The deck was covered with golden-toned mosaics, like a sandy beach lining the water. Palms and ferns dotted the periphery, interspaced with cacti. A beige canopy stretched over half the pool, providing shade. Lounge chairs of all shapes and sizes littered the deck; they'd clearly been brought here piecemeal, but they added to the quirky charm.

And there, in the shaded area, several people lounged. They sat up to greet us, and I recognized him immediately.

This time he was in a T-shirt and shorts instead of that puffy black coat, but his mussed curly hair, broad shoulders, and lazy grin were all on full display.

It was Jonah the PI.

21

"Oh, wow! Dudes!" Mikki waved.

I stood frozen in place as Mikki, Grace, and Karen continued towards them. Forcing myself to move, I kept my expression neutral even as my thoughts spun. How was he here? Had he also made the connection between Catherine and the Center? Had Officer Kim told Catherine's parents about my frenzied call?

Jonah smiled, squinting, as we approached. This motherfucker wasn't even wearing sunglasses. Nothing to hide. He shook Mikki's and Karen's hands, then turned to me.

"Hi." He stuck out his hand. "I'm Jonah."

So we were pretending not to know each other. Okay.

"Thea." I tried to inflect some poison into my voice as I grasped his palm, but he just nodded and turned back to the group. The other man stepped forward. He was shorter, with close-cropped dark hair and a genial smile. "Hi, I'm Ramit."

I tried to seem warm, normal. The third in their group, a tiny fortysomething woman in a strappy pink bikini, bounded forward and wrapped me in a hug. "Hi! I'm Dawne with an *e*!" She wore a thick, flowery perfume. When she stepped back, I got a closer look: high ponytail with extensions, shimmering bronzer, and lip filler.

"Thea," I said, but she was already back by Jonah's side. He was saying they'd gotten there that morning.

"And we've just been *unwinding*." Dawne gave a happy sigh. "It's so special to be here."

"Where are you from?" Mikki asked.

"LA." Dawne nodded serenely, her hand pressed to her ample chest. She looked like someone who could've been on *Last Chance Love*.

"Let's finish the tour, and then you all can hang out before dinner!" Grace's enthusiasm was unflagging. I glanced at Jonah and found he was looking at me. He gave me a reassuring smile. I suddenly wanted nothing more than to punch him in the face. Just seeing him was unlodging the anger from our last conversation.

"What is that?" Mikki pointed. On the far side of the deck sat what looked like an enormous barrel. "Is that a hot tub?"

"It is!" Grace grinned. "Japanese-style. It's filled with water from the natural springs on this property, which feed the fountains too. You're going to love using it at night."

Jesus. Hanging out in a hot tub with Jonah?

I kept a pasted-on smile as we bid farewell and continued the tour. As we walked, a new thought struck me: Was it possible Jonah was somehow connected to the Center? Had they sent him to New York to gather intel? Was he now here pretending to be an attendee to manipulate me?

Or was that completely paranoid?

Either way, his presence was definitely a sign that I was on the right track, whether he'd come here of his own accord or not. If he was working for the Center, though, then my thin cover was definitely blown. No way yet to know.

Grace led us past the pool to another canopied area with tables and chairs. "This is the veranda. We usually eat here if it's nice out. But there's also a dining area inside."

"Ooh." Mikki craned her neck. "I'm so hungry. I didn't get a chance to eat lunch."

"Don't worry, we're putting together some snacks for you guys now." Grace led us down a gravel path further into the desert, behind the castle, which was dotted with several large structures.

"That's the yoga pavilion." Grace pointed to a large, circular khaki tent. "We'll hold our sessions there."

Beyond the tent was . . . nothing. Just flatland, then gently swelling hills, then the mountains. The air was so clear I could see the crinkles and curves of their peaks. They didn't even look that far, though they had to be hundreds of miles away.

"That's our ceremonial space." Grace pointed to a circular area marked by benches. A huge stack of logs sat in the center, presumably for a bonfire. "And past it is the greenhouse." The glass structure sparkled in the sun. "We grow a lot of our own food. We're hoping to expand soon. One more thing." Grace led us towards a line of smaller circular tents. "Your rooms!"

"Tents?" Mikki sounded unenthused.

"Semipermanent yurts," Grace said. "They're actually very comfortable."

"We can't stay in the permanent building?" Mikki gestured. I was surprised at her boldness.

"There's no space." Grace shrugged. "The rooms are taken by residents."

"All of them?" Karen clucked. "That place is huge."

"Well, a lot of the rooms are studios."

"Studios?" I echoed.

"Like I said, almost everyone here is an artist." Grace nodded. "So we each get our own space to create."

"Well, good." Karen patted Mikki's arm, her mouth quirking at the corner. "We wouldn't want to interrupt anyone's creating, would we?"

Mikki rolled her eyes but smiled back.

"How many residents are there?" I asked.

"Currently . . ." Grace looked up. "Well, there's Moon and Sol, of course. Steven's here full-time." Steven—the mosaic guy? Was he living here?

"And we have three other full-time residents who like to leave during retreat weekends," Grace finished.

Could one of them be Catherine? If so, where was she now?

If only I could just ask Grace. But not yet—first I had to spend more time with her, to see if I could trust any answers she'd give. Because so far, at least, she seemed like Team CRH all the way.

The yurt was actually larger than it looked from the outside. Beyond the cot, there was a beat-up dresser with a battery-operated lamp, a round mirror, and a squat cushioned chair by the window. The window was just an open square—no glass, no way to close it, just an embedded screen with a roll of fabric tied at the top. A warm breeze blew in, lifting my hair.

Outside, facing away from the tiny yurt village, was that endless desert landscape.

I felt a twinge of unease as I perched on the bed, mindlessly opening my backpack and pulling things out. I'd assumed this would all be larger, fancier, like a bougie yoga retreat—dozens of people sitting in rows of folding chairs, watching speakers pontificate from a stage. This was small, eclectic, even a bit dumpy. And much more intimate. Which meant I would have less of a chance to hide during whatever healing sessions were going to take place. Somehow I hadn't even considered that aspect of the retreat when signing up.

"Knock, knock." Mikki opened the thin wooden door and wandered in, gesturing with a vape pen. "Looks like we're neighbors. If you hear any primal screams coming from my yurt . . . I'm just considering how much money I paid to stay in a tent."

"We are kind of roughing it, huh?" I chuckled.

"Yep. You want?" She held up the pen. "It's just nicotine. I can't even imagine being high here. Can you?"

"At the castle? No way. Too overwhelming. And thanks, but I'm good."

She passed me in a cloud of sandalwood perfume and peered out the window. "How are you feeling about this place?"

"It's . . . interesting," I said. "Different from what I expected."

"Me too. They must work miracles to charge what they do." Mikki watched me, blowing out a plume of mint-scented smoke. "What are you here for?"

Oh, not much, just doing some amateur sleuthing around a missing child actor I met in a psych ward.

"Um, you know. Dating issues and stuff. You?"

"Same." She shrugged. "I'm sure you'll hear all about it soon. But as a therapist, you're probably used to talking about this stuff."

"Well, not in a group setting like this." My chest tightened. "I'm kind of dreading it, to be honest."

"I'd rather get a root canal. But my therapist pushed me to go."

It felt calming to commiserate. But I should also be doing said sleuthing. "So you heard about this place from your therapist?"

"Yeah. She said they were doing 'cutting-edge' work." Mikki used finger quotes. "Whatever that means. What about you?"

"I heard the podcast."

"Oh yeah. I got sucked into that too. We'll see what the famous Moon and Sol are like in real life. No one can be *that* happy." She paused, hands on hips. "Do you think it's weird that we haven't seen them yet? Like, where are they?"

"No idea. We should ask Grace."

She glanced at her phone. "We still need the Wi-Fi password."

"Yes. We do." Not having any connection to the outside world was making me feel even more on edge.

"What's that?" Mikki pointed to my eighth-grade diary, which I'd tossed on my bed.

"Oh." I put a palm over the cheekily grinning cat, embarrassed. "It's an old diary. Where it all began, you know?"

She scrunched her nose and smiled. "I do."

A male grunt from outside made me jump and Mikki spin around.

"Hello?" he called. Not Jonah or Ramit.

Mikki pulled the door open. "Hi?"

"Suitcase." A man with a reddish, scruffy beard and a black baseball cap waited on the other side. "Which color?" His voice was sharp, almost gruff.

"Mine's blue. Oh, thank you." I grabbed the handle and pulled it in the yurt.

"Mine's the black one." Mikki strode outside. "Wow, how'd you bring all three?"

I'd seen only one photo on that art site, but our luggage carrier did in fact appear to be Steven Leister, the mosaic artist. I leaned out the doorway to watch him follow Mikki to her yurt next door.

An hour later, I was lying in a lounge chair, my stomach filled with homemade hummus and cut veggies and buttery popcorn, a ginger lemonade sweating on the tiny table next to me. Karen and Dawne were in the heated pool, chatting and laughing. Mikki, on my left side, was fully engaged with the now-shirtless Jonah beside her. She'd changed into a black bikini that made my flowery one-piece feel childish. Ramit had left to shower before dinner—maybe he had anxiety about being naked in front of everyone too.

Despite Jonah's proximity, I felt drowsy and relaxed in the sunshine. A flowering bush nearby released the sweet scent of honeysuckle, and a wind chime tinkled delicately. When was the last time I'd been on vacation? Not for years—COVID, grad school, and my first social work job had kept me homebound. Now, my body felt heavy and immobile, like it was melting onto the plush beach towel.

Grace had gotten us the Wi-Fi password—*healing123*—and I'd immediately texted Dom that Jonah the PI was here too. She'd responded with a series of exclamation points. And then: Hmm well maybe you really ARE on to something . . .

I'd responded: What if he's a spy for this place?

That'd be CRAZY. Can you question him about it?

I can try. Not that I had detective skills . . . but maybe my clinical skills would help?

What are they like? Dom had asked, sending emojis for the sun and moon.

I'd responded: No sightings yet. Grace had told us Moon and Sol were indeed around but "preparing" for us, and that we'd see them at dinner.

I knew I had to do much more surveying, more sleuthing. But I also had to fool everyone into thinking that I was here for the right reasons, didn't I? And if that meant hanging out by the pool for an hour or two . . . then maybe that was okay.

Mikki got up and wandered towards the pool.

"So, how are you doing?" Jonah settled into her vacated chair, his voice low.

"Oh, I'm fine." The relaxation vanished; now my body was as tight as a spring. "Just loving that I get to spend more time with you."

"I appreciate you keeping everything under wraps. And also . . ." He angled himself towards me. "I wanted to apologize for what happened."

The words surprised me, but I recovered quickly. "'What happened'? That's what you're calling it?"

"Fair. What I did." He ran a hand through his curls. "I didn't mean any harm, but I can see how intrusive that was, coming into your home like that. I should've kept us at the bar."

Gross. It made me feel like a chess piece, one he could move around at will. I didn't answer, and he went on. "It's a weird field. I don't break the law, but there're a lot of gray areas. And when I get wrapped up in a case—that's always my focus, above everything else."

I stared out at the pool. Mikki was deep in conversation with Karen and Dawne.

"And for the record," he went on, smiling faintly, "I've had more than my share of one-night stands. So I'm really sorry for sounding like a judgmental, sexist pig. That was an extremely shitty thing to say."

"I appreciate the apology." I paused. "But how can I believe you? For all I know, you work for Moon and Sol."

His eyebrows shot up. "You think they hired me to go to New York, talk to you, and then come back here and pretend to be a guest so I can put you off the scent?"

"Well . . . yeah."

He scratched his chin. "Think about it. If they're doing anything shady, why would they have me here conspiring with you? Wouldn't it be easier for them to just host a normal-seeming retreat and expect you to go away after?"

That stumped me.

"You've heard of Occam's razor, right?" he asked.

"Please don't ask me if I've heard of Occam's razor," I snapped. Any goodwill from his apology melted away. God, he was condescending.

"Sorry." He shrugged. "It just seems unnecessarily complicated. But maybe it makes sense to you." He turned to me, lowered his voice even further. "I understand if you don't trust me. That's fine. We can keep our distance from each other if you want. I just thought it might make sense for us to pool our resources."

"Okay, then tell me this—why'd you end up here?"

He opened his mouth, but suddenly Mikki appeared over us, water droplets glistening on her shoulders. Jonah relinquished her chair, and she sat, wrapping herself in a towel.

"Sorry to interrupt." Smirking at me, she winked.

22

As we left the pool to get ready for dinner, anticipation hummed in the air. I wondered if Moon and Sol's absence was a tactic, a way to get us to revere them before they actually appeared.

I headed back to my yurt, relieved I'd stayed dry so I didn't have to brave the showers. My brain whirred as I got dressed. As much as I hated to admit it, Jonah's explanation made sense. His presence was making me more suspicious of the Center, not less. It wouldn't be logical for Moon and Sol to plant him in this group, not if I already knew him.

I thought back to his phrase: *pool our resources.* Did he have information about Catherine that I didn't?

Another question: When were we going to start "the sessions," and what exactly would they entail? My chest squeezed with anxiety as I plopped on the bed. I picked up my diary and flipped through it, noting the rounded letters amongst an abundance of drawn flowers, hearts, and smiley faces. I stopped and read from a random page.

I am SOOO mad I'm shaking. Melissa is acting like such a b-word!!! We were supposed to have a sleepover this weekend and watch Stargirl and I was really looking forward to it. Adam and his idiot friends have been really mean this week. And then on FRIDAY MORNING she tells me that she has to go to a family thing and can't do the sleepover anymore. And then . . . I overhear in the bathroom that ASHLEY'S having a sleepover that night. Guess who's going. My BFF. Right.

I had no memory of that, but it didn't surprise me. Melissa and queen bee Ashley had started hanging out during basketball camp the summer before eighth grade. Throughout that next year, Melissa had slowly but surely moved into the cool girls' orbit. But not all at once. Maybe that's what had made it so painful—sometimes she'd act like everything was normal between us.

I turned to another page.

I had an AWESOME dream last night about Sebastian Smith. He was in my class and we were assigned to do a project together and he was always coming over. We liked each other and even snuggled under a blanket once (with our clothes on of course!!). Then we were walking through school holding hands and Mike was joking and singing "Sebastian and Thea are getting married!" It was SUCH a great dream!!!

I thought back to the podcast where Moon had been talking about her crush, how her aloneness had led to its intensity. *I think a lot of young girls in particular are told that all we need is our prince to feel better.*

"Thea . . . coming?" Mikki called from outside my door.

"Yeah." I set down the diary, feeling disoriented, like I'd been ripped out of another world. I grabbed a jean jacket; the temperature was dropping with the sun. "Be right there."

The dining room was lined in wooden panels, the one respite from the mosaics covering the rest of the castle's walls. The high-ceilinged room featured a giant stone fireplace and a long wooden table set with a rainbow of ceramic plates. Two large chandeliers made of colorful glass parrots cast a warm light. Tantalizing smells emanated from the kitchen: roasted vegetables and clove and cardamom.

"That smells *so* good," Mikki muttered. She'd changed into a long black dress and slicked on lipstick. I locked eyes with Jonah, who sat between Dawne and Ramit. He looked away, nodding at something Dawne was saying. I squared my shoulders and followed Mikki to the table as she settled across from them.

"Hi, girls!" Dawne beamed. She'd also dressed up, with smoky eye makeup and a pleather blazer. "Ready to meet our gurus?"

"Ready as I'll ever be." Mikki poured us glasses of water from a pitcher.

Ramit raised a hand to greet us, his eyes darting down to the table. He seemed a little nerdy, a little shy. I knew how he felt.

"So it's just the six of us?" Mikki asked. She pointed and named everyone. "Ramit, Jonah, Dawne, Thea, me, and . . . where's Karen?"

"I'm here!" Karen flew into the open chair next to Mikki. "Hi, all." She shrugged off her fleece, revealing a T-shirt that said *I'M A KNIT-TER NOT A QUITTER.*

"All right." Mikki leaned back in her seat. "Let's get this show on the road."

As if summoned, Grace strode in. "Hi, guys!" She paused at the empty seat at the head of the table, then smoothed back her neon orange hair. Beads of sweat lined her upper lip. "Food's almost ready, so I wanted to share a few announcements. First, we're a substance-free retreat. So no drugs or alcohol, and if you're found using anything, we have to ask you to leave. It's on the website, but if you missed it and brought something, just put it away. We need everyone to be totally clearheaded as we do this deep work."

I guess I hadn't been expecting copious cocktails, but . . . nothing whatsoever? No *wine*?

"And now." Grace grinned. "It's time to introduce you to the people you came to see." She gestured to the door. "Please welcome . . . Moon and Sol!"

But only one person strolled into the space: Sol. He was more attractive than the pictures had suggested, or maybe it was his energy— confident, calm. He was tall and rangy with a yoga body, shaggy blond hair, a trim beard, and bright blue eyes. His grin dug furrows on either side of his mouth, his eyes crinkling.

He also looked slightly familiar. Who did he remind me of?

The room hushed with expectation.

"Hello." Sol grasped the back of the chair at the head of the table. A silver wedding ring glinted. "How's everyone doing today?"

The smooth, drawling voice from the podcast—it was strange to hear it coming from a live human being.

We muttered back *his* and *hellos.*

He held up an invisible mic to his face and cried: "I *said*: How's everyone doing today?"

"Great!" Dawne and Karen both shouted, and everyone laughed.

"Good, good." He chuckled, looking down for a moment. "Ohh, that's obnoxious, isn't it? You guys like my motivational speaker impersonation?"

Dawne clapped, grinning widely, and Mikki gave a joking fist pump.

"Well, let me just say: welcome to the Center." He leaned down, casually resting his arms on the back of the chair. His expression became serious, and without the scaffolding of a big smile, he looked older. "I want to first acknowledge the land we're on: the unceded territory of the Mescalero Apache. As a white man it's important to me that we remember the devastation that our forefathers have wrought. Let's have a moment of silence." He dipped his head. Everyone else looked down, though I caught Mikki studying him. She appeared to be the only woman of color here.

"All right." Sol raised his head. "I also want to start tonight by saying this: If you *do* see me acting like a motivational speaker, please let me know. Because I'm not here to motivate anyone. If you're here, then you're here for a reason. My job is to help facilitate the change that you came to make. So." He straightened and clapped his large hands. "Let's hear some reasons why you're here."

There was silence.

"Relationships!" Karen finally called out.

"Yes." Sol angled his upper body towards her. "What about relationships?"

"Well, I'm divorced and single." She shrugged. "So clearly I suck at them."

Everyone chuckled, relieving some of the nervous tension.

"Oh yeah?" Sol grinned.

"Yeah. A friend suggested I get my butt here pronto."

"Gotcha. What's your name, dear?"

Dear. Yuck. That was condescending.

She didn't seem to mind. "Karen." She shifted. "From Tempe, Arizona."

"Karen from Tempe, Arizona. Thank you for speaking up first. That's a good answer, right? I imagine a lot of people here can relate. Anyone else have a different answer?" His eyes roamed the table, passing over me, startling me with the intensity of his gaze. I felt suddenly anxious, like I might be called to come up in front of the class.

"I'm here for the same reason," Dawne said. "Except I always find *other* people who suck at relationships."

Sol's eyes trained on her. "And you are?"

"Dawne." She nervously twirled a lock of hair. "With an *e*."

"Dawne with an *e*," he echoed. "You feel like you're attracted to the wrong partners."

"Exactly." She said it emphatically.

"Do you know why?"

She shrugged. "Something to do with my parents?"

"Good." Sol nodded approvingly. "You're on the right track." He drummed the back of his seat. "Anyone *not* know why they're here?"

No one moved. It might've been Sol's strong presence, or just the nature of people opening up about themselves, but the energy of the room felt charged. A cool wind rushed in through the open doorway, making me shiver.

"I ask because those without a goal are the ones to give up first." He scanned the table, his eyes stopping on me. "Anyone else want to share?"

My stomach growled, embarrassingly loud, in response. I slapped a hand on my belly as if to quell it.

"Can we do this after we eat?" Mikki murmured.

Sol trained on Mikki. "Say that again?"

She smiled sweetly. "I was just wondering about dinner. It smells amazing."

"And you're hungry."

"Yep."

His dazzling smile returned. "So you're saying you're feeling a little uncomfortable right now?"

"Sure?" She was smiling back, but a new, fraught tension filled the space.

"What's your name?" Sol asked.

"Mikki."

"So, Mikki." He plopped into his chair, one arm on the back. "Why are you here?"

"You want me to say it in front of everyone?"

"It's all going to come out this weekend." He lifted a hand. "You're just getting a head start."

"Fine." She sat back in her chair and crossed her arms. "I'm here because I'm a sex and love addict."

"Great!" Sol looked thrilled. "You have a defined problem. You're ahead of the game."

"Wonderful." Mikki continued to smile, but her eyes were watchful.

"And what made you come *here*?" Sol asked. "There are programs, treatment centers, groups, what have you, all over the place."

"My therapist recommended it." Mikki shrugged. "And I needed a vacation."

Karen snorted. Dawne looked horrified.

Sol leaned forward. "Oh, Mikki, no. No, no, no. This is the exact *opposite* of a vacation. This is boot camp. This is going to be one of the most difficult weekends of your entire life—if not *the* most difficult. Everyone's going to fall apart here. Everyone. And you know what? It's going to be fucking great."

Mikki studied Sol.

"How's that to hear?" Sol asked. "You can tell me to fuck off, if you'd like. No wrong answers."

"No." She looked thoughtful. "I have no problem falling apart. But I don't know about the boot camp analogy. I'm not one to take orders."

"And you don't have to. There's only one rule here, and that's to be invested." Sol smacked the table lightly. "If you treat this as something foolish, then you're going to waste your—and my—time. But I don't think you'll do that, Mikki. I think you actually want to be here. There's just a part of you that's suspicious. And tonight, fine, you can feel ambivalent. But don't let it take over the whole weekend. Promise me you'll try. Okay?"

After a second, she nodded. Sol leaned back, satisfied.

"Mikki has a good point, though," he said. "You must all be fucking starving."

We laughed.

"So I'll shut up in a moment," he went on. "But the last thing I'll say is that your being here is important. Figuring out your romantic issues will actually help you with *all* of your relationships. Our society pushes this obsession with finding 'the one,' but we want to expand your view. We want you to find intimacy in all of its forms, including what I consider one of the most important: community." He gestured around the table. "Okay, I'll stop. Any last urgent questions?"

"I have one." Karen cleared her throat. "Is Moon coming?"

Sol stared at her without speaking. The silence stretched.

"She's not feeling well tonight." His smile returned. "But she's a fighter. I'm sure she'll be back to her old self by tomorrow. Now, let's eat."

Grace and Steven came out of the kitchen, carrying platters piled high: tart chicken masala, rich vegetable biryani, gingery palak paneer, crispy samosas, fresh garlic naan. I was surprised they served meat, but

it was probably free-range, organic, etc. The dining hall filled with boisterous voices and laughter. Everyone apparently felt chatty after Sol's
introduction. I was relieved I'd managed to escape his initial questioning. I accidentally caught eyes with Jonah across the table and wondered if he felt the same way.

I watched Sol, who was talking animatedly with Dawne and Karen.
If he did know anything about Catherine, I had the sense it wasn't
going to be easy to find out.

"Let the games begin," Mikki murmured as she paused to sip her
water. She gazed at me. "You ready for this?"

"I guess we'll see." I looked again at Sol, and suddenly the vague
familiarity clicked into place. I knew exactly who he reminded me of.

It was his looks, but also his energy: calm, paternal, charismatic, a
little challenging.

He reminded me of Pastor John.

23

After dinner: the "initiation ceremony." The temperature had plummeted, and we returned to our yurts to grab extra layers. Inside, I stood there for a moment, feeling off-kilter. This glittering mosaic world, the feeling of being watched in the courtyard, Jonah's unexpected appearance, and now Sol reminding me of Pastor John . . . It was like entering a fun house where the normal rules didn't apply.

We walked as a group towards the firepit; thin electric lights revealed the path. The sky was a bright royal blue at the horizon, fading into a rich navy above. The stars winked overhead; I hadn't seen a night sky like this since living upstate. But here, there were no chirping crickets or croaking frogs. Apart from the rush of the wind, it was dead silent.

"What's your name again?"

I looked over to see the tiny Dawne, who wore a short fur coat.

"Thea," I said. "You're Dawne, right?"

"That's right!" She grinned up at me. "Have you been on this type of retreat before?"

"No, never. Have you?"

"Not this one specifically, but a *lot* of other relational retreats. They're *so* helpful."

So helpful you have to keep going to them? I pushed the unkind thought down.

"You'll be amazed at the progress you make this weekend," she went on.

Mikki's sputtered laugh rang out in front of us. She was walking with Jonah, so close their hips were almost touching. *Watch out, Mikki. He's not who he's pretending to be.* I felt a sudden loyalty to her, even though we'd just met. But I couldn't warn her to be careful—unless I wanted to blow Jonah's cover.

Blow his cover. What was I, a freaking spy?

We neared the bonfire, which danced with massive flames. Grace waited just inside the circle of ankle-high rocks marking the space. Her fluorescent hair softened to copper in the darkness, she directed us to the benches. They were set back about twenty feet, though the warmth of the fire still radiated like sunlight.

Mikki took the first seat. I sat next to her, and Dawne settled next to me. Jonah was at the end—good. I wanted to be as far from him as possible if we were doing group work. Sol was crouched down closer to the fire, ruffling through a large tote bag.

Dawne grabbed my wrist, her long nails digging in like talons. "There she is!"

We all turned to stare at the figure approaching out of the darkness.

In defiance of the cold, Moon wore a fluttering, diaphanous white dress. Lit by the flames, the shadowy outline of the castle behind her, she looked like a frame from a fantasy movie. She could've been an elfin queen, but not a particularly nice one. Her lips were pressed together, her expression determined. Her long dark hair trailed behind her, ruffling in the breeze.

Steven, resident mosaic artist and bag handler, strode beside her, a marked contrast to her otherworldly appearance in his baseball cap and scruffy beard. Slightly hunched, he stared at the ground, avoiding eye contact with all of us, as if he were an antisocial sound guy who'd arrived to help set up the show.

I glanced over; Sol had straightened and was watching their approach with a clear frown on his face. He'd gone completely still, like an animal aware of an approaching predator—or prey. When Moon and Steven reached the edge of the stone circle, his face broke into an enormous grin.

"You came!" He jogged over and bent to kiss her on the cheek. She looked away, a small, polite smile on her face. Something glinted on her chest—a diamond on a thin gold chain. A full sleeve of tattoos covered her left arm.

"We're ready?" she asked. I recognized her voice from the podcast, but it was stronger, clearer, projecting over the crackles of the fire.

"Yup. Would you like to . . ."

"Yes." She turned, taking the bag from Steven.

We all watched, fascinated audience members to the exchange. Moon's annoyance towards Sol was obvious, at least to me. Throughout the exchange, Steven continued to gaze silently at the ground. Sol reached out suddenly and clapped him on the shoulder, making him jump.

Moon advanced towards us, the fire at her back, and cleared her throat. She still looked elfin up close: anime-large eyes, strong brows, heart-shaped face.

"Hi, everyone," she said.

"Hi!" Dawne called out with delight.

Moon's eyes dropped down to her and she smiled. Her front teeth were slightly crooked, bookmarked by sharp cheekbones and dimples. She was, like Sol, markedly attractive in person. Her body was small and curvy, her nipples visible underneath the thin white dress. I felt that combination of judgment and admiration that arose whenever I saw a woman brave enough to go braless.

"Welcome," she said. "I'm sorry I couldn't make our first meal; I needed to gain strength for our initiation ceremony tonight." Her voice, with that lilting Mexican accent, was richer in person. Dawne and Karen cheered. Sol and Steven settled onto the sand at the other edge of the group, next to Jonah.

Moon cocked her head. "That's it? Two people are excited?"

The rest of us clapped and yelled. She smiled. "That's better. I would like to open the ceremony by thanking my ancestors, the proud and ancient line that stretches back through the ages. I thank them for the practices they have given me." She pulled a pouch out of her bag and walked towards Mikki. "So, we're going to start with accountability partners."

"Accountability partners?" Karen echoed.

"Yes." Moon bounced the pouch in her hands, mixing whatever was inside it. "You are going to check in with your partner. A lot. I'm sure Sol had told you that even though we started off a little slow today, the rest of the time is going to fly by. We're going to have group sessions, and we'll also sit down one-on-one with all of you. But in the meantime, we ask that you process as much as you can with your partner. We'll start with you . . ."

"I'm Mikki." She zipped up her leather bomber jacket.

Moon pulled out a small folded piece of paper. She opened it, squinted. "Dawne."

Dawne waved. "Yay!"

Mikki smiled back, less effusive.

Moon stepped in front of me, glancing up. "Name?"

"Thea."

"Thea." Her eyes were a warm amber. She reached into the bag.

Even before she opened the paper, I had a sudden certainty of who it would be.

"Jonah," she read. He dipped his head in acknowledgment.

Of *course* I'd be paired with Jonah. But maybe it wouldn't be the worst thing. If we were both looking for Catherine, no one would be suspicious if they saw us talking quietly. *Processing.*

"So, you two." Moon gestured at Ramit and Karen. "You'll be together. Okay?"

Karen raised her hand and Ramit slapped it.

"Tonight we are going to connect and set an intention." Moon gestured. "To connect, you're going to share something with your accountability partner that you've never told anyone before. You won't need to share this with the rest of the group. Just each other. Okay? You can go sit wherever you want so people can't overhear."

Jonah and I dropped into the sand on the opposite side of the fire. He wore a knit ski cap, and his curls escaped from the bottom. I wasn't sure where to look; he was staring at me intensely. Did he mean to smolder, or was that just his face?

"Still mad?" he asked.

"What?" I said stupidly.

"You ignored me all through dinner." He frowned. "Someone might notice, by the way."

"I was just talking to Karen and Mikki. Anyway." I shook my head; I wasn't going to *bicker* with him. "You never answered my question at the pool. How did you know Catherine was connected with this place?"

"Facial recognition software."

"From . . ."

"Facebook." He shrugged. "Tech is my specialty. I'd scanned before—multiple times—but someone just put up public photos of a retreat they went on last year. Catherine was in several of them."

A chill went down my spine. "So there're pictures linking her here. Evidence."

"Exactly."

"Can I see them?"

"Of course." He nodded. "But they're in a password-protected folder on my laptop."

"Which is . . ."

"In New York. I thought it might be a little suspect to bring it along." It was the same reason I'd left my own laptop back home.

"But hey." Jonah smiled faintly. "Quid pro quo. How did *you* know to come here?"

I briefly explained Catherine's note, the logo, and the *come home* podcast episode.

"So you think Moon and Sol sent her a message using the podcast?" he asked when I finished. "And she wanted you to hear it?"

"Yes. I mean, otherwise that's a huge coincidence, right?" I exhaled. "I don't know what I was expecting, though. Now that I'm here . . . I don't know what to do. How to go about this."

He dug into the sand, picking up a palmful and dropping it again. "I say we spend tonight and tomorrow getting as much info as we can directly. Tomorrow night, we case it out."

"Case it out." The term sounded foreign.

"Search the building."

"So you think she might be here?" The thought made the back of my neck prickle.

"You don't?" he asked.

"I don't know. I did feel like someone was watching me in the court-yard this afternoon. But I didn't see anything. I could've just been making it up."

He continued to watch me. I knew it was a technique, and yet I couldn't stop the words tumbling from my mouth. "I called one of the officers who came to the unit after Catherine left, and she made me feel like such an idiot. She told me that Catherine also disappeared five years ago, but that she was pulling out money the whole time."

His eyebrows drew together. "Why does that make you an idiot?"

"Well, because maybe Catherine just *does* this. Disappears."

"But why?" He leaned in. "She's caught up in something. That's why her parents hired us—and a hacker to try to break into her bank's system. We couldn't find anything. Until now. Catherine's *here*, Thea. She left—maybe got away?—but now she's back."

"Two-minute warning!" Moon called from the other side of the fire.

"So you think they're involved?" I lowered my voice further. "Moon and Sol."

"Absolutely."

"What do you think of them?"

He stared at me. "What do I think? They're cult leaders. This is a cult."

"You're that sure."

"I mean, they're just getting started, but yes."

"So do we question them at some point?"

"After we search the building. Until then, we keep quiet. Don't let anyone know why you're here. Why *we're* here." He softened his voice. "Okay?"

"Obviously." I paused, my stomach fluttering with a new thought. "You don't think Moon and Sol . . . could they have been the impostors who picked Catherine up? I saw some video footage. He was tall; she was short. Though his body shape was different. And she had blond hair. Though of course she could've worn a wig . . ."

Jonah nodded approvingly. "I wondered that too. So I sent pictures of Moon and Sol to Killian and Lisette, who forwarded them to . . . what's her name? Diane? She confirmed that the couple who came in *wasn't* them."

"Oh." The flash of inspiration faded into disappointment. Then again, it was a long shot. I couldn't picture Moon and Sol flying to New York, somehow making fake IDs, and sneaking in with disguises like undercover restaurant reviewers at the hottest new bistro.

"One minute!" Moon called.

"Why would they even have a retreat weekend if they're hiding Catherine?" I gestured towards Moon. "Isn't that risky?"

He shrugged. "To keep everything seeming normal? Or maybe they need the money. They're making what . . . 24K in one weekend?"

Moon called us all back together, handing out wooden slats and Sharpies.

"Okay!" Moon held up one of the pieces of wood. "We're now going to write our intention in one word. Something we want to let go of this weekend. And go deep. No one else will see it but you."

I paused only a second before writing *SHAME* on mine, then held it face down on my lap.

Moon pulled out a round, skin-stretched drum whose sides were covered in feathers. She started a slow, dramatic tattoo and nodded at me to go first. I walked towards the heat of the bonfire, then heaved in the wood. It crashed down in a shower of embers. Everyone cheered. I felt a small thrill at the applause, and couldn't help but grin as I went back to my seat.

Jonah was gripping his slat, his fingers covering half the word, but I was still able to make it out as he jumped up and moved towards the fire.

The word was, strangely, *DOUBT*.

24

I'd thought the night would wind down after the ceremony. I was wrong.

After Ramit threw the last piece of wood into the fire, Moon led us in a processional back towards the castle, still banging her drum. We marched down the path, past the yurts and yoga tent, across the veranda, beyond the pool. Finally, we arrived at the wooden hot tub. Someone had turned on twinkling fairy lights that illuminated the space.

"Time to submerge!" Moon relished the words, beaming. "Get in!" Her drumbeat quickened, taking on an ominous tone.

"What?" Ramit said quietly.

"Submersion time, folks!" Sol pulled off his sweatshirt, revealing a taut, bare chest. He pulled the cover off the top of the tub, releasing billows of steam into the chilly night.

Moon stopped banging with a final thump and for a moment, everyone stood there in shock. We could hear Grace and Steven as they crossed the veranda, chatting softly while hauling Moon and Sol's bags. The sounds faded as they went inside.

"Well, okay," Dawne murmured as Sol shucked his pants and skipped up the steps, his white ass shining in the fairy lights. He gave an appreciative sigh as he slipped in the water.

"Guys, it feels fucking amazing." He rubbed his face.

Moon set down the drum and drew up her white dress, showcasing the downy tufts in her armpits. Yep, there were those nipples, now attached to full breasts. More tattoos dotted her chest and ribs. She wore black hipster-style underwear that she tugged down. I glimpsed a triangle of dark pubic hair before realizing I was staring and looked away.

Dawne gave a small "Whoo!" and bent to unzip her platform boots. As if a button had been pushed, everyone started to tear off jackets and clothes. Even Karen, who was cackling and muttering, "Nothing we haven't seen before!" Even Ramit, who looked alarmed.

Mikki rolled her eyes at me, suddenly in just her black bra.

Wait. Was this happening? Was I expected to get naked in front of people I'd met hours before? It felt suddenly hard to breathe.

I thought of Jonah's words: *This is a cult.* Was this part of it, forcing people to be naked together, to increase their vulnerability or something?

In a flurry of skin, people were slipping into the hot tub, under the cover of the water. I suddenly realized that if I waited too long, everyone would be sitting there staring at me, watching my own personal strip show. Dawne and Jonah were already in the tub, which was larger than it looked from the outside.

Ramit—more muscular than I would've guessed—tried to casually cover his penis as he got into the tub. A nude Karen swung her shirt around her head.

"Party time!" she cried, then thundered up the steps and plopped in with a splash.

I still hadn't made a move, stunned. It struck me that I could refuse, that I could say I wasn't feeling well and go back to my yurt. But as Moon stood there, waiting patiently, I had a feeling it wouldn't be that easy.

She came closer, her breasts jiggling with every step. "You okay, Thea?" The diamond necklace gleamed at her collarbone.

There. The symbol tattooed on her chest, in the same position as Catherine's.

"Um." I tore my eyes away. Jonah had proof that Catherine had been here, but this was the first evidence I'd seen with my own eyes. It couldn't be a coincidence, them having the same tattoo in the same place.

"It's all right." Moon put a ringed hand on my shoulder. This close, her spiced rose scent entered my nostrils. I glanced around. Mikki, the last to go in, had abandoned me, leaving her clothes in a neat pile.

"These are just our meat suits." Moon grabbed a handful of flesh at her hip. "They don't really mean anything."

Well, I wouldn't go that far. It wasn't that I was particularly precious about my body; in college, I'd actually signed up to model nude for other art classes. While I had physical insecurities like many women, that wasn't necessarily what was holding me back.

What bothered me was the lack of sensitivity. What if I had an eating disorder, or body dysmorphia? There was seemingly no regard for how triggering this could be for people.

And even if I didn't have those particular issues, it wasn't like I was magically cool with people—especially strange men—*especially* Sol and Jonah and Ramit—seeing every part of me.

"I'll go with you." Moon gestured to the hot tub. "Ready?"

"I'm sorry." It was hard to protest—almost impossible—but I forced the words. "I'm not sure I'm comfortable with this."

"Thea, if you don't want to, you don't have to." Moon's golden lioness eyes were hypnotic. She held both my arms in a parental way, her naked flesh filling my vision.

"Okay, great." I kept my eyes on hers.

"*But*," she went on, "we really encourage radical vulnerability here. Exposure in all possible ways. You understand?"

"Yeah, I just . . ." To my horror, frustrated tears filled my eyes. I ordered them not to fall. Everyone was quiet in the hot tub, surreptitiously watching.

"Just a sec." Moon let go of me and walked off, her bare feet slapping against the mosaic floor. Suddenly, the fairy lights around the pool area turned off. There was still the moonlight, but it was much darker than it had been a second ago.

"Everyone, close your eyes," Moon directed as she came back.

"Closed!" Sol cried.

"Better?" Moon put a palm over her eyes. "I won't look either. Promise!"

"It feels so good," Karen called. "You'll love it once you get in."

What else could I do? Moon wasn't going to give up, and this was just going to get more and more awkward by the second. And I *wasn't* a prude, or anything like that—that was the aggravating part, that everyone now probably thought so.

"Fine." I unzipped my coat. Numbly, I pulled off my sweater and bra, then pushed down my jeans, almost tripping as I kicked off my shoes. The brisk breeze raised goose bumps on my arms. I swept past Moon, up the steps, and down into the water.

"Yay, Thea!" Moon cried, clapping. Everyone broke out into cheers. It was like a dam had burst, all the tension I'd caused—well, Moon had caused, really—suddenly defused.

And it did in fact feel amazing to be in the hot, steaming water, breathing in the bracing air.

"Good job, honey!" Dawne slipped an arm on my shoulders. "None of us should be afraid to be natural."

I hid a smile at the "natural"; Dawne's breasts seemed clearly fake. "Thanks." The frustration was now shifting quickly into embarrassment. Maybe I had made too big a deal over it. After all, no one else seemed to mind.

"I like it better like this anyway, without the lights." Mikki floated over and tipped her head back. "You can see the stars."

Moon gathered into a little group with Sol, Ramit, and Jonah across the tub. I couldn't see the tattoo in the steam, but knowledge of it put me on high alert. *Remember why you're here.*

"Hey, hon." Next to me, Karen spoke in a low voice. "You okay? I wanted to tell Moon to lay off, but I didn't want to overstep. You're a grown woman from New York; you of all people can take care of yourself."

Was that how she saw me? "Yeah, no, thanks. It's fine."

"You know, when I was your age, I wouldn't have been so happy with this either." Karen shrugged. "I actually lived in a nunnery from my twenties into my thirties."

"Really?"

She laughed at my surprise. "Yep. Right after college. I started grad school and was doing this project with nuns living in an abbey outside of Tucson. And something about their lives—they just seemed to have this sense of peace. I'd never seen anything like it. So I dropped out and moved in. I'd grown up Catholic, but it hadn't ever meant that much to me."

"How long were you there?" I asked.

She sighed. "Oh, about ten years. Towards the end I was at a conference and feeling less thrilled with the whole thing. Disillusioned. With any group there's going to be discord and power struggles, but I felt like we weren't able to sort it out, and it just festered. So I ditched the conference to go to a bar, and that's where I met my husband. Art was a nice man. A little wild too. He's the one who started signing us up for these nude cruises."

"Did I hear the phrase 'nude cruises'?" Mikki sidled up, grinning.

It relieved me that we'd moved on from my dramatic moment.

Dawne joined and told us about a nude beach party at a Costa Rica retreat the year before.

"You'd be surprised which guys had the biggest *hmm*-hmms." She bobbed her head back and forth. "It's always the quiet ones."

Sol let out a huge guffaw and we all giggled. Maybe this naked-hot-tub thing was meant to loosen us all up? The air felt celebratory, especially when Moon appeared with a huge unmarked bottle and passed it around. Could it be? My kingdom for a swig of tequila. But when it came my way—Moon was watching; I had to sip, saliva and sickness be damned—I found it was ice-cold pineapple juice. I handed it to Mikki, who was talking quietly to Moon. She chuckled and nodded as Moon grabbed her arm. Fast friends, huh?

Sometime later—a half hour? More?—Moon raised her hands. "Everyone, a few announcements before bed. First, a breakfast buffet will be in the dining room starting at seven. Sessions will start at eight in the yoga pavilion. Okay?"

"Also!" Sol spoke between cupped hands, which was really not necessary. "If you have any dreams tonight, please let us know."

"The veils between the worlds are very thin out here," Moon added. "People often get messages from the other side." She climbed out of the hot tub, her body shining like a seal's, with Sol close behind. I noticed Jonah and Ramit watching them—her, most likely. The couple picked up their clothes and started walking back to the castle, still naked. He said something and she pushed him, flirting. Whatever tension had been between them earlier was gone.

Dawne got out next. "Night, everyone!" Mikki and Karen quickly followed suit. Jonah climbed out, and I couldn't help but glance at his streamlined, muscular body. Who would've thought that we'd end up getting naked together, after all?

I wanted to leave, but something was holding me in place. The rest of the group drifted off to the yurts or showers. The stars winked above, blurring when I looked at them directly. There was still that eerie silence underneath the rush of the wind.

"You want to go first?" Ramit asked. His expression was unreadable in the darkness. "I'll close my eyes. Or I can go."

"Oh, thank you." It was thoughtful to offer. I realized I hadn't spoken to him much yet. "What brought you here, Ramit?"

He shrugged. "Well, first I got hooked on the podcasts. Then I went to this luncheon, where I met Sol, and we really hit it off. He let me know about this retreat. So . . . here I am. What about you?"

"Oh, similar story. The podcasts." I wondered how big their listenership was. It seemed like a pretty genius (and low-cost) way for a cult to spread the word.

"All right, you go." He held a hand over his eyes. "I'll get out last and put the cover on."

"Deal." I slipped out of the tub and pulled my clothes on over my wet, shivering skin.

"Well, good night," I called. "I'll see you tomorrow."

"You will." His voice was low, trepidatious, and maybe even tinged with doom.

I knew the feeling.

25

I did dream that night.

I was in the middle of the desert, sitting on sandy dirt that seared my naked skin. The merciless sun beat down, frying my back like bacon. God, it was hot. The heat felt tangible and heavy, crushing me like swaths of velvet. I swallowed and my dry tongue shifted like a small, dead animal in my mouth. Even breathing hurt, like inhaling boiling water.

There was someone lying beside me. She was still alive, but barely. Someone had betrayed us, left us here, but the shock and sorrow had long since drained away. Now, we were just animals, same as the lizards that shimmied by, or the vultures that wheeled overhead.

Something caught my eye in the distance, more a motion than anything: an undulating through the gentle shrub-dotted hills. I squinted, unable to tell what it was.

But it was coming towards us, and fast.

I woke with a gasp. Rolling over, I nearly tumbled out of the cot. I reached out wildly until my fingers connected with the battery-operated lamp.

I sat up in bed, forcing myself to take deep breaths. Okay. I was in a yurt at the Center. Not dying in a desert.

I couldn't remember the last time I'd felt such physical agony in a dream. But I rarely remembered my dreams, and maybe that was a good thing.

I glanced at the window. In the time it took to swing my head, I saw a face, solid and reflecting back the lamp's light behind the window screen.

But when I blinked, my eyes focusing, nothing was there.

I turned off the lamp and crept to the window, scanning as my heart pounded.

There was just that expanse of empty land, bathed in the faint opalescent glow of moonlight.

—————

My phone's alarm pulled me out of darkness. Sun beamed in from the open window. It had taken hours to fall back asleep after my scare, and as I sat up, my body felt heavy with exhaustion and disquiet. The memory of the face in the window came back to me.

It had to have been my imagination, primed by the *Stargirl*-like nightmare. I remembered now that I'd had nightmares after the movie too. Catherine's death scene in the desert had been a whole montage, ending with a long shot of her corpse. I couldn't remember if the dreams had included another person—presumably Catherine?—beside me.

In any case, I needed to focus. My throat felt like sandpaper from the dry desert air, and my water bottle was empty. My phone's battery was also almost out; there had to be outlets in the castle. I dressed quickly and stepped outside.

It was still chilly, but the ascending sun warmed my shoulders, shining out of another unbroken cerulean sky. The bathroom was empty, though showers rushed in the room beyond. I brushed my teeth, hoping I wouldn't come face-to-face with any cheerful, naked attendees first thing in the morning. I myself would wait until an off-peak time to shower.

On the way to the dining room I waved at Dawne and Karen, sipping from stoneware mugs on the veranda. Inside, a simple but hearty buffet awaited: cinnamon-flecked oatmeal, hard-boiled eggs, warm stacks of toast, salted butter, homemade jams, local honey. I filled up a plate and poured a huge mug of coffee, then headed back outside.

"You ladies ready to get started?" Karen smiled as I took a seat.

"Absolutely." Dawne tipped her face to the sun. She wore pleather leggings and another pair of towering heeled boots.

"Totally." I swallowed a bite of toast. "How do you think the 'sessions' will go?"

"No clue." Karen shrugged. "This is my first time at this type of thing."

"I'm sure we'll start slow," Dawne said. "That's how it usually works. Maybe some morning vinyasa to wake us up and get us in our bodies?"

Steven, in the same worn baseball cap, zoomed past us with a cardboard box.

"Hi, Steven!" Dawne cried.

He barely dipped his chin as he passed.

"Not the friendliest, huh?" Karen mused.

"I think he's cute." Dawne smirked. "And based on dinner, an amazing chef."

"He made dinner?" I asked.

"That's what Grace told me. Apparently, he lived in India for a few years and knows how to make everything from scratch." She twirled a lock of hair. "I'd love to meet a man who can cook."

I approached the yoga tent with dread curdling in my gut. A memory flashed: sitting in the car as Dad drove us to church feeling this same apprehension. Knowing I'd have to watch Pastor John give the sermon and then shake his hand on the way out of the sanctuary. Knowing he'd stare past my shoulder, smile through me like I was a ghost.

Inside, it smelled like sage. Grace was setting out a half circle of cushions while Moon bent over a plate, blowing on the smoke coming from the dried leaves. Sol sat with his eyes closed in meditation.

"Hi!" Grace whispered. She wore a vintage sandwich shop T-shirt and her tangerine hair was gathered into two braids. She gestured to the cushions, and I sat and waited as the others filed in. Dawne's laugh rang out, causing Moon to flinch.

"Quiet, everyone!" Grace called softly.

Jonah nodded hello as he sat on my right side. What was that woodsy scent he wore? Or was it just him? I breathed it in hungrily. Mikki plopped on my other side, looking grim.

Moon walked around the circle, flapping the smoke towards us with a feather. I knew from my yoga days that sage was supposed to cleanse. My chest constricted. What was going to happen? My only hope was to fly under the radar as long as humanly possible.

Sol opened his eyes and smiled. "Good morning, everyone."

"Good morning," we echoed.

Moon settled next to him. "How'd everyone sleep?"

"*Great,*" Dawne called out.

"Good. Any dreams?" Sol scanned the room. His eyes stopped on me. I looked down.

"Not yet, huh? That's okay. We've got one more night." He got to his feet. "We have a lot of work to do today, friends. The plan is to have four sessions with a lunch break in the middle. Sound good?" Sol clapped his hands together. "So with that said, who'd like to go first?"

No sound, no movement; we all sat there frozen.

He chuckled. "*Go first and do what?* I can hear you asking. You'll see. This is your opportunity to be courageous."

"I'll go." Karen spoke. Relief flooded my system.

"Wonderful. Come on down, Karen." He beckoned, then gently clasped her shoulder. "So I'm going to ask you a series of questions. Please try to answer everything, even if the answer is *I don't know*."

A gentle pulsing sound: Moon was tapping a soft metronome into her drum. It felt discordant to see her acting as the quiet observer instead of the animated leader of the night before.

"Will do." Karen smiled nervously.

"So." Sol started walking in a slow circle around her. "Last night at dinner you told us you suck at relationships. Right?"

"That's correct." She sounded as if she were being questioned on the witness stand.

"And you mentioned a friend suggested you come."

"Yes."

"What made your friend do that?" The drumbeat added a sinister quality to the questioning, a horror movie soundtrack warning us to pay attention.

Karen smiled ruefully. "Well, he knows my dating issues. Specifically, that I'm too picky."

"Too picky," Sol echoed. "After you start dating people—well, men; you indicated on your paperwork you're straight—you decide they're not good enough?"

"Sometimes. Oftentimes."

"So, who's the last person you left?"

Karen squeezed her eyes shut. "Oh, goodness. Well, the last person was him."

"Him!" Sol glanced over at us with surprise, a comedian riffing with an audience member for a laugh. "Your *ex* suggested you should come here?"

"Yes. Well, we'd been friends for many years. We decided to try dating, and it just didn't work out." She shrugged.

"Interesting choice of words." Sol moved his hand in a straight line, like reading from a book. " 'It just didn't work out.' " My stomach dropped. Was my "work" going to look like this, a bad comedy routine?

Sol paused, glancing right at me as if he could hear my thoughts. "So, I'm being a little facetious, Karen. And there're a few reasons for that. The first is that I know—or I feel—that this is in fact the way to break through to you. Because the issue is that you're disconnected from your feelings."

Disconnected? The woman who was reading self-help books on the plane?

Sol turned back to her. "Is that right?"

After a second, she nodded.

"You're being honest with me, right, Karen? You're not just telling me what I want to hear?"

"Of course not." She scoffed.

"Good." Sol crossed his arms. "Now, some might ask: What happened to cut you off from your emotions? And that's an important question. But what I'm most interested in right now is the behavior. You say you're too picky, but I think you're actually picking these people on purpose. Just not consciously."

"Okay . . ." She sounded unsure.

"I bet they're all reeeeeally niiice." Sol drew out the words. "Good guys, huh?"

She nodded. "Yes."

"And they bore the living shit out of you!"

She groaned and dropped her head. Now we all laughed.

"I mean, let's take the last guy. You dumped his ass, and he's still trying to take care of you!" Sol tipped his head, like he was hearing something the rest of us couldn't. "He might've even . . . oh shit. Karen, did he . . . did he pay for this retreat?"

Her head was still in her hands. She bobbed her head once. Dawne gasped.

Moon watched everything neutrally, continuing her soft drumming.

"That makes sense." Sol nodded. "You take the care from the caretaker, and you don't understand why it doesn't feel good. I'll bet you're very confused. You have the best intentions, but . . ." His hand fluttered downwards. "You're just not into them."

When Karen raised her head, tears glittered in her eyes. "It feels awful."

"I'll bet it does." Sol's voice lowered. "Hurting the people who love you, over and over again. It feels like torture."

"It does." She swiped tears off her cheeks. My chest squeezed with sympathy.

"But that's why you're here," Sol went on. "Regardless of who paid your way, you're here to break the pattern." He turned to face us. "Our *patterns* are the relational dynamics we get caught up in. They feel normal to us. But if we step back, we can recognize them. And with that knowledge, decide if we want to break them." He turned back to Karen. "What's your pattern?"

"Like you said. Dating men I should like, but I don't." She watched him, wary but interested.

"Good." Sol gestured towards us. "It's time to pick someone from the group to channel your ghost lover."

"What?" She looked startled.

"Yes. Gender doesn't matter. Just whoever you feel is the best fit."

She gazed at us, evaluating. I wanted to hide, but I forced myself to return her eye contact. She was brave for going first, and if she wanted me to be a part of this, I would.

"Jonah," she said.

Sol beckoned. "Come on up."

What could he be feeling as he took his place next to Sol? After all, he was here for the same reason as me. To dig for information on Catherine. Not to get deep with a group of strangers.

Sol motioned. "So Jonah will represent your *ghost lover*: everything you yearn for in a partner. You chose Jonah because he has some of those qualities. Can you tell me what they are?"

"I'm not sure." Karen's voice sounded different, younger.

"First thing that comes to your mind."

"Confident." She glanced at Jonah, almost shyly.

"Confident, good." Sol walked around them both. "What else?"

"I don't know . . . He's a good-looking guy, I guess?" Karen shrugged.

"Yes." Sol nodded. "Confident, attractive . . . smart too."

Jonah smiled uncertainly.

"And what are some of your worst qualities, Jonah?" Sol took a step back.

"You're asking me?" he said.

"I am." Sol grinned.

"Okay." It was the first time I'd seen Jonah look unsure. "Well . . . I've been told I can be cut off from my emotions."

This was awkward. I wanted to look away, but couldn't.

Sol nudged Karen. "Sounds like someone else I know." She chuckled. "What about anger?" He retrained on Jonah.

Jonah nodded. "I do get angry sometimes."

"And what do you do when you get angry?"

Jonah paused. "I used to throw things. Punch things. People, sometimes. I don't anymore."

"You figured out how to hold all that anger in." Sol crossed his arms. "How do you treat people romantically?"

"It depends." Jonah shoved his hands in his pockets. "Sometimes I really like someone but it burns out quickly. A few times I've met someone that feels like the perfect fit, and I do everything I can to keep them. But . . . you know, it doesn't last."

"Good." Sol leaned towards Karen. "Who is he reminding you of?"

"My father," she said quietly.

"Okay." Sol clapped. "Thanks for confirming. I'm assuming your father had more power in the household; is that right?"

She nodded.

"Often we pattern ourselves after the parent in charge." Sol rested his hand on Jonah's shoulder. "Tell me more about Dad."

"Well, he was really charming," Karen said. "And everyone in town loved him. People knew he could be a little hotheaded, but no one knew the extent of it." She sniffed. "They didn't know he beat my mother. Once he broke her arm. He'd beat on my two older brothers too. But I was the youngest, and if I hid he wouldn't look too hard for me. So that made me feel guilty."

Sol nodded. "So there was violence. Chaos. Inside this popular, handsome man."

"Exactly. Not that I think you would do anything like that, Jonah."

"Tell me this." Sol stopped in front of her. "What did you learn from him? What traits does it take to have power in this world?"

"Well." She gestured. "Like we said, I disconnect from my feelings. But I'm not sure what else. I don't think I'm angry."

"Oh, you're fucking *furious*." Sol raised his voice. "I can feel the rage vibrating within you. It's very deep down. But why do you think you go after these passive men? It's because you get a certain pleasure out of flattening them. Men who beg you to let them pay for a trip after you discard them. How powerful does that feel?"

Karen stared at Sol, dazed. Finally, she nodded. "Maybe you're right. I never thought of it like that."

"We do everything for a reason." Sol turned back to us. "It may not make sense to other people, but we all follow an inner logic. It's hard for women to show anger in our society, isn't it? So they have to get creative—how to expel anger in sanctioned ways. How to punish men."

"Come on," Mikki murmured next to me. I was reminded, suddenly, of what Ace had said back in art therapy. *Because men are physically stronger, y'all have come up with your own weapons. Mental ones.* Was Sol peddling the same misogyny?

"Here's the problem." Sol stood behind Jonah, grasping his upper arms. "This is the lover you really want: strong, all-powerful. Someone to tell you what to do. But you know how toxic and smothering that would feel. If you pick men of the opposite temperament, you get to keep those traits for yourself. In a sense, you've *become* your ghost lover."

"Oh god." Karen bent over, covering her face. Moon's drumbeat picked up, becoming louder, more insistent.

"No, Karen." Sol pulled at her arm. "Tap into that power!"

She stood, her face red and wet.

"What do you want to say to your father?" Sol gestured at Jonah.

"He's dead," she choked out.

"Good! That means he's here, in spirit, with us right now."

Goose bumps pimpled my arms.

"I can't speak ill of the dead." Karen wrenched her head back and forth.

"He's not dead!" Sol cried, his voice filling the tent. "Karen, I just said he's here with us right now. What's his name?"

"Oscar."

"Oscar!" Sol pushed Jonah back and he stumbled, looking surprised. "What the *fuck* is your problem, man?"

"I—I don't know," Jonah said.

"First thing that comes to mind," Sol said.

"Um . . . okay." Jonah squared his shoulders. "My problem is that I'm sick of this, people clinging to me."

"Why?"

"It makes me feel claustrophobic."

"Are you from a big family, Oscar? Small?" Sol asked.

Jonah considered. "Big? But I think I was one of the younger siblings."

Karen gasped, a hand over her mouth.

"You don't like people clinging to you." Sol nodded. "So why'd you get married?"

"I had to. It's what people expected of me. And . . ." Jonah closed his eyes. "I'm not sure, but she might've been pregnant? My girlfriend. We had to get married."

"How did that make you feel?"

"Trapped."

Karen's hand remained over her mouth while fresh tears poured down her cheeks. What was happening? Because as they went back and forth, Jonah riffing from Oscar's point of view, his stature changed: his shoulders slumping, his head moving forward. Even the set of his jaw looked different.

"Karen!" Sol shouted. Moon's drumbeat increased in volume, her expression placid. "It's time to cut the cord. This shadowy figure of Oscar is no longer your ghost lover. It's time for an exorcism. Face him."

Karen turned towards Jonah.

"Say what you need to say," Sol directed.

"I love you, Dad." Her voice quavered. "Despite everything, I do. But you have to go. You have to let me live in peace."

"But I know what's best," Jonah growled.

"You *don't* know what's best. For me or anyone else. You're a small, scared man who lashed out at us. That's not how I want to be."

Jonah dropped to his knees. "Don't send me away."

"You need to move on." She kneeled in front of him, grasping his hands. "It's time, Dad. I'm going to be okay. Please. It's time for me to live my own life."

The drumbeat thudded, so loud and fast we could barely hear their words.

Sol stood behind Jonah, placing a hand on the top of his head.

"Oscar," he hollered. "We ask that you move into the next phase of your incarnation. Be gone!"

The drum stopped. Sol pushed Jonah's head down into a prone position, his forehead pressed to the wooden floor.

Sol backed off, and slowly, Jonah sat up. He looked around, confused, as if he didn't know where he was. Sol touched him on the back and pointed at his cushion. His breath was audible as he dropped beside me. I stared at him—*What the actual fuck?*

"Karen." Sol placed one hand on her shoulder. "He's gone."

She wiped more tears away and took a deep breath. "I know. I can feel it."

Ding. Moon was holding up a leather string that attached two metal cymbals. The clear, sharp note from their being struck together reverberated.

"Let's take a break." Sol pointed at the doors. "Karen and Jonah, stick around."

I got unsteadily to my feet. My left foot tingled; it had fallen asleep, but I hadn't even noticed. Dawne, Ramit, Mikki, and I exited the tent into the blinding sun. Something tugged at me—this felt familiar, what I'd just witnessed. But from where?

We walked silently towards the veranda. I waited for someone to speak. But all four of us were, for once, at a loss for words.

26

"What did we just watch?" Mikki asked. The four of us were on the veranda, where someone had laid out a sweating pitcher and stack of glasses. She sat stiffly in her chair, sucking on her vape pen. "What the hell was that?"

In that moment, the answer came to me.

"Constellation therapy." I leaned forward. "We saw a video in my art therapy class."

"That's a sanctioned type of *therapy*?" Mikki asked.

"Yes. Well, usually you include more people and you assign them all roles from your life—family members, partners, or whatever. It's a way to process things without the actual people present." Karen's session had been intense and even a little frightening to watch, but the fact that I could put a name to it felt calming.

"But what's the point, if it's not really them?" Mikki asked.

"From what I understand, it's cathartic to speak your truth and be heard and validated by a group. Though some people believe you're actually channeling the energy of your family members, even if they're not there." I thought of Jonah's posture changing. "Of course, that's a little woo-woo."

"I think it's amazing." Dawne swirled her cucumber water. "There was a huge shift for Karen just now. I could feel it. It was magic."

"Magic?" Mikki scoffed. "Sol's just a great performer."

Dawne slammed down her glass. "Can you please stop? I'm so sick of you shitting on everything. God." She closed her eyes. "I can't believe you're my accountability partner."

"I'm just stating my personal opinions." Mikki raised her hands. "You don't have to agree with them."

"Whatever." Dawne marched off towards the bathrooms.

"And all that talk about patterns," Mikki went on, as if nothing had happened. "Is that a real thing?"

"Well, yeah." I straightened. "It's called repetition compulsion. People tend to get drawn into relationships that match their childhood dynamics until they resolve them. Although some people never do."

"Hmm." Mikki picked at her nails. She looked at Ramit, who was sitting silently a few chairs down. "What do you think about all this, Ramit?"

He jumped, then looked over at us. "Uh . . . I don't know."

"Are you ready to take the stage?" Mikki looked afraid. She knew that she—all of us—would soon be put in the same position as Karen. "Give everyone a great show?"

"Well . . ." He adjusted his Ray-Bans. "I don't think it's a show. Not exactly. Whatever happened with Karen . . . I think it helped her?"

Mikki pressed her mouth shut.

"Listen." I touched her arm. "It's just us. None of us know each other. And after this weekend is over . . . we'll probably never see each other again."

She smiled wanly. "Let's hope not."

I felt pleased to have calmed her, but was still surprised when, back in the yoga pavilion for session two, she raised her hand as the next volunteer.

I'd been wondering when I'd be able to check in with Jonah. He had to have been acting—but how had he guessed those things about Karen's father?

"Great." Moon got to her feet. "Mikki, come on up."

I snapped back to attention as Mikki walked to the front.

Moon appeared to be in charge this time, and had shed her caftan to show a black crop top and yoga pants. The spiral symbol peeked out of her strap.

"We're going to do something different," Moon said. "I can tell that all this . . ." She waved her hand around. "It's not really your scene."

Mikki shrugged and adjusted her oversized button-down. "Not really."

"But you do go to therapy, right?" Moon sat down on her cushion, motioning that Mikki should sit across from her. Sol jumped up and sat next to me, in her place.

"Yep."

"What's your therapist's name?" Moon's voice was soft today, non-threatening.

"Zaila."

"How do you feel about her?"

"She's all right. My last therapist went on maternity leave and didn't come back, so at least she hasn't done that. Yet."

"That's frustrating." Moon shifted, placing her feet on the floor, her arms crossed over her knees. She was mirroring Mikki's posture.

"Yeah, well. That's business, I guess." Mikki stared back, challenging her.

"So did Zaila suggest this retreat?"

"Yes."

"How so?"

"Well, I was talking about all my issues, as usual, and she brought it up."

Moon nodded. "Does she suggest things often?"

"No." Mikki smiled slightly. "She actually doesn't say a lot, just lets me ramble. So I thought maybe I should listen to her."

"You said the first night that you're a love and sex addict. Tell me about that."

Mikki blew out a long exhale. "Can I smoke?" She pulled out her vape pen.

"No." Moon said it sharply. "No substances. Sorry."

Mikki slipped it back in her pocket. "Well, it's something I've dealt with for a long time."

"*It* means . . ."

"I guess the best way to say it is seducing people."

"Who was the first?"

"It started in high school." Mikki pulled her knees in closer. "Sophomore year, I made out with my friend's boyfriend. I don't know, it felt like this challenge. It was all I could think about. And the second we hooked up, it all went away. But I think it got worse in college. I went after one of my professors. She rejected me, which made me depressed. But then I switched to another professor—the father of a friend, actually. But when we started sleeping together, I got turned off."

"So when it happens, the urge goes away."

"Exactly. Before, it's like needing to scratch an itch."

"It's compulsive."

"Right." Mikki bit her lower lip. "And I don't even have to be attracted to them."

"But they have power. And/or they're out of bounds. Is that the pattern?"

"I guess so."

"How does it feel?"

"When I'm pursuing someone?" Mikki considered. "It feels . . . not good, exactly. More like I feel alive."

Moon nodded.

"It's ridiculous." Mikki threw up her hands. "I'm way too old to act like this. And I could really fuck up my life."

"What do you do again?"

"I'm a stylist."

"So this could affect your career, your reputation."

"Exactly."

"When's the last time you felt this way?"

The silence expanded, ballooning in the space.

"The last time . . ." Mikki cleared her throat. "Was an issue. But I don't want to talk about it."

Moon scooted closer to her. "Good. This is what we need to talk about."

"Not like this." Mikki motioned to us. "Like I'm telling a story on the fucking Moth."

"This is the most important part," Moon insisted. "Being witnessed. Trust me, Mikki. This will change everything."

"No." Mikki shook her head. "I haven't even told my therapist."

"Fuck your therapist."

Mikki looked up in surprise.

"I mean, she couldn't even get to the heart of it, right?" Moon tilted her head. "And we got there in . . . what, five minutes?"

Mikki smiled faintly.

"It's time for it to come out," Moon went on. "It *wants* to come out."

Mikki shook her head. "I can't. It's too . . ."

"Break through the shame." Moon's voice rose. "It's just shame. We all have it! There's a reason you did what you did."

"I know, but . . ." Tears glistened in her eyes. "It was unforgiveable."

I shifted, shrugging off my jean jacket, feeling suddenly hot. A therapist would never push a patient like this, much less someone they didn't even know. Mikki seemed stable, but still. This was sensitive work. Forcing people to go places they weren't comfortable with could have negative consequences, to say the least.

"So it was unforgiveable," Moon prompted.

"Yeah. It was . . ." Mikki let out a deep, shuddering sigh. "Fine. It was my best friend's husband. At their wedding."

"What?" Dawne whispered.

Mikki looked over uncertainly, but Moon grabbed her hands. "Look at me."

Mikki did, her eyes wide.

"You said it out loud," Moon said. "The worst is over."

"But it's not." Mikki lowered her head.

"What happened?" Moon asked.

"Don't make me do this," she whispered, wrenching away a hand to press it to her eyes.

"Come on, Mikki, you're almost there." Moon was so close their foreheads were almost touching. Due to the acoustics of the space, we could hear every quiet word.

"Tell me," Moon cooed.

Mikki sniffed and straightened, wiping at her face. She stared at the floor. Moon handed her a fresh tissue from her pocket, but she just held it.

"She brought me back to their suite." Mikki's voice shifted into a monotone. "A part of her must've known."

"Known what?"

"That we were attracted to each other." Her voice was suddenly stronger. "She wanted me to have one last glass of champagne with them. We were so drunk, though . . . She passed out on the couch, like, immediately. And I crashed in the bed. He climbed in next to me. Told me I was the most beautiful woman he'd ever seen. How he'd fantasized about me." Her eyes squeezed shut. "It wasn't just that he was off-limits. Maybe a part of me wanted to ruin this thing she had that I didn't. I don't know." She shrugged. "It happened and I left. He must've told her something—maybe that I hit on him. She avoided me at breakfast, stopped answering my texts. And that was it. They're still together, months later."

A bird cawed suddenly, right outside the tent.

Moon got to her knees and pulled Mikki to her. "You're going to be okay."

Mikki murmured something back that I couldn't hear.

"No, you will," Moon responded. "There's a reason this is happening. Why you're doing these things. We're going to help you get to the bottom of it. It won't be solved this second, but it's going to happen. Do you believe me?"

After a second, Mikki dipped her head in a nod.

Moon leaned back to look at Sol. He held up the prayer bells. *Ding.*

"Everyone, you can head to the veranda for lunch." Moon looked up over Mikki's head like a distracted parent. "Good sessions this morning. Nice work."

27

"Man," Ramit said softly as we walked away from the yoga tent. "That was intense."

"Poor thing." Karen crossed her arms.

"I wouldn't call her that." Dawne flipped her long ponytail over her shoulder.

I glanced at her in surprise.

"Don't judge, hon." Karen shook her head. "All of us have done stuff we're not proud of."

I remained silent, conflicting thoughts swirling through my mind. On one hand, it seemed dangerous for two nonprofessionals to force people to talk about difficult and sometimes traumatic moments in front of a group of strangers.

At the same time, Moon did have a point: *Fuck your therapist. We got there in . . . what, five minutes?*

But that was because she'd pushed. Therapists let clients get to those deep, painful places in their own time. What would it do to rip off the Band-Aid—no, the tourniquet—like that?

Was that what had happened to Catherine? Had the work retraumatized her, caused her brain to become overwhelmed, shut it down?

Ramit and Karen went to the veranda while Dawne and I walked on to the bathrooms.

"I've been cheated on a few times." Dawne stared straight ahead. "So that was kind of triggering to hear."

"I get that. I'm sorry."

"And my mom's boyfriends . . ." She blew out her breath. "It's just caused so much pain in my life. I don't know how Mikki could live with herself."

"I think that's why she's here," I said. "To change it."

"Yeah."

At the sink, Dawne smiled up at me. "What do you think Steven made for lunch?"

"Ooh. I don't know." I pulled my phone from my pocket; it was at 4 percent. "I need to charge this first, though."

"There's an outlet in the lobby."

"Oh, thanks." I'd brought my cord in my jacket so headed over. In the hall to the courtyard, I studied the framed photos. In a cluster of group pictures, there were several blank spaces, like several had been taken down. Had they contained Catherine?

In the courtyard, I passed the merrily bubbling fountain and turned in a full circle. The creepy eyeless heads stared back at me. I crouched to take a closer look. The older woman and younger boy, both impressively realistic, looked slightly familiar. Maybe I'd seen photos of these people when I'd studied the Center's site.

I approached one of the mosaic-covered doors. Inside was a desk piled with stretched canvases and crumpled tubes of oil paint. The chemical smell caused a pang of nostalgia. I'd loved oils but hadn't used them in years. The next room was a similar size and shape but looked to be a photo studio.

I stopped in front of the purple door and tried to peek through the lace curtain in the window, remembering how I'd felt someone's eyes on me during the tour. The room beyond was dark and opaque. I tried to open the doorknob. Locked. I went to the next door, and the next: they were all unlocked.

What could be beyond the locked door? Or . . . who?

I continued to the musty-smelling, taxidermy-filled lobby. Behind the front desk, I spotted the wall socket. A new text from Dom popped up:

Any updates?

Not yet. We just started our "sessions" today. Constellation therapy–esque.

I plugged in the phone, then considered the desk. Quietly, I pulled open the top drawer. Two sets of shiny car keys sat atop a jumble of rubber bands, paper clips, and pens. It felt strangely reassuring to see them. If I needed to make a quick getaway, I knew where to go.

I started a slow walk around the room, eyeing the muddied paintings and staring into the dead animals' glass eyes. Tucked into a corner was a framed black-and-white photo of Moon and Sol, sitting naked together in the hot tub. She was in his lap, an arm latched around his neck. They beamed at each other, and unlike the posed photos in their online interviews, these smiles looked real. I thought back to the tension between them by the bonfire the night before. What had that been about?

A metal scraping sound came from the courtyard. I slipped though the hallway just in time to see Steven locking the purple door. He glanced around and I ducked back. If he was coming into the lobby, he'd see me immediately. But instead, he exited through the opposite hallway towards the bathrooms.

I approached the purple door and tried to turn the knob even as I knew it was useless.

The back of my neck prickled. That same feeling of being watched arose. Was someone behind the diaphanous shield of the curtains, staring at me?

I knocked softly. "Hello?"

No response.

"Catherine?" I blurted out.

Nothing.

A creak from above. I took a few steps back, scanning the second-floor walkway that wrapped around the courtyard. I hurried to the stairs and raced up.

No one there.

Adrenaline zipped through me. I felt suddenly conscious of a whole unseen crowd in the castle. Grace had said their three full-time members left for retreat weekends. But who knew? This place was huge. They could be spying on me at this very moment.

I tried all the landing doors. They, too, were locked . . . except for the last one. It opened to reveal a rickety spiral staircase winding upwards. It wobbled beneath my weight as I climbed. Childlike paintings of colorful monsters hung close on the walls.

The staircase opened into a landing. Sunlight filtered through the dusty windows onto cardboard boxes, stacks of paintings, sheet-covered furniture. A storage room? The staircase continued upwards, so I climbed more steps until I reached another door.

It opened onto the roof. More precisely: the castle's tallest turret: a flat, uneven black surface, about twenty-by-twenty feet, at least sixty or seventy feet aboveground. After leaving a shoe in the door to prevent it from closing, I walked carefully around the perimeter, which was ringed by about four inches of raised adobe—certainly not enough to keep you from tumbling over the edge.

From here you could follow the gravel road until it reached the needle-thin highway. Grace had said it was three miles away? An hour's walk? In the same direction, two dark specks sailed through the cloudless sky. Hawks: I recognized their grand swoops from hikes back home upstate. I turned around. On the other side of the turret, the castle blocked the pool and veranda, but the yoga pavilion, firepit, greenhouse, and yurts were visible beyond. Sound carried here, and I could hear the burble of the fountain and the distant jangling of the wind chime by the pool.

A bell clanged below: a literal lunch bell. There, like roving insects, Moon, Sol, and Mikki walked back from the yoga pavilion. Mikki and Moon were holding hands. I paused, trying to make out their faint words, but the fountain covered it like white noise.

I hurried back to the door and down the staircase. On the junk room landing, I paused.

I needed to get back for lunch, but something was tugging at me. I circled the storage room, picking my way around the boxes and furniture.

A black-and-white painting on the ground caught my eye. A geometric border encircled several figures, painted in a simple indigenous art style. The two largest ones had skull-like heads and faced forward, their hands raised. A snake that twisted in a spiral separated them from the smaller people below. One was crouched and facing sideways, its body covered in stripes. Two others held staffs, a wavy line connecting their mouths. Two at the bottom were mostly covered by a patterned square that looked like a blanket. Above them, a figure with large eyes held an arrow.

I couldn't look away. Why did this feel important? I reached into my pocket for my phone before realizing I'd left it downstairs. I tried to memorize the painting before pulling it towards me so I could see the others stacked behind it.

In the blank space behind, Catherine's pale, severed head stared back at me.

I jerked back, the painting clattering to the floor. "What the *fuck*?"

It was a sculpture. Like the ones in the courtyard, though this one was even more realistic. It still had blank holes for eyes.

I reached out to touch the sharp cheekbones, the slightly prominent upper lip. The likeness was remarkable.

"Uh . . . hey." The peeved male voice caused me to scramble to my feet. Steven stood in the doorway, light filtering in from behind him.

"Hi!" I squeaked.

"What are you doing in here?" I'd barely heard his voice, but it was gruff, menacing.

"I'm sorry, I . . ." I tried to laugh. "I was charging my phone and I heard something and . . . I just ended up here."

"This room is off-limits." His face was absolutely unreadable.

"I'm sorry. I didn't know that."

He strode towards me and I backed away; he bent to push the paintings back into place, hiding the sculpture.

I gestured at them, feigning ignorance. "Did you paint these?"

"No." He straightened. "We've had lots of artists here. They've all left stuff behind."

"But you did the mosaics?"

He looked down. "Yeah."

"They're incredible." I tried to sound awed, which wasn't hard— they really were. "How long did it all take?"

He stared at me for a beat. "A long time."

He was answering my questions, at least. Now might be my only chance to speak with him one-on-one.

"How long have you lived here?" I asked.

"Since the beginning." He held my gaze.

"That was, what . . . five years ago?"

"Something like that."

"And you knew Sol."

That made him scoff. "Nope."

"Moon?"

"She wasn't calling herself that back then." He said it quietly, as if to himself.

"What was she calling herself?"

"You know, you signed an agreement." His mouth turned downwards. "I don't know why you're sneaking around, but whatever you're looking for, you're not allowed to share it. If you're, you know, a journalist or something."

I held up my hands. "I'm not a journalist. Just curious."

"We just put out lunch." He turned, and I hurried to follow him down the stairs, out onto the walkway, back down to the courtyard.

"I just have to get . . ." I gestured with my thumb. He nodded and I scurried down the hall, grabbing my phone and charger from the lobby. He was still waiting for me when I got back to the courtyard.

"Dinner last night was incredible, by the way," I said.

He didn't smile, but made eye contact. "Thanks."

"Grace said you lived in India?" I asked as we headed down the hall.

"I spent a few years there." He paused. "With Moon."

Had they been together romantically back then? I wasn't sure how to ask without spooking him. He paused in front of the door that led to the kitchen, judging by the smells.

"Thanks for walking me," I said. "Sorry again."

He gave me one last indecipherable glance before he slipped through the door.

28

The statue burned in my mind all through lunch. Steven had prepared a New Mexican feast—crispy sopapillas, enchiladas in rich green chile sauce, gooey cheese quesadillas—but I could barely taste it. Mikki and Karen both seemed high on their sessions, laughing and joking around as if a great weight had been lifted. And maybe it had.

Sure, it was possible that someone here had randomly decided to sculpt Catherine O'Brien, but she hadn't really been in things as an adult. Combined with Catherine and Moon's matching tattoos and Jonah's Facebook pictures, it seemed clear proof that she'd been here.

"You okay?" Jonah leaned in.

"Yeah." I cleared my throat. "I have to tell you something. Later."

He nodded. Across the table, Karen watched us.

"Something I want to talk about in my session," I said in a louder tone.

"As your accountability partner, I'm happy to assist."

That made me crack a smile.

"You have any tips about channeling the deceased?" I asked quietly, now that Karen had turned to Ramit.

His eyes crinkled as he took a long gulp of botanic-infused water. "Don't knock it till you try it."

"Seriously. What *was* that?"

"They clearly like theatrics." He nodded at Moon and Sol. "So I put on a show."

"But how did you know that stuff? Like her dad marrying her mom because he got her pregnant?"

"I don't know." He frowned. "I was just making everything up. And Karen seemed to go along with it."

"Hmm." Maybe Karen had been swept up in the energy? And telling Jonah he was incorrect might've felt like ruining the moment?

After lunch, most people headed for the pool, but Jonah and I walked to my yurt. He sat on my bed as I filled him in on the locked door in the courtyard and the statue of Catherine upstairs.

"Let me see the pictures," he said.

"I didn't get any pictures. My phone was charging."

"Oh." His forehead creased.

"I can tell you where it is." Did he not believe me? "You can go see for yourself."

"So Steven can catch me?" He leaned forward, forearms on his knees. "Didn't we agree to wait until tonight to look around?"

Irritation permeated my chest. "It wasn't planned. I heard something, and I went up to see what it was."

Jonah's dark eyes bored into mine. "And Steven caught you snooping."

"I mean, sorry." Remorse and defensiveness rose in equal measure. "It was an accident. I'm not a professional like you."

"I'm just saying, we need to be careful. This is our only chance to find out what's going on."

"Well, I found out that Steven and Moon used to live in India together."

"*Really*," he said.

"Yeah. I have no idea when." I mused. "Do you think they could've been together? Like in a relationship?"

"It's possible."

"And—what. Now he acts like her butler? Her and her *partner's* butler? That's messed up."

"I think that's a cult thing." He shrugged. "Maybe being around her is enough."

"Romantic," I said sarcastically.

"I know." He leaned back on my bed and his hand connected with my diary. "What's this?"

"My middle school journal."

He held the sunglassed cat face up to cover his own, and I chuckled.

"Why'd you bring it?" he asked, handing it to me.

How to respond? "Well . . . I was just thinking about some things I went through at thirteen. I mean, I'm going to have to share *something* with Moon and Sol. We're not all grade-A actors like you."

"You think I'm going to act my way through my own session?" He watched as I slipped the diary into my backpack. "I wish I were that good."

It felt like we'd already spent days in the yoga pavilion instead of hours. At Sol's request for a volunteer to start the third session, Dawne sprang to her feet. She started crying immediately, announcing that she was afraid she'd never find love. Sol disagreed. Through his questioning, he invoked her ghost lover, whose energies were in line with Dawne's mother: dismissive, cruel. She chose Karen as the stand-in and ended up weeping in her lap.

Moon's constant drumming and Sol's endless questions, along with the rising heat in the airless tent, started making me feel woozy. I was relieved when Dawne's session ended (*ding*), ready for a break.

"Ramit?" Moon beckoned. "Your turn."

No break, then. Ramit stood and exchanged places with Sol. His jaw was tense, his eyes wide. He looked terrified.

"So." Moon smiled as Ramit sat next to her. "What brought you here?"

"I met Sol at an event and thought it'd be a good idea to come. I just . . ." He rubbed the back of his neck. "My business partner and I—we're developers—we sold some games recently to Apple. So I've been trying to slow down and date and stuff. But it's been harder than I thought."

Moon nodded. "What's been hard about it?"

"People are just so flaky." His lip curled, a sudden twitch of annoyance. "And when they do show up, I don't know . . . I feel like they just expect all this stuff. I dated this one girl for a few weeks and she wanted me to pay for everything. Which was fine; I can pay for dinners and whatever. But then she started hinting that she wanted this super-expensive purse. I guess she wanted me to buy it for her? It felt like she was using me."

Moon glanced up, her eyes meeting Sol's. She looked away immediately, but it felt like something, a message.

"So people—women—are using you," she said.

"I don't want to sound like a dick. But . . ." He looked down. "Most of these women wouldn't even look at me if they didn't know I had money."

"Money," Moon echoed. "From developing games? What games?"

"Well, the most well-known one is *Killer Kangaroo*."

Moon nodded, seemingly unfamiliar with it. But my ex Ryan had played it nonstop for a few weeks over the summer. There was a bright, random spark of excitement to tell him—*I met the developer!*—that quickly died out.

"So let's focus on your childhood for a minute," Moon said. "Tell me about it."

"Oh." Ramit shrugged. "I don't know, I was born in India, in Delhi, and we moved to the US when I was seven. I'm an only child. My parents have been trying to convince me to let them hire a matchmaker. Thirty-seven is pretty old not to be married."

"In your culture," Moon added.

"Yeah. But I don't feel all that connected to my culture. It just sucks that I'm disappointing my parents."

"Even though you're doing well in your career?" Moon asked.

"Well . . . they thought developing games wasn't as respectable as other jobs. But they've accepted it. Now they really just want me to get married. They want grandchildren."

"So you talked a little about your childhood." Moon leaned forward. "But I couldn't get a sense of what it was *like*."

Ramit shifted, seeming to settle in. "It was normal. My parents were pretty happy, and financially did okay."

"How was school?"

"It was fine. I went to boarding school for a while when I was young."

"What age?"

"Uh, I think I was four."

"Four," Moon echoed. "A sleepaway boarding school?"

"Yeah, but I'd come back on the weekends. It wasn't that far."

"Why were you sent away?" Moon's brows knit.

"Well . . ." His voice faltered. "From what I've put together, my parents were going through a hard time in their marriage. They were fighting a lot. My mom was kind of depressed for a while. They didn't want me to be around that."

Moon was quiet.

"But it wasn't a bad thing," Ramit went on. "I mean, it wasn't like I had a traumatic time at boarding school. It was fine."

"What do you remember? Specifically?"

He squinted. "Well, not that much; I was so young."

"Hmm." Moon watched him.

"It's not like . . ." He shook his head. "Look, I know you're trying to tell me that my parents fucked me up by sending me away that young. But that's not true. Really."

"Ramit?" Moon's voice was light, delicate. "When's the last time you were in a relationship? A long-term, solid, committed relationship?"

"I guess . . . high school?"

"High school doesn't count."

He considered. "Well, I dated someone in college, but we were more on and off."

"After that?"

"Well, that's when my friend and I started our company. Things just got crazy. I didn't have time for a relationship."

"Ramit!" Moon thundered, causing us all to jump. "You are telling me that for the past fifteen years you have not had time for a relationship?"

"Well, no. Honestly."

"And now that you do, you're being hunted by horrible women who want Fendi purses?"

Ramit's mouth hung open. "I mean—"

"Stop." Moon jumped to her feet and stood over him. "Just take a breath. Think about the fact that you've completely avoided relationships for your entire adult life."

Ramit stared up at her, silent. The tent was so quiet it felt like being underwater.

Moon crouched down and pointed to us. "Who's your father? Who's your mother?"

"Um . . ." Ramit gulped. He looked stunned. "I guess I'd pick . . . Sol? And Thea?"

Whoa. It was like watching an intense play and suddenly being invited onstage. Sol stood and held out a hand to me. I took it and followed him to the front. Karen, Mikki, Jonah, and Dawne watched us from the cushions.

"We know your parents were doing their best." Moon gestured at us. "We know they loved you. But unfortunately, because of their suffering, you suffered too. Why don't you remember anything from that time? Because you've locked it away. Can you imagine how scared you felt? How alone?"

"All right, that's enough." Ramit got to his feet, scowling. "I don't appreciate you talking shit about my family."

"SIT DOWN!" Sol's voice boomed. He pointed at Ramit's cushion. To my surprise, Ramit sat.

"Stop with this nonsense." Sol stepped forward. "How dare you act so disrespectful?"

"But—" Ramit started.

"No! I won't have this. Look what you're doing to your mother." Sol gestured at me. "Do you know how badly she's feeling? And you act like *this*. So selfish. So dramatic."

Ramit went rigid, his lips parted.

"Do you know how hard I have to work just to keep this woman alive?" Sol cried. "And all you can do is sit there and complain?"

A wave of sadness crashed over me. It felt physical, like water filling up my lungs. I put a hand over my ribs, gasping for breath.

"See?" Sol sounded triumphant. "Do you know how harmful you are, Ramit? Do you know how much you're hurting her?"

"Stop." Ramit held up a hand, which was shaking. Moon slipped her arm around his shoulders.

Sol laughed. "You're telling me to stop?"

Moon whispered in Ramit's ear, and he shot up to stand.

"You can't blame me for this," he cried. "It's not fair."

"But it's your fault!" Sol poked his finger against Ramit's chest.

"It's not my fault! It's *your* fault!" Spittle flew from Ramit's lips. "You're the one who kept pushing her! You're the one who caused her to . . . to . . ."

Moon wrapped her arms around him. "It's okay. Just say it."

The visceral sorrow swelled, and tears filled my eyes. Ramit was crying softly.

Moon looked at me. "Mom. Come here."

I took a few hesitant steps towards them.

"You need to talk to your son," Moon said.

I knew exactly what she wanted me to say. "It's not your fault." I took a deep breath. "You didn't do anything wrong. You were just a little kid."

Moon nodded, her eyes glittering.

"But he made everything so hard." Sol's voice was ragged. "This little monster, just *wanting* all the time. Wanting all her energy, her attention. He just wouldn't stop."

"He's a child," Moon yelled. "That's how it works." She looked at

Ramit, whose quiet sobs had faded into shuddering breaths. "And Ramit had absolutely nothing to do with her suicide attempt. That's not something a child should be blamed for. *Ever.*"

Suicide attempt? Mikki's mouth fell open. Dawne's and Karen's eyes were wide.

"Ramit." Sol raised his hands in supplication. "I'm sorry. I was in a bad place. Trying to keep everything together. But I never should've put that on you." He pulled Ramit into a bear hug.

Moon gave me a slight nod.

"I'm sorry too." The words came easily, like I was reading lines. "I wasn't able to get the help I needed, and it affected you, and I wish it hadn't."

Moon guided me towards them, and Sol brought me into the hug. The three of us breathed one another's breaths, our heads close together.

Ding. Slowly, we pulled back.

"Good work." Moon stood with her hands on her hips, nodding approvingly, like she was overseeing a home improvement project. "Let's break. We'll regroup for dinner. Ramit and Thea, please stay here."

29

Quietly blindsided, I watched as Jonah, Dawne, Mikki, and Karen filed out. Dawne threw a last look back at Moon and Sol, maybe because she hadn't had her postsession processing time like everyone else. But she slipped out too.

I settled onto a cushion, my chest still swirling with emotions: the sad, achy feeling now overlaid with a bright splash of surprise. How had Moon and Sol known about Ramit's mother's suicide attempt? I was assuming it wasn't public knowledge.

The rest could be attributed to intuition and therapy practices. I knew I hadn't channeled Ramit's mother; Moon had been gently nudging me so that I'd known what to say. And the heavy sorrow? That was simple induction and projective identification. Clients could unconsciously place their difficult feelings inside of you like sticking a bag of rocks in your lap. If a therapist wasn't aware of it, they could get caught up in it, thinking the feeling (fear, rage, disgust) was their own. In this session, Ramit had unknowingly transferred his own despondency to me.

"That was wild." Ramit raised his eyes to Sol. "You sounded *just* like him. How'd you do that?"

Sol settled beside him. "I tap into the energy. I sounded like him?"

"I mean, without the accent, but yes."

"Thea." Sol turned to me. "How are you feeling?"

"I'm good." The sadness was melting away. I needed to get answers from Moon and Sol, but maybe not in front of Ramit.

"You both did such an amazing job." Moon sat so close that her spiced rose scent was cloying. "I'm so impressed."

Her praise pleased me, despite my determination to remain distanced. There was something about Moon's approving gaze that felt warm as sunlight.

"Ramit," she went on. "I applaud you opening up. I know it's not easy to feel exposed like that."

"Yeah, it was . . ." He chuckled. "Supremely uncomfortable."

"That shows we're getting into those deep places."

"So what happens now?"

"Good question." Sol clapped his shoulder. "Now we have a great jumping-off point for your one-on-one tomorrow."

I'd forgotten about the one-on-ones. That might be a good chance to dig further.

"Thea, do you have any reactions to Ramit's session?" Moon clutched my hand; hers was warm and moist.

"Um . . . just glad I could be a part of it."

"You're a therapist." Sol steepled his fingers. "You must have *some* thoughts about our methods."

Everyone stared at me.

"They're . . ." I shrugged. "Effective." *And possibly unsafe.*

Moon chuckled. "You don't believe it, do you."

"Believe . . ."

"You've heard of the collective unconscious, yes?" She glanced at Ramit. "Well, first let me start with the individual unconscious. It's the part of our brain that operates below our conscious awareness. We can only interact with it indirectly—dream analysis, freewriting, trance work. Jung thought there was also a *collective* unconscious, a great pool of information we all have indirect access to. We think this work dips into that well. Because we're much more interconnected than we think. You wouldn't believe how many attendees have a session where they channel a parent who then reaches out to them, sometimes for the first time in *years*. They can feel it, what we do here."

"That's really trippy." Ramit shook his head.

"That makes sense." I tried not to sound skeptical. Maybe they could make a case for this work, but it still didn't excuse their lack of training.

Moon smiled. "Our patterns are powerful. They're dynamics that go much deeper than we realize. Ramit's pattern was particularly strong." She tapped the top of my hand. "I have a feeling yours is too."

Back in my yurt, I continued to puzzle over Moon and Sol's knowledge of the suicide attempt. Or at least Moon's knowledge—she was the one who'd named it. I thought of old-timey mind readers who could quickly suss someone out by reading their body language. Even today there were famous "mentalists" who claimed to read people's thoughts. Could Moon be one of them, using a combination of techniques and intuition to pull out people's family secrets?

If they were using tactics of psychics and mediums, then another possibility came to mind. I even knew the term—"rigging"—though I couldn't remember where I'd learned it. It meant planting actors in the audience to "prove" your skills.

Was it possible that Ramit was a plant? That his session had all been planned beforehand? I'd briefly considered Jonah in that role, after all. Uneasiness clawed my gut.

A new Facebook message popped up on my phone. Wait—John Holloway? I clicked open the messenger app to see Pastor John's tiny avatar.

I'm sorry you feel that way.

My breath caught in my throat. I scrolled up to see what I'd sent him.

You fucked up my life.

He'd decided to write back to me . . . and this was his response? The most infuriatingly gaslight-y phrase a man could say?

"Oh hell no," I muttered and grabbed my backpack. I had evidence of our inappropriate relationship. I had fucking *proof*. I was going to take pictures of my diary and send them to this motherfucker and threaten to post them publicly. Would he sound so calm then?

Rage crackled as I dug around my backpack. I was an adult, not a middle schooler. He wasn't going to mess with me, not anymore.

The diary wasn't there.

I checked again, then opened the zippered pockets. I stood, looking around the small space. But even as I searched frantically underneath the bed, behind the desk, I knew:

Someone had taken it.

30

After searching my yurt for the third time, I took a deep breath and decided on a calming shower. Hopefully, no one would be in there at this weird, pre-dinnertime.

But Moon was in the shower room, surrounded by a cloud of steam.

"Hi!" she cried as I came in. She stood with her chest out, rubbing shampoo into her hair.

"Oh, hi." *Shit.* I could still use the protected shower, but it'd be embarrassing to scurry in there, especially after what had happened at the hot tub last night.

"I'm so glad you're here. I wanted to talk to you." She gestured with her chin. "You can put your stuff on that chair over there."

All right. This was happening. I'd always felt reasonably comfortable around naked women anyway; I regularly went to a spa in Brooklyn with a swimsuit-optional area. I stripped quickly, setting my clothes and towel on top of Moon's. I turned on the shower next to her, setting down my toiletries.

She stared at me, smiling, as I played with the temperature. She seemed incredibly comfortable, probably more so than when she had clothes on. And for good reason: she looked great. I felt jealousy mingling, at both her appearance and her confidence.

"So you wanted to talk to me?" I squirted shampoo into my hand, feeling resigned. If anyone else came in to shower, they'd see our bodies head to toe.

"Yeah. I'm just so, so happy you're here." She soaped up a shower pouf, then rubbed it over her neck and shoulders. She tilted her head, still gazing at me. Was she flirting?

"Me too." I could play along with the positive, peace-vibes bullshit— I was good at that. And with the shock of the stolen diary still swirling in my mind, I wasn't up to anything more complicated. "This place you've created . . . It's just incredible."

Could she and Sol have taken the diary? Of the other attendees, Jonah and Mikki had both remarked on it. But anyone could've come in and searched my yurt.

"Thank you. A lot of people worked really hard on it." She soaped her breasts. I looked away, my cheeks growing warm. "So I wanted to ask you: What made you come here?"

"Oh." The easy question relieved me. "Relationship issues. Like everyone else." When I opened my eyes, she was scrubbing her armpits, looking thoughtful.

"Hmm." She swabbed her stomach.

"You wanted a different answer?" I tried to sound playful, but a shiver of paranoia ran up my neck.

"Steven said you were in the storage room." Her amber eyes flicked back to mine. She widened her legs, started soaping between her thighs. I averted my gaze.

"Yeah, sorry. I heard something upstairs . . ." I washed my arms and belly over and over. I couldn't clean anything else with her watching me like that.

"You said you listened to the podcast," she said.

"That's right."

"Which episode called you here?" She turned, still smiling.

"The last one. The one where you were talking about that boy you had a crush on."

"Oh yes." She nodded. "Carlos. You had a crush like that too?"

"Yeah, in a sense. He was an actor, though. I didn't know him personally."

"What actor?"

"Sebastian Smith?"

"Ah." She grinned hugely. "I remember him."

"Yeah. He was in that movie *Stargirl*." After hesitating, I gestured. "You must've seen it, too, right?"

Her eyes remained blank.

"Your tattoo." I pointed to her shoulder. "That's from the movie."

"Oh." She laughed. "Coincidence. This symbol is from a dream I had as a kid."

"What does it mean?"

"Who knows?" She shrugged. "I used to draw it over and over. It felt like a map I didn't want to forget."

I wasn't sure if I believed her. But she continued: "Were you an only child, Thea?"

"I was, actually." How did she know?

"I was too." She stood. "Well, after my brother died."

The words jarred me. "Oh. I'm so sorry."

She shrugged. "A lot of people died in Ciudad Juárez. Carlos? He died too."

"I'm sorry," I said again, though it felt ineffectual. "That's awful."

"It was awful. And it wasn't my brother and Carlos's fault." Her eyes grew red. "They couldn't have avoided it. The drugs there . . . and the drug lords' greed . . . it's unfathomable. But you know what? At least I got to know them before they transitioned. And I'll see them in the next life."

"For sure." Catherine had brought up reincarnation too. But it wasn't that strange for the New Age set.

"You know." Moon grabbed my hand. "I lost people I loved, and it was hard. Almost impossible. But for you . . . there was no one there, was there? Just empty space. A void where love and affection should've been."

The words grabbed my throat.

"It was hard for you too," she went on.

I managed to swallow. "It was."

"I know." She stepped forward and grabbed me in a hug, her breasts pressing against my ribs, her head nestling in my neck. She stroked my back. It felt shocking and strange . . . but as I realized she wasn't letting go, I relaxed into it and felt unexpectedly soothed.

Some time passed—how long, I had no idea—until she pulled back with a warm smile. "Thank you for sharing this with me. I can tell that you do want to be here."

"I do." My eyes were red now, too, but I was able to keep the tears at bay. The last thing I wanted was for someone to come in and see me crying in the nude.

"Okay." She squeezed my arm, wrapped herself in a towel, and left. I finished up, feeling bewildered. How had I gone from feeling supremely uncomfortable to embracing a naked Moon in the space of a few minutes?

Maybe *none* of this was ethical. But I had to admit: Moon had something, some ability to leap into people's deepest, tenderest parts with just a few words.

31

I hurried back to my yurt wrapped in the overlarge towel, not wanting to put on my dirty clothes. But on the gravel path, an arm suddenly encircled my upper chest from behind.

"Don't move." It was Sol's breath in my ear, a warm vetiver scent in my nose.

What the fuck?

"Um." I struggled, but he wouldn't let go, the hard plane of his chest pressed against my back.

"See that?" He let go and I whirled around. But his eyes were on the path in front of me. I turned back to see an impressively large brown snake coiled on the path. I'd been so deep in thought from my conversation with Moon that I hadn't even seen it. In the silence, a shivery maraca sound arose.

"Is that . . ." I was in awe.

"Rattlesnake." Sol touched my arm. "Why don't we give him some space? They usually keep moving, but I like to respect their timeline."

"Yeah, definitely." We walked off the path onto the dirt, giving the snake a wide berth. It was the biggest I'd seen in real life, its coloring helping it blend into the dirt and gravel, but now I could make out the rings and geometric patterns on its back. I couldn't believe I'd been about to step right onto it. My heart still thudded.

"Sorry to grab you." Sol strode next to me. "But they can be spooked by noise, so I didn't want to yell."

"No problem." I tightened my towel.

"You know, I wanted to check in with you." We slowed at the door to my yurt. He pulled a pair of yard-work gloves from his back pocket. "Join me in the greenhouse?"

"Sure."

"Great. See you there." He tucked a lock of blond hair behind his ear and gave me that megawatt grin before loping off.

I dressed quickly and threw on some mascara, trying to calm my still-vibrating nerves. It was from the rattlesnake, right? But something about Sol's grabbing me had felt . . . I don't know, erotic?

God. First I'd wondered if Moon had been flirting with me—and now Sol? Was it them, or did I just need to get laid?

The greenhouse was a contrast to the desert, humid and filled with rows of plants and even some small trees. Sol waved me over to a table filled with buckets and planters.

"Try this." He held out a closed fist, then dropped several glowing raspberries into my palm. I tossed them in my mouth. They burst with flavor, both tart and sweet.

"Wow," I said. "Delicious."

"Yeah." Sol gestured around. "I thought Steven was a little nuts when he wanted to set all this up, but it's been amazing. In a couple years I think we'll be self-sustaining. Moon wants to get some goats and cows too."

"Very cool." I nodded. This close to him, staring directly, it struck me again how much he looked like Pastor John. Moon was the more charismatic one, but Sol had plenty of his own confidence.

Sol gestured to some folding chairs, and we both sat. He continued to smile at me, so I grasped for something to fill the silence. "So where are you from? I'm realizing I don't know that much about you."

He crossed his arms. "My story's not that interesting. Boy grows up in Michigan. Boy moves to LA to be a rock star. Boy fails, but ends up meeting the love of his life."

"How did you two meet, exactly?"

He chuckled. "It was an audition. The most stereotypical place to meet in LA. It was for laundry detergent; I read for the part of a complaining dad, and Moon was the long-suffering mom. We saw each other in the parking lot after and made fun of it."

So Moon had been an actor. It wasn't a surprise, given her flair for the dramatic. But it was interesting that none of the articles had mentioned it.

"Neither of us was traditional in that way," he went on. "Moon never wanted children. Which makes sense, after the childhood she had."

"She went through a lot," I supplied.

"Oh yeah. Her single mom wasn't the best caretaker after her brother died. Depressed, neglectful. My mom was the opposite: super anxious and controlling."

"That must've been hard." Back to social worker mode.

"It was. But!" He slapped his knees. "Let's not talk about me. I want to know more about you." He leaned forward, and I had the sliding sensation that I was back in Pastor John's office, winning the full brunt of his attention. It had felt incredible then and still felt good now. Though I didn't fully trust Sol, it seemed harmless enough to tell him some basics.

"Well, I'm from a town in upstate New York . . ."

"And your parents?"

I straightened. "My dad was a manager at a pharma company."

"What was he like?"

Was this turning into an impromptu session? "Strong, silent, Christian type. He traveled a lot when I was growing up. And my mom was a stay-at-home mom."

"Did she like it?"

"Um . . . she wanted more kids. I think she was disappointed with just one."

"But you're amazing," Sol said, his eyes guileless.

"Thanks. I don't know, it's kind of ironic that what she wanted most in the world—to be a real capital-M mother—she wasn't great at."

"Give me an example. Of how she wasn't great at it."

I paused. The memory jumped into my mind in full color. "Well, when I was thirteen I got a UTI. I didn't know what it was at the time. I was sure God was punishing me—I'd just had my first sexual encounter. I was too scared to google the symptoms on my dad's computer. But then it got worse, so I finally told my mom. She took me to her gynecologist, who was a man. When the nurse told me to get undressed, and I saw those stirrups . . ." I shook my head. "I just couldn't do it."

Sol nodded, shifting and crossing his legs. Now he was playing the therapist.

"When I refused to take off my clothes, my mom got *so* angry at me. She even started crying, saying I'd embarrassed her. Luckily, I guess the nurse told the doctor and he came in and said my urine test showed I had a UTI. He prescribed something and we left and my mom refused to talk to me for the rest of the day, even at the pharmacy."

Sol rubbed his chin. "Why was she so upset?"

"I don't exactly know. Basically whenever I needed help of any kind, she acted like it was this huge inconvenience or embarrassment for her." To my horror, tears sprang to my eyes.

"Oh, Thea." Sol reached out and took my hand. "I'm sorry."

"It's fine." A tear leaked, and I wiped it from my cheek. "Honestly. I went to therapy for all that."

"But clearly it's still painful." Sol squeezed my hand. "Listen, I want you to know something. That was her problem, not yours."

"I know."

"And I think that story shows something significant. You could've just shoved down your discomfort and let the doctor examine you. But you said no. You used your agency. Even if your mom didn't like it."

"That's true." And it was, I'd just never thought of it that way.

"I had issues with my mom too; as I mentioned, she was controlling and manipulative. It made me feel powerless. So later on, I'd take out that anger on other women." He glanced at me. "Not, you know, physically. But it really messed up my relationships. I'm telling you because we're all trying to work through this stuff. It's not like Moon and I have all the answers, you know? But when a group like this comes together and agrees to be open and honest, it facilitates immense change. I treasure what you just shared with me. And I hope you can bring the same vulnerability to your session."

His blue eyes were more slate gray up close.

I swallowed. "Thanks, Sol. I'll try."

"Good." He stood, then held out a hand to pull me up. "You want to help me carry some fruits and veggies to the kitchen?"

"Sure." As he handed me a basket of peppers, I felt the same sense of whiplash that I'd experienced after talking to Moon. As we again skirted the rattlesnake, Sol chatted about other creatures they'd seen: lizards, deer, coyotes. Apparently, one attendee had brought her dog, an elderly chihuahua named Dionysus who had half-blindly chased jackrabbits bigger than him—at least when his favorite prey, Steven, wasn't around.

I laughed, wondering at the expansiveness that filled my chest. Was it because of what I'd shared with Sol? I knew from therapy sessions how much of a relief it could be to share a shameful story and feel validated and supported.

But that had just been a taste. One small story to one person. After dinner, we'd have the final session, and it would finally be my turn. I had no idea what Moon and Sol would pull from me in front of everyone, and I dreaded finding out.

32

"Do you think the soulmate thing is true?" Next to me, Dawne waited for an answer, blinking her plush eyelashes.

"Huh?" I paused, the homemade pizza halfway to my mouth. We were having dinner, but I was lost in trepidation verging on panic. I'd always had stage fright, and this felt like the worst possible version: pouring out my issues in front of an audience. I'd been remembering a grade school talent show in which I was supposed to recite a poem, but ran off the stage instead.

"I don't know if you saw this, but that's the guarantee. That if you come here you'll meet your soulmate after." Dawne speared a forkful of salad, looking thoughtful.

"I did see that." Being here, I was even more skeptical of the claims.

"I mean, I've done all this work," she went on. "I've been to so many retreats. I've read so many books. Podcasts. Therapy. I really don't know what else I can do." Her eyes became shiny, and she pressed a hand to her chest.

"You've done a lot," I acknowledged. I understood her frustrations, all the pain that came from constant dating disappointments. Feeling like something was being kept from you—something that could make you feel so much better. Before Ryan, I'd made two other relationships "official," but they'd both crumbled quickly, burning out in around six months.

"It will happen at the right time," I went on. "And it'll be better than you could've imagined." It sounded like something she'd like to hear.

"You're totally right. It will. Thanks." She gave me a tiny, relieved smile.

Jonah caught my eyes once across the table. He was also on the healing docket, and I wondered if he felt nervous. He'd claimed he couldn't act his way through a session—so what was he going to share?

I was the first to arrive at the yoga pavilion. Inside, Grace was setting dozens of small electric candles around the perimeter, which gave off a cozy glow. Moon and Sol conferred quietly on cushions.

As I sat, nerves—no, terror—reared up. As with the talent show, I wanted nothing more than to race back outside. Grace sat next to me, smoothing a few stray orange hairs. Interesting—she hadn't been at the other sessions. The others filed in, and I was also surprised to see Steven take a seat.

"Why the extra people?" Jonah asked. His voice sounded tight.

Moon smiled at him. "You'll see."

Mikki sat on my other side. She reached out to squeeze my forearm.

"So." Moon clapped her hands on her thighs. "Let's begin. We have a very special session to look forward to tonight. We weren't sure if this was the case, but after meditating today I'm feeling pretty confident. We have two attendees here whose patterns overlap."

What?

Moon gazed at me. "It's quite rare. Which tells me that Thea and Jonah were brought here for this specific purpose. To co-heal their patterns together."

Jonah and I glanced at each other, our faces mirroring confusion. Every time I thought I had a grip on what was happening here, something shifted, throwing me off-balance.

"So what does that mean for our session?" I asked. "Will it be different?"

"You don't have to worry about it. I just ask that you let me lead, and keep an open mind." Moon brushed her air-dried waves over her shoulder. "We're going to start with you, Thea. Could you stand, please?"

My heart galloped in my chest. Sol took my empty seat.

"Let's walk." Moon slipped an arm around my waist. She led me in slow steps around the circle of cushions, like a horse. "Where have you gotten stuck with relationships?"

"Um . . ." I cleared my throat. *Let's start with the obvious.* "Well, relationships have always been tricky for me."

"In what way?" Her sharp rose scent filled my nostrils.

"It's just hard to get them to last," I said. "But I think that's pretty normal in New York."

"Who was your last lover?" We were walking a little faster now. There was no ominous drumbeat, just silence, but I heard it underneath her words anyway.

"This guy Ryan. We dated for a little over three months."

"What happened?"

I glanced at the others watching me from the cushions. Their eyes followed us in the dim room. Now that this was actually happening, my breath came easier. Waiting had been somehow worse.

"We broke up," I said.

"Why?"

I pictured his shocked face. Maybe I could offer something just right of center. "I think he was scared of intimacy. Of really knowing me." That sounded good. Maybe I'd be able to survive this after all.

"But something happened. Right?" Moon tightened her grip. "Something to set him off."

Damn. She really did have a sixth sense. She could smell it, like a shark detecting blood in the water.

Internally, I steeled myself. I was going to have to throw her some meat.

"I told him about a fantasy I had." My voice faltered, and I cleared my throat. "He didn't like it."

"Good." Moon loosened her grip. "What was the fantasy?"

I hesitated.

"Thea, whatever it is, it's been fantasized about a million times before."

I forced myself to say the words: "Well, it's less a fantasy than a memory. Something that happened when I was thirteen. I actually don't like thinking about it, but . . . I have to. In bed."

She looked at Sol, a glint of triumph in her eyes. What had I said to cause that?

"Go on," she said.

"It's a little complicated." I exhaled. "But basically it was my first sexual experience. First anything—I hadn't even kissed anyone before. And it was with this guy who bullied me. Well, a lot of people, including me."

"There was a man involved too." Moon's tawny eyes glowed. "Not just the bully. Right?"

"Well . . . kind of." A flash of confusion: Had I told her? Told anyone here?

"An authority figure?"

"Do you mean Pastor John?"

"Yes." She nodded.

The answer focused into clarity: she'd seen my diary. This was how she knew. Instead of anger, I felt sudden calm. Moon would draw it out of me, slowly but surely. All I had to do was follow her lead.

"What happened with him?" she asked.

Now she was playing dumb. "Well . . . I don't know if he was ever planning on trying anything physical with me. But it felt like an emotional affair. Totally inappropriate on his end. Abusive, really." I shook my head. "I wish I could've realized that back then."

"He knew how to draw you in," Moon said. "By seeing you, paying attention to you."

"Exactly. We'd have these long conversations in his office and . . . yeah. No one had ever listened to me like that before. It felt . . . intimate? And then he started telling me things about his life too. Including, at some point, issues he was having with his wife."

Moon snapped her fingers at Sol. "Where would you like John to stand?"

I felt startled. How had Moon known to ask Sol? After all, I could've named Jonah or Ramit or even one of the women. But somehow she knew Sol was the right one.

"Thea?" Moon sounded impatient, as if we were on a deadline.

"Um, right there is fine." I pointed to the other side of the impromptu stage.

"Good. And where would *you* like to stand?"

"We can stay here, I guess."

Moon broke away from me and went to stand behind Grace, touching the two orange braids overlapping on her crown. "Who is she?"

"What do you mean?" Now I felt thrown off.

Ignoring my question, Moon asked: "Gracie, where would you like to stand?"

"By him?" Grace indicated Sol. A flicker of excitement shone in her eyes as she joined him.

Moon turned back to me, hands on hips. "Who is she?" she repeated.

"Jamie." As soon as I said her name, a heavy feeling settled in my gut. "Pastor John's wife."

"Good." Moon went to stand behind Jonah. "And he's the bully, yes?"

A shudder went through my body. Just a second ago I'd been in control. But now, I'd stepped into an empty elevator shaft and was in free fall.

Because Jonah looked like Adam. Somehow, I hadn't noticed it before. The same glossy, curly hair, the same dark, watchful eyes. The same cruel curve of his lips.

Grace didn't look like Jamie, who'd been—and still was—blond and voluptuous. Grace, with her candy-corn hair and guileless eyes, would be my anchor to reality.

"Who is he?" Moon insisted.

"Adam," I said faintly.

"Adam." Moon turned to Jonah. "Where should you go?"

"Maybe here?" Jonah took a step towards me.

"No!" I cried involuntarily. "Don't come near me." My chest squeezed with fear, like it really *was* Adam.

"Good." Moon touched my arm. "Where would you like him to go?"

"Over there." I pointed to the far end of the pavilion. "The others too."

At a nod from Moon, the three of them backed away.

"Thea." Moon pulled me in and down so that our foreheads were nearly touching. "We're going to enter the memory. Where are you? What's going on?"

I stared at Sol and Grace, standing side by side. They were holding hands. The image brought tears to my eyes.

"It was an accident," I said softly.

Trees grew in the space around us, stretching high above. It was a clear night, stars glinting overhead. I'd run away from the group, from the campfire, where Adam had taunted me in front of everyone. Where Mrs. Iona, our teacher, had as usual pretended not to hear.

Melissa, by this time 80 percent into Ashley's group, had also heard. She hadn't laughed like Ashley and the other girls. But she'd still smiled mechanically, staring at the ground.

I took off, jogging into the darkness. I felt a desperate need to find Pastor John, the one person in my life who actually gave a shit about me. I couldn't tell him that the taunts were about me and him together, but just seeing him, just seeing him see *me*, would ease this horrible twisting feeling in my gut.

He and Jamie were staying in the main building, like all the adults, while we students were in cabins scattered around the campground. This was the end-of-eighth-grade graduation trip that everyone talked about since the start of junior high.

I burst through the front door and looked for #4.

Wasn't that interesting, that he'd given me his room number? Told me to come find him if I needed him?

Of course I hadn't planned to actually take him up on this offer. But Melissa spurning me at the campfire had broken the fragile arch holding everything up.

I *did* need him.

I raced through the hall, past the cheap faux-wooden siding and crookedly hung deer antlers and pulled at the door of #4, forgetting in my desperation to knock . . .

This was the part that burned to recall, that lived behind a wall in the back of my mind.

Why hadn't they locked the door? If so, it never would've happened. But they'd forgotten. Or maybe they liked the risk. Whatever the case, what I'd seen had momentarily baffled me. They were on the floor, and the view of their naked bodies was like the late-night channel I'd come across while babysitting at a neighbor's house.

They turned to me. Jamie's nipples were pinker and larger than the woman I'd seen on TV. She shrieked, trying to pull the edge of the rug over her. He'd pulled back from her—out of her—and I stared at his erect penis, which he quickly covered with one hand.

I was momentarily stunned: Hadn't he just told me they weren't having sex? How was I seeing what I was seeing?

He was shouting something, and finally I tuned in.

"SHUT THE DOOR!"

I closed it.

My chest, my stomach, everything was churning, and I could barely get a breath. I just stood there for a moment, immobile. And then I heard it: a laugh.

Jamie was *laughing*.

Woodenly, I turned and walked down the hallway. Out the front door.

"Hey." Someone was walking up out of the darkness with a flashlight.

It was Adam.

"What?" I managed to say.

He pointed the beam at me, and I threw my hands in front of my eyes. "Damn, Thea. Did you tell on me? Did you run to your boyfriend and tell him what an evil sack of shit I am?"

"No."

"Oh. Okay. Good." He paused. "I was just kidding, you know."

"Uh-huh."

"You really can't take a joke, can you?"

"Guess not." The inner storm was calming. The hurricane energy froze into numbness.

I kept seeing the look in Pastor John's eyes. The horror, the anger, the undeniable implication: *Get the fuck out of here.* Jamie's laugh. She wouldn't be laughing if she knew what he'd told me about her, in addition to the lack of sex: that she was controlling. Nagging. Constantly complaining. I'd actually felt bad for him, this kind, loving, and patient man, having to contend with a wife like that.

But all of that was over now. He'd never be able to look me in the eyes again. I knew that, as sure as if he'd warned me. The long conversations, the secret smiles. Gone like they'd never happened at all.

I turned and walked towards the lake.

"Where are you going?" To my faint surprise, Adam followed.

"I don't know." I stumbled over a branch.

"Here." Adam shone the light in front of both of us. "You know, I can't figure you out, Thea. I can't tell what you're thinking."

"Why do you care?" I was strangely grateful for this conversation. If it weren't happening, if I were here alone, I'd peel off the face of the earth and float off into space.

"I don't." He scoffed.

We approached the dock. The waves lapped below us, a soothing sound. I sat at the end, wrapping my arms around my knees. The sliver of moon reflected in the black surface of the water.

Adam clicked off the flashlight as he settled beside me. "You're shaking. Are you cold?" Without waiting for an answer, he put an arm around me. It felt warm, solid. I wanted to cry, but all I felt was a deep, black nothingness.

This void had always been there. When I was on the bus, or sitting in class, or trying to finish my math homework at the kitchen table. It had even been there when things were better with Melissa, peeking out after she'd fallen asleep and I was still awake in my sleeping bag.

I'd never had such direct access to it, though. Now, it vibrated, a gaping hole in my chest.

"You know, I joke about you and Pastor John and everything," Adam said quietly. "But I see the way he looks at you. It's not, like, normal."

"Hmm."

"Whenever he comes in the classroom he always looks for you first. He finds you and his eyes light up."

It was nice, I guessed, for someone else to validate it. To know I wasn't just making everything up. On some level I'd known, but it had also felt confounding. How was I to understand what attraction looked like?

"One time he was talking to you and I think he even got a little bit of a boner. I think he thinks you're hot." Adam's hand moved to the back of my scalp, massaging. I tensed and then relaxed. It actually felt good. How could it feel good coming from someone I hated?

"You *are* kind of hot." His hand tangled in my hair, he turned my head towards him and kissed me. I kissed him back. My first kiss. *Huh.* His tongue snaked into my mouth, but it was gentle, with more finesse than I would've expected. His breath was faintly minty. He shifted and pulled me closer. The kiss felt nice, distracting. Then he pulled me down onto the dock, pressing his body to mine. The hardness of his erection poked into my thigh.

Suddenly, I was flooded with desire. It filled the void, pulsing and urgent. I kissed him harder, pushing myself into him.

"Whoa." He pulled back. "You really want it, don't you?"

I didn't know what I wanted. But when Adam stood up and held out his hand, I took it.

"Come on." He led us confidently to the shed by the dock. To the floor, where he set down a musty, crumbling blanket. He was fourteen, but he must've been having sex for a while. He knew exactly what to do, how to set me up, where to touch me, how to get me to touch myself. And I couldn't have been the first girl he'd said those kinds of things to:

You're so fucking ugly.

You're such a slut.

Say you're my bitch.

Pretend I'm him. Say it.

It was all over quickly. I sat on the blanket for a long time after he left. It was all so much: my first kiss, my first make-out, my first fuck. And all interlaced with Pastor John's eyes, so appalled, so alien. *Shut the door!*

Eventually, I'd gotten up, noting the pain between my legs. Adam had left me the flashlight—a kind act, or maybe he'd just forgotten it. I used it to examine the swipe of blood on my thighs. I got dressed. Folded up the gross blanket. Left the shed. Went directly to the shower building, where I scalded my skin and got back in my clothes.

They were singing campfire songs. Those fucking idiots.

I went back to my cabin, to my bunk, which was directly over Melissa's. Still wet, I got into the damp sheets, pulling them up to my chin. I felt wide awake, but within seconds, I fell blessedly asleep.

33

The feelings reared up as if I were still there, twenty years in the past. The numbness had melted, and sharp knives of shame and hurt and humiliation sliced into my chest and belly as I cried. Moon murmured— *It's okay, let it all out*—while wrapping me in her arms.

Eventually, the tears stopped. I took shuddering breaths. I didn't want to open my eyes, to see the others staring at me. But when I did, everyone's faces were filled with softness and warmth. Grace and Dawne's cheeks were wet with tears.

Moon thanked everyone and invited Mikki, Dawne, and Ramit to step out.

"Is the session over?" I glanced at Jonah. "What about Jonah? His work?" I'd taken up all of our time in the session—when would he share?

"Don't worry." Moon pushed back my hair in a motherly gesture. "That was his pattern too. Jonah treated someone the way that Adam treated you."

Jonah nodded slowly, staring at the floor.

Sol grasped his shoulder. "How do *you* feel?"

"Like shit." Jonah smiled faintly. He'd already apologized to me during the session; Sol and Grace had too.

And though they weren't actually Pastor John and Jamie and Adam, it had shifted something to hear it. Like I'd been living with a dislocated shoulder for twenty years, and it had just been popped back in place.

"And you?" Moon trained on me. "How do you feel?"

"Good." Already parts of me were rearing up, questioning what had just taken place. Moon had been able to facilitate this because she'd stolen my diary. That was clearly wrong.

And yet . . . something momentous, maybe even mystical, had just happened. The memory had felt *real*. My knees ached from the shed's wooden floor under the thin blanket.

Moon rubbed my arm. "We've taken a big step in breaking the pattern. There's still more to do, but it will no longer rule you."

I nodded, wiping under my eyes. There must be mascara all over my face.

"Let's take a break." Moon checked her watch. "Sol and I have to get ready for the bonfire ceremony, and you both may want to rest a little."

Soon, Jonah and I were outside, walking in the direction of the yurts. I felt raw, like an exposed nerve.

I started: "That was . . ."

"Wild," he finished.

"Were you acting again?" It felt unbearable to fathom, though it had to be the case.

"Actually, no." He cleared his throat. "Sol was right. I did treat someone like Adam treated you."

"Oh." I was both surprised, and not.

"I should tell you what happened to me," he went on. "Or rather, what I did."

"You don't have to."

"I want to." He looked grim. "So yeah, I was a bully. My parents were fighting all the time, and I think I was taking it out on other people. I targeted this one girl, Hannah. She was obsessed with our teacher. And he gave her special treatment, for sure. But he or she must've crossed some line because he started avoiding her. And I took advantage of that. I invited her to parties, got her drunk. And one night I had sex with her." He paused and we trudged in silence for five seconds, ten. "I was drunk, too, but that's no excuse. I was pretty cruel to her after, and I'll always regret that. At some point she disappeared. Her parents transferred her. I looked her up many years later; she was living somewhere in Tennessee. Married, two kids. I still think about her."

We stopped outside of my yurt. His arms were crossed, his shoulders hunched. Staring at the ground, he looked miserable and somehow young, like a little boy who'd done something unforgiveable. Jesus. How were these boys allowed to have this kind of power over us? To cause us so much pain?

"I don't understand how they know about our pasts." Jonah's eyes darted to mine. "Moon and Sol. There has to be an explanation, but I can't think of it."

"There is." I cleared my throat. "At least for me. They stole my diary."

"What?" He frowned.

"Yeah. It disappeared. And it was filled with stuff about Adam and Pastor John." Though not what had happened at the camp—I'd been too depressed or ashamed to record that.

"Okay. But how did they know that my 'pattern' overlapped with yours?"

"Did you mention anything in the application for the retreat?"

"Nope. Just some vague bullshit about dating issues."

It made me think of Ramit's session, how Moon had known things she couldn't have known. And this time, she'd seemed to know them even before we started the session.

"I think they're really good at reading people." I shrugged. "Moon especially. That has to be it, right?"

"I guess." He rubbed at his chin. "In any case, it doesn't change what we came here to do. In fact, it makes it even more important. Moon and Sol are good. Catherine could've easily gotten caught up in their—whatever's going on with them."

"I agree. You still want to do the search tonight?"

"Yep. An hour after everyone goes to bed, let's meet at the hot tub."

"Sounds good." I rubbed my temples. "I think I need to lie down for a few minutes."

He nodded. "I'll see you at the bonfire."

My sense of time was off. The hours and intensity of the sessions made it feel like we'd been here for weeks instead of days. I needed something to ground me, to remind me of my normal life. The Wi-Fi wasn't working—Grace had mentioned it could go in and out—so I opened up my photos instead. I looked at pictures of Ryan: Exaggeratedly excited over a giant burger. Sticking out his tongue at me in bed. Kissing my cheek in a selfie as we waited to ride the Cyclone at Coney Island. For the first time, I didn't feel that sharp pain of longing and shame.

Maybe if Ryan had been more open, it would've helped me undo the handcuffs holding my sexuality hostage. But I also could've started that work on my own.

A deep calm settled over me. I'd finally told the story. About how after my best friend failed me, I'd searched for support from my pastor, who had groomed me and then almost literally slammed a door in my face—and slammed it for good. How that loss had opened me up to Adam's predatory advances. Sure, I'd kissed him back, followed him willingly enough. But I'd also been in a state of shock, and I never would've done anything physical with him in my right mind. He was intuitive; it's why he was such a good bully. I felt sure it was why he'd come on to me in the first place.

I cried a little more, for the thirteen-year-old who'd felt so lonely and unloved. It had started much earlier, of course—I'd known, even as a child, that my mom was disappointed in me. Her quiet, shy daughter had just reminded her of the boisterous family her body had refused to give her. But maybe she would've been the same with more kids: faintly disgusted and put upon by their needs. I didn't know. Dad had been a presence more than a person, either absent or controlling. The few people I'd bonded with—Melissa, Pastor John—had cut me off. No wonder relationships were so hard for me.

I wanted nothing more than to stay in the yurt, but forced myself to reapply mascara and walk to the bonfire. Moon had us sit across from our accountability partners and gaze into their eyes for five full minutes. The flames reflected in Jonah's dark irises. Such a short time, and yet it seemed to last forever. It was awkward initially, but melted into something else: a connection or an understanding.

Moon had us stand, embrace our partners, and then hug everyone. She called upon her ancestors to bless our work together. Sol set up speakers and played drum-heavy music. And then we danced. Something in me felt electric, like I needed to shake some stale energy out. We laughed at one another's wild moves. Dawne tried to grind up on Moon, and she laughed and went along with it. Sol pumped his fist like a club kid. Ramit surprised us all, whipping his head and hips with abandon. Grace and Mikki undulated, their arms over their heads, while Karen *woo-hoo*ed into the night.

Somehow I found myself in front of Jonah. He grabbed my hand and twirled me like we were at a wedding reception. We laughed and swung each other around in a circle. His palms were warm and strong, keeping me from spinning out into the darkness.

34

I was back in the cave.

It was tiny, too small for me to stand. I was curled up on a ledge, listening to the rushing of water nearby. My body was numb with cold. There was something dead in the water near me; the rotting stench reached my nose when the current buoyed the corpse to the surface.

She'd pushed me. But they'd all betrayed me. I tried to scream, but my throat was too sore; nothing came out. I moaned and shuddered.

Someone—something—was hissing at me. I could just barely make out the words over the gushing of water.

Save her?

My eyes flipped open. My alarm trilled on the pillow next to me. I'd kept it turned down, not wanting to wake up anyone nearby when I got up to meet Jonah.

I sat up slowly, still disturbed by the nightmare. I'd had a similar one a few weeks ago, when I'd distractedly drawn a cave in art class (*Is this a cunt?*). This time, it had been more visceral. If I closed my eyes I could imagine the frigid water, the rotting smell.

I got up in the dark clothes I'd worn to bed and shrugged on my jacket. Outside, a crisp wind blew into my face, helping me fully wake. I shook off the last remnants of the dream. Time to focus.

Jonah leaned against the hot tub, silently watching me approach. In his leather jacket, he looked like James Dean waiting by his motorcycle. I felt a tug in my stomach, a sudden desire to grab him, pull his lips to mine. For him to lift me onto the edge, unzipping my jeans.

Whoa. Calm down. He'd never even hinted at being attracted to me. There was just something about this place. It had to be coming from Moon and Sol, the erotic energy in the air.

I tried not to look flustered as I walked up. "Hi."

"Hi." He stood, clicking on a flashlight and handing me a second one.

"Oh, nice. Thanks." I turned it on.

"We're lucky." His voice was low. "High winds tonight. We'll still try to be quiet, of course. But I was worried about someone hearing us."

"Totally." Sound traveled so easily in the desert. I paused, listening to the rushing and whistling of the wind. "So where do we start?"

"The spaces that we know for a fact people aren't sleeping in. Save the riskiest for last."

"Sure." I followed him across the veranda and through the dining room. The normally cheerful space felt creepy and watchful, like shadowy people might be crouching behind the chairs. In the kitchen, Jonah opened a few cabinets, which were packed with huge bins of rice, flour, and other cooking supplies. I eased open the door to the walk-in pantry. The shelves held stacks of cans and plastic jugs of water.

"They're ready for the apocalypse," I said softly.

"No kidding. Let's keep going."

We continued down a hall off the back of the kitchen that opened into the lobby. Jonah quietly opened the desk drawers, pausing as he noticed the car keys.

"They just leave them here?" he muttered.

"I guess if different people are using the car, it makes sense to keep them near the front."

After a quick search, we approached the courtyard. Against the backdrop of the burbling fountain, I wandered around, shining my light. The eyeless heads were even creepier in the dark.

So was the purple door. Had the curtain in the window moved? When I looked more closely, it was completely still.

"I want to see the statue." Jonah leaned in, his breath tickling my ear.

I nodded, leading him up the stairs to the second floor, down the walkway, and towards the last door that led to the spiral staircase. We went slowly to avoid loud creaks and stepped out on the landing. The junk room. It felt like we were playing a game. *Cold . . . warm . . . warmer . . .* There was an energy in the air, gathering around us.

I went immediately to the black-and-white painting of the figures and pulled it back. But when I shone the light behind it, there was nothing. Just a dusty open space.

The sudden absence shocked me. "Someone moved it."

Jonah held up a hand, listening. Then I heard it too: similarly careful, quiet footsteps up the rickety staircase. He turned his flashlight off and motioned for me to do the same. We moved back into the room, crouching behind a pile of cardboard boxes.

The person walked into the room. They ambled slowly around the perimeter, shining their own flashlight into every crevice. They were getting closer.

I tensed, grabbing Jonah's arm. At the last second, he shot up and aimed his light at them.

"Whoa!" She threw up her hands.

Jonah lowered his flashlight. "Mikki?"

She lowered her own, her voice hushed. "Jonah? And *Thea?*"

"What are you doing here?" Jonah asked quietly.

"I could ask you the same thing." Instead of her usual fashionable attire, she was in a sweatsuit and sneakers.

No one spoke.

I glanced at Jonah. I wanted to trust Mikki, but how could I? After all, I'd just been musing about the idea of plants. I knew Jonah was a good actor; Mikki could be even better.

"What, you think I followed you in here?" she asked.

"I don't know." I glanced at Jonah, who watched her carefully.

"Well, you clearly weren't following me, so I guess I'll tell you. I'm a journalist."

Steven's words came back to me: *Whatever you're looking for, you're not allowed to share it. If you're, you know, a journalist or something.*

"Investigating . . ." Jonah prompted.

"Moon and Sol. You?"

"A missing person," I said. Jonah shot me a warning look.

"Oh." Her eyebrows jumped. "Okay, that's interesting."

"Why don't we find somewhere better to talk?" Jonah gestured.

"The roof?" I asked. "There's a platform that's pretty high up. And with the wind, I don't think anyone will be able to hear us."

"You've been up there?" Jonah looked surprised. He and Mikki followed me up the rickety staircase and out the door. I again slipped off a shoe to prevent the door from closing. Up here the wind was more intense, and I settled myself onto the ground by the door. No way was I getting near the edge.

It was a beautiful night view, the crescent moon and stars shining over the flat, rolling landscape.

"So how do we do this?" Jonah asked. The three of us instinctively huddled together; it was cold up here.

"Why don't we share what we know?" Mikki asked.

"I can't believe you're a journalist." I shook my head. "You seemed so . . . *suspicious* of everything."

She smirked. "I thought it'd be a good cover."

I thought of her session, how she'd slept with her best friend's husband. Had that all been a lie?

"Who do you work for?" Jonah asked.

"I'm freelance." She pulled her hood over her head.

"So what are you investigating about Moon and Sol?" I asked.

"I used to live in LA, and my friend and I would go to this bougie yoga studio. Well, she'd go, because she could afford it, and I'd use her guest passes. There was this teacher that my friend loved, but I found kind of intense. Fast-forward ten years. I'm listening to this relationship podcast that Apple recommended to me—don't judge—and I recognize the voice. It's her. Sarah. But she's calling herself Moon. And . . ." Mikki paused for dramatic effect. "She has a Mexican accent."

"*What?*" I said.

Jonah leaned forward, his forehead creased. "So when she was teaching yoga . . ."

"No accent. Well, a very faint Southern one." Mikki shrugged.

"Wow." Moon's whole persona was built on her traumatic past, growing up in a dangerous city in Mexico where her father had disappeared and her brother and childhood crush had died. Had she made everything up? The thought made me feel suddenly nauseous.

"She'd been presenting as white up until a few years ago," Mikki went on. "Obviously, other people have done things like this, but no one's found out yet. The podcast is in the top fifty in the relationships category; their audience is big and growing. This is going to be a huge story when it comes out."

"Do you have any proof?" Jonah asked.

"I was able to get her last name from the yoga studio. Unfortunately, she was going by Sarah Smith—pretty impossible to track with normal search methods. But I did find her picture on an acting profile from eight years ago."

"Sol told me he and Moon met at an audition." I glanced at Jonah.

"Sorry I forgot to fill you in. But I was thinking they must've met Catherine in LA."

Jonah nodded, then turned to Mikki. "What else did you find out?"

"Well, I saw this negative comment on Reddit—"

"I did too!" I broke in. "I even wrote to them. But they never wrote back."

"Maybe he's having second thoughts after talking to me." Mikki rolled her eyes. "He was a little cryptic but said he wanted to help me. Apparently he was living here for a while, a few months. He didn't know Moon was lying about her background, but he said he wasn't surprised. He also told me that Moon and Sol use tactics to keep people in line. They have some kind of philosophy that he found disturbing, though he didn't say what it was. But he did send some photos from his time here."

"Can we see?" I asked. Maybe there would be some of Catherine. Jonah had already found proof on Facebook, but the more, the better.

"Yeah, I'd actually like to show you one in particular." She tapped at her phone and held it out. It was one of the ubiquitous group shots—two rows of people, arms slung around one another, identical grins.

"There she is!" I pointed to the redhead in the back. Relief surged through my chest. I was finally seeing it with my own eyes: Catherine had been here.

"Yup." Jonah zoomed in on her. Her smile was big but somehow fake-looking; it didn't extend to her eyes. Her necklace sparkled, catching the sunlight. A gold chain with a diamond: the same exact necklace that Moon always wore.

"Go to Moon," I directed. Jonah did and I pointed. "They're both wearing the same necklace."

Jonah zoomed out; no one else appeared to be wearing one.

"Oh my god." I pointed to the man next to Catherine: shaved head, broad shoulders, with a deep cleft in his chin. "That's him!"

"Who?" Jonah asked.

"The Australian guy who came to the hospital claiming he was Catherine's therapist. Clint."

"Yeah, Clint. He's my source from Reddit." Mikki glanced at me.

If he was spilling to journalists, clearly he wasn't working on Moon and Sol's behalf. So why had he shown up at the hospital? Had he known people would drag Catherine back here? Had he been trying to warn her?

"Keep looking." Mikki gestured at the screen. "There's someone else you need to see."

Moon and Sol were in the front and center, arms wrapped around each other. Steven stood next to Moon with his usual trademark scowl, even in this happy scene. Grace was also in the back row, though her hair was neon pink instead of orange. Another woman stood next to her, her face almost hidden underneath a baseball cap. Middle-aged? Slightly older? She was smiling, that much was clear.

"Her?" I zoomed in. The sun was bright and her face was in shadow, but the mole just below her mouth was unmistakable.

My breath locked in my throat. It couldn't be.

But it was.

The woman in the back row was Karen.

35

"Whoa," Jonah murmured.

"Yup." Mikki nodded, her expression stony. "I recognized her right away."

"So she came for a retreat?" I studied Karen's wide grin, feeling disturbed. "Or did—does—she live here full-time? Did Clint say?"

"I don't know." Mikki took back her phone. "I texted him, but he hasn't responded yet. At least not before the Wi-Fi went out."

"She made it sound like it was her first time here, right?" Jonah asked.

"Absolutely," Mikki said. "From that first moment in the airport. Which—who knows. Maybe Grace just dropped her off. None of us actually saw Karen getting off a plane, right?"

"So she knows Grace." The revelation chilled me. I could still picture it: Grace walking up to us with her cardboard sign. "She acted like she was just meeting her."

"But why?" Jonah asked.

"Well, think about it." Mikki counted off on her fingers. "Karen was fine with the shitty accommodations. She jumped her ass in that hot tub last night. And she volunteered to go first this morning. We're so influenced by the people around us. If this nice older white lady is cool with everything, it feels like we should be too."

Was that the reason? Or did it have something to do with Catherine? I'd considered the idea of a plant or plants, but Karen was the last person I would've suspected.

And this brought up another question: Were there more?

"I tried questioning Grace." Mikki slipped her phone into her pocket. "She's like a perky brick wall. Same with Steven. I even tried flirting with him, but it just freaked him out. In any case, I'm going to confront Moon tomorrow. You guys can come along if you'd like."

"Is that wise?" Jonah asked. "We're out here in the middle of no-where, looking for a missing person . . ."

"Yeah, so: missing person?" Mikki looked back and forth between us.

I quickly filled her in on everything, starting with the hospital and ending with the missing sculpture.

"So when did you guys meet?" she asked when I finished.

"I met Jonah in New York." No need to explain how. "But I wasn't expecting him to show up here."

"And now you're teaming up?" Mikki looked back and forth between us again.

"Yeah." I glanced at Jonah, who nodded in agreement.

"Did you search the rest of the castle?" she asked.

"We still have a ways to go," Jonah said.

"And one place we definitely still need to look is the purple door." I pointed down.

"What purple door?" Mikki asked.

"In the courtyard. It's the only one that's locked. And I've had this weird feeling, like someone in there is watching me. First on the tour, and then yesterday when Steven walked out and locked it."

"You think Catherine's in there?" Mikki asked.

"I don't know. Maybe."

Mikki jumped up. "Let's go, then."

Jonah nodded. "We just need to be careful. For all we know, Steven sleeps in there."

"No, he doesn't. Everyone here sleeps on the second or third floor." Mikki threw a glance back as she headed to the staircase. "You sure you're a PI?"

Jonah glared at her.

He redeemed himself when we got to the purple door, pulling out lock-picking tools with a flourish. In under a minute, the door clicked open. Jonah shot a triumphant glance at Mikki as he opened it and crept inside, his flashlight beam cutting into the darkness.

My chest ballooned with dread. Now that we were here, I really, really didn't want to go in.

For a minute I waited in the open doorway, watching as Jonah and Mikki shone their lights around the room. It was an art studio, same as the other rooms off the courtyard. There was a long table along one side, scattered with dozens of pieces of ceramic and glass. A standing desk. A wall of buckets. It smelled of paint and other chemicals.

It had to be Steven's mosaic studio. By why was it locked?

I forced myself to take a step inside, then another. The air was at least ten degrees colder than outside. Mikki and Jonah pulled out drawers in the table and desk.

I had to fight the urge to leave. After all, I was the one who'd pushed us to come here. But now that we were here, I could feel it. A badness, warning me away.

"What's this?" Mikki stopped at a door in the back of the room. It was painted the same white as the wall, and I hadn't even clocked it at first.

"Closet?" Jonah stood in front of it, considering. "It feels like cold air coming from it."

"And why's it locked?" Mikki indicated the dead bolt above the knob.

"Wait," I said.

Jonah looked back. "Are you okay?"

"I'm sorry. I just . . ." I wrapped my arms around my torso. "I'm fine."

As Jonah opened the dead bolt and turned the knob, I thought of how in my twenties I'd forced myself to watch horror movies and go to haunted houses. They always seemed like the best idea, up until I was hit with the reality: sharp, physical fear. Then I wanted nothing more than to be far away.

Jonah swung the door back towards himself. "Holy shit."

He and Mikki stared inside.

I propelled myself forward. My breath shallow with dread, I stood on my toes to see over their tall shoulders. The door opened into a room about the size of a large walk-in closet. The floor was covered in dark, sandy dirt. Two steps in, there was a gaping hole in the ground. It had to be six feet by six feet. And within it, steps carved out of rock descending into darkness. Cold, dank air flowed up the stairs like water.

The cave nightmare reared up in full color.

I stepped back. "No fucking way."

"What is this?" To my horror, Mikki lowered her foot onto the first steeply cut step, shining her flashlight down. "How far down does this go?"

"Pretty fucking far." Jonah stood at the lip.

Mikki took another step, then looked back. "Are you guys coming?"

I couldn't tell them about the dreams; they'd think I was crazy. How could I stop them?

"Maybe we should call the police?" I clasped my hands at my chest.

"And tell them what? We found a creepy staircase?" Mikki turned. "I'm going down."

"Wait!" The darkness was already swallowing her.

"Thea." Jonah placed a hand on my shoulder. "Just stay here. We'll check it out."

"I just don't think it's safe." The fear felt like a snake squeezing my neck.

"It's okay." Jonah patted my shoulder and turned away.

I watched as he descended behind Mikki, their flashlights bobbing. The tunnel down was slanted; soon I could no longer see them.

I slowed my breath and the spiky terror evened out. I sat on the edge of the hole, my feet on the first step, the damp cold seeping through the seat of my jeans.

I rubbed my eyes with my palms. It felt like my dreams were leaking into reality, like this hole existed only because of my imagination. Moon's words from the night before came back to me: *The veils between the worlds are very thin out here.* What worlds was I brushing up against?

I leaned down; Mikki and Jonah were talking, but their voices were faint.

It had to be a coincidence. After all, the cave I'd dreamed about had been tiny, and this seemed to lead down into a larger chamber. Obviously, I wasn't going to wriggle into any tight spaces. The very idea made me shudder.

I'd come all the way here, traveled thousands of miles to find Catherine. She could potentially be down there right now, suffering in the dark. And I was going to just sit here because of a dream?

It took another few seconds, but finally I stood. If I stayed, then I was giving up, and I shouldn't have come in the first place. Mikki had been scared too—I'd seen the tensed jaw, pursed lips. She just hadn't let it stop her.

I took one step down. Small pieces of rocks went skittering over the edge. The steps were worn, the sharp edges rounded with age.

Another step. *Careful.* I shone the light down and pressed my other hand flat against the wall. Tumbling down these steep steps would lead to broken bones, if not worse.

Slowly, incrementally, I made my way down into the earth.

36

The further down I went, the colder it got. Damp, chill air wrapped around me like a straitjacket. It smelled musty, slightly bitter. I took each step mechanically, forcing myself to take deep breaths.

Finally, after what felt like forever, I was at the bottom. I swept my flashlight around; I was in a cavern the size of a small room. Mikki and Jonah were walking around the perimeter, their beams swirling like mini floodlights. The stone ground was bumpy but overall pretty flat.

"Hey!" Mikki glanced at me. She might be nervous, but she was also excited: her dark eyes flashed, taking everything in. She stopped in front of a huge squarish slab across from the stairs. It was like a weird parody of the lobby upstairs. I pictured Grace behind the stone desk, cheerful in devil horns: *Checking in? Welcome to hell!*

Beyond the slab was a six-foot-tall tunnel. Mikki and I shone our lights into it, but they were quickly swallowed up by darkness.

I gulped audibly. There was nothing on this earth I wanted more than to turn around.

"What do we think?" Mikki peered into the corridor.

"Do you have any idea what this is?" I needed to stop her, to pause for one freaking second. "You've been researching this place, I'm assuming? Wasn't it supposed to be a resort?"

"Yeah." Mikki turned to me and Jonah. "I actually tracked down one of the original investors; he's now in Florida. He told me the management company had inflated their numbers and run out of money pretty early in the process. But instead of continuing investment rounds, they wanted to abandon the property, which he thought was strange. They ended up selling the land to one of the builders." She paused for dramatic effect. "Steven's father."

"Steven's father owns this place?" Jonah asked, clearly taken aback.

"He used to. He died seven years ago and left it to Steven, who started building the castle during early COVID. The guy I spoke with couldn't figure out where he'd gotten the money. Steven's dad—his family—wasn't rich."

"Catherine," I said. They both glanced at me. "She was withdrawing large amounts from her bank account during that time. Maybe she funded this place."

Mikki nodded slowly. "That makes sense. But what seems weird to me is that no one mentioned *this*. A cave system underneath the resort—I didn't hear about that anywhere."

I glanced up at the dim square of the doorway high above us. If someone shut and locked the door, we'd be trapped down here.

"Should we keep going?" Jonah nodded at the tunnel. He seemed on edge too.

"Let's go." Mikki walked ahead of him.

Steeling myself, I followed them. My jaw vibrated, from cold or fear, but I clamped my teeth together. I was going to do this.

The tunnel went about twenty feet and then opened into another space. We shone our lights, but the ceiling was too high for us to reach. This felt like a much larger cavern. And it was less smooth, rocks of all sizes scattered before us. The rough ground was wet, covered in small pools. There came the delicate, rushing sound of running water.

"Look." Mikki pointed. "Can you see that? All the way back there?"

A small point of light flickered far off.

"Let's check it out." Mikki started picking her way across the bumpy terrain.

"Be careful," Jonah called as her sneaker skidded into an ankle-deep puddle.

She stepped out of it. "Damn, it's slippery."

As they went ahead, I remained frozen, primal terror climbing up my spine. Being in this space, this cavern, was giving me déjà vu. The sound of the water, the damp mineral smell: it reminded me of the dreams.

But even if I told them—it wouldn't change anything. Lots of people dreamed about caves. They were fucking Freudian.

I took a slow step, then another. *That's it. One foot after the other.* I approached some larger rocks, used my free hand to climb over. *Okay.* I could do this.

The flickering light gradually grew bigger; it appeared to be a candle near the far end of the cave. Squinting at it, I slipped, falling onto my knees with an "oof."

"You okay?" Jonah called.

"Yeah." I got gingerly to my feet, my knees aching. *Focus.*

The ground sloped downwards like we were in a giant amphitheater, moving towards the stage. The small pools turned into rivulets. I concentrated on each step. When I looked up again, Mikki and Jonah had reached the back wall and were shining their flashlights on something white and round that looked like a skull.

"Jesus," I muttered, my heart thumping away in my chest.

Near the end and bottom of the cavern, the rivulets widened further into streams, cutting through the rocks and flowing downwards. The rushing sound was loudest here, white noise filling my ears. I paused to see Jonah's flashlight shining on a space at the wall—or rather, lack of space. The streams converged, flowing as one into a hole that was about five feet across. It was like a giant drain, gurgling and sucking, shooting bubbles and spray. I thought ridiculously of the hot tub upstairs.

This is our cold plunge! I pictured Moon at the edge of the hole, naked and gleeful. *So good for your circulation!*

I climbed towards its left side, where Mikki and Jonah were standing. My foot slipped and dropped into the water. I cried out with the sudden terrifying possibility of being sucked down into the hole, never to be heard from again.

Jonah grabbed my shoulders, supporting me until I was back on the rock.

I choked back a sob filled with frustration and fear. I was fine. I was doing fine.

"This is it, right?" He shone his light on the white skull-like object. It was the sculpture of Catherine's head set on top of a plank of wood near the hole's entrance. A large lit candle burned beside it.

"Yes," I gasped. Who had brought the sculpture down here? Lit the candle? And why?

"This is the missing girl?" Mikki bent to study it. "It kind of looks like *you.*"

"They look alike." Jonah bent to take a picture with his phone.

"No eyes. Creepy," Mikki muttered. "And these." She bent to pick up one of several ceramic shards on the other side of the candle. "What are these?"

"They look like the painting." I peered over her shoulder.

"What painting?" Jonah asked.

"One I saw in the junk room." This shard had the two largest figures on it, their square arms pointing at the sky. The other shards showed the torso of the striped figure, the bottom half of the couple behind the patterned square.

Mikki lifted the sculpture, grabbing something beneath it. "Oh." She held up a shining gold necklace. "This looks like Moon's."

"It's Catherine's." It suddenly felt hard to breathe.

"This is that symbol, right?" Jonah shone his light between the sculpture and candle; someone had painted a red spiral trapped in a triangle, the spiral's line dotted with circles.

Moon's excuse—that she'd dreamed about the symbol as a kid, that it had no connection at all to *Stargirl*—suddenly seemed very thin.

"We have to leave." The words came out in a whisper. No one heard me over the rush of the water. Now Jonah was examining the necklace.

"Guys!" My voice came out sharp, jarring. "We have to get out of here."

Mikki's and Jonah's eyes were wide.

"What's the matter?" Mikki asked.

"What's the *matter*? This is a fucking *shrine* to Catherine."

"It might not be hers," Jonah said quietly. "Maybe all the women at the Center have this necklace."

"But why is her *head* here?" I cried.

"So I don't want anyone to freak out." Mikki held up a red-tipped finger, the whites visible around her irises. "But I think this is blood." She dipped it again in the water, rubbed it against the spiral, and held it to her nose. "It smells like blood."

I pressed a hand to my mouth, suddenly nauseous. An image arose, superimposed on the shadowed rocks: Catherine standing in front of the hole. Someone coming up behind her, pushing her in.

You tricked me! How could you do that to me? It should've been you!

I backed away, my foot slipping and plunging again into cold water. It sucked at my ankle, pulling me towards the black void, stronger than I would've imagined. I turned and scrambled over the wet rocks, my breath ragged in my throat.

I had to get out of here.

Who knew if the vision of Catherine was a good guess or just a random theory offered up by my imagination. What I did know was that this place held a darkness—an evil—that I needed to escape immediately.

I slid over the rocks, again slipping and banging my left knee. I pushed myself up and kept going, barely registering the sharp, stinging pain.

Halfway across the hundred-foot chamber, I paused to look back. Mikki and Jonah were following twenty feet behind, their lights bobbing. *Keep going.* Now that we knew what was down here, the possibility of being shut in seemed much more realistic. We had to get out of this underworld as quickly as possible.

My hands shook, and I felt the dark edge of a panic attack. I tried to keep it away with deep breaths and mental encouragement. *You're doing great! Awesome! Amazing job!* Finally, I reached the tunnel, the blessedly walkable floor, and raced through it. Then I scurried up the stairs. The open doorway at the top shone a warm, buttery yellow.

I think this is blood. It smells like blood.

I was going to call the police. I didn't care if Mikki and Jonah thought I was crazy, or if it took two hours for them to get here. The second I had service, I was going to call 911 and tell them about Catherine. I couldn't contain or push away the possibility—it blared like an alarm—that they'd done something horrible to her here.

In the meantime, I'd lock myself in my yurt—*The yurts don't have locks.* I'd barricade myself in my yurt, then. Did I need a weapon? Should I stop in the kitchen to grab a knife first?

My thighs quickly started burning. It was harder going up the steep steps. Halfway up, I started coughing and couldn't stop. I bent over the stairs and vomited up water. Dripping back down the steps, it seemed like a lot. Where had it come from? I hadn't drunk anything recently, apart from a glass of sparkling yuzu juice at the bonfire.

"Are you okay?" Jonah caught up to me.

"Yeah." I continued upwards. My right calf spasmed, but I didn't slow.

Jonah was saying something behind me, but I could barely listen. All I could focus on was that square of light, steadily growing. I was almost out of this place—a place that felt ancient and cold and not of our world. A place that could break away from reality like an untethered boat drifting out to sea.

It was only when I reached the last few steps, my momentum launching me up through the hole, out through the door, and back into the studio, that the thought struck me:

We didn't leave the light on.

37

I stopped short, but Jonah barreled into me and we both stumbled forward.

They were all there, waiting for us.

Moon and Sol stood in the middle of the room in pajama pants and sweatshirts, their hair rumpled with sleep. Moon's arms were crossed, but she looked open, curious. Sol had an amused half smile on his face, hands clasped behind him, waiting patiently.

Grace and Steven flanked them on either side. Grace's eyes were wide and round; she looked scared. Steven wore his usual half frown.

Mikki let out an "Oh!" behind us.

"Welcome back!" Sol clapped his hands. "Looks like you guys gave yourselves the self-guided tour tonight."

I jerked my phone from my pocket. "Stay back. I'm calling 911."

"Thea." Sol sounded incredulous. "Please calm down. I don't know what you think is going on."

"We saw it." My voice was shaking as I unlocked the screen.

"Saw what? Listen, I'm sure we can explain everything."

"The Wi-Fi . . . it's still not working." No bars, but there was that SOS in the upper right.

"It went out. Like it often does." Sol rubbed his eyes.

I pinched the side buttons and several sliders appeared on the screen, including *SOS Emergency Call*.

"You found the cave." Moon said it calmly, the lilt of her fake accent filling the space. "What did you think?"

"So cool." Mikki widened her eyes at me. From fear or admonishing me to calm down? My finger hesitated on the slider.

"It's incredible, isn't it?" Moon smiled. "A cathedral. You saw our temple."

I couldn't keep the words in anymore: "What did you do to Catherine?"

Moon watched me, still smiling. Her diamond necklace glinted at her throat.

"Where is she?" My stomach clenched; for a moment I thought I'd vomit again.

Grace and Steven exchanged a glance.

"Look." Sol shook his head. "I don't know what you think happened to Catherine, but—"

"So you admit you know her." Jonah stepped forward. "Is she here?"

"If she is, you better let us see her," Mikki added.

"Sure." Moon shrugged.

"What?" I asked.

"Come with me." Moon beckoned. "All of you. I promise you will feel a whole lot better."

Was this a trap? Being in the cave had done something to me, thrown off my internal compass. A distant part of me wondered if I was acting irrational, overdramatic. But that altar, the sculpture, the necklace, the *blood* . . . I glanced down at my phone, those small white letters— *Emergency Call*—waiting patiently.

"Or you can leave." Sol glanced at Moon. "If that's what you'd rather do. Grace can start driving you to the airport right now."

"Yes." Moon blinked. "But they won't. Because they want to see Catherine."

"Have you been *hiding* her?" Mikki asked.

Moon's expression sharpened into irritation, a look I'd rarely seen from her. "Of course not. She's undertaking an intense regimen of meditation. An internal vision quest. Which you do alone."

Was it true? Had Catherine been in the castle this whole time, *meditating*? I wanted to laugh wildly. I didn't trust Moon, but she seemed so sure, so untroubled.

"Take us to her." I kept my phone at the ready in my hand.

"Wonderful." Moon turned and walked out the door. I hurried after her, through the moonlight-streaked courtyard, up the wooden stairs to the second floor. Jonah and Mikki followed, their faces uncertain. Moon paused in front of one of the doors and unlocked it; a skinny hallway led to a whole different part of the castle. The walls were hung with photographs.

This part of the building was a maze. We walked down some stairs, though another, smaller courtyard with a fountain, up other stairs, though a room dominated by a dusty piano. In the next hall, Moon stopped. She knocked on a door, then opened it. She gestured for us to go inside.

The room was lit by a crystal-laden chandelier hanging lopsided from the ceiling. There was an unmade twin bed shoved in the corner, a freestanding air conditioner beside it. In the middle of the room was a table covered with books and papers. The room smelled like unwashed sheets mixed with incense.

A woman came out of a doorway in the back. She wore a fuzzy zip-up fleece and biker shorts, and her hair was up in a messy bun.

Even though I recognized her immediately, it took a second to sink in.

She looked fine, good even—her face fuller than at the hospital, her skin golden-hued with a tan.

"Thea?" Her blank face shifted into an expression that hit me like a gut punch: eyes stretched open with fear, lips pulling back into a rictus of horror.

Almost immediately it melted into something else: the fearful eyes now wide with excitement, the grimace now a pleased grin.

"What are you doing here?" Catherine bounded forward and pulled me into a tight hug. I stood there, stunned and confused, as her arms tightened around me.

Part Three

38

I stood stock-still as she pulled away. This new, healthy-looking Catherine took me in, and it struck me, lightning-quick, that I'd taken her place: disheveled, dirty, confused.

"Are you okay?" I asked. Her brief, horrified expression had imprinted on my brain. It seemed so at odds with how she looked now: content, relaxed. Had I mistaken what I'd seen?

"Of course." She grinned. "How are you? This is so random. I'm so happy you're here!"

I glanced behind me. Near the doorway, Moon was beaming, beatific. Jonah and Mikki both watched us, uncertain.

"We'll give you two a little time to catch up." Moon shooed them out as Mikki gave me a last questioning glance and shut the door behind them.

So Catherine *had* been here the whole time. It felt odd to be standing in front of her, like seeing a cartoon character in real life. As soon as the door closed, Catherine's smile fell. She stared at me, and I noticed the dark circles under her eyes.

"Want to sit and chat?" Her words were light, at odds with the heaviness with which she slumped at the table. I sat across from her, and her smile reappeared. This time it looked slightly wooden. Goose bumps stippled my arms. Something wasn't right here.

"Catherine, seriously. Are you okay?" I sat across from her, feeling disoriented, fuzzy. That constant question banging in my head — *What happened to Catherine?* — had dissolved in the blink of an eye. But other questions, many more, were rising to take its place.

"Yeah, I'm fine. I'm great." She squinted. "Oh, you want something to drink? Water? Tea? Actually, the teakettle just broke, so —"

"Wait, stop. What the fuck is going on?" I asked.

She blinked. "What?"

I scoffed, raising my hands. "Are you really surprised to see me?"

"Yeah?" She smiled uncertainly.

"You left me a secret note pointing me here. After you were basically kidnapped from the hospital."

Her forehead creased. "I wasn't kidnapped."

"Yeah, but they used fake IDs to get in. Who were those people?"

"Thea . . ." She stretched out her hand. "I wasn't kidnapped. Really. But I'm glad you're here. It means a lot that you were worried about me."

"I was." Saying the words, I felt suddenly embarrassed. Had I been paranoid, reading into clues that didn't even exist? "In the note you said you'd made a mistake and had to deal with the consequences."

"Which was true. I ran away from the Center, and I shouldn't have." She shrugged. "I had to come back."

"But why write me in the first place?"

"Because I wanted to thank you." She scratched her nose. "Really. I didn't have ulterior motives."

"Why did you hide it like that, in the crayon box?"

"Because I didn't trust anyone there," she said. "And you told me you did that art class, so I figured you'd see it."

"But why did you thank me for using my headphones? They were Amani's."

"Oh." She drummed her fingers on the table. "I guess I forgot whose they were."

So it hadn't been a subtle clue. She'd truly just forgotten. Something I'd suspected briefly and moved on from, too excited by the other possibility. She'd been overwhelmed, on meds . . . of course she hadn't remembered (or cared) whose headphones she'd borrowed.

I sat back, deflated. "Okay. So who were the impersonators? How did you contact them?"

"I didn't. They just showed up. People who used to live here who are now in New York."

"With fake IDs?"

She shrugged. "They knew it was the only way they could get in."

"Why didn't they just ask you to see them?"

"I didn't leave on great terms." She grimaced. "I think they knew I'd be too embarrassed."

I paused. "So why'd you tell your parents you'd leave with them?"

"I was planning to. But when CRH people showed up, it seemed like it was meant to be." Her leaf-green eyes were wide, guileless.

"Why not tell your parents? They were really freaked out."

"My dad is super controlling." She shook her head. "If I'd told him where I was going, he would've come here and taken me back by force."

"You're an adult. No one can force you—"

"You don't know my dad." Her face went vacant and she stared past my shoulder.

I decided to drop it.

"What about that guy Clint?" I asked. "The one who said he was your therapist? He lived here, too, right?"

"He's a former member." Catherine nodded. "He also lives in New York now. He must've come when he heard I was in the hospital."

"He seemed—concerned."

"He cares about me. He wanted to make sure I was okay."

"Did you get in touch with him?"

"No. He would've tried to convince me not to come back."

"Why?"

She shrugged. "Things don't always end well with people here. It happens."

"But when I tried calling, his number was out of service."

"I don't know, Thea. I'm sorry." She looked down.

I felt a whisper of disquiet. She had an answer for almost everything, and yet I was sure she was lying. She didn't even seem all that surprised to see me.

"Why have you been hiding this whole time?" I asked.

Her eyes retrained on me. "I wasn't hiding. I was meditating."

"Why?"

"Because I've been trying to get better." She smiled wanly.

"Here?" I gestured. "Catherine, you just had a psychotic break. Moon and Sol aren't licensed. I doubt they have any type of training whatsoever. This is not the best place for you."

Her eyes grew red and glassy. "It is, though. This is where I'm supposed to be."

"A place where there's a weird, bloody altar to you in a cave?" I leaned forward. "Is that part of the healing process too?"

"You don't understand." She lifted the bottom of her T-shirt to her eyes. "There's a process in place. You don't get it because you're not part of this community."

She smiled widely, still mechanically wiping at her tears. The discordance was jarring.

"Do you know what happened before you had the break?" I asked softly.

"Oh, you know." She attempted a laugh. "The work here is intense." She let her shirt fall. She was back in control. "You've been here—what, two days? Imagine being here for years. You go so much deeper. And it's incredible, it really is. But sometimes it's too much. I wasn't strong enough, and it cracked me open. But it's okay." She folded her hands. "I'm better now. And I'm feeling stronger every day."

"How did you end up on the expressway in New York?" I kept my voice neutral.

"Oh." She stared down at the table. "I . . . I don't know. Someone must've taken me to New York. It's all . . . fuzzy. I don't know what happened."

For some reason, I believed her.

"Thea." She smiled, her eyes dry, as if she hadn't just been crying a minute ago. "I know you want to help. But I'm fine, really."

Oh really? She'd just had a psychotic break, memory loss, and catatonia—and she was claiming to be fine?

"Oh, look." Catherine pointed to my arm; blood was leaking from my elbow. I must've cut it on one of my falls in the cave. She jumped up and pulled a first aid kit from a cabinet. I watched as she ripped open an alcohol wipe.

"Here." She went towards my elbow.

"I can do it." I snatched the wipe from her and swabbed my elbow, wincing at the sting. Then I wiped my left knee, which was also bleeding.

"I'm sorry you came all the way here." She bit her lip. "Are you going to stay?"

"Stay?" I leaned forward to grab a bandage from the kit.

"Oh. I just meant—you're not staying, of course. When are you leaving?"

"Tomorrow. Well, today, technically." I had no idea what time it was—two in the morning? Later?

"Have you had your one-on-one yet?" Catherine was gripping the edge of the table.

"Not yet." I pressed the Band-Aid down.

"Thea." Catherine said it in a whisper. When I looked up, her eyes were again wide and frightened. I had the distinct feeling of vertigo. Her terrified look before—I *had* seen it. I hadn't made it up.

"What?" My stomach flipped.

She leaned in so that her solar plexus pressed into the table. *"You should leave."*

She said it so quietly I wasn't sure if I'd heard her correctly. But before I could respond, the door swung open.

"Hi, beauties!" Moon strode in. "I don't want to interrupt, but I was thinking we should all get to bed if we're going to be able to function tomorrow."

When I glanced back at Catherine, she was grinning widely, as if Moon had just told a hilarious joke.

"Totally," she agreed in a normal voice. "Sorry to keep you up, Thea."

"No problem." Slowly, I got to my feet. Now that the adrenaline was wearing off, my cuts and scrapes radiated with pain. But I wasn't tired at all. In fact, I was at my most alert.

Catherine might be alive. But she wasn't okay. She needed actual mental health treatment. But clearly she hadn't been given that option.

If this was a cult, Catherine wouldn't have much of a say about anything.

"Will I see you tomorrow?" I asked at the doorway.

Catherine's eyes went to Moon like a small child looking to her mother for permission. *Can I?* My scalp tightened.

"Of course, if you'd like." Moon winked at Catherine. "You could probably use a break from your meditation practice anyway."

I followed Moon down the winding hallways, up and down the sets of stairs. Questions I could ask rose and fell in my mind, and unease ballooned in my chest. I didn't want Moon to think I was suspicious of her, of the Center. But there was still so much that didn't make sense.

The shrine, Karen's pretending to be a new attendee . . . There was something off here. Catherine's fear and tears had proved it. She not only felt unable to leave—she'd had to look to Moon to know if she was even allowed to see me again.

You should leave.

By the time we reached the courtyard, I'd come to the firm conclusion: Catherine was mentally unwell, and the solitary confinement wasn't helping.

I had to get her out of here.

"Thanks for walking me." I smiled sweetly as we paused by the fountain.

"Sure." Moon pulled me into a tight hug. She leaned back, her arms still around me. "And don't worry, we forgive you three for snooping. I totally understand why. Your love and care for Catherine is so admirable. She was a patient for what—just a few weeks? The fact that you showed up here looking for her—it's incredible. It shows how much you connected."

"Thanks." I grinned down at her, pretending to be comfortable at this close range. Everyone was acting here; I could too.

Finally, she let me go. "We'll have a big discussion tomorrow. I'm sure you still have a lot of questions. And there are some things I'd like to share with you too. Including why you're having the dreams you're having."

The words jolted me. "What?"

"About the desert. And the cave too?" She patted my arm. "Try to get some rest. We'll talk more in the morning."

39

I stand in the open doorway.

There they are, Moon and Sol, their naked bodies gleaming in the candlelight. They're on an animal-hide rug, treasures glittering around them. She's on top, gazing down, lips parted in pleasure. Then she sees me and smiles. She holds out a hand, beckoning me. I step forward and Sol cups the back of my calf. But when I take her hand, something changes.

It's not Moon anymore; it's Jamie, Pastor John's wife. And she's already snatched her hand away, sneering with disgust. We're not in a palace, we're in a cheap hotel room, and they're on a towel that barely protects them from the nubby, stained carpet. I try to back away, but Sol—now Pastor John—clamps down on my calf. At the sharp pain I fall to the floor. Pastor John stares at me, grinning hugely, and it makes my blood run cold. Jamie gets off him, muttering, and grabs my left arm. Pastor John stands and grabs my right arm. They start pulling me forward, towards—what?

Then I see it. A whirlpool in the middle of the hotel room, the water sucking inward, downward, making a sickening noise. The hotel melts away. We're in the cave now. It was all a trap. I try to brace against the ground but they drag me forward and skin scrapes off my feet. I'm bleeding, and that makes the hole excited; the sucking noises get louder. As they push me to the edge, Pastor John places a huge hand on my lower back, and I look into the water and see rows and rows of teeth.

Not a hole.

A mouth.

"No!" I gasped, my eyelids flipping open.

Familiar golden sunlight streamed into the yurt. My phone beeped its alarm. I sat up slowly and picked it up. Still no Wi-Fi. My body was still tense from the nightmare, and now new apprehension flooded my system. What was wrong with the Wi-Fi? Didn't that seem suspicious?

At least I still had SOS. The satellites reached even this remote place.

As I dressed, I tried to shake off the dream—a clear manifestation of the unease I felt in this place, where I'd spilled a traumatic memory to literal cult leaders. Catherine's terrified face still shone in my mind. *You should leave.* And I would. I just had to figure out how to get her to leave with me.

I had a feeling trying to talk to Moon and Sol would be a lost cause. They were utterly convinced of themselves and their methods. I could try, but maybe I should focus more on Catherine herself. And I had very little time. Grace was set to drive us all back to the airport after lunch.

Walking to the bathroom, I remembered Moon's parting words about my dreams. How had she known I was dreaming about the desert and the cave? Maybe the desert dreams weren't that wild of a guess, given that we were *in* the desert. But the cave? I'd dreamed about it— twice—before we'd even found the cavern.

"Thea!" Moon accosted me as I exited the empty bathroom. "There you are. Ready for your one-on-one?"

"Oh." I clutched my toiletries bag. "Right now?"

"Yes. The sooner the better." Her tawny eyes shone. "Why don't you grab some breakfast and bring it to the yoga tent?"

"Sure." I tried to match her smile. This would be my chance to see if I could talk some sense into Moon and Sol. And, if not, try to gather as much intel as I could.

"Hey," I said as we walked outside together. "I noticed the Wi-Fi still isn't working."

"I know." Moon rolled her eyes. "It happens a lot, unfortunately. I'll see if Steven can take a look at it."

"Thanks." I paused in my yurt to consider my plan. If I could convince Catherine to come with us to the airport, then what—I'd send her on a plane back to LA? In an ideal world, her parents could help set up treatment. But given that she'd used words like "force" and "controlling" to describe them, they clearly weren't the right people to ask.

There were also private treatment centers in New York; maybe Catherine would agree to go to one of those?

"Hey!" Mikki was sitting alone at the dining room table. "Finally. What the fuck is going on?"

"Yeah." I settled next to her. "It was a weird night."

"So Catherine's been here the whole time?"

"She has." How to tell Mikki about what I'd seen? And *should* I tell her? After all, Mikki was a journalist. She hadn't yet recognized Catherine was a celebrity, but when she did—what then? Mikki wasn't bound by any rules of ethics. She could spread the news immediately, interfering with my plans to try to quietly get Catherine out.

"What's going on?" She could tell I was holding back.

"I'm just trying to figure out how to get Catherine to come with us this afternoon." I bit my lip. "I think she needs help."

Mikki picked up her coffee mug. "She seemed . . . not-okay to you?"

"Yep. Like . . . scared and brainwashed at the same time?"

"Yikes." Mikki blew out her breath. "Do you think she'll listen to you?"

"I don't know." I scratched at the already heavily scored wooden table. "I have to go to my one-on-one with Moon and Sol. I'm not super hopeful, but maybe I can convince them that Catherine needs a higher level of care."

"Hmm." Mikki took a sip. "Did we ever find out why they had that bizarre altar?"

"Good morning!" Dawne swept into the room, her long highlighted braid streaming behind her. "That fire ceremony was so fun, right? Dance party!"

The night before felt so far away, of a totally different time. Mikki and I met eyes.

"Did anything happen after I went to sleep?" Dawne called over her shoulder at the coffee carafe.

"Nothing at all," Mikki sang back, her voice light.

"Thea, come in!" Moon jumped up as I walked into the yoga tent.

I'd expected Moon and Sol, but the whole gang was there: Grace, Steven, Catherine . . . and Karen. She smiled warmly as I sat on a cushion. I looked away. It struck me that I wasn't just surprised that Karen, a seemingly kind and kooky woman, had been lying to my face this whole time. I was also hurt.

"How are you feeling this morning?" Moon asked with that lilting accent. I wondered if Mikki was still planning to confront her about it today.

"I'm okay." I felt the same sensation as when we'd started my session:

anticipation tinged with fear. Not that I was going to share. "How about you?"

"Well . . ." She blew out her breath. "Terrified."

"Terrified?" I echoed. Sol scooted closer to her, rubbing her back.

"Absolutely." She shrugged. "We were planning to have this conversation with you today. To connect you with Catherine. But last night things went a little . . . off track."

Catherine's legs were crisscrossed, her elbows resting on her knees. Sure, she was tan. But hunched over, with greasy hair and wide, unblinking eyes, she again looked strange.

"You were planning to connect us?" I echoed again.

"Yes. Catherine was doing her internal vision quest, as we said, but she was also sequestered in order not to influence you. We had to figure out if you were who we thought you were." Moon gestured at Karen. "It's also why our resident Karen did what she did."

"Oh, so your name is actually Karen?" I was unable to keep the bitterness out of my voice.

"It is. I'm sorry, hon." Karen looked dejected. "I hate lying, but it was necessary. I needed to figure out if I felt the right way about you."

"The right way?" I shook my head. "Why do I feel like everyone's talking in riddles?"

"Thea, it's okay." Sol held out a hand. "We're going to share everything with you."

"Great. I can't wait."

No one said anything for a moment. Finally, Moon nodded at Karen.

"What do you think happens after we die?" Karen asked me.

I scoffed at the unexpected question. "I have no idea."

"You were raised . . ."

"Lutheran."

Karen nodded. "So you were taught about heaven and hell too. I always found it so severe. Not to mention unfair. What if I'd been born a Muslim? A Jew? It didn't make sense that being saved was a matter of being born into the 'right' religion."

This topic seemed like a random tangent, but I nodded. I'd had similar thoughts during my own crisis of faith in high school.

"Even after years in the convent, no one could give me a good answer." She smiled. "The other sisters questioned my lack of faith. I'd always felt drawn to Jesus—his great sacrifice, allowing himself to be murdered to save the world. That seemed beautiful to me. But I couldn't get past the concept of good people being condemned to eternal damnation. When I left, I considered myself agnostic. Until the dreams." She noticed my expression and nodded. "Mine started when I moved to Arizona. Something about the landscape. And when Gracie came to visit, they were even more vivid."

"Grace is Karen's niece," Moon explained.

Grace nodded, tugging at the end of her orange pigtail, her blue eyes on me. A chill trickled down my back. So not only had Grace and Karen known each other at the airport. Karen was her *aunt*. And now that I knew, they did look vaguely related, with the same round cheeks and high foreheads.

"So Gracie told me about this woman in LA who was really helping her." Karen motioned at Moon. "When the retreats started, Gracie asked me to come. I wouldn't have ever expected it, but I felt so at home here that I never left. And when Moon started talking about reincarnation, it wasn't that much of a stretch for me. Early Christians actually believed in it too."

I glanced at Catherine, who was staring at the ground. That day in the hospital, she'd asked me: *Do you believe in reincarnation? Don't you feel like we've met before?*

"So you think we all knew each other in a past life or something?" It felt strangely relieving for the puzzle pieces to start locking into place.

"We talk a lot about patterns here, right?" Moon leaned forward. "How certain relational patterns keep showing up in our lives until we solve them? Well, it happens on a larger scale too. Sometimes we experience something that's so traumatic that we bring it with us into our future lives. With our cohort, of course." Moon gestured around the group. "All of us experienced the trauma together. That's why we all have the dreams. That's why we all ended up here. Because it's time to finally resolve the pattern."

I nodded. Now it was clear: These people were completely delusional. My plan to calmly discuss Catherine's mental health now seemed laughable.

"So what's the pattern?" I needed to get as much info, as much ammunition, as I could.

"You've already experienced it." Moon shrugged. "Past life patterns show up in our current lives, but really they're pale imitations. Echoes.

Your experiences with your pastor and your bully—you must've recognized the crossover with *Stargirl*."

The movie title shook me. So Moon was admitting it: *Stargirl* had something to do with all of this.

"Didn't *Stargirl* intersect with your life?" Moon pushed. "The pharaoh and the guard? Pastor John and Adam?"

I swallowed, suddenly unable to speak. Because: yes. I'd noticed the similarities back then too. But it had to be a coincidence.

"Catherine dreamed it first." Moon stared at me without blinking. "She told her father, who asked question after question so he could turn it into a big-budget film. You connected with it not only because of the current-life echoes. But because you lived through it." She broke our gaze. "All of us did."

"Moon," I protested. It felt necessary to push back against this, if only to steady myself.

"Look. It happened right here." Moon pulled out something from behind her: the black-and-white painting from the junk room. "Catherine found shards in the cave. I know you saw them down there. They're from the Mimbres people, who disappeared almost a thousand years ago. We knew the pottery pieces were special—because they showed *us*. Gracie was able to channel the full design in this painting. Look." She pointed to the two larger figures at the top. "You and Catherine. The twin priestesses, connected to the spirit world." Her hand moved down to the figures with the staffs. "Me and Sol. The leaders." She pointed out the figures behind the square. "Karen and Steven. Your mother and father." She touched the striped, crouching figure. "Grace, the sorcerer." She tapped the lone figure holding the arrow. "And Jonah, the guard."

My head spun. Karen and Steven—my mother and father? Grace as the sorcerer? And *Jonah*?

"So Jonah's part of this too?" I asked.

"Yes." Moon gently set down the painting. "We thought we'd talk to you first, and that you could share this with him. He's here, of course, as he should be. But he's resistant. We can feel it."

Taking a deep breath, I thought back to the story of *Stargirl*: the priestess Thuya falling for the guard Hapi after initially disliking him. Her growing relationship with the pharaoh. The sorcerer telling the queen about Thuya's connection with the pharaoh and her plans to run off with Hapi. The pharaoh—surprise!—stopping them, having Hapi killed immediately and Thuya left in the desert to die.

And then that strange last scene in the spaceship: Thuya holding a knife as she approached a new version of the queen. The camera pulling out to show a whole spiralic galaxy matching Thuya's birthmark.

I hadn't clocked it at the time, but *Stargirl* had been about reincarnation all along.

"But there was just one priestess in the movie," I managed to say. My brain suddenly felt full, slightly foggy. This wasn't real, of course. But it also awakened something in me, some excitement that burned like a pilot light in my chest.

"Yes. That was a mistake." Moon gestured at Catherine. "Her earliest regressions—dreams—were of dying in the desert. But her eyes were closed. She didn't see you, so she didn't know you were there. But since then, she's dreamed about you many times. Right, Catherine?"

Catherine nodded mechanically. Her wan smile looked painted on.

"Are you okay?" I asked her.

"She's tired, Thea." Moon sounded suddenly cross. "This has all been incredibly draining for us. Especially Catherine, calling for you in the spirit world, praying to open your mind. You showed up, yes. But we didn't know if you'd stay. You have resistance too."

I thought back to the times I'd sensed someone watching me through the lace curtain of the purple door. Had it been Catherine after all? Had she been meditating in the *cave*? The idea of it made me shiver.

You should leave. I was pretty sure Catherine hadn't been praying for me to stay.

"Thea." Moon leaned in. "Do you remember what happened in the desert? Before you died?"

"Ah, no." I shook my head. "I don't."

"*Think.*" Moon's voice lowered. "Your desert dreams. Can't you see something off in the distance, coming towards you?"

And all at once I remembered: that undulating movement slipping over the hills.

"You can see it, can't you?" She smiled and leaned back. "This is an enormous opportunity. Because it goes beyond our cohort. Sometimes something happens that's so egregious, so agonizing, that the energy affects not just the individuals but the collective. That's what happened when you and Catherine were brutally killed."

"By you, right?" I cocked my head.

"Yes. In that incarnation, I was a taker of life. That was my role to play." Moon's eyes glittered with intensity. "And your role is much greater. You don't remember, but something happened in the desert. You were offered something. A choice."

"I don't remember, Moon. I'm sorry."

"But that's why you need to stay." Moon jumped up and crouched in front of me, grabbing my hands. "Just two more days. Until Ostara— the spring equinox. You're here on the most balanced day of the year in order to bring balance to humankind. Once we resolve our healing work, everyone on earth will feel the effects." Her honey-colored eyes pleaded.

"How do you mean?" I asked.

"Think of it like this." Moon let go of my hands and sat on the floor, still too close. "If you're a person with unresolved trauma, you might experience physical symptoms. Headaches, stomachaches. Right?"

I nodded mechanically. It was true: the mind and body were closely connected. I'd worked with a few patients whose health issues had improved or cleared up after they processed painful experiences.

"We believe that the same thing happens on a collective scale. Suffering, war, poverty: these are the manifestations of our psychic trauma. Our cohort went through a trauma together. If we're able to heal it, there will be a ripple effect. Fewer people will suffer. Fewer people will die." Tears shone in her eyes. I thought of the deaths she'd claimed: Had any of them been real?

"This is huge, Thea," Sol piped up. "Bigger than you could even imagine."

Catherine peered up at me through her curtain of hair.

"We know how this sounds," Karen said. "You've only been here two days. This is all brand-new. But can you just take some time to think about it? If any part of you resonates with what we're saying, then stay. At least for one more session. You'll be amazed by what happens, I swear to you. And once we work through it, that's it. The pattern's broken. We can all move on."

"And if I say no?" I asked.

"Then we'll have to wait for our next opportunity, who knows how far into the future." Moon smiled sadly. "And the pattern will haunt us for the rest of this lifetime."

"We need you," Grace pleaded. I glanced at her smooth, bare face. Grace was the sorcerer? How had they come up with that?

"We know this is a lot." Moon got to her feet. "So we'll give you some time to process. But if you want to come talk to me—or anyone—we'll be around."

"Okay." I stood, a headache lurking.

Moon embraced me without hesitation. They all waited in a line to hug me—even Steven, who smelled like fried dough.

Catherine was last. She gave me that same weak smile, but this time it struck me as real.

You should leave. Was she happy because she thought I was planning to?

40

"Can I talk to you?" I asked Catherine quietly.

"She actually needs to go rest." Sol slipped an arm around her. "As Moon said, this all has taken a lot out of her." He walked her out of the tent and Moon, Karen, and Steven followed. Grace gathered up the cushions to set in a corner, and I helped her. The others were all clearly behind Moon. But maybe Grace would have a crack.

"Some great actors here," I said.

She looked up in surprise, then chuckled. "Well, a lot of them are from LA."

"Yeah. So, wait—how did you meet everyone again?" I now remembered Grace telling me on the drive here she was from Santa Fe and had come for a retreat.

"Well, I am from Santa Fe originally." She tossed the last cushion down, straightened. "But I met Moon in LA." She smiled, rueful. "I'd just dropped out of college."

"Oh yeah?"

"Yeah." She brushed back a neon strand. "I was trying to pay for it myself with all these shitty jobs, and I just couldn't do it. Not even after . . ." She smiled, looking embarrassed. I waited and she finally continued. "I went on this app for sugar babies. My friend told me about it; she was seeing this guy who paid her rent. She was happy, and it seemed like this great opportunity. But when I did it, it didn't feel like that. It felt . . ." She exhaled. "Maybe it was the guys I met. But it wasn't a good experience. And I didn't make that much."

It was hard to imagine fresh-faced Grace as a sugar baby.

"How did you meet Moon?" I asked.

"She lived in my building. It was perfect timing. I was pretty depressed." Grace shrugged. "She got me to see that if you're hopeless, you let the evil win. If you join with others, you can be a force for good. She gave me something to live for."

So Moon had been preying on people looking for answers. That was the very definition of a cult.

"Grace, do you think Catherine . . ." I considered how to phrase it. "She doesn't seem quite right to me. I know Moon said she was tired. But . . . what do you think?"

Grace's smile disappeared. She looked suddenly fearful, the same exact expression I'd seen on Catherine's face the night before. "What do you mean?"

"Well, how long has she been living here? Has she been like this the whole time?"

"Like what?" Now Grace's mouth turned downwards.

"Um . . ." *Out of it? Sad and scared? Clearly not well?*

"Catherine's fine, Thea. Trust me. She's more than fine." Grace's words were sharp, and she abruptly took off, disappearing through the canvas doorway.

"Okay, then," I said in the resulting quiet.

I took the opportunity to look for Catherine's room, but when I finally found it, after many wrong turns and dead ends, no one answered my knock. I called to her softly and tried the knob, but it was locked. Finally, I left.

I had to talk to Catherine one-on-one. Maybe everyone else here was brainwashed, but I felt sure I could talk some sense into her. I *had* to.

I decided to take a quick shower, defiantly using the curtain-protected stall. The hot, steaming water cleared my head. So Moon et al. were obsessed with past lives. That wasn't necessarily shocking—again, a lot of the spiritual set was into that. At one point, I'd even dabbled in the esoteric arts. After Ryan's ghosting, I'd contacted a tarot reader Dom loved. And the session had seemed to be weirdly accurate, though it was very possible my brain was just using the symbols to create meaning. It mattered less to me if it was "real" and more that it was helpful.

I had to admit that people could find real refuge in spirituality—and religion. The problem arose when people used their beliefs to harm. Think of the Crusades. Think of the Inquisition. Think of certain religious communities right *now* denouncing queer and trans people.

Then the beliefs became more about control and oppression than anything else.

Grace shutting down at my questions, Catherine *and* Karen looking to Moon for permission to speak . . . all of it gave me a bad feeling. This wasn't just a group of hippies and hipsters having fun in the desert. Moon and Sol held power here. I knew from various cult documentaries that leaders often stopped their members from getting help, whether that meant seeing a therapist or going to a hospital for medical treatment. I wasn't going to allow them to let Catherine decompensate, to deteriorate. Not if I had the chance to stop it.

When I came out of the showers, Jonah was brushing his teeth at the row of sinks. He was in sweatpants, shirtless, his curls mussed.

We locked eyes in the fog-ringed mirror. He leaned forward and spit.

"Good morning." He said it so neutrally that we both laughed.

I tightened my towel, aware of our near-nakedness. His sweatpants were low, revealing his lower abs and V lines.

"So." He rapped his toothbrush on the sink. "What have you been up to?"

"Oh, not much. Just learning about how you and I are part of a past life cohort based on the movie *Stargirl*."

"*What?*"

I explained everything I'd learned from Catherine and from the group. When I finished, he burst into laughter.

"What?" I asked, as he caught his breath.

"Sorry. Just—damn. It's even wilder than I thought." He shook his head. "What'd they say when you told them you were leaving?"

"I didn't." At his confused expression, I continued. "I need to talk Catherine into leaving with us first. But she's not answering her door."

"Leaving with us?" He frowned. "To go where?"

"Ideally, an inpatient treatment center."

"Hmm." He leaned against the sink, crossing his arms. Muscles rose on his biceps.

"Did you call her parents?" I asked. The thought struck me with a flash of anxiety.

"No Wi-Fi." He shrugged. "But I will as soon as it's back on."

"I don't think you should tell them. Catherine seemed scared of them. Especially her dad."

His smile was humorless. "They're my clients, Thea. That's the whole reason I'm here."

"Well, let me ask you this. If you found out your client was an abusive husband, would you still tell him where his wife was?"

Jonah rubbed the edge of the sink, eyes worried. It felt encouraging that he was listening.

"Just let me talk to Catherine first," I went on. "Before you do anything."

"And how are you going to do that? They're clearly keeping you away from her."

"Well." I shrugged. "They want me—us—to stay. So that gives us some leverage, right?"

He nodded slowly. "It could."

"I'll tell Moon that I need a one-on-one with Catherine. I think I can convince her to leave with us."

"What makes you so sure?"

I didn't know how to explain it, because the answer that arose sounded just as ludicrous as everything Moon and Karen had shared. I felt connected to Catherine; I had since the first day we'd talked at the hospital. She trusted me. I knew, somehow, that if anyone could convince her, it'd be me.

Of course, I couldn't say that out loud.

"Just wish me luck," I said instead.

41

After dressing, I went back to the yoga tent and peeked in a window. Sol was crouching beside Ramit, rubbing his back, while Moon held Ramit's head between her hands, eyes closed, murmuring something. I backed away, disturbed. In the midst of all this, Moon and Sol were still running their retreat. Ramit and Dawne had no idea what was happening here behind closed doors.

"Thea." Karen walked up to me on the path. "How are you feeling?"

God, I was sick of people asking me that.

"I'm fine." I said the words coldly.

"Look." She raised her hands. "I'm sorry that I lied to you. I really am. But my intentions were good. Don't let your anger at me keep you from staying here." She paused, her turquoise eyes jumping around my face. "*Are* you thinking of staying here?"

"I don't know." I cleared my throat. "I'm considering it, but I want to be able to talk to Catherine alone first."

"Great." Karen gestured. "Let me take you to her."

"Really?"

"Yes. If you stay, it needs to be of your own free will. You deserve to have all the info you need." She continued on the path towards the castle. "Just . . . maybe don't tell Moon and Sol."

"Deal." So Karen, at least, still had some sense of agency. I followed her. "During that group meeting, you said something about needing to figure out if you felt 'the right way' about me? What did that mean?"

Instead of answering, Karen gave me a long look. "You have children, Thea?"

"No." It always felt strange when people asked me that, although there were plenty of people younger than my thirty-three years who did.

"Me either. But it's strange, because for my whole life I've felt like a mother." She shrugged. "When my sister had kids, I assumed that would fulfill it. But no. I love Grace and her brothers very much, but they don't feel like my children. There was even this point where I thought about adopting in my forties. But Art and I decided against it. It was weird, this feeling, like . . . what do they call it? Phantom limb? Like I already had kids, but I didn't know who they were. When I came here and met Catherine . . . well." She smiled, sticking her hands into her cargo pants. "I felt it immediately. This sense that Catherine was my daughter."

"And when you met Steven, you felt like he was your husband?" I broke in.

Karen scratched her chin. "He annoyed me, in a really personal way, even though he didn't do a thing to me. I don't think our marriage was a happy one."

"Okay. But you felt motherly towards Catherine."

"Yes. Straightaway." She glanced at me. "I feel the same way about you."

Her words made me uncomfortable. I hadn't really thought about it, but I had felt a warmth, even a protectiveness, from Karen this weekend.

But it was just her, right? Wouldn't anyone feel this way towards an older woman with twinkling eyes and a kind smile?

"Why did you have to pretend to be new here?" I asked.

"I needed to be able to interact with you intimately. So I could know." She leaned in, eager to explain. "You didn't hang out much with Grace or Steven, right?"

"Right," I conceded. A new question arose. "By the way, your session—were you just making all that up?"

"Not at all." She sounded firm. "I've broken my pattern, but it's not hard to tap back into it. It will always exist inside of me."

We arrived at the courtyard, and Karen walked us confidently up flights of stairs and down halls until we reached Catherine's door. She knocked. "Hon? It's me, Karen. Thea's here with me. She wants to talk to you."

After a second, the door opened. Catherine waited, her face blank.

"Okay." Karen nodded at me. "I'll talk to you later."

Back inside Catherine's room, I had more time to process what I was seeing. It was messy in here: piles of clothes on the floor, sheets hanging off the bed. The table, scattered with books, held a full plate of untouched food: eggs, toast, yogurt topped with berries.

"Not hungry?" I sat at the table and touched the nearest book: *The*

Chalice and the Blade, a vintage paperback with a rounded goddess statue on the front.

"No." She plopped across from me, looking much the way she had in the yoga tent: drained, deflated.

"So . . ." I wondered how to begin. This was my one chance to convince her; I had to do so delicately.

"You should go, Thea." Her gaze flicked up to mine. "You shouldn't be involved in all this."

"Why is that?" I leaned forward. "You told me we were connected in a past life when we were back in the hospital. You don't believe it now?"

"I . . ." Her mouth hung open. She shut it abruptly. "It's complicated. But just trust me."

"Okay. But Catherine." I opened my palms. "I have to be honest. I'm a little concerned about you."

"Oh yeah?" She stared down at the table.

"Yeah. You seem a little . . . off. You've been through a lot in the past few weeks, and that can be really destabilizing."

She chuckled weakly, shaking her head.

"How *are* you feeling?" I pushed.

"Fucking great." She rolled her eyes; that felt more like the Catherine I remembered from the hospital.

"I know that this is your community. And that you care a lot about these people. And—that you're all doing really important work together. But . . ." I took a deep breath. "I wonder if this is the best place for you at this moment."

The dark eye circles set off her bright green eyes; they looked almost lime in the dim light. "What are you saying?"

"I think you should come with me today." I pressed on as her eyes narrowed. "Just for a little bit. Just until you're feeling better. Less tired. You know? I think there may be some . . . pressure that you're feeling here."

She continued to stare at me.

"Maybe it takes an outsider to see it," I went on. "But I can tell that you might be struggling. Which totally makes sense."

"So where do you think I should go?" She pulled the plate in front of her and started shoveling eggs into her mouth. I winced; they must be cold.

"Well, you could go anywhere from the airport. There are places all over the country that would be good for you. You know, if you have the money—"

"I have no money." Yellow flecks flew out of her mouth.

"Okay. Well, maybe your parents—"

She pushed the plate away roughly. A piece of toast flipped over onto the table. "You want to know about my parents? My dad was a fucking creep."

I waited. After a moment, she continued more softly. "He didn't act like a father's supposed to act with their kid. At least after I turned twelve. He'd barge into my room when I was changing, try to get me to sit on his lap, hug me in a weird way . . . And the one time I tried to talk to my mom, she grounded me. Said I was lying. So." She shrugged.

"I'm so sorry." The suspicions I'd had hardened into reality. Catherine's father had abused her. And her mother, instead of helping, had punished her.

"Yeah." Catherine rubbed at her eye viciously. "The only person I ever told was Sebastian. Until Moon, of course."

Sebastian Smith: her costar in *Stargirl*. My former crush.

"That's my pattern." She stretched her lips, but it wasn't a smile. "Moon calls them *echoes*—past life patterns showing up in this life. But it doesn't feel like an echo. It feels real."

"Of course," I said.

"I'm sure you had it too." She gestured to me. "The pattern. Mine was with my dad and Sebastian. The pharaoh and the guard. Sebastian tried to protect me, but he couldn't do much. But Moon . . ."

"She was the queen, right?" I asked softly. Maybe I could use this delusion to convince Catherine to come with me.

"Yeah."

"Why does she call the shots?" I asked. "Why do you trust her?"

Catherine just shrugged.

"I'm your sister, right?" I went on. "Maybe you should listen to me."

Her eyes filled with tears. One rolled slowly her cheek.

"You can trust me," I continued, feeling encouraged. "I want to help you."

"It's too late." She wiped the tear away.

"What's too late?"

"I can't leave."

"Why not?"

She didn't respond, and I continued. "I can tell something's not right here. That *you're* not all right. I'm a social worker; let me help you figure this out. Come back to New York. You can stay with me."

"New York?" she said uncertainly.

"Yes. We'll find a place where you can get help, and then after, we'll do all the things—go to art museums, movies, Central Park . . ."

She stared down at the table. Some inner calculation was happening behind her eyes.

"You like shopping? We'll go shopping . . ." I said the words as a kind of lullaby. "Broadway shows . . . or off Broadway, whatever you prefer."

A slight smile. I had her; I could feel it.

"All you have to do is come with us after lunch," I said, then held my breath.

"No." Her eyes snapped up at me, a new determination behind them. "We have to leave tonight."

I exhaled. "Tonight?"

"We have to leave secretly. They won't let me go otherwise."

"You want us to drive away in the middle of the night?"

"Yes." She gazed at me, defiant. "You think this will be easy?" Her volume increased. "That they'll just let me fucking leave?"

"Okay." I held out a hand, placating. "Fine. We'll leave tonight. If that's what we need to do." I wasn't thrilled about the prospect: taking one of the Center's cars and leaving it at the airport. But they had a second vehicle; they could come get it. Catherine's mental health was more important.

"Really?" She looked uncertain but hopeful, like a child who'd gotten a whole cake she'd pointed at.

"Really." I pulled out my phone. "What time should we leave?"

"Let's leave at four a.m. The keys—"

"Are in the lobby. I know."

"Okay." Her whole body relaxed—shoulders slumping, head lowering. It was like she'd just completed a marathon.

"You're going to set your phone's alarm?" I asked.

"Don't worry." She stood unsteadily and went to the bed, where she collapsed. Her words were half mumbled into a pillow. "I'll be up."

42

"So you're really staying?" Mikki's eyes were wide behind chunky glasses I hadn't yet seen her wear. I'd caught her in the midst of packing, and her suitcase yawned next to me on the bed.

"Just until tonight." I'd told Mikki that Moon and Sol had asked me to stay, but not why. If I told her about the "disturbing" belief system her source Clint had mentioned, then that was definitely going in the article. And maybe that would be okay, but my first order of business was to get Catherine out of here.

"Ah yes, the car-stealing plan." She nodded, sitting on the chair and pulling out her vape.

"I mean, it's probably Catherine's car anyway, right? She's been the one funding everything around here."

Mikki took a pull. "Touché."

"If it's the only way she'll leave, that's what we have to do," I said. "Someone will come get the car from the airport, anyway. We're not actually stealing it."

"But Thea . . ." Mikki tugged at the tangle of necklaces around her neck. "What if she doesn't go? And you're already missing your flight . . . I don't know. This all sounds weird."

If only she knew.

"I trust her," I said finally. "I can read her; I don't know how to explain it. Maybe it's my clinical skills."

Mikki leaned forward, her arms on her knees. "Do you think it's safe?"

"How do you mean?"

"If Catherine's too scared to leave during the day, what does that say about this place?" She stared down at her combat boots. "And Karen playing pretend . . . I don't know. It all feels shady."

"I know. But I don't think it's, like, dangerous."

"Why not?"

I considered. "Catherine's afraid to leave, but those car keys have just been sitting in the desk. She could've taken off at any time. She's not locked in her room—there's a lock on the inside. This place is cult-y, for sure. But I haven't seen evidence of anything illegal."

Mikki sat back and crossed her legs. "Remind me why Catherine was in your psych ward again?"

"She was catatonic. I think she had a psychotic break beforehand."

"How did that happen?"

"Catherine said it's because of the work they do—how intense it is. And I can see that. I just had one session and it was overwhelming."

Mikki blew a white plume towards the window.

"Did you . . ." I started. "I mean, in your session, was that true?"

She stared at me. "No."

"Oh." I tried to chuckle. "You're a good actor, then."

"I do what I need to do to get the story." Mikki jiggled the vape pen. "I was laid off from a media company six months ago. I've been eating through my savings. It's not easy to be a journalist these days."

"I can imagine," I said.

"These companies are hiring fewer and fewer people full-time. So we all have to compete against each other for freelance stories. Most of them with shitty pay." Her lips pursed. "I'm behind on my rent. New York is just so fucking expensive. My sister wants me to come to Atlanta. My mom and dad want me to move into their guest bedroom in St. Louis. But you know what that would feel like? It'd feel like a failure."

"I get that," I said, thinking of the sticker shock as I'd looked for apartments. And I had a full-time role with benefits.

"But you know what this is?" Mikki gestured around. "This is a capital-S *story*. A top-tier news source paid for me to come here. This reveal about Moon will be huge; people love a con artist. And I'll make actual money. Get other assignments. This is everything, Thea."

"I understand."

"So if I have to pretend to be a sex and love addict, then that's what I'll do." She smiled. "It's not that far off, anyway."

"Did you ask Moon about her fake accent?" I asked.

"No. Not yet." Mikki sat up straight. "We just did more 'work.' They both pushed me to come back next month."

"Oh, wow."

"And I will, if I can get my editor to pay again." She shrugged. "I'm starting to see that this story might be even bigger than we expected. Oh, I wanted to ask—do you think Catherine would speak to me? Once she's out?"

"Maybe. I can give her your information."

We traded phone numbers. Still no Wi-Fi, which meant I couldn't even try to move my flight. I'd have to email Diane from the road as soon as I had service, letting her know I was calling out Monday. Hopefully, Catherine and I could find an early morning flight.

"Are you sure you want to stay?" Her gaze was like a laser beam. "This Wi-Fi situation is concerning."

"I'll be okay." I held up my phone. "I can still reach emergency services."

"All right. Well, I'm going to stop in Silver City for a few days." Mikki stood, hands on hips. "See if I can talk to someone about the cave, maybe from the university. I also want to dig on Steven a little more."

"Steven said he's known Moon a long time." I remembered from our brief conversation after he'd caught me in the junk room. "They were even living together in India for a while. If you find more info on him, maybe you'll find out more about Moon."

"Good idea."

I stood to leave, but at the doorway Mikki said my name.

"Yeah?"

Lines appeared between her eyebrows, and it struck me this was the first time I'd seen her look truly worried. "Just be safe, okay?"

Lunchtime came and went, and soon Mikki, Ramit, and Dawne were rolling their suitcases to the entrance. I felt a tightness in my chest— the reality of my decision to stay was starting to sink in. Jonah and I hugged the departing: the official story was that we were flying out the next morning. No one questioned why we hadn't gotten flights for that evening, as the retreat instructions had specified.

"Let's stay in touch." Dawne gave me a tight hug, before Ramit did the same, along with a sunny smile. We'd all traded numbers, and I felt a pang of sadness as they got into the SUV. Despite the disturbing nature of the weekend, I'd really bonded with these people. It was amazing how quickly that could happen when you went through something intense together.

As the car retreated down the dusty road, Moon wrapped an arm around me.

"I'm so happy you're both here." She squeezed. "We're going to start setting up for our session tonight."

"Tonight?" I repeated. I'd thought I'd be long gone before having to do another one.

"Yep." She grinned. "It's going to be so special. You'll see."

"Thea." Sol tapped my arm. "Want to join me on the veranda?"

"Sure." I followed him, glancing back to see Moon grasping both of Jonah's hands. She'd been thrilled when I'd told her we were both planning to stay, but not particularly surprised, as if she'd expected it. Jonah knew the plan; we'd both leave with Catherine at 4:00 a.m.

Sol leaned in towards me. "I asked Steven to make us some kava. Have you had it?"

"No, I don't think I have."

"Oh, you're in for a treat. It's a root that relaxes the body. We mix it with chai. Delicious."

When we reached the veranda, he motioned to the chairs and continued his confident lope into the kitchen. The flat-topped pool was still; it was a breezeless day. The scent of honeysuckle tickled my nose. Sol returned with two glasses clinking with ice cubes. The tan-colored drink was flavorful, sweetened with honey but retaining a sharp bitterness underneath.

"So." He slipped in the chair next to me. "I wanted to check in with you because I know we laid a ton on you this morning. It's a lot to take on faith, right?"

"I don't know." I said the words lightly. "Maybe it is."

"I think we both know the real reason you're staying." He smiled. "Catherine. Your bond runs deep. It proves our point, though, doesn't it? After all, if she was just a patient, it really wouldn't make sense for you to be here."

"How do you mean?" I met his gaze, feeling like I'd suddenly entered into a game of chess. I had to be careful. I couldn't reveal anything that might tip off our plan to leave.

"Well . . ." He scratched his chin. "You tell me. Is it normal for social workers to travel thousands of miles to search for former patients?"

"It's not," I acknowledged.

"Catherine told me you listened to the podcast." Sol straightened his sunglasses. "That was what tipped you off?"

How much had Catherine told him? I realized I had no idea. Something else I had to be careful about.

"Yeah. Well, you invoked a Catherine while directing listeners to come home."

He chuckled. "Fair. Maybe I was trying to call her back. But it was a pseudonym. I was talking about a member named Talia. She's traveling, but she'll be back soon. You'll meet her, if you decide to stay longer-term. Has the cutest little dog, Dionysus."

Longer-term? Was Sol really trying to recruit me right now? I kept my face neutral.

"You mentioned him." I smiled. "The one who likes to chase jackrabbits and Steven, right?"

"Right." Sol laughed. "Poor Dionysus is just jealous. Steven and Talia are together, you know."

"Oh, nice." I felt strangely happy to hear that Steven had a partner. He seemed so quiet, so grumpy, so . . . subservient. Especially to Moon.

"It was a long time coming." Sol lifted his face to the sun. "Moon didn't like it at first. She gets jealous too. Wants all Steven's attention."

I hadn't expected the conversation to go in this direction.

"Not that they've ever been romantic," Sol went on. "That's just who she is. We're in an open relationship, so I deal with that too. But it's a natural part of being nonmonogamous. You have to be really good at communication."

His eyes were still squeezed closed, so I took the opportunity to study him. Was this his way of letting me know he was available? I'd never considered myself nonmonogamous, even though I knew people—like Dom—who it seemed to work great for. This, however, seemed like way more of a danger zone, given Moon and Sol's healership positions.

"Do you meet people on retreats?" I asked casually.

He rolled his head in my direction, peeked open one eye. "Sometimes. But only when they're here longer-term. And only when they've done a lot of processing first. Otherwise, I'm just taking advantage, right?"

Right! This was the reason it was beyond unethical for therapists to date clients. There was a clear power differential, as well as a common phenomenon called "erotic transference." This was when clients became attracted to their therapist because of the dynamics stirred up in the work. But since Moon and Sol weren't licensed, their licenses couldn't be revoked. There was nothing holding them back but their own morals.

"That's great that you're so thoughtful about that." I smiled sweetly, sure he wouldn't sense my sarcasm.

He raised his glass. "We try to be thoughtful about everything we do here." He took a gulp. "You know, I heard you're an artist. We could set up a studio for you. All you'd have to do all day is make art, eat good food, and relax in the hot tub."

In another world, one in which this was just a community and not a cult, that would've actually sounded tempting. After all, what did I have to look forward to back in New York? A stressful job? Moving in with strangers? Dating apps? It all felt so gray, compared to the bright colors and gentle breeze that I woke up to here daily.

Living in a place like this was a nice fantasy, but just that—a fantasy.

"Thanks." I nodded. "That's a really generous offer. I'll think about it."

"Good." He finished his glass and stood. "I need to go help set up. But feel free to relax, use the pool. Whatever you'd like. We'll have our session before dinner."

Sol left his glass on a table, so as soon as I finished mine I carried both through the dining room and into the kitchen. Steven was washing an enormous pile of dishes. He'd served more Indian food for lunch, and the smell of ginger, garlic, and turmeric filled the small, hot space.

"Hey." I set the glasses on top of more glasses on the counter. "Can I help with that?"

"No," he grunted back without looking at me. A boom box that looked like it was from the 2000s blasted heavy metal.

I leaned against the counter. "So when's Talia getting back?"

His head whipped towards me. "What?" His mouth was tight, his eyes wide with shock.

"Oh, sorry." I took a step back. "Sol was just telling me about her. That she was traveling. So I just wondered when she was coming back."

Steven stared at me for a few more seconds, then dropped the pot he'd been scrubbing. Bubbles flew up as he turned and stalked out of the room.

So maybe Talia *wasn't* coming back. But then why would Sol tell me that? So that I might mention it to Steven and upset him?

Who knew what dynamics were here beneath the surface. As I left the kitchen, an icy chill traversing my shoulders, I focused on one thought:

Four a.m. couldn't come fast enough.

43

"Everyone! Time to gather!" Moon popped out of the dome in a bikini top and shorts.

"Wonderful," Jonah muttered sarcastically. We both stood. From the veranda, we'd watched them build the dome over the last several hours, the activity so frenzied that I'd asked if Jonah and I could help—which Moon had nixed with a dismissive wave. First the rounded wooden skeleton had gone up, like the spine of a huge tent. Then they'd covered it in blankets and finally sheets of canvas. Sol and Steven had carried in large stones on pitchforks; they'd heated them in a huge fire at the pit.

Now, I could feel the heat coming off the structure, radiating like a sunburn. I could only imagine what it felt like inside.

Apparently, our "special" session was going to take place in a sweat lodge. I was someone who avoided saunas at the gym: the thick heat made it too hard to breathe.

How was I going to get out of this?

"Moon." I cleared my throat. "I really appreciate you guys going through the trouble. But . . ." God, this felt like the hot tub all over again. *I'm not really comfortable.*

"Let me guess." She grinned. "You hate hot spaces like this."

"Yes." Her words felt like a relief.

"Well, of course you do." She blinked. "You died in a desert."

I glanced at Jonah. "Okay . . ."

"Listen." Moon touched my arm. "This is going to make the regression so much faster and easier for you. And the solstice is in two days; we don't have much time. This *temezcal* will wake everything up. I know you've been dreaming about it a little, but it's time for a boost. Now." She glanced around her. "Let me grab Catherine."

Catherine had stayed in her room that afternoon. I'd wanted to check on her, but I also hadn't wanted to say anything that might accidentally change her mind. I had the feeling it wouldn't be hard for that to happen.

Jonah rubbed his face as Moon left. "I hate this kind of shit too."

"It's just so *hot*." I paused. "Haven't people died in sweat lodges before? You know, ones that are run by people who don't really know what they're doing?"

"Well, that's encouraging."

"Hi, guys!" Sol came out of the tent, his shirtless chest shining with sweat. He slicked back his hair. "You ready to get started?"

"Yeah . . ." I winced. "I'm sorry, I really don't like saunas."

"I feel you. But you can step out at any time. We encourage people to check in with their bodies and take care of themselves." He squinted, his blue eyes matching the clear sky.

At least it was a mild day, probably in the low sixties. I glanced at Jonah, and he shrugged. Sol held the canvas flap back for me to enter.

It was hot, but at least I could breathe. It didn't look like they were pouring water on the rocks, so the heat felt dry. The cushions were set in a circle, and I took one next to Karen. It was dark in here, the only light from the sunlight filtering in through the doorway. Grace was moving the rocks with a stick, while Steven glowered at me from the other side. *Yikes. Sorry, dude.* He had to know I hadn't meant any harm by mentioning Talia, didn't he?

I felt unnerved again; the last thing I wanted to do with this group delusion was another session. But maybe I could think of it like field research. How many people got to witness something like this? Shared psychotic disorder, mass psychogenic illness otherwise known as hysteria . . . People could deeply affect each other in an unconscious but very real way. There was one I'd been particularly fascinated with after hearing about it in school: *choreomania*, which referred to crowds bursting into spontaneous fits of manic dancing in medieval Europe.

"Okay!" Moon ushered Catherine inside. To my relief, Catherine looked slightly better than she had that morning: more awake and alert. She sat across from me, near Steven. Her eyes met mine, but she said nothing.

"So." Settling next to Catherine, Moon looked at each of us in turn. "I'm going to start by telling you a story. We think of how things are today—the massive amounts of suffering—as normal. But they weren't always that way. Modern female scholars realized that ancient artifacts proving tribal violence were actually misread. Because it's all interpretation. And so of course we'd see bones and rocks as arrows and weapons. We now know that up until a certain point in prehistory, humans lived together more or less in a state of harmony. There was still conflict, of course; it wasn't perfect. But communities were much more equitable. Women held positions of power. There were priestesses." She looked meaningfully at Catherine and me. "Everyone mattered. But then nomadic groups started taking over these peaceful communities. And they had to defend themselves to survive. Now our societies descend from those legacies of violence." She paused, blinking. "It leads to so much unhappiness. Emptiness, loneliness, fear. Those in charge sell us stories about soulmates as just one way to placate us. We do need connection, but not in the way we've been told."

"Hear, hear," Karen muttered softly.

"Thousands of years ago, our past life selves gave in to the fear and violence. But today, we've been given the opportunity to make it right." She got to her feet. "Thea? Catherine? Can you come here?"

Here we go. I went to stand beside her. The tent just accommodated my head; Sol and Jonah would have to stoop. With the space now enclosed, it was definitely hotter. Sweat was already beading at my temples. I forced myself to take a deep breath. I could do this. I would take a break, just not literally one minute in.

Moon took our hands. "Catherine, when you were thirteen you dreamed of a male and female leader. In the movie version it was a pharaoh and queen, but I believe Sol and I were much less than that. Likely elected leaders of a village. And you and Thea were the twin priestesses. There was something special about you two. Your mother knew, didn't she?"

There was a beat. Then, Karen got to her feet. Her face glowed with sweat. "I knew."

"Thank you, Mother." Moon nodded with her chin. "Did Father know?"

Steven stood. "No, but I trusted my wife."

It felt strange to watch him participate. A little embarrassing, like watching a disgruntled grandfather forced to do improv.

"Because . . ."

"Because she was smart." He shrugged. "Calculating. She wanted them to have a better life than us."

"Did she." Catherine's voice was bitter. I glanced over; she was glaring at Karen.

"You doubt that?" Moon asked her.

"I think she did it more for herself than for us." Catherine's tone was scornful. "She wanted that respect. That esteem."

"I'm sorry." Karen's voice was a pleading warble. "I didn't know what would happen."

"Where did you live?" Moon turned to Catherine. "After she gave you away?"

"The temple." Catherine looked at me. "Right, Thea? Can you see it?"

And the stunning thing was, I could.

It appeared suddenly in my mind's eye: the quiet square pool, its surface glass-like. The trees with tiny jade leaves shimmering in the breeze. The nearby buildings, low square blocks made of a light-colored stone. Was this a scene from *Stargirl*? No, the temple there had been grand, filled with candles and statues and piles of gold objects. This visual had to be coming from somewhere else.

"We felt trapped," Catherine went on. "But it was tolerable until *she* came." She pointed at Grace, who blanched. "The sorcerer wanted you to get rid of us so she could take our place."

"Stand up," Moon directed. Grace got to her feet. She was wearing a swimsuit and gray linen pants already dotted with sweat.

In *Stargirl*, it had been a male sorcerer showing the queen visions, convincing her to kill Thuya. Were we going to go through the full plotline together?

Moon went over and put an arm around Grace's shoulder. "What did my advisor tell me?"

Grace cleared her throat. "To get rid of them."

"And how did I do it?"

She hesitated.

"How did I get rid of them?" Moon asked again, louder.

Grace's eyes filled with tears. "Um, I guess—"

"Don't guess!" Moon shouted, her yell overwhelming in the small space. "Tell me what you know!"

I glanced at Jonah. He'd pulled off his shirt and a bead of sweat ran down his chest. He was staring at Moon as if entranced.

"I'm sorry." Grace covered her face.

My clothes were completely molded to my body. I pulled off my shirt, since I was wearing a sports bra underneath, and felt a millisecond of relief.

"Focus!" Moon shouted again.

"Please stop," I said. They both turned to me. "You left us in the desert to die, I'm assuming." I went rigid, sure that Moon would freak out at my use of the word "assume." But instead she grinned.

"Yes." She let go of Grace and came towards me. "And what happened?"

"Well . . ." I glanced at Catherine. "We died."

"And before?" Moon grabbed my upper arm, her fingers digging in. "What did you see?"

A new image grew in my mind: something sliding through the endless dunes, coming closer. Unlike in my dream, I could see it clearly. It was a snake, its onyx scales sparkling in the sun. But this was no normal snake: even from far away I could tell it was huge, thick as a tree trunk.

"You see it?" Moon asked in a whisper. She pushed down, and I sank to the floor. Catherine sat, too, lying down and curling into the fetal position. This was exactly how we'd been positioned in my dream. A wave of horror washed over me. What was happening? How was I seeing what I was seeing?

"It's coming closer, yes?" Moon crouched next to me, still gripping my shoulder.

I wanted to race out of the tent into the cool air, suck in huge breaths. But I was frozen in place, watching the vision unfold. I knew if I went outside it would disappear.

"Tell me what you're seeing," Moon urged.

"Uh . . . it's a snake." It was coming unimaginably fast straight for us, and I had the distant thought that perhaps it'd swallow us up in a gulp and keep going. The idea felt like a relief—at least it'd get us out of this unrelenting sun.

The heat was a bridge. Even though I knew I was sitting in this sweat lodge, I was also there, near death in the desert, watching the creature approach.

"A snake." Moon sounded triumphant. "What does it look like?"

"It's huge." I sucked in my breath. "It just stopped right in front of us." Its head—about the size of a watermelon—floated at my level, its eyes large as marbles. A thin purple tongue darted in and out of its jaws. Its scales reflected the sun so brightly I could barely look at it.

"What's it doing now?" she whispered.

As I sank further into the vision, my body cried out in agony; the sun was baking us alive. And then, right when I thought I couldn't stand a second more: sweet relief. An animal hide stretched over us, providing shade.

"We're under a tent," I said. "I think the snake made it appear."

On the floor next to me, Catherine murmured in gratitude.

"What's the snake saying to you now?" Moon asked.

I could hear the words, a conversation unfolding. The snake's voice was low and booming, but coming from inside my head. I was answering in kind, too weak to speak out loud.

"It . . . I'm asking it: Is this tent real? And it's saying: In a sense, yes."

"And now?"

"It's telling me that we were put in its path for a reason." I swallowed, my bone-dry throat swollen. "That normally it can't communicate with our kind, but that we're special; we're able to connect to other worlds. It's saying it knows that our entire community betrayed us because they were scared of our power."

Can you help us? Catherine asked; she was involved in this psychic conversation too.

It is too late for this lifetime. The snake's eyes were like stone. I had the sense it had been here long before humans and would remain long after we were gone. *You will soon be bones and dust.*

The words filled me with heavy sorrow and regret.

But I can give you an opportunity, it went on.

"What's the opportunity?" Moon asked when I relayed the statement.

"It's . . ." Here the conversation glitched, the words not quite making sense. "Something about how being betrayed by our entire community gives us power . . . that we can make the decision to sacrifice ourselves in the future, and that act can cause a shift in humanity. Or a jump ahead, or something like that."

There was a repeating high-pitched rasp; I realized it was me wheezing. Catherine and I were so close to the end.

"What's your response?" Moon's fingernail pierced my skin and the bright pain brought me back into the tent. They were all staring at me, eyes wide, faces red and gleaming.

I tried to pull away. "It's too hot." I started to get up, suddenly desperate.

"No!" Moon wrenched me back down.

"I need to get out." White spots sparkled at the edges of my vision.

"Keep going." Sol was on my other side, holding my arm, keeping me in place. "We're almost there."

"What did you say?" Moon hissed.

I squeezed my eyes closed. And there they were: the watchful eyes of the snake.

Fuck humanity. My inner voice was scornful, and rage surged up through my belly. *They deserve to burn.*

Don't die with hate in your heart. Catherine's psychic voice was almost too faint to hear. *There will be consequences.* She was usually the impulsive one, the selfish one. What right did she have to chide me now?

There isn't much time. There was a touch of some emotion in the snake's resonant voice, maybe pity. *What is your answer?*

"Thea!"

I plunged through a dark tunnel into wakefulness. Someone was grasping my shoulders. Dom? Had I missed my alarm?

Moon let go of me and Sol and Jonah blinked down at me. Consciousness rushed in: I was at the Center.

"Are you okay?" Jonah asked. He and Sol both looked concerned, their faces drawn. Moon's expression was blank. I thought suddenly of the snake, the stonelike eyes.

"Yeah." I started to sit up. The rest of the group stood in a larger circle around us. We were on a sandy patch of dirt just outside the tent. My body and hair were completely soaked, my hands clammy. "What happened?"

"You passed out." Jonah shot a glance at Sol.

Sol and Moon had been holding me in place, forcing me to stay even when I'd said I wanted to leave.

"I'm so sorry, Thea." Now Moon's eyes were filled with tears. She brushed back my wet hair. "I'm so sorry I pushed you. I just—we were so close to getting a confirmation."

A confirmation of what?

The memory of the desert and the snake and Catherine still loomed behind my eyelids. My body felt strange, but I was also relieved to no longer be in searing pain. The memory of it made me suddenly nauseous. I leaned over and retched, but nothing came up.

"You poor thing," Moon muttered. "Grace! Go get Thea some water."

I just wanted to get away from everyone, especially Moon and Sol, to try to figure out what had just happened. The fastest way would be placating them. I held up a hand. "I'm okay."

Even though I was most assuredly *not* okay. At first it had started almost like a game, saying what I thought Moon wanted me to say. But then I'd actually seen things, heard things, so lifelike that I could still remember every detail. Had it been some kind of hypnosis? But Moon hadn't been speaking; she hadn't even been pounding her drum.

"Take it easy." Sol peered into my eyes like a suspicious doctor.

I tried to stand, but my legs gave out underneath me. Sol and Jonah grabbed my arms and lowered me back to the ground.

"Told you I didn't like saunas." It was a dumb joke, but I couldn't help but glance accusatorially at Moon.

She bit her bottom lip, having the decency to look ashamed.

"I'd say we have our confirmation." Sol rubbed my shoulder gently but looked at Moon. "Right?"

She ignored him. "Let's get you back to your yurt. Unless you'd like to rest in the main house?"

"No, it's fine." I tried again to stand. They held my arms, but I was able to stay up. "I—I just need to rest."

Sol insisted on keeping his arm around my waist as we started down the gravel path.

I glanced down at my arm. Blood smeared around the red crescent Moon's fingernail had pressed into my flesh.

44

On my cot, still bewildered, I tried to figure out what had just happened. Somehow, Moon had predicted the vision I'd have in the sweat lodge. *You don't remember, but something happened in the desert. You were offered something. A choice.*

How had she known? Guessing my dreams was one thing, but there was no way she could've known something I hadn't yet seen.

My body still felt strange, off. I'd briefly dated a guy with a VR headset: after running through ruins on a distant planet, I'd taken it off to feel dizzy and displaced. This time, though, the sensation was much stronger.

God, I wanted a drink. Maybe two. Just to bring my buzzing nervous system down.

"Hey." Moon peeked in the door. "Can I come in?"

"Sure." I was both curious and loath to talk to her. I couldn't forget how she—and Sol—had held me down after I'd indicated I needed to leave.

"I brought you this." She set down an iced matcha in a clear glass on the desk, then sat on the edge of the bed. She was freshly showered and wearing a waffle robe.

"Thanks." I wrapped my arms around my legs. Our positions felt weirdly mother-daughter.

"So, what was that?" I asked when she didn't speak.

"It was a past life regression. It's where you slip back into a past life." Moon played with her necklace. "Time is a construct, right? So these lives are all happening at the same time. It's like stepping into another dimension."

"Ah." There had to be a simpler explanation, like the shared group delusion. But that still didn't explain how Moon had known what I would see.

"Have you guys done—regressions before?" I asked.

"With Catherine, yes. That's how we knew that you two met a spirit in the desert when you were dying. Since her eyes were closed, she never knew what the spirit looked like." Moon blew out a breath. "But now, thanks to you, we know. A snake spirit. I wish I could've seen it. I'm sure it was magnificent."

I shivered. Those marble eyes still burned in my mind, like too-bright lights lingering in my vision.

"But I'm sorry." Moon put a hand on the bedspread. "I thought I was helping you cut through the fear, the pain. But maybe I pushed you too hard."

Was she sorry? Her face looked sincere, but then again she was an actor.

This was yet another example of why Catherine shouldn't be here. Moon and Sol didn't respect people's limits. No wonder Catherine had broken down.

"Thanks for the apology." I forced a smile. "So was that part of the healing work?"

"Of course." She smiled back. "One more session tomorrow night, then the last one on the equinox. And the healing work will be completed. You can go, or stay, if you'd like. We'd love that."

"What do the next two sessions look like?" I asked. "Because the sweat lodge—"

"No, no more in there." She shook her head. "They'll be in the cave."

My body froze. "The cave?"

"Yes." She scratched her bare knee. "It's a powerful energy vortex. A portal to another world. So for the most important work, we meet down there. Don't worry, we'll make it cozy."

"What will happen?" Sol's words came back to me: *I'd say we have our confirmation.* "Does this have to do with the sacrifice thing?"

"It does. You agreed to offer yourself as a sacrifice to heal the world. So you'll do that." She brushed back a long strand. "Symbolically, of course."

"You think I agreed to the snake spirit's offer?"

"Yes. Catherine refused; we were pretty sure, but now it's clear."

Maybe it was the heat, or having passed out, but I was having trouble keeping everything straight. "So I agreed to come back in a future lifetime—this one—and somehow sacrifice myself for the good of the world? And the snake gave me that opportunity because it somehow knew I'd been betrayed by my entire community?"

"Exactly."

"But why the future? Didn't we already die? I mean, think of the story of Jesus—he sacrificed himself in his lifetime. He didn't have to come back thousands of years later."

"Jesus is a good example of this. But his situation's different. He was already enlightened during his lifetime. He *could've* saved himself, but he chose not to." Moon explained slowly and patiently, like an elementary schoolteacher. "Now, you and Catherine never fully came into your powers. You weren't able to save yourselves. So the *choice* to sacrifice yourselves was offered for a future lifetime. When you could actually make the decision."

"Gotcha." There was a certain logic to it. I had to suppress a wild giggle. "So how am I going to *symbolically* sacrifice myself on the equinox?"

Moon shrugged. "Obviously, we're not going to ask you to do anything crazy. I need to meditate on it more, but we'll come up with something everyone's comfortable with."

"Great." Wow. Did she really believe I'd be cool with that? After what had happened in the sweat lodge?

Of course, I didn't think I was in real danger of Moon and Sol forcing me to cut my heart out with a dagger or anything like that. But I was still extremely relieved that I was leaving soon—before the next session.

"Thanks for explaining everything." I smiled, wishing her away.

"Sure. Try this." She handed me the matcha, then watched until I took a sip.

After she left, I went to take a shower. I waited for some heaviness to fill my limbs, for my body to slump to the ground.

But nothing happened. Of course. Moon hadn't drugged my matcha. I was being paranoid. This group delusion was strange, and Moon and Sol were cult-y boundary-pushers, but it seemed like a jump to believe I was in actual physical danger.

When I walked into the dining room, the place settings looked different. It took me a second to figure out why: there were wineglasses by each plate. For mocktails, I assumed.

"Thea!" Sol jumped up from the table. He wore a wreath of leaves in his shaggy blond hair, which contrasted with a blue band T-shirt. THE RA RAS. "I'm so glad you're feeling better. Welcome." He leaned down to kiss my cheek. "You were incredible today."

"Uh, thanks." That was a weird thing to say.

"Sit right here." Arm around my shoulder, he directed me to the head of the table. "You're the guest of honor tonight."

"Oh no—"

"Yes! No arguing." His eyes were wide, a little wild. "Now that we're all together, our power is so strong. Can you feel it?"

I wasn't sure if it was the physical aftereffects of the sweat lodge or the imminent escape plan, but I felt slightly giddy too. "I can."

What would they think, waking tomorrow to find Catherine, Jonah, and me gone? It made me feel both a tug of guilt and a buzz of excitement. Trickster energy. Moon and Sol thought they knew everything; what would their shock look like?

Grace walked out of the kitchen, carrying several bottles of wine.

"We're celebrating tonight." Sol gestured at her. "You'd have to ask Steven—he's the expert—but these are some of the jewels of our collection."

"Thea, you have a preference?" Grace asked. "Cabernet? Burgundy?"

"Wait, I thought you guys were dry?" I asked. The sight of the wine bottles was doing something to my body, like a dog spotting a bag of treats.

"Only during retreats. The rest of the time, we partake." Sol slid his glass to the edge of the table. "Alcohol can actually be a great medicine, if used responsibly. Why don't you give her the cabernet."

Grace leaned over me to pour.

I opened my mouth to stop her—I could tell them I didn't drink. And I shouldn't drink here, not around these people I couldn't really trust. But after everything that had happened over the past few days, I needed it. Just one glass. I could smell the dark, earthy aroma. Okay. I'd have one glass, and I'd drink it very slowly, and that would be it.

Sol didn't touch his wine, so I waited too. Moon entered the dining room, Catherine and Jonah behind her. Leaning over, she grasped me in a hug from behind. "Our beautiful savior!"

Jonah nodded at me, his eyes serious. He hadn't come to the yurt to check in with me. But maybe he also wanted to act delicately until we were on the road out of here. Catherine's cheeks were tinted with pink, and she avoided looking at me as she sat.

Moon settled on my other side. "A toast!" She raised her filled glass. "To our long-lost sister, a seer with unimaginable powers. Thank you, Thea, for giving this—for giving us—a chance. We're going to do something spectacular together. We're going to heal the world! Cheers!"

I couldn't help but smile at Moon's childlike enthusiasm. I clinked glasses and took a sip. I wasn't a huge red wine person, but this was delicious; rich and complex, it melted on my tongue. As I swallowed, my entire body relaxed. I hadn't drunk since last Thursday, after drinking pretty much daily for the past year. I'd seen articles that said alcohol was physically addictive; I didn't quite believe it was true, but my body was responding in kind.

Just one glass.

Steven and Karen carried out large pans that they set onto the table: roasted chicken and grilled zucchini, charred ears of corn, fresh corn bread.

"Watch your fingers, Joe," Karen said as she put a steaming tray down where he was picking up his water glass.

"Jonah." He smiled at her.

"Not a nickname guy, huh?" She winked, then settled by Moon.

I took another small sip. Damn, this was delicious.

Three hours later, near midnight, I was in Moon and Sol's room. It was a large, sumptuous space: four-poster bed, faux-fur blankets, plush Turkish carpets. Sol messed with the record player on a side table, shirtless, his hair still wet from the hot tub. Tonight felt like it had lasted days, starting with dinner, where I'd drunk a glass, and then another, and then another. I knew I shouldn't, but the warm, fuzzy buzz just felt so fucking good. When was the last time I'd felt this good? It had been weeks, if not months, if not years.

And the last few days had been so stressful. I craved this, some small opportunity for release.

On the way to the bonfire, Jonah walked next to me. "Are you good?"

"Yeah. I'm great." I leaned in, breathing in his scent. "Your alarm set?"

"Yup."

"And you can drive tonight?"

"Of course." He'd had a few glasses with dinner, too, and now his dark eyes gleamed. "I'm sure we'll all go to bed soon. I'll get a few hours of sleep."

It struck me that we were similar, Jonah and I: hard workers. So hard on ourselves too. We cared too much. Did too much. No wonder we turned to alcohol to relax.

Around the fire, Moon played her drum and Sol sang and strummed his guitar. This time he played fast classic rock songs, and Grace pulled Jonah up to dance. He moved his shoulders, glancing at me with an embarrassed grin, and I couldn't help but laugh. Karen grabbed my hand, lip-synching and shimmying. No Catherine or Steven. I tried to remember when Catherine had left, but then Grace appeared—when had she gone?—with a bottle of whiskey.

This I knew I definitely should not drink, but that trickster energy reared up. *Just a few sips. It's okay.* Jonah's eyes met mine as I took a pull, and something in his expression made my stomach taut. I handed him the bottle, as if daring him. He kept his eyes on me as he drank.

After, Moon had led us to the hot tub to the beat of her drum. She dropped it to shuck her clothes. The rest of us followed suit; no hesitation this time. Jonah hopped in the tub fast but was watching me as I pulled off my shirt. It felt sexy, illicit, for him to see me. For everyone to see me. No longer did I care. After all, I knew these people! I'd known them for thousands of years, apparently. The ridiculous thought made me giggle.

You're getting drunk, Thea. No more whiskey. So I abstained—*Good job*—but then Moon disappeared and came back with bottles of white wine: my favorite, cold and tart. Sharing the bottles felt like a bookend to the pineapple juice from two nights before. Sol told more funny stories, but I could barely concentrate with Jonah next to me. He was so close the energy vibrated between us.

I was making this up, whatever attraction I was sensing. I had to be. But then Jonah's hand found my leg, just above my knee, and squeezed.

Desire shot up through my belly. I looked at him; he was nodding at Sol. But then he glanced at me and smirked.

Was this really happening? I had the vague sense of needing to plan how I was going to get Jonah back to my yurt. But then we were following Moon and Sol back to their room to listen to records. Grace and Karen disappeared somewhere along the way, because it was just the four of us in here. I was in my wet underwear and bra, wrapped in a thick blanket, sitting on Moon and Sol's bed. Jonah was beside me, clothed but damp, and we were passing a wine bottle—another red, this time—back and forth.

I was beyond stopping. That trickster part of me had shifted into outright defiance: *Stop being such a good girl. Stop being a martyr. Just enjoy yourself for once in your fucking life.*

Sol had put on soul music and Moon was dancing around the room topless, in just her underwear. She'd clearly been a dancer or a gymnast; there was something natural about her movements. I felt like I was watching a cabaret show, at least until she danced up to me and grabbed my hands.

"Thea, come on!" Her accent was stronger than ever. I smiled as I imagined confronting her about it right now. Of course, that would stop the party, full force. Mikki should be the one to out her, anyway.

I threw off the blanket and joined her. Normally, I felt awkward dancing, but this time the music—and the alcohol—made it easy to let go. Sol sang along, rolling his shoulders. Jonah watched me from the bed, his eyes burning.

"Come on!" I beckoned to him. "Come dance!"

He shook his head, smiling. Moon danced over to him, in between his legs, giving him an impromptu lap dance. I glanced at Sol, but he just swooped in, slipping an arm around my lower back.

"Hi!" He grinned, our faces suddenly close together.

"Hi." In my blurry state, it felt like dancing with Pastor John. Were they the same age? Maybe they had the same birthday too!

He leaned in, breathing into my ear. "You're so sexy."

Sol's words were both surprising and not.

"I think I need more wine." Uncertainly, I broke away, looked at Jonah. Moon was now leaning down and kissing him.

What was happening? Moon pulled away and looked back at me.

"Let's do this right." She pointed to the door. "Thea, stand there."

I went to the door. Confusion mixed with so many other sensations: excitement in my chest, fear in my gut, a pleasurable ache in my groin.

"You too." She pulled at Jonah's hand, and he got up and stood next to me.

"How was it, Thea?" Moon asked as Sol walked up behind her, slipping his arms around her belly, kissing her neck. "When you walked in on them. Who was on top?"

My mouth gaped open. "Huh?"

"The pastor and his wife." Moon reached up and caressed Sol's cheek. He slipped a hand into her underwear.

Should we leave? I wanted to ask Jonah, but he was gazing at Moon. Should *I* leave? I wasn't sure I could find my way out of the mazelike castle in this state.

"Um. He was on top."

Jonah pushed the bottle into my hand, and I automatically took a swig.

"Should've guessed." Moon laughed. "Well, we're going to switch."

Sol climbed onto the bed, pushing down his boxer briefs. Moon slipped out of her underwear and straddled him. I watched, eyes wide with shock, as she leaned down to kiss him, her breasts just brushing his chest. He continued to touch her, and she moaned. She stroked his penis—larger than the flaccid version I'd seen in the hot tub would've suggested—and guided it inside her. They started moving together. She leaned back, tossing her hair, gazing down at him.

"Oh my god." I glanced up at Jonah. He took another swig of wine, then bent to set it down. When he stood, he grabbed me and kissed me.

For a moment, the kiss blanked everything else out, even what was happening on the bed mere feet away from us. We pressed against each other, opening our mouths, letting each other in. His hands slipped down under my underwear, cupping my ass. One hand moved to the front. His touch was confident, strong, and I gasped at how good it felt. I palmed his erection straining against his pants.

"Thea." We broke away from each other at Moon's voice. She was still on top of Sol, holding a hand out to me. "Come join us. Both of you."

Jonah grabbed my hand and moved towards them. I thought suddenly of the dream—the scary one that had woken me up this morning. Seeing Moon and Sol together, her beckoning me towards them.

Déjà vu rattled as Sol reached out to cup my thigh. How did the dream go? Something about Pastor John and Jamie, and a cheap hotel room, and a whirlpool filled with teeth.

Moon pulled me in and kissed me. Her lips were softer than Jonah's, her tongue more gentle. It felt so normal, so natural. And why not? Anyone would want to kiss Moon, who was so gorgeous, whose eroticism seeped from every pore.

She got off Sol and moved back so that we could all fit on the bed. On the silky sheets, hands caressed and mouths kissed, delicately at first and then harder: fingers grasping my hair, palms opening my legs, the pressure of Sol's beard between my inner thighs.

This felt like a do-over, a chance to swipe the old memory of Pastor John and Jamie clear, to fill it with something new. This was therapeutic! I laughed into a mouth—Jonah's mouth. Moon was teasing my nipples, running her tongue around them. She looked up at me, grinning, then slid up to kiss my earlobe.

"You're so beautiful, Thea."

I thought I was grasping Jonah, thick in my hand, but when I looked down it was Sol. He pulled Moon's chin to him, kissing her. Such a jumble of body parts: arms, fingers, hair. I caught a glimpse of us in the window's reflection: we looked like an undulating sea creature.

"Come here." Moon was pulling at me. She grabbed condoms from the nightstand and tore one open, fitting it over Sol. I straddled him and then he was inside me, moving beneath me. I exhaled and leaned down and kissed him. Moon was behind me, caressing me, her fingers revolving. She was moaning too—being fucked by Jonah from behind, I saw with a quick glance—and the sounds and pressure and vetiver scent combined into a blur. I was in a trance, my brain empty, sensations taking me over like I was no longer human, just pure animal.

I was getting close, and the thought struck, sharp and illuminating as lightning: I was going to orgasm without the shed, without Adam, without the shame. And then my brain switched off again and I felt it coming towards me, that inevitable release racing ever closer.

Just before I came, something made me look at the door. It was slightly ajar, and in the split second before my eyes squeezed closed, before I cried out, I saw it in the dark space: a single, staring green eye.

45

I woke in my yurt, my phone pressing into my hip.

My head was on fire. I moaned, touching my temples. Wine. Whiskey. All going down like water. All leading to . . .

Oh my god. I curled up in a ball as the images rained down on me. I'd had a drunken foursome with Moon, Sol, and Jonah. Hadn't I? For a moment I considered that it might've been a particularly vivid dream. But then I shifted and felt the telltale soreness between my legs.

Shit. I was not one of those girls. I was not sexually adventurous: hooking up in public, in bar bathrooms, on Ferris wheels. Going to sex parties, which Dom had told me about with relish. Even embarking on one-night stands. There'd been a handful during and since college, and that was it.

So what had happened last night? Had Moon and Sol drugged me?

No. I knew they hadn't. I had no one to blame but that part of me that hungered, that wanted to be out of control, *selfish* even—instead of always helping everyone else.

Add that to the erotic energy that ran beneath the surface here. I'd seen it that first night when Moon had pulled off her dress. The nudity, the touching, Sol making sure I knew he and Moon were open . . . had it all been intentional? Had they been grooming me for this? Or was it just their thing, and I was so lonely and horny that I'd allowed myself to be swept up into it?

I didn't remember coming back to the yurt. I was in my crinkled underwear and a T-shirt—THE RA RAS. Sol's shirt. Along with anxiety and regret, the hangover was making my head pound so badly I could barely think. It felt like someone had sliced out a chunk of my brain with an ice cream scoop.

And yet, underneath it . . . there came a flutter of something electric. Because as shocking as the experience had been, I *had* let myself go. I'd done things I never would've expected myself to do. There had been something primal about our bodies coming together.

I shifted, digging out my phone.

And then I remembered.

I stared with horror at the blank screen; it had run out of battery and turned itself off. I hadn't woken up at four as planned. I hadn't left with Catherine and Jonah.

Fuck!

Catherine had been there last night—now I remembered the flash of her eye in the doorway. When I'd looked again, she'd disappeared. What had she been thinking? She had to be alarmed that I was entangled with these people I was trying to protect her from. Goddamnit. I never would've done any of that sober.

Tears of frustration filled my eyes. I tried to sit up—I needed to talk to Catherine—but sank back down to my pillow and moaned. It was too painful.

Had Moon and Sol somehow known about our plan? It didn't make sense, not unless Catherine had told them. And after all, they hadn't known my phone would die. No, this time the culpability lay firmly with me.

A few minutes later, I managed to sit and grab my pill packet from my purse. As I dry-swallowed Tylenol, a new thought struck me: Had Catherine had sex with Moon and Sol too? Was everyone having orgies? Steven? Grace? Karen? I truly had no idea.

As I managed to dress, I considered how I'd been able to have orgasms—multiple ones—without any thoughts of Adam or the shed.

Moon's earnest voice arose in my mind: *The pattern's broken.*

Was it broken for good? I felt a tiny spark of wonder, which was quickly submerged by foreboding. Even if Moon and Sol were getting results, the paths there were not just unethical—they were totally out of control.

I showered in the covered stall; I was done being naked. I didn't see anyone until I dressed and left my yurt to find Moon approaching with a coffee.

"Good morning!" she trilled. Beyond the dark circles under her eyes, she looked none the worse for wear. She wore short black bike shorts that showed off the tattoos on her tan legs.

Damn. All I wanted to do was get to Catherine. My head felt slightly clearer. We were leaving today; I was sick of this sneaking around. Moon and Sol couldn't hold any of us here against our will.

"Hey." I hesitated, but she barreled into me, grabbing me in a hug.

When she broke away, her gold eyes were wide and curious. "How you feeling, sweetie?"

I inwardly blanched at the term of endearment as I took the mug. "I'm okay." I knew I didn't look okay; I looked like a hungover mess. How was Moon able to drink the amount she did, especially as such a small person, and look fine? She wasn't even wearing sunglasses!

"Good." She put her hands on her hips. "Let's have a chat?"

"Um, sure." I followed her to the veranda. Images from the night before flashed through my mind. I couldn't believe the things I'd done to her. The things she'd done to me. We'd been wild creatures, handling, sucking, and biting each other.

"So." She exhaled as she sat. "I wanted us to have an opportunity for aftercare, to check in about everything. What happened last night— that's not something we have a habit of doing with new guests. But it just felt . . ." She spread out her hands. "Right. Didn't it?"

My head still felt gripped in a vise. "I . . . um, yeah." I wasn't going to argue with her, not when I was planning on leaving as soon as humanly possible.

"Normally, we do that type of healing work very intentionally."

"So you've done that before." Of course they had.

"It's rare." She shrugged. "But sometimes people do need hands-on sexual healing. I'm sure you know that a lot of people hold trauma in their genitals. As you've seen from our sessions, the work has to be really tailored to the client."

So Moon and Sol were sexual surrogates. I'd come across the term at school but had had to google it that night to make sure I'd heard correctly. While controversial in a lot of circles, it was a type of therapy that could include sexual contact, in order to help people with sex and intimacy issues.

"What happened last night . . ." Moon shrugged. "None of it was planned. But I hope it provided some healing for you. Being invited in instead of shut out. Being praised instead of verbally abused."

"A corrective experience." I stared at her. "That's what you mean, right?"

"Exactly." She grinned. My mind whirred; Moon actually seemed proud of having done "work" when we were wasted together. She was more off the rails than I'd suspected.

"But I want you to know that it was more than that." She grabbed my hand. "I mean, you felt it, right? How deep it was? Because we've done it before. Thousands of years ago."

"We've done . . ."

"We were all together. The four of us." She nodded. "Last night proved that you and Jonah are both who we thought you were."

"But . . ." I paused, confused. "Was it Catherine who had the affair with the pharaoh and the guard? Or me?"

"I believe it was you." Moon paused. "But I'm not totally sure. It's hard to differentiate. You know, I think in certain lives you've been in the same body. Like the collective unconscious, our soul energy exists in a great pool. Souls rise up and melt back down, merge and separate. Have you ever felt like something or someone is missing? It's because in some lives you and her are split into two."

Of course I felt like something was missing: it had fueled my search for a soulmate up until now. But didn't most people feel that way?

"We do all feel like that sometimes, because we've been separated from the pool." Moon's answer to my unspoken question jarred me. "But with you two, it's different. It's why you were drawn together at the hospital. It's why you followed her all the way out here based on nothing. It's why you couldn't stop watching *Stargirl* at thirteen." She shrugged. "You're two sides of the same coin: Catherine's the entertainer, outgoing and impulsive. You're the gentle artist and healer. It makes so much sense that *you* turned out to be the savior."

"Moon." I took a deep breath. It was time to be honest, to stop playing games. "I'm sorry, but I don't think I'm going to be able to stay."

Her smile disappeared. "What?"

"I need to go to the airport today." I wasn't going to mention Catherine, not yet. Not until the last minute, when Jonah and I would ferry her into the SUV. They weren't going to physically restrain us. There was nothing they could do.

"Oh. Are you sure? The visions—"

"I know, but even with the visions, I think . . . I don't know, maybe this is a group belief system, a kind of mythology, that I've been tapping into." I shrugged. "That kind of thing can happen, you know."

Her face was blank; all warmth was gone. "And you just want to leave?"

"Yes." It was a relief to say. "Jonah and I would like to head back today."

"Oh. Okay." She looked down, her face twisted by a frown. "Well, if that's how you feel, then we have to respect that. We'll just have to wait for Steven to get back. Then he or Grace can drive you to the airport."

"Steven's gone?"

"Yeah, he went to get supplies." She continued staring at the ground.

"What about the second car? Can't we take that? Maybe Grace—"

"Grace is preparing for tonight." Moon's voice rang out in the silence. She cleared her throat. "And anyways, that car is broken down. It doesn't work."

"Oh." The reality of the situation descended, heavy as a weighted blanket. For now, at least, there was no getting away from the Center. "When is Steven getting back?"

"I don't know exactly, but I'd guess around dinnertime?"

That was hours away.

"And when he gets back—" I started.

"Yes. He will turn around and drive you out." Moon patted my hand, smiled again. The stormy look was gone. "Don't worry, sweetie. We're not going to kidnap you."

46

Jonah didn't respond when I knocked at the door of his yurt. So I took my dead phone to the lobby and plugged it in. It lit up. God, it was after two in the afternoon. Had I really slept that long?

Still no Wi-Fi.

I went to Catherine's room; finally I was getting the layout of this place down a little more. But no matter how much I knocked and called to her, she didn't answer.

When my phone was charged, I headed to the dining room. My stomach was still rumbling, but maybe I could settle it with some toast. My mind whirred. Where was Jonah? Why wasn't Catherine letting me in? Was she furious? Sleeping?

This was the second time I'd failed her. The memory arose: *She asked for you.* The night before she'd left the hospital, I'd also dropped the ball after drinking.

As I crossed the veranda, I felt more than unsettled, like I wanted to crawl out of my skin.

The lack of Wi-Fi, the disappearance of the SUV, the other car not working . . . Were Moon and Sol trapping us here? I hadn't thought they were dangerous, just unethical and overconfident. But maybe I'd been willfully ignorant. After all, Catherine had refused to leave unless she could sneak away. She knew a lot more about this place and its inhabitants than me.

The dining room was empty, and as I neared the kitchen I heard voices behind the door. I slowed and crept closer.

"I just don't know if I can do it." Grace's voice was low. A hiccup: it sounded like she was crying.

"Oh, it's okay." Sol crooned the words. "Come here, baby."

Nothing for a minute. Then Sol: "You're so strong, Gracie. You're stronger than you know."

"But I'm afraid."

"Don't listen to your fear. It comes from the primitive self. What does your higher self believe?"

"That . . . I don't know." She paused. "Do you think I should do it?"

"Well, that's not my decision." Sol sounded thoughtful. "It's really up to you."

"I know. But what do you think?"

"It makes sense to me. You know, taking responsibility like that."

"But then . . . I won't be able to see you." She started crying again, her sobs cutting into my chest.

"Of course you will. Gracie, nothing can keep us apart. You hear me? My love for you transcends all worlds." He paused. "You know, you're the bravest person I ever met. No one would've expected that you'd be able to do this. The others, they think you're a coward. But I know what you're capable of."

She took a shuddery breath. "Thank you."

"Thank *you*. For inspiring me."

There was quiet, then. At least until Grace made a soft moaning sound. I backed up, then turned and hurried out of the dining room onto the terrace.

The running kicked up the headache, which interfered with my ability to puzzle out what I'd just heard. Grace and Sol were lovers. Fine—I wasn't all that surprised Sol was sleeping with other members. But what on earth was Grace so scared to do? And why was Sol pushing her to do it?

Don't listen to your fear. It comes from the primitive self. Gaslighting the natural fear response was a classic cult technique. It was so effective because it cut people off from their intuition. If your brain was able to argue with what your body was feeling, then you could be convinced to do anything.

Jonah was walking down the gravel path from the yurts.

"Where have you been?" I asked, approaching him.

His hair was mussed, his eyes bleary. "Sleeping." He rubbed his hair, making it even messier. I remembered running my hands through the curls, grasping them hard.

"Listen, I have to talk to you," I said.

"Okay, I just really need water."

"No." I held up a hand. "Please, just for five minutes."

We went back to my yurt, where I filled him in on the car situation and the conversation I'd overheard between Grace and Sol. He listened, stroking the stubble on his chin.

"That is weird," he said when I stopped.

"Right? What do you think they were talking about?"

"I don't know." He exhaled. "But I don't like the sound of it. Any of it."

"Me either. And I can't stop wondering . . . I mean, what if Moon's lying? What if that second car actually works?"

"Well." He shrugged. "Why don't we try it?"

"Now?"

"You know a better time?" He clasped his hands. "We know where the keys are. If the car works, then that's that. Grace can drive us, or we can fucking drive ourselves."

"But what about Catherine?" My heart slammed against my breastbone. "We can't leave without her."

"You don't think she'll come?"

"I don't know."

"Listen, let's take it step by step. We check the car first." He was already halfway out the door. "Come on."

As we approached the lobby, I wondered what everyone would think, hearing the car turn on in the heavy silence. But what did it matter? It'd prove they'd been lying to us. They couldn't stop us from leaving, and if they tried, I'd call emergency services.

Jonah pulled open the drawer and snatched the lone set of keys. He sailed through the glass doors, and his movements were quick enough that I wondered if he felt scared too.

He unlocked the car, which beeped softly, and we both quietly pulled open the doors and got in. I felt a wild leap in my chest. On this plot of land, nothing fit neatly into place: people lied convincingly, things went missing, and supposed past lives floated in the air. But this was concrete, undeniable. The car would either work or not.

I clutched the front of my shirt as Jonah inserted the key in the ignition. He turned it.

Nothing happened.

Frowning, he tried again.

Silence.

"Okay, then." He hopped out and I followed suit. We locked the car and went back into the lobby. Jonah dropped the keys in the desk drawer.

A deep disappointment filled my torso. "Shit."

"Yeah. We tried." He massaged his eyes.

"It doesn't seem safe, does it? To be stuck here like this?" My headache resurged. Being trapped was making me feel hot, almost feverish.

"I don't think safety is these people's number one concern." He slumped over the desk.

"Well." I took a deep breath. "What are our options?" I counted them off. "We could wait for Steven to get back. We could contact emergency services . . ."

"And tell them what? We need a ride?" Jonah shook his head. "There's no way cops would drive hours out here to pick us up."

"We could say Moon or Sol's threatening us."

"It's illegal to make false statements to police officers."

"Well, what about walking out to the road? We could try to hitch a ride."

"You want to walk to the road?" Jonah lifted his head. His eye circles were darker than usual, a deep violet. "'Bye, guys! We're just going to drag our suitcases down this gravel road for an hour or two!'"

"Well, they wouldn't physically drag us back."

"Maybe not. But you think Catherine would be on board with that?"

I had to concede. "She wouldn't. I think there's a chance we could've convinced her to drive out with us. But not walk."

Jonah drummed his fingers on the desk. "It's also really deserted out here. I don't remember seeing other cars on the road when we got close. It could take a while to see someone and way longer for someone to actually pick us up."

"Yeah." I felt the urge to scream and pull out all the drawers, fling the stuffed owl off its perch. "*Fuck.*"

"Hey." He came around the desk. "We're going to be okay. I have a gun—"

"You have a *gun*?" I jerked away from him.

"I do. And I'm going to start wearing it on me."

I sank down to the ground. This—all of it—was too much to process. Jonah sat quietly beside me.

"So what do you want to do now?" he finally asked in a low tone.

I lifted my head from my arms. "I want to talk to Catherine. But her door's locked."

He bumped my shoulder with his. "Well, let's go break in."

Ten minutes later, we heard the telltale click and Catherine's door swung inward. I didn't love having to talk to her this way, but there was no other choice.

"Catherine?" I said softly, stepping inside.

It was dim, curtains mostly covering the two windows. It smelled even more sour and stale than before. I felt a jolt of déjà vu as I clocked Catherine's prone form in the bed, facing away from us.

"Hey." I switched on the lamp on the bedside table. Standing over her, I could tell her eyes were open, staring at the wall.

Oh no. Was she catatonic again?

But she finally shifted, looking up at me. "Hey."

"Sorry to come in like this." I sat on the edge of the bed. "But we had to talk to you."

She glanced at Jonah behind me.

"Tell him to leave," she said in a flat voice.

"Sure thing." He raised an eyebrow at me as he left the room.

The metal bed creaked as she sat up. Her greasy copper hair hid her face.

"So I told Moon we wanted to get a ride to the airport," I said.

She closed her eyes.

"Not you," I went on. "Just Jonah and me. But Steven's out with the SUV and the other car doesn't work—we checked. We were thinking of maybe walking to the road to try to hitch a ride. Even though . . . I don't know. Do you think someone will pick us up?"

"You're asking what I think?" A puff of air—a tiny scoff. "I think you're fucked."

"What?" Needles pricked the back of my neck.

"This happened last time too." She lowered her head. "You always fuck things up."

"I know, at the hospital—"

"No. With Sol. When he was the governor or whatever. I told you to stay away from him. And the guard. They wanted us, but they hated us too. They hated our power. Why didn't you listen to me?" Her eyes glistened.

Okay. We were in group delusion territory here. I had to tread lightly.

"I'm sorry," I said. "I messed up. But this is our chance—"

"There is no chance." Catherine coughed, a phlegmy sound. "It's over."

"What's over?"

She just leaned her forehead on her knees. Her shoulders jerked and went still, as if she was too exhausted to cry.

"I tried." Her voice was muffled. "I really tried."

"I know you did." I rubbed her back. The knobs of her spine were too prominent.

"Well." She lifted her head. "Maybe it will reject you too."

"What will reject me?"

She just stared straight ahead.

"Catherine, what will reject me?" Her strange, disoriented face in the shadows was making the hairs rise on my arms.

"You should know. You're the sacrifice."

I jumped up. "Okay, I'm getting out of here. Even if you're not coming with me. You're freaking me out."

She lay back down.

"And we'll come back," I went on. "We'll rent a car and come back and get you. Okay?"

No answer.

"Okay, Catherine?" I wanted to grab her, shake her silent form. But instead I turned and left.

47

"Thea!" Sol caught me in the courtyard.

"Hi." I watched him approach, shirtless and shoeless, clad in just navy swim trunks.

"Hi, beautiful." He leaned in. For a moment I winced, sure he was going to kiss me on the mouth. He gave me a peck on the cheek, instead. "How are you feeling?"

"Super," I said.

"Good. I'm a little . . ." He waggled his fingers. ". . . myself. But sometimes we need a Dionysian night, right?"

Dionysus—why did that word keep coming up? It had been the name of the dog too. Talia's. Steven's absent girlfriend.

"You hungry? You want Grace to make you something?" Sol pointed towards the castle. "She's starting to prep dinner." He chuckled. "To be honest with you, I can't even look at food right now."

Where Moon had appeared fresh and cheerful, Sol's face hung in folds, his eyes puffy and red. He looked five or even ten years older. I felt a sudden repulsion towards him.

"But I heard that you and Jonah are ready to fly the coop," he continued. "Steven should be back by dinnertime. So he can drive you guys to the airport then. I think there's a late-night direct flight to New York, right? Hopefully, you can hop right on that."

"Sure." I tried to sound calm. If he knew I'd just broken into Catherine's room, or that Jonah and I had tried to start the other car, he wasn't showing it. "And where *is* Steven?"

"He's picking up a satellite phone. We're sick of this shitty Wi-Fi situation." Sol shook his head. "It's unsafe to not have a line out, you know?"

"Right," I said slowly.

"You know, I'm really bummed that you're leaving." Sol's face went solemn. "But you know what's best for you. And you're the one driving the bus with this whole situation. So we have to accept that. Anyway." He waved a hand. "I'll save my goodbyes for later. I'm going to have a soak; it's the best cure for a hangover. See you there?"

"Maybe. Enjoy."

He loped off, and I froze when I saw the angry red claw marks on his back.

I went to Jonah's yurt, opening the door to find him lying in bed.

"Hey." He blinked blearily at me. After a second, he held out an arm. Despite my frustration and fear, a small, giddy feeling rose in my stomach. I went to him and climbed in. He spooned me, molding his body to mine and slipping his arm over me. I pulled his hand under my chin. Our bodies fit together perfectly.

"This is the worst hangover I've had in years," he murmured into my ear.

"Me too." I sighed. "Catherine won't walk out with us. She's saying really weird things. I'm worried about her."

"Did Sol tell you about Steven?"

"That he was coming back at dinnertime? Yeah." I paused. "You think we should stay?"

"I think we should consider it."

"But it still just feels . . . sketchy."

"I know. But there's a chance we're seeing things that aren't there. We have to consider the facts."

"Like what?"

"Well, we didn't tell them we wanted to leave today, so it makes sense they didn't keep the car here for us. And the second car doesn't run, sure, but it's not like it was running before. And the Wi-Fi—it's really not working. I asked Grace to reboot it earlier, and I sat with her when she did it. Maybe we're putting more meaning into all these things than we should."

"But what about all this bizarre sacrifice stuff? And that conversation between Sol and Grace?" I shivered. "It's creeping me out."

"Moon said it'd be symbolic, right? And who knows what Grace and Sol were talking about. Maybe it's a weird sex thing."

"Oh god," I groaned, pressing my hand to my eyes.

"And like I mentioned . . . I have protection for us."

"Where is it?" I asked.

"It's in my suitcase. Under the bed."

I sat up, pulled it out, and opened it. I pushed aside the jumble of clothes. Underneath was a hard plastic case.

"Is this legal?" I asked, my stomach twisting. I'd never been this close to a gun, unless you counted the cops patrolling the subway. Friends' parents had been hunters growing up, but my dad had never owned one.

"You think I'd be able to get a gun on the plane illegally?" He propped his head on his hand, watching me. "Yes, it's legal. I just had to check the bag."

"So you're going to wear this on your person?"

"On my person?" He smirked. "Yes. That's exactly where it will be."

"Okay." I shoved the suitcase back and lay down. "You think Moon and Sol have any?"

"Those hippies? You think they're packing?"

"I don't know." The idea did seem ridiculous. I couldn't imagine their drums and dried sage bundles swapped out with pistols or shotguns.

"I have a holster. Just stay near me until Steven gets back. As a precaution." He rewrapped his arm around me.

"How do you feel about last night?" I asked in a whisper.

"Well . . . I wasn't planning on it," he replied softly.

"Me either." Did that mean he regretted it?

"Have you done something like that before?" I asked.

"Group sex?" He chuckled, his chest vibrating against my back. "No way. I'm boring. But . . . there's something about this place."

"Yeah."

"There's something about you too."

"Really?" I perked up.

"Yeah." He kissed the back of my neck, which sent a jolt of electricity down my spine. "I think I like you. Can't you tell?"

"I mean . . . not really."

"I know I can be hard to read." He was quiet for a second. "Can I take you out when we get back to New York?"

"Yeah. Definitely." Maybe I should've played it cool, but the words leapt from my mouth. I waited for him to speak again, but then a snore rumbled in my ear. He was asleep.

The irony amazed me. The last thought I had before I drifted into sleep:

I'd come to this relational retreat to search for a missing woman.

I'd encountered an actual cult.

And I'd met someone.

48

The dinner bell chimed, slicing through the nothingness of sleep. I pushed my face into the pillow. Jonah shifted behind me.

"Should we go?" he asked.

"Yeah." I sat up, reluctant to leave our cozy cot. I definitely felt better with a few hours' sleep. My head, while still sore, didn't feel like a wide-open wound.

Jonah gazed up at me, his expression serious.

"What?" I asked.

"Nothing." He smiled slightly. "You're cute."

"So are you." I leaned down, hesitated. He pulled me in and kissed me. The world slowed down, until . . .

Clang!

"We'd better go." He sat up. "Steven should be back by now. You all packed?"

"I am. Except for my diary." The words made me suddenly sad. I was going to have to leave that part of myself behind here, apparently.

"I'm sorry."

"It is what it is." I sighed. "Are you bringing your stuff to the lobby?"

"I'll wait. Don't want to piss them off by seeming too eager." He rolled his eyes, then pulled me in for one more kiss.

"Welcome!" Sol cried as Jonah and I entered the dining room. "Grace made her famous lasagna. It's incredible. Good for hangovers too."

I glanced at the others: Moon, smiling and animated. Catherine, staring down at her plate. Grace, calmly cutting clean stripes into the huge, steaming pan. Several bottles of red wine waited in the middle of the table; the sight made my stomach turn.

"Where's Steven?" I asked.

"Oh, I'm sure he'll be back soon." Sol shrugged.

"He's still not back?" I exchanged a glance with Jonah.

Sol straightened. "I didn't want to say anything, but I wouldn't be surprised if he stopped to see Talia."

Moon, Grace, and Catherine all whipped their heads to look at him.

"Didn't you say she was traveling?" I asked when no one said anything.

"No." Sol stood to grab a wine bottle. "She left, to tell you the truth. Lives in a nearby town."

Moon's expression was suddenly thunderous. "Babe, please shut the fuck up."

"Sorry, babe." He shrugged, unbothered. "It's the truth. Steven misses her, you know."

"So when is he getting here?" My body was on high alert. It struck me that I really had expected Steven to come back, to show up at the appointed time. The fact that he was still gone made my anxiety sky-rocket. Where was he? Was he okay?

"I'm sure he'll be back any minute." Sol took a plate from Grace. "Right?"

"Right." Moon smiled softly, suddenly back to her baseline equa-nimity. "We can count on him, Thea. Don't you worry."

There was another empty chair.

"Where's Karen?" I asked as Grace set a plate of lasagna in front of me. The garlic, basil, and tomato smell and oozing cheese made me suddenly ravenous.

"She's not feeling too well." Moon shrugged. "She might join us for the session, but we'll have to see."

"The session?"

"Of course." Moon's eyebrows dipped. "You didn't think we were going to stop our sessions just because you were leaving, did you?"

"But now that you're here, you can participate." Sol smiled, a drip of red at the corner of his lip.

"If you'd like." Moon shot him a sharp look.

"Um . . ." Something was definitely off. About Steven still missing. About the others' reaction to Sol mentioning Talia. And about Cath-erine sitting there like she was shell-shocked.

"We weren't planning on it." Jonah squeezed my knee.

"It's totally up to you." Moon shrugged. "This session is really for Grace, anyway."

"What do you mean?" The cheese burned the roof of my mouth, but I couldn't stop myself from wolfing it down.

"It's an amends." Moon took the wine from Sol, poured herself a big glass. "For what she did last time."

"You mean . . ."

"As the sorcerer." Moon gave me a tight smile, as if she was tired of explaining it. She stood and leaned to pour me a glass, which I wasn't planning on touching. She then poured one for Jonah, who took a sip.

My mind spun as Sol and Moon kept up the chatter throughout dinner. Grace seemed perfectly normal, smiling and even ribbing Sol at points.

This session had to do with the conversation I'd overheard. Didn't it?

Sol's voice arose in my head: *You're the bravest person I ever met. No one would've expected that you'd be able to do this. The others, they think you're a coward. But I know what you're capable of.*

This was it, then. The thing that Grace's body was telling her to be afraid to do.

"We'll attend." I pushed my leg into Jonah's. "Wouldn't miss it." After all, Jonah held the trump card: a gun. If anything started happening that didn't feel right, we'd be able to stop it.

Even my worst fear—getting trapped down there—wouldn't happen. Not with a gun that could help us bust through a flimsy wooden door.

"Great." Moon beamed at me.

Catherine looked up at me. She hadn't touched her food. Her eyes were still deadened, exhausted. But now they also looked sad.

"You sure you want to do this?" Jonah asked. We were in the courtyard. Everyone else—barring Steven and Karen—was down in the cave. The square of the sky above was deepening into a royal blue as the sun set, the stars already shining bright. For a second I was reminded of the end of *Stargirl*: Thuya on a spaceship, getting ready to take revenge on the queen. Had Catherine dreamed that part too?

"Yeah." I forced myself to focus. "You have the . . . thing, right?"

He lifted his baggy sweatshirt; there it was, holstered to his belt. It looked fake, like a stage prop. I had the sudden urge to grab it, just to know what it'd feel like in my hands. He let his shirt drop.

"Do you think this is, like, dangerous?" I asked. "Like, where is Steven?"

"I don't know." He shook his head. "Look, we can skip this session if you feel weirded out."

"I do. But that's why I want to go to it. I don't want anything bad to happen to Grace. Or Catherine." I glanced at the sculpture of the woman's eyeless face and shivered.

"What do you think will happen?"

"I don't know. But she sounded scared, Jonah. About this 'amends' or whatever Moon called it." I paused. "And why aren't Moon and Sol doing fucking amends? *They're* the ones that supposedly killed Catherine and me, right?"

"Good question." He shrugged. "Maybe they're planning to do them too. Maybe they already have. Who knows how this works. We really don't need to be a part of it."

"No. We need to keep an eye on Grace and Catherine." I headed towards the purple door. Inside the room, the door to the stone steps yawned open. Two battery-operated lanterns waited for us at the edge.

I stopped above the hole and took a deep breath. The cold, musty air enveloped me. But this time I felt stronger. I knew what was down there. I knew Catherine was alive. I knew Jonah could protect us.

So I started down the steps.

Everyone was at the far end of the larger cavern. They sat in a circle, their lanterns beside them. Jonah and I started down the sloping, rocky floor. With the lanterns hanging over our arms, it was easier going than last time, trying to navigate the damp darkness with a flashlight. But I was still careful about where I stepped, avoiding the tiny pools.

As we got closer, it smelled like incense. Moon was fluttering a white feather over a bowl to blow the smoke towards people.

"Hey!" She grinned as we approached. "You made it!"

They were uncomfortably close to the hole. The burbling noises made me shudder.

"We did!" The words felt anachronistic, like we'd swung by a house-warming. I was glad I'd worn several layers; it was even colder than I remembered.

Moon directed the bowl's smoke at my face and down to my ankles. She did the same to Jonah. "There. Now you can join the circle."

I avoided looking at the hole, but saw the flash of white: the sculpture of Catherine's head was still there on the little altar. I never *had* found out who'd made it. There were two empty cushions between Catherine and Sol. I took the seat by Catherine, who was staring miserably down at her lap.

Grace smiled; her hair was loose over her shoulders, and she was wearing the same floaty white dress Moon had worn the first night of the retreat. For some reason, it creeped me out. I looked towards the entrance of the cavern. In the dark, I couldn't even see the tunnel out. Had it been the right choice, coming down here? Witnessing whatever was planned?

"Tonight, we're here to rectify a mistake." Moon sat across from me, pushing up the sleeves of her slouchy sweater. "For a long time, we thought Catherine and Grace were the priestesses. And that cost us, didn't it? Of course, everything happens for a reason. Catherine had to end up in New York to meet Thea. But still, that doesn't excuse Grace's lies."

"I'm sorry." Grace looked down into her lap.

"We're not surprised." Moon laughed. "After all, the sorcerer deceives, right? That's who she is. That's her nature."

Even in the dim light, I could see Grace's cheeks redden. I didn't like this: Grace being blamed for not knowing her role in a play that Moon had made up.

"Because Grace pretended to be the other sister, we wasted time and energy. We went ahead with a ceremony we never should have embarked on. We sacrificed the wrong person."

What?

"Wait, who did you sacrifice?" I asked, cutting into Moon's monologue.

"Me." Catherine said it in a small, childlike voice.

"But because it was the wrong person, the portal sent her back," Moon went on. "Catherine rose from the dead. It's a miracle that hasn't happened for thousands of years."

"Rose from the dead?" I tried to exchange a scared look with Jonah, but he was gazing at Moon. "What are you talking about?"

Catherine's shoulders shook; was she crying? I couldn't tell behind the curtain of hair. Goose bumps sprang up on my arms.

"And tomorrow," Moon went on, ignoring me. "When light and dark are balanced, the rightful savior will fulfill her sacrifice. She'll bring the world back towards equilibrium, exponentially increasing good. She'll shrink the evil that has overtaken men's hearts, the greed that allows them to kill." Moon's breath was ragged, and she paused to swallow. "Tonight, Grace will vanquish the evil that lives within her. She will go through the portal first and prepare the way for our priestess. She will magnify Thea's great sacrifice with her own."

"Stop." I stood, knowing that something was wrong, that we were barreling towards a place with no return. Then everyone else stood in tandem, including Jonah.

Suddenly, Sol was by my side, his hand heavy on my shoulder. "You okay?"

I jumped up and pulled away from him. "I'm leaving."

Sol's hand returned to my arm, tightened. "I think you should stay."

His grip was viselike, and I cried out.

Jonah was already stepping closer, confused. "What's wrong?"

"Sol—let me go!" Couldn't Jonah see? Why wasn't he helping me?

But instead, Jonah gripped my other arm, even more tightly than Sol. My entire body went cold as if dunked in ice water. Now Jonah looked straight ahead, ignoring me.

No. This wasn't happening. Jonah wasn't—

"It's okay, Thea." Sol sounded faintly irritated, like I was killing the vibe. "Just cool it."

My voice returned. "Stop!" I tried to pull away, but they were both too strong, their fingers pressing deep into my flesh. It felt like something was unraveling, the solidity of Jonah, of who he was to me, disintegrating into dust.

"Please," I cried, now desperately trying to wrench out of their grip. The more I struggled, the harder they clamped. Terror filled my body with energy; I felt like I could detach my arms, leave them behind.

"I wish you'd skipped this session." Finally, Jonah was looking at me. His eyes looked dull and tired. "We could've had one more night."

I gaped at him, speechless once again.

"Aww, that's sweet." Sol chuckled. "And I agree. She's a partier. Who knows what shenanigans we could've gotten into?"

"Would you both shut the fuck up?" Moon stood by Grace, an arm around her shoulder. "This is a very important ceremony."

"Help me!" I turned my pleas to the rest of the group. But Catherine was sobbing into her hands, and Grace was staring determinedly at the ground. "Someone, please, help!"

"Thea!" Moon's voice was sharp. "You'll have your time tomorrow. Could you please give Grace the attention she deserves?"

In response, I screamed. It did nothing; Sol and Jonah continued to grip me as if I were a piece of furniture they had to secure in place. I screamed again, unable to stop, the horror bubbling up my throat.

"For fuck's sake." Moon bent to pick up a scarf she'd originally unwound from around the incense bowl. Though I pressed my lips together, she managed to stuff it into my mouth.

"I *told* you we should have the zip ties ready." Sol's voice was cold.

"I didn't realize she'd act this way." Moon gave me a pointed look, then turned. "Grace, you ready?"

"Yes." Grace ran her hand over Catherine's head, petting her. "It's okay, Cath. I've been manipulating people my whole life. This is my chance to make it right." She approached me, her wide blue eyes determined. "It's an honor to open the portal for you, Thea. Thank you for your sacrifice." She touched my shoulder, then turned and walked towards the hole where the rocky wall met the ground. Moon followed, holding a lantern aloft.

I yelled, the scarf muffling my words. I struggled anew, no longer feeling the bright pain from Sol and Jonah's grip. I knew then what was going to happen. What I should've known all along.

Grace walked carefully to the edge, her back to us. The slurping sounds seemed to get louder, as if straining to suck her in.

"*Grace, stop! No!*" My yells came out as garbled moans, a weird and inconsequential soundtrack to the proceedings.

Grace looked back, somber and scared. But then her eyes trained on someone—Sol, right next to me—and a rapturous smile pulled at her lips.

"No!"

She turned back and jumped. Catherine shrieked once, the piercing crack echoing around the chamber. The crown of Grace's head was the last to disappear: a flash of tangerine, and she was gone.

49

We all stood there for a moment, silent and still. The hole's burbles sounded merry, like it was pleased to have been fed.

"Well." Moon's voice was subdued. "That's that."

Catherine sank to her knees, sobbing quietly.

"I know it's hard." Moon smiled bravely, rubbing her back.

My mind was blank, my body rigid.

Every atom in my body screamed at me: *THINK!*

Okay. I needed to figure this out. Jonah's gun. If I could just wrench a hand away, I could stick it under his shirt, grab it. But I didn't know how to shoot a gun. Maybe training it on them would be enough? Then I could back up across the cave, run upstairs, and use the phone in my front pocket to call emergency services. Down here I doubted there was satellite access. And then—

As if listening to my thoughts, Sol reached into my pocket, pulled my phone out, and slipped it into his back pocket. Shit. I let out a sound, which was muffled by the gag.

"Thea." Moon approached me, looking exhausted but happy, like she'd just come from a great workout class. "I don't want this to scare you. I know what it looks like, but you have to trust me. This portal leads to a beautiful realm. There's no pain, no suffering. You'll finally get to rest. Gracie wanted that too."

The words washed over me, and my brain was banking them, but I felt suddenly disconnected from my body. I couldn't feel the cold stone underneath my feet. A desperate thought arose: *Is this a nightmare?* Maybe if I could just pinch my thigh, I'd wake up.

Her expression softened. "I know you're scared. That's normal. But it's your destiny. And we'll help you through it." She reached out and tucked a strand of hair behind my ear.

She started across the chamber, towards the tunnel out, and Sol and Jonah dragged me after her. It was hard to walk over the slippery surfaces without use of my arms, and at points they hauled me along as I stumbled. My arms and shoulders were on fire, overstretched. Catherine's quiet sobs followed us.

Where were they taking me? As we finally entered the flatter cavern, I tried to form a new plan. Maybe on the stairs . . . they couldn't *both* hold me, could they? But if I tried to shove them down the steps, wouldn't they take me with them?

"Oh, I *did* bring a zip tie!" Sol paused us at the foot of the stairs. Jonah pinned my arms behind me and sharp plastic bit into my wrists.

"Onwards." Sol walked me up the steps, grasping my bound wrists. It was hard to walk with my hands behind me; it threw off my balance. I had to concentrate on not tripping. It was slow going, and on the way I visualized Grace's head disappearing beneath the surface. Where was she now? Stuck in some underground aqueduct? Had she drowned? Did the hole lead to another cavern? Was she still alive? Panic simmered underneath my thoughts.

I stumbled.

"Careful!" Sol sounded irritated. I was sweaty with exertion, and the gag made me feel like I couldn't breathe. I jabbed at it with my tongue, and it fell out just as we entered the studio. Okay. We were out of the cave. It was time to get away now. But how? My breath rasped in the quiet. I was actually amazed I wasn't having a panic attack, but some animal part of my brain was keeping me in the present, taking in every detail.

Sol marched me through the courtyard, up the stairs, and into Catherine's room. Inside, he sat me on the bed, bending me forward. The zip tie came loose, but immediately something cold and metal clamped on my left wrist. He closed the other end of the handcuffs on the metal bedframe.

I rolled my free wrist, realizing there were tear tracks on my face.

"You guys don't need to do this." My voice shook, and I swallowed. I needed to use my words; that was my only chance. "I get it. I agree with what you're doing."

Sol stood in front of me. "Sorry, kiddo."

Kiddo? The flash of indignation helped, felt solid, and I grasped at it like a flotation device. "Did you do that to Karen too?" I asked, my voice a little stronger. "Steven?"

"Of course not." Moon sat at the edge of the table. It was just the three of us now; Catherine and Jonah had broken off. "Steven was staying away with the car so you didn't have an escape option. And Karen is fine. She's resting. She's tied to Grace in this lifetime, and we thought it'd be too hard for her to watch."

"Did she *know*?" I asked. "That Grace was going to do that?"

"No." Moon shrugged. "But she'll understand."

"So that's what you're going to do to me tomorrow." Terror rose up through my throat.

"Thea — oh, good." Moon glanced at the door. Jonah walked in with a bucket and set it on the floor next to me. I stared imploringly. But he was no longer the person I'd cuddled with an hour ago. This new version avoided my gaze.

Sol gestured. "Here's your bathroom, for now. We'll get you some TP too."

Moon smiled softly. "If there's anything you need . . ."

"Just yell." Sol grinned, his eyes flashing with contempt. Whistling softly, he left the room. Jonah hesitated at the doorway, finally looking at me.

His eyes weren't hard like Sol's, or soft like Moon's. He looked despondent yet determined, like a rancher who was gearing up to shoot his injured horse.

"Please," I said. There had to be a way to get through to him.

"I'm sorry." Strangely, his own voice was pleading. As we stared at each other, the full reality of the falsehood reared up. Jonah had been a part of this the entire time. Like Karen, this was his home. He, too, had been asked to play a role, and he'd played it well.

He opened his mouth to say something else, but Moon touched his arm and they walked out together, closing the door behind them.

"Okay," I said out loud after they left. I stood and tried to pull the bed; it didn't move. My arms ached, and my right wrist chafed painfully against the metal. I peeked underneath the bed and saw the legs were bolted to the floor. There had to be a way I could twist and pull the thin bar on the headboard. But though tarnished, the headboard was strong, all one piece of metal. There was no way I could bend it, let alone break it.

I strained at the handcuff for a few minutes, trying to slip my hand out, but it just cut into my skin. Now I was bleeding, bright red smearing onto the white duvet. Someone had put on fresh sheets and made the bed.

I lay down, staring up at the ceiling. The horror of the situation felt muted, hanging out at the edges of my periphery. If I allowed it to move in, to envelop me, I'd be completely useless.

I had to think. What had Moon said down there about Catherine? Something about coming back from the dead?

But because it was the wrong person, the portal sent her back. Catherine rose from the dead. It's a miracle that hasn't happened for thousands of years.

So they'd sent Catherine into the "portal," but she'd survived. That meant there had to be a way out. The thought helped ease the blank fear back beneath the horizon. Maybe at this very moment, Grace was crawling through a tunnel, back up towards the light.

But—and I didn't want to think about this, I really didn't—even if Catherine had survived, she'd reappeared changed. She'd had a psychotic break. I had no idea what she'd seen down there, what she'd had to go through.

She'd sobbed to see Grace go in. So the path out hadn't been easy.

The thought made me stick my face in the pillow and scream.

Whatever horrors she'd been through now awaited me.

For a few hours I lay there, my brain calculating, trying to puzzle a way out. At some point I passed out, falling deep into a dreamless sleep. When I woke, it was dark. Pain flared in my wrists, arms, and back. A wave of terror rose, and I pushed it back down. *Focus.* I slipped out of bed and squatted over the bucket, then pushed it as far away as I could reach.

Maybe, if one of them came in, I could throw the urine in their face. And then what?

Before I sat back on the bed, I paused. This was Catherine's room. Maybe there was something in or around the bed that could be of use. I threw back the covers, pulled off the fitted sheet—not easy with one hand. Nothing there except an old striped mattress, yellowed and dot-

ted with stains. I pulled the mattress up off the frame, peered underneath.

The sunglassed cat grinned back at me.

My diary.

I grabbed it and sat heavily. Its disappearance felt like it happened so
long ago. The retreat itself felt quaint, like a trip I'd taken years before.
Had Catherine taken it? Why?

I moved into a small patch of moonlight so I could see it. A torn
scrap of paper marked one of the pages.

*M and I are going to the Stargirl next week, I'm so excited!!!! We're going
to buy tickets to The Drama Queens and sneak into Stargirl instead. I
know!!!! It's a lie and I'm already praying for forgiveness from God. But
I have to see it. I don't know why, I just have this feeling. I HAVE to.
I've even been having dreams about it. So you know how the poster for
Stargirl shows the actress in this desert staring off into the distance. Last
night I dreamed that she and I were in the desert together. At first we
were in this really nice tent that had rugs and golden cups and stuff, and
people were treating us like ROYALTY. And then we woke up and everyone was gone. They'd left us there!! It was really scary because we knew
that we were going to die of thirst!! We just had this little pouch of water.
And then this snake appeared and maybe it was because we'd started
hallucinating (sp?) but it started talking to us!! It asked which one of us
wanted to be a sacrifice. We were like: ??? And the snake explained more
but I don't remember what happened/what we decided. Then I woke up.*

I let out a deep breath. I didn't remember this dream, but if Catherine had read about it, she could've told Moon. But if she had—why
was the diary hidden? And besides, even if Moon had known I'd had
this dream at thirteen, how had she known I'd be dreaming about it
here? It was also slightly different: I hadn't remembered being out in
the desert with a group, but now it felt familiar. I could almost hear it,
feel it: the clang of wine goblets, the shout of tipsy laughter, the soft fur
underneath my elbow.

It was different from *Stargirl*, in which guards had unceremoniously
dumped her and left.

The moon shifted; the whole room was now dark. I slipped the diary back under the mattress, tried to fashion the sheets and blankets back as they'd been.

A new wave of despair washed over me, and I sobbed into the pillow until it was soaked. After, I lay on my side, staring into the pitch-black room. There had to be a way out of this. There had to be. Determination surged into my belly.

There was no way I was going down that hole.

50

"Good morning." Moon swept in, carrying a tray. She looked particularly radiant in a long marigold dress that set off her eyes.

I'd woken up hours earlier, unable to fall back asleep because of the ache in my arms and wrists. So I'd watched the room turn from black to silver to gold. My mind had jumped around constantly, probing and prodding, searching for a way out.

Now I sat up warily.

"You want some breakfast?" Moon gently set the tray next to me: a steaming omelet, butter-drenched toast, a fresh banana.

"Is there any way we could put this on my nondominant hand?" I held up my shackled right wrist.

"I'll help you." She dragged a chair over and picked up the banana, peeled with deft fingers. "How are you feeling today?"

"How am I feeling?" I stared at her. She was acting like this was completely normal.

She nodded. "I know this must be a lot to process."

My stomach growled. Moon held the banana up, and after a second I took it with my left hand and bit. The sweetness filled my mouth.

"Everyone goes through this." She watched me. "The period of resistance. I went through it once too. But when you get to the other side, you feel so much better. Everything makes sense. All the pain lightens when you know it's not your fault. It's just your pattern."

I picked up a piece of toast. "That sounds nice." I said it sarcastically, but Moon nodded fervently.

"It's like waking up. You're finally living in alignment with your authentic self."

And your authentic self has a fake accent? The words were on the tip of my tongue, but I held them in. I needed to do everything I could to get Moon on my side, to change her mind.

"For me, it was always a question." She stared at me with her signature expression: I'd thought of it as intense, but now it looked deranged. "I had these impulses that didn't make sense to me. I was a yoga teacher, trying to help people, trying to bring more peace and love into the world. But every so often I would just get this urge to destroy. To say something hurtful. To laugh at someone's pain. Once I realized my past life pattern, it all fell into place."

"Okay." I tried to sound thoughtful. "Or maybe you're just human. Everyone has aggressive impulses. And the more we push them down, the more they come up."

"I was a murderer, Thea. And that thread still runs through me." She heaved a sigh. "This is my opportunity to atone for my mistakes."

"By harming more people?"

"By facilitating a sacrifice that will help the human race leap forward. Do you know how slowly humans evolve? The soul patterns we bring with us from lifetime to lifetime—they take so long to break. There aren't many of these opportunities. I'm not going to let you waste it." She held up a forkful of omelet, which I awkwardly took.

"I thought it was my choice?" I asked.

"It is. But you already said yes. And if you'd had enough time here, to fully open yourself up to the process, you'd go as willingly as Grace. But this is supposed to happen on the equinox." Her eyes glittered. "I can feel it."

Reasoning with her wasn't helping. So I tried a different tack. "How did this all start? When did you meet Catherine?"

"LA." Moon crossed one leg over the other, jiggling her slipper-encased foot. "She was really suffering over the death of her friend Sebastian Smith. I helped her, but it wasn't until we moved here that I realized what my role really was."

To throw her in a hole.

"So Catherine was—she went in that portal, too, right?" I asked.

"She did." Moon nodded.

"Willingly?"

"Oh yes."

I remembered Catherine's anger at the hospital, her screams. *You tricked me! How could you do that to me?*

Moon was lying. Catherine had not gone willingly.

"And then," I prompted, "she just appeared?"

Moon's smile slid off her face. "I know you're trying to get information to save yourself, Thea. But I'm confident the portal will take you. So: yes. We had no idea until we started seeing headlines that she was hospitalized in New York."

"How did she get there?"

"No idea. But it doesn't matter." Moon studied me. "She came right home."

Because you left her no choice.

She stood. "I need to see to preparations for tonight."

"Wait." You weren't really supposed to point out a person's delusions to them, but I'd run out of options.

"What if this is all in your head?" I asked. "I work with people who experience this type of thing. One patient was convinced he had to save the world from aliens. You need help, Moon. You—"

"Stop." Moon snatched the plate and backed away. "I'm not delusional, Thea. I see how things actually are. I'm living in more reality than you could possibly comprehend."

"Oh yeah?" I scoffed, unable to hold my anger back any longer. "Does that reality involve a fake Mexican accent?"

Her eyes widened with surprise.

"You're an impostor, Moon." The words poured out. "For whatever reason—probably to sound more 'exotic,' to help you stand out, to grow your business—you're doing something wrong. Stealing something that doesn't belong to you. Do you know how offensive that is? Do you know what people are going to say when they find out?"

Her face was blank.

"Mikki's writing a huge exposé at this very moment," I went on, my voice loud, filling up the room. "You're going to be a laughingstock. A meme! People will dig up every morsel they can about you. And at some point, someone will figure out all this insane shit you've been doing. To Catherine. Grace." I shuddered. "To me."

Moon walked to the door, and when she turned around, she was smiling sweetly, her golden eyes glowing like a flame. "What have I done?" Her voice was accentless—no, it had a faint Southern twang— and it dislodged a burst of fear in my chest. "I didn't make anyone come here. Y'all showed up of your own accord. You know what needs to be done. I'm just here to give you a little push."

51

Hours after Moon had left, sick of my pulsating anxiety, I'd pulled out the diary and started reading through. One entry stood out, from a few weeks after we'd started communion classes with Pastor John.

Something crazy happened today. Pastor John got MAD!! He is usually so cool and calm but he LOST IT. So PJ was talking about Jesus's decision to sacrifice himself to save us and Adam was laughing with Scott and PJ said: Is this a joke to you?? And Adam said no and PJ YELLED: You think it's so funny!! Would you have had the guts to do what Jesus did!! Knowing how horrible it would be!! Would ANY of you do it!! No one said anything. He said: I didn't think so. Then he went back to teaching. But I thought about his question for the rest of the day. WOULD I have done it? Probably not. But maybe? I don't know. It made me truly understand how brave Jesus was to go through so much pain, knowing he could stop it at any time but dying anyway to save us.

I paused, looking at the flat blue sky outside the window. Was this where my martyr tendencies had originated from? My wanting to help Catherine so badly that I'd stayed in a clearly threatening situation at the Center? Had she sensed this trait in me in the first place?

The door opened. I shoved the diary behind me.

Catherine peered in.

"Hi." I tried to keep my voice soft, even as my heart thumped in my chest. "Come in."

She walked in slowly, uncertainly, like a toddler just starting to use her legs. She held up a bag. "I brought you some granola."

"Great. So, listen." I pressed my hands together, feeling like an elementary schoolteacher trying hard to hold it together. "I need you to call 911. You can use the SOS function. I can show you if you bring me a phone."

Catherine slumped into a chair at the table. Her eyes were red, her cheeks flushed. She tossed the granola bag, which landed by my feet.

I tried to smile, knowing it must look like a scared rictus. "Can you do that, Catherine?"

"I'm sorry." She lowered her head into her arms. "I'm so sorry."

"It's okay. Just get—"

"No." She picked up her head, wiped at her wet face. "I wanted to be wrong, you know. I prayed in here every day that you wouldn't show up. But I knew you would. I shouldn't have left that note. I shouldn't have done it."

"So that *was* you sending me a clue?" I asked.

She nodded. "But even after you got here I wanted to be wrong." Her lips pulled down, a sad clown face. "I searched your room and took the diary so Moon and Sol wouldn't get it. But it proved who you were. So I started praying that you'd leave. But when they brought you to my room, when I saw you, I knew. I knew it was too late." She shook her head. "I should've known you wouldn't leave, no matter how many times I told you. But I wanted to protect you." She curled into her lap and sobbed.

"Thank you." I tried to make my voice as soothing as possible. "Thank you for trying to protect me."

"But . . ." It took her a minute to be able to talk. "I couldn't. I couldn't get you to leave because you were worried about me."

And it was true. I *had* been worried about Catherine. But as I watched her crumpled-over body, a new surety arose: it hadn't been purely that which had kept me pinned here.

So what else was it? Had I been so excited to jump into a juicy mystery that I'd ignored danger at every turn? So bored with my life I'd jetted off on a wild-goose chase of a celebrity I didn't know? So ridiculously overconfident that I'd imagined myself to be her sole savior?

I could've gotten in the car with Dawne, Mikki, and Ramit. I could be in New York at this very moment.

But no. I'd been seduced by Catherine's mystery, then literally seduced by Jonah, Moon, and Sol. It had felt *good* to be called special, even by people who were clearly not well.

"You were the one watching me?" I asked, my voice dull. "From behind the purple door? And looking in my yurt that first night?"

She nodded, her eyes squeezed shut.

Catherine wasn't going to call the police. That was suddenly very clear. All I could hope for was more answers, more info that might help me.

"Did they push you into that hole?" I asked.

"Yes." She shuddered.

"What's in there?" My scalp shrunk in fear, but I kept my voice steady.

"Nothing. It's just this tiny space. I pretended I was in a womb." She sniffed. "It made me feel better. I told myself I was waiting to be born."

"How did you get out? Was there a tunnel?"

"There's no way out." She wiped at her nose.

"Then how did you get out?" Frustration surged through my chest.

"I don't *know*," she cried. "I was in there, and then suddenly I was with you. I thought you were Grace for a second. That's why I tried to . . . I was upset. They tricked me. They pretended Grace was going to go, and then they pushed me. *She* pushed me." Catherine nibbled at her thumbnail. She looked suddenly young, a brooding preteen.

"So you have no memory of leaving the tiny space," I prompted.

"It must've spit me out." She pulled at a greasy lock of hair. "I wasn't the right one."

"Catherine." I could hear the quiet desperation in my voice. "You're a good person. You don't want to do to me what Grace did to you, right?"

Catherine just stared at the table, the ends of her hair in her mouth.

"Why are you listening to Moon and Sol?" This was my last chance, my Hail Mary. "They lied to us in that other lifetime, right? Why is everyone trusting them now? They're bad people. We know that."

"But it really happened." Catherine glanced at me, her face haggard. "You remember it. In the desert, that spirit offered us the choice."

"But how do you know I accepted it?" My voice rose. "I didn't get to that part because I fucking passed out!"

Catherine stood, stumbling slightly. "Because you're a better person than me."

"I'm not!" The exasperation jumped out, an uncaged animal. "I'm a self-involved piece of shit just like you! Just like everyone here!"

"I'm sorry." Catherine backed towards the doorway. She was shaking, her shoulders vibrating. "I'm sorry, Thea. I'm sorry. I'm sorry."

"Catherine, wait!" I was half standing, straining against the handcuff. "Wait, just talk to me! Stop, just—"

She shut the door quietly behind her.

52

The light changed, golden-hour hues painting the walls. I stared at the ceiling. I'd had one last chance to convince Catherine to help me, and I'd blown it.

My last molecule of hope was Karen. They'd kept her—by force?— from attending Grace's session. So where was she now? Locked up? She might be just as trapped as I was.

Eventually, my brain went quiet. I watched a fly buzz around the room as if looking for something. Once in a while I heard the faint mutter of voices out the open window. So quiet here. A pity that I could scream and scream, my voice extending for miles, and never be heard.

The door opened; Jonah appeared. I sat up and painted on a smile, survival energy engaging my facial muscles.

He sat at the table. "Hey." His voice was solemn. "We don't have much time. But I just wanted to talk to you. To—apologize."

"For what?" I asked, as if I didn't know.

He stared at his clasped hands for a long time, his lips pressed together.

I had to get him talking.

"When you were waiting outside the hospital that day, you wanted to run into me, right?" I asked gently. I was actually curious. "To make me think you were working with her parents?"

"Yeah." He scratched his cheek. "I thought I'd have to wait longer, maybe until the end of the day. But you came out pretty quickly."

"Who picked Catherine up?"

He pushed back his glossy curls. "Moon and Sol."

"Are you serious?" I thought back to the video footage: the man tall and hunched, with a paunch. Her, tiny and blond. "So they were, what? In disguise? Wearing *wigs*?"

"Uh-huh."

I'd considered this once, but someone had disproven it . . .

"You told me you'd sent photos of Moon and Sol to Diane," I said as it clicked into place. "That she'd confirmed it wasn't them."

He just nodded. My stomach clenched at the level of organization that had taken place.

"Did you really find me with LinkedIn and Instagram?" I asked.

"Yup." He tapped his fingers on the table. "I remember being shocked at your pictures, how much you looked like her. But my goal was just to talk to you and find out when Catherine was leaving the hospital."

"So that Moon and Sol could get there first, right?" I felt disgust with myself for spilling this information so easily.

"Right."

"So they didn't think she'd come with them if they just showed up as themselves?"

"Well . . ." He shrugged. "We didn't know what state Catherine was in. If she'd even say yes to seeing them. So when you said her parents were coming, it seemed like the easiest way."

"Fake IDs and all."

"It's not that hard to make them." He must've seen my expression, because he continued. "But for the record, I didn't have anything to do with you signing up for this retreat."

"But you agreed to keep playing the PI."

"Yeah. They thought you'd open up to me. So we could find out if you were really her. Which, clearly, you are." He held out a hand. "Those were *your* visions, your dreams. And your decision to stay."

"Oh, you all would've just let me leave?"

"When everyone else left? Of course."

I wasn't sure I believed that.

"But what about after?" I asked. "You trapped me. Steven left, and the other car . . . someone disabled it, right?" I was certain of it, as if I'd watched it happen in front of me.

"Well, at that point . . ." He rubbed at the table. "Moon was getting nervous about what Catherine was telling you. I mean, you're sisters. She knew Catherine had mixed feelings about what was going to happen. But still—no one held a gun to your head. If you'd started walking out to the road, I would've gone with you."

The words made me shiver. "Jonah—"

"It's Joe."

The name sounded vaguely familiar. *Watch your fingers, Joe.* Karen had said it to him at dinner two nights ago, but I'd been distracted by those jewel-toned bottles of wine.

"Joe." I forced myself to take a deep breath. It meant something that he was here. That he was talking to me. "How did you get involved in all this?"

"Well." He shifted, lifting one ankle over his knee. "It's like I told you the night I met you. I used to have a crush on Catherine."

"When?"

"As a preteen. But I followed her through the years. And when I saw that Sebastian Smith had died, I knew she'd be devastated. So I drove to LA. I felt like she needed me. I tried to figure out where she lived, but she wasn't on social media."

My stomach dropped. The truth was dawning on me. Jonah—Joe—wasn't just a part of this cult. He was also a stalker.

"But I caught a lucky break." He smiled softly. "I found out where Sebastian's funeral was and waited outside. Eventually, she came out and got in a car and I followed her to her house. The next day she came out and went to this yoga studio. All I had to do was give them my credit card and I was in. She seemed like kind of a zombie in class, so I decided to give her more time before I tried to approach her. You know, I slept in my car. Showered at the yoga studio. And just went back and forth, every day. She always went to the same class. Finally, at one point I got the nerve to put my mat next to hers. That was the day Moon was the substitute teacher. Catherine switched to her classes, and they'd talk afterwards. So I made sure to get there early and chat with Moon too. One day she asked if I wanted to get a smoothie with her and Catherine. And that was it. I was a part of Moon's group."

I nodded throughout, like this all made so much sense. "Then what?"

"I don't know." He frowned. "Catherine wasn't what I expected. She was pretty cold. I wasn't hitting on her or anything like that— I just wanted to get to know her. But Catherine was so focused on Moon. It wasn't healthy, you know? I mean, Sol loved it. He thought he had this little harem or something." A sigh. "And then we came here when COVID started. Moon got into the past-life cohort stuff, and it explained everything. Why I'd always felt so drawn to Catherine. But then when I met you . . . I realized I'd been wanting to be with *you* all this time. Not Catherine. I wish we had more time together. But I guess that's what a tragedy is, right?" Joe was different from Jonah: hunched over, uncertain, his fingers picking at hangnails. Even his voice was a little different: higher, softer.

I thought suddenly of the opening ceremony. When we'd written what we wanted to release on those thin pieces of wood.

Joe/Jonah's had confused me. *DOUBT.*

"Joe." A warm feeling suffused my chest. "You don't really believe in this stuff, do you?"

"What do you mean?" His dark eyes darted to mine.

"All of this." I spread my free hand. "I work in mental health. I know shared psychotic disorder when I see it."

He shook his head, his face going pale.

"Listen to me." I made my voice confident, hard. "This is all make-believe. Moon has brainwashed you into a fantasy. A part of you knows that. And if that's the case . . . Joe, you're really hurting people. Grace could be dead. Catherine is not well. This needs to stop. *Now.*"

He stared at me, as if considering my words. Then he shook his head. "I wish I could believe that. But think about our patterns, Thea. They fit. What I told you about the girl at my school—that was all true."

A cheerful knock at the half-open door. *No!* My hands clenched into fists as Sol sailed in.

"Aww, are the lovebirds having a goodbye sesh? Cute." Sol clapped Jonah's back. "It's time, my friend."

This was my last chance. I couldn't let them take me down there.

"Thea, would you be so kind as to put your arms behind your back?" Sol pulled a zip tie from his pocket.

I held up my free hand. "Sol, wait."

He tilted his head, watching me like I was an animal whose noises he couldn't understand.

"Please don't do this." I remembered the conversation I'd overheard between him and Grace. "Look, I know you convinced Grace; I heard you in the kitchen. She didn't want to go into that hole, and you ma-nipulated her into doing it."

Jonah's eyes sharpened on Sol.

Sol chuckled. "I didn't do anything, darlin'. It was her decision."

"No, it wasn't. You kept telling her how brave she was."

Sol's gentle smile didn't waver. And that's when I felt it: a new cold fear spreading through my belly. Sol knew exactly what he'd done. He was the best liar of them all.

"You know, Thea"—Sol crossed his arms—"I had my doubts. In fact, Moon and I got in a huge fight the day you all got in. I wanted to let the pattern go, leave it for another lifetime. But when you showed up, you were the spitting image of Catherine. And it was like, *Oh, okay. Maybe it is time to handle this.* But I'm ready for it to be over now. We need to move on and focus on the business."

"The *business?*"

"Of course. Do you have any idea how big our podcast is getting?" He shook his head. "We're set to really take off this year."

So that's all Sol really cared about. Money. Power. And if he had to harm people in the process to keep his cash cow, Moon, happy, so be it.

"You're a loser," I spit out, unable to stop the words. "You know that? You failed as an actor and musician, and now the only reason you have this 'business' is because of Moon."

Sol glowered at me with contempt. Then the expression drained and he smiled pleasantly. "All right, then. Time to go." He put his hands on his hips. "So, you want to do this the easy way or the hard way?"

Twenty minutes later, battered and bruised from my attempts to jerk, scramble, and pull away, I was back in the cave. They'd had to zip-tie my ankles, gag me, and haul me like a rolled-up rug all the way down. At the top of the stairs to the cave, I'd wriggled so much they'd dropped me. Sol had had to grab me under the arms as I'd started tumbling down.

After that, I'd stopped struggling. Carrying me over the rocky terrain, Sol had dropped me once—maybe on purpose. My head had hit a rock so hard I'd seen stars.

Now I was sitting in one of the tiny streams of cold water, facing the hole. My whole body shook. There were voices behind me, but I couldn't hear them over the water's gurgles.

Moon pulled the gag from my mouth. "Are you going to be nice and quiet?"

"Moon, listen to me." The words felt stuck in my throat, but I choked them out. "I'm not the sacrifice, okay? I don't want to be. The sacrifice has to be willing, right? I'm not willing. I'm sorry, I'm not."

"Let's turn her around." Moon glanced behind me.

"All right." Sol picked me up underneath the arms. As I swirled around, my eyes landed on Karen sitting across from me. Her head was bowed low.

My last shred of hope disappeared. Karen was a willing part of this.

Even so, I called out to her. "Karen, please! Help me!"

She lifted her head. Her face was ashen, her eyes red. She looked like the corpse of herself, devoid of all life. Maybe she hadn't known about Grace's plan. But she knew now. And even though the knowledge had destroyed her, she was still here.

The others were here too: Catherine, Steven, and Joe.

I trained my eyes on Catherine. "Catherine! Please!" Her head was slumped onto her chest, her hair covering her face.

"We had to sedate her." Moon patted my shoulder. "She cares about you so much, she's getting confused."

"Steven, please!" But he stared determinedly at the ground, and Joe watched me with bleak sadness in his eyes. "Please! Joe! Help me!"

A slap to the back of my head, which made me gasp in pain, sparkles exploding.

"Hey." Moon glared at Sol. "Don't do that."

"We need to finish this." He sounded irritated. "Can we, please?"

"Yes." She sighed. "Joe?"

He came closer, and he and Sol grabbed me under the arms, lifting me to stand.

"No, *no, no!*" My voice rose into a wail. I tried to sag back to the ground, but they started carrying me towards the hole, like a roller coaster lurching into movement.

My screams reverberated through the cave. My mind went blank, a pure white burst, as my bound bare feet dragged over wet rock and dipped into the bubbling ice-cold water. I pulled up my legs as if that would help.

"O-kay," Sol muttered as if they were in the midst of a handyman project.

My legs swung free, then the zip tie snapped open. As Sol held my wrists, Moon stood in front of me, setting down garden shears.

"Stop!" I shrieked, with renewed energy. "Please! No! Stop!" I kicked and tried to wrench away from Joe and Sol, but their grip was like iron.

Moon leaned forward and kissed my cheek. I snapped at her like a rabid dog.

"Thank you." Her fingertips pressed into my heart. She tore her eyes away from mine and nodded.

Karen stood behind her. She moved forward and squeezed my shoulder, slipping something hard and small into my front left pocket.

"Don't lose faith, hon." She managed a half smile. "Everything's going to be okay."

Behind her, Catherine stood. Her eyes were dilated, barely any green showing. "I love you, Thea." Her words were slurred. "I'm sorry. I love you." She hugged me.

Steven remained where he was sitting, head low.

"All right." Moon nodded firmly at Jonah and Sol. I shrieked as they lifted me over the swirling, sucking water. There had to be a way to stop myself from going into the tunnel—maybe by bracing my legs or arms.

Focus. Strong legs. Strong arms.

But the hole was too large, too slippery. Too hungry.

When they let me go, I dropped into the mouth and it swallowed me whole.

Catherine

"Catherine?" Moon smiles at me sweetly. "You want to go for a hike?"

It's too hot for a hike. It's just past noon and the sun is blazing in the sky. But you don't say no to Moon.

"Sure." I get up from my bed, where I've been meditating. It should be nice to see someone—I've been kept in here for the past four days—but the planes and angles of Moon's heart-shaped face fill me with a thick, syrupy fear.

I quickly grab sunglasses and sunscreen and race to follow her; she's already heading down the steps to the courtyard. I get a whiff of her rose perfume oil and something deep in my gut twists. Sometimes I think about those early days, back when the castle was just a skeletal structure stretching towards the unending blue sky. Back when we slept in two campers and made cowboy coffee over the firepit and didn't have any agenda aside from our healing sessions. Sure, the radio would spit out news about the rising death toll, how bodies were being stacked in refrigerated vans because the morgues were so full. But I was happy. Everyone was surprised, especially David—now going by "Sol"—since I'd admitted I'd never gone camping before.

"Just the two of us?" I ask as she walks straight out to the SUV.

"Just the two of us." She hops in. She's using the Mexican accent full-time now, has since they started the podcast, but it still sounds strange to me. Apparently, she could use it easily after spending so much time there doing yoga trainings. When I made the mistake of questioning it—Moon grew up in West Virginia, the daughter of two white parents—she patiently explained that she felt more at home in Sayulita than she ever had in the US. That her body might be American, but her soul and ancestors were from there. Later on, Sol cornered me and called me paranoid and cynical for "interrogating" her. My probing revealed my maladaptive thought patterns and how much work I still have to do.

Did Moon bring water along for this hike? I hope so, but know I can't ask. She sings along to the satellite radio, and I try to relax. She's not the best driver, but luckily there are very few cars this far out. The diamond sparkles at her throat—same as mine. I got it for her back in LA, brought it to that first Christmas party at Moon's apartment where I met David/Sol, her boyfriend. At that point she and I were already doing healing work together, usually after yoga classes in one of the treatment rooms. The hours of talking and hands-on Reiki would pass in what felt like minutes. And after, I'd actually feel better. The guilt over Sebastian's death— the fact that I hadn't been there for him, hadn't even known he was struggling—would feel lighter. Moon had known deep loss too; her older brother and several friends had gotten hooked on opioids in the late nineties. He'd died when she was sixteen, and her mother had never recovered.

Moon's intuitive abilities helped her get to my deepest, darkest places. It took only a few weeks for me to tell her about my father, the inappropriate way he'd treated me as soon as I turned twelve. No wonder I'd never had an orgasm. No wonder sex had never felt particularly pleasurable for me, and that I needed substances to bear it. Before this, Sebastian—my PR boyfriend, secretly gay— was the only person I'd ever told about the abuse.

"How are you feeling?" Moon glances over at me.

I'm still feeling sick, but I can't tell her. She calls illness a parasitic method of seeking attention.

"I'm great." I force a grin.

"Good." She reaches out and squeezes my hand. "I've been worried about you, Cath."

Really? Because I'm pretty sure I've been banished to my room so she doesn't have to think about me. Ever since Talia arrived, she's been focused solely on her. They even talked about getting matching tattoos. I touch the one Moon and I share on my chest.

"You don't have to worry," I say woodenly.

"I feel like we hit a wall." Moon drums her fingers on the wheel. "With the past life sessions. We need something to jump-start us."

For a while the sessions were lasting all day, into the night. I'm the only one who can properly channel, but the moment that Moon wants me to see—when I'm near-dead in the desert—I can't. My eyes were closed back then. I just hear my sister talking to someone with a low, deep voice. It gives one of us the opportunity to sacrifice ourselves in a future life. But then the vision fades. Maybe I died at that point.

"I'm sorry." It's usually better just to apologize.

"Don't be sorry! I know you're doing your best. But we just need to *know*, Cath. If we know, then we can figure out what to do."

For the thousandth time, I curse myself for having picked up the white, black-lined shards in the cave. *I found something!* Painted ceramic pieces from the long-lost Mimbres people, according to Steven, who told me it was almost common to find them in the area. They would smash their pottery and leave it behind when moving on to a new area. How was I to know that the pieces I found would set Moon on this obsessive path?

I'm not sure she knows where she's driving. But eventually she makes an abrupt turn onto a side road, then cruises until we hit a small parking lot.

"Okay." She gets out of the car without a backpack, without anything. Definitely no water. I swallow; my throat is already dry. But I just have to deal with it.

She passes the wooden trail map stand without looking. I hurry to keep up; she's tiny but moves so fast. I quietly spread sunscreen on my arms, hoping she won't turn around and castigate me. She thinks all lotions are filled with deadly chemicals, but Karen has been secretly bringing me sunscreen from town for my pale skin. We walk over some hills, the trail so thin I follow a few feet behind her. Her calves are strong and tan. There's no shade, of course, and even with sunglasses I have to squint.

For some reason I can't stop thinking about the cave. Moon has been spending most of her time down there, communing with some energy she claims to feel. A few days ago she called it a portal, and the word made my stomach cramp. I hate being down there. It makes me feel trapped, even more so than when I'm confined to my room.

Rings glitter from Moon's hands. It's hard to imagine now how she once caressed me so lovingly, her square, elegant fingers running over my body, waking it up. How she gave me my first orgasm, then many more. How she told me she loved me.

"Here!" She stops abruptly and turns in a slow circle. It doesn't look different from anywhere else on this trail. "Come on!" She steps off the trail onto the sandy dirt, which makes my stomach drop.

Where are we going? We've been walking now for at least an hour. My throat is so dry it feels hard to swallow.

Twenty minutes later, we're far from the trail. Far from anything. Here you can't even see the far-off mountains; we must be on higher ground, and the surrounding hills are hiding them.

She unties the bandanna from around her neck. "Squat down, sweetie."

She ties it around my eyes. It smells like rose-tinged sweat.

"Now stand up."

I stand. She whirls me around in a circle: once, twice, three times, humming a tune to herself. Then she whispers: "Plug your ears." As I do so, she pulls me down to the ground. I'm dizzy from the twirling, and I lean my head over my crossed legs. I hear faint crunching sounds, then nothing.

Finally, I unplug my ears. "Moon?" No reply.

My hands hesitate at the bandanna; Moon could be sitting right there, watching me. This could be a test. She conducts a lot of them. Often I fail and am not allowed to eat for several days.

After a few more minutes, I pull the bandanna down. I jump to my feet. "Moon?"

Nothing—no one—in any direction. The sun's just starting to lower in the sky. So that way is west, right? But what direction did we come from? I have no idea.

She has to be close by. I'll walk to the top of that hill over there so I can see the trail.

My feet grind over the dry earth. Fuck, I'm thirsty. I also have to pee. I remember a show from years ago where the main guy gets lost in the New Mexican desert and is forced to drink his own urine.

Even as I reach the top of the hill, I can tell it's not going to help. There are just other, larger swelling hills all around. No sign of the trail.

What should I do? I take a few deep breaths. Moon taught me that, early on: the simplest way to regulate your nervous system. I could pick a direction and start walking, but what if it turns out to be the wrong way? What if I walk further into the wilderness? There's so much of it out here, miles and miles of sandy dirt and scrubby brush. No shade anywhere.

I'll stay here.

An hour later, feeling fried from the sun, my panic electrifying me, I start to walk.

The sun's falling lower in the sky. Will I be out here all night? Or . . . forever? Is this a way for Moon to get rid of me? She's clearly sick of me. I don't know why. I gave her all my goddamn money. The Center now exists because of me.

I want to cry but force it down. I need those tears.

I stop walking and sit. I laugh loudly. Am I going to die in the fucking desert *again*? Have I been betrayed by the same old people in new bodies?

I lie down and play with a long, thin yellow plant. It looks like a mini stalk of wheat. I wonder distantly if I should try to eat it. That feeling's coming over me again, where it's like I'm in 2D. Not really here. I've been experiencing it since we started the past life sessions. Sometimes I feel imprisoned between lifetimes, not in this one, but not in the old ones either.

The sun sinks below the horizon. I lie on my back, watching the aquamarine fade into navy. The stars are brighter than I've ever seen them before. I think briefly of the dreams I sometimes have of being in space. Dad twisted them for the last scene of *Stargirl*, but they could've been a whole different movie. Some emergency's happening and I'm racing towards something, through a metal structure, while someone runs beside me.

I push the nightmare away. I'm so, so thirsty. I wonder how long I have left without water.

A low purring sound. I lift my head.

It grows louder—yes, a car. I scramble to my feet. I try to call out, but all that leaves my throat is a wheeze. I throw my hands over my eyes as bright headlights find me.

"There she is!" A far-off voice. I keep my hand pressed over my eyes, my shoulders trembling. Is this real? Is this really happening?

"God, Cath." Moon sounds annoyed. A door opens and footsteps walk up to me. "You really scared me." She pulls my arm, and I let my hand fall.

I really scared *her*? I barely question these reversals anymore. "I'm sorry."

Sol's in the driver's seat, fiddling with the radio. "Hey, lady."

"Hi." I do the math: Moon must've looked for me at some point, failed to find me, and left and got Sol.

Inside, Talia's waiting with a bottle of cold water. I grab it and drink it all the way down.

"What were you doing out here?" she asks, her brow furrowed. She doesn't understand yet. She's only been here a few weeks.

"Cath wanted to go back to the scene of her death, to see if it helped with her regressions." Moon turns in the front seat to smile at me. "But she went a little further away than she should've, so we had to rescue her. Right?"

I nod.

The blood is so vivid against the dirt. The vermillion comes from her nostrils, her mouth, little rivulets like those in the cave.

I stand over her, studying her. She's wearing one of Moon's linen dresses. Sage green. Her neck, left arm, and right leg are all bent at unnatural angles.

I was in the lobby, processing retreat applications, when I heard the barking, then the scream. I appear to be the first one to hurry out front, to see this. I look up. Moon is peering over the ledge, standing on the tall tower where she and I used to sit and watch the sun set. When there were clouds, the sky would light up in reds and oranges and pinks.

Next to Moon, Talia's dog Dionysus is also looking down, little freaked-out yips coming from his tiny throat. Moon sees me but doesn't say anything. She picks him up and coos, trying to soothe him.

"This is your chance, love." Clint's eyes are wide with frustration. "Do you want to come with me, or not?"

If only it were that easy. I can picture it clearly: sitting in the SUV while Grace disappears inside, only to reappear with Moon and Sol. Their fond smiles. *Silly Cath.* It's not up to me. I'm not going anywhere.

I haven't been off the property in what—three years? Four? Sometimes I envision sitting on a plane, gazing out the window. My old apartment feels too distant to remember, but sometimes there are flashes: a claw-footed tub. A walk-in closet with rows of chic, neutral-toned clothes. That sleek Italian espresso machine I bought but never once used.

"Cath?" he urges. Oh, Clint. The Aussie. Our latest member. Grace met him at a bar in Truth or Consequences, where she was attempting some casual recruiting. He was living in New York but had come to New Mexico to go cave diving at Blue Hole in Santa Rosa. He told me the sheriff's office put a locked gate over the hole's entrance because so many cave divers would go in, get lost, and die. But if you go through the official channels, they give you a key. Afterwards he came to T or C for the hot springs. Clint's a wanderer, so it wasn't hard to get him to come check out the castle. And he'd seen *Stargirl*, so he took my celebrity presence as a good sign. We really put on a show for him, since Talia had just died.

We called it an accident. But we all know Moon pushed her off the tower. Steven, previously quiet, is now basically silent. Talia wanted him to leave with her. I don't remember how I found out. But everyone knows everything here. Talia couldn't have expected Moon to just let that happen. Steven, in a strange way, belongs to her.

Joe came into my room, drunk and rambling, the night after they buried Talia. I can't believe he used to work in some high-powered tech job; he's such a little boy. Trading his profession to be a low-level videographer and photographer, recording every amazing thing Moon and Sol do. He started crying, asking me what to do. I kept my mouth shut. I don't trust anyone, but him specifically—he hasn't been sleeping with Moon in a while, but he still does whatever she wants. It could've been another test.

Clint, though, seemed like a possible savior. I had to be careful, not revealing too much too quickly. He'd always wanted to live on an artist commune, so I kept up the charade, showing him my sculptures. I've been too exhausted to make any for a long time, but I still have the three from years ago: one of my head, one of my mother's, and one of Sebastian's. I made a sculpture of my father, too, but threw it off the tower so it would shatter below.

But Clint's smart; he started to see it after only a month or so. How we all smile on cue, but it doesn't reach our eyes. How Moon and Sol control literally everything we do. He also thought the cave was creepy, especially after Moon sent Dionysus's stiff body into the hole. The poor dog was old, yes, but Talia's death devastated him. A week later, he died in his sleep. Moon was heartbroken, crying for days.

We had a funeral down there, where Moon howled over Dionysus's body and then tossed it into "the portal." She thought he was now in some other world, energetic and free.

"Are you listening to me?" Clint snapped a finger in front of my face. I do this—drift off—more and more. It's not unpleasant, actually.

"I want to come with you." I'm sprawled on his bed as he packs. "But I already told you the only way I can do it."

"I'm not going to steal a fucking *car*."

I bought the car. But if I say it and it somehow gets back to Moon, she'll be furious.

"Then I'm not leaving," I say instead.

"Why?" He stops, staring down at me. He's handsome, with broad shoulders and that deep cleft in his chin. I slept with him, not out of attraction but as a way of making him feel more committed to me. Like that worked.

"They won't let me." I've already explained this to him.

"Catherine, you have agency."

I've explained this too. It's clear he doesn't want to really take it in. So I force myself to smile. "It's fine, Clint. It's time for you to go. It's okay."

"But . . ." He touches the back of his head, agitated. "Fuck. Here." He opens a book on the table, tears out a scrap, and scribbles something down. "Here's my cell phone. My email. I want you to contact me if you need anything. All right?"

"Sure." I don't have a phone—I lost my cell service and then the phone itself years ago. But if it makes him feel better.

"That ceremony with Grace—that's tomorrow?" he asks.

"Yeah." It's finally happening. Moon has for whatever reason declared that Grace is the good sister who offered to sacrifice herself. I wondered if she would have let Clint watch the ceremony, given what's going to happen.

"Seriously, call me anytime." He sits beside me. "I'll fly back from New York if you need me. Yeah?"

"Sure."

He kisses me. "They don't get to control you, you know."

"I know."

"Here." Karen sets a bowl in front of me. "Hon, you need to eat. You didn't have anything for dinner."

I nod, unable to speak. Moon just shoved Thea into the hole, and now everyone is shoveling food into their mouths. We're having a nice little late-night snack. Disposing of people is apparently hard work. Moon is chatting about something, her tone normal. My brain refuses to translate the words; they sound like a foreign language. Whatever Sol made me take seems to be wearing off, but slowly.

The loop keeps playing in the back of my mind like a flickering TV screen: Thea's arms pincered by Jonah and Sol. Her shrill screams echoing in the rocky chamber. The sound abruptly cutting off as her head disappears into the water.

I raise a spoonful of beans to my mouth, but my lips won't open. Karen continues to watch me across the table. She still looks awful. Joe looks dazed, eyes glassy like he's high, which maybe he is. Steven stares down at his plate. He's moving his food around but only pretending to eat. Is this how he felt after Talia? Wondering why he didn't do anything to stop it?

I touch the diamond at my throat. Before the session where Grace pushed me in, Moon asked for it, saying metals couldn't be near the vortex. Maybe she wanted a memento to remember me by. But tonight she grabbed it from the altar and it's back around my neck, like a shackle.

Sol watches me, eyes at half-mast. He looks unconcerned, but I know that's a trick. He's always lying in wait, a snake waiting to strike.

"You okay, dear?" he asks.

I manage to understand his words, to nod.

"I know that wasn't easy."

Moon glances at him sharply. "It was beautiful, Sol. We didn't have enough time to help Thea understand, but it had to happen. And you can already feel it, can't you?" She wiggles her fingers. "She's in the next realm, looking down on us. Helping to start the shift."

"Sure." Sol nods. "I'm just glad we're moving into this next phase. Did I tell you all that Ramit's coming back next month? And bringing some of his friends." He smiles, delighted. "And Dawne's going to connect us with someone she knows, this girl on a reality show. She has *millions* of followers."

Moon's frowning. "I don't know if we need to talk about that right now."

"I know, I'm just excited." He leans over and kisses her on the cheek. "It's a big deal. Now that we've gotten through this—uh, process, we can finally concentrate on the Center."

She gazes at him. "Well, let's keep the focus on Thea for now. We owe her a lot."

I sit on the bed in the gathering dusk. I stare at the handcuffs that are still fixed to the bedframe.

I did this. I brought her here.

But it was meant to happen. I knew as soon as I saw her in the hospital, walking up to me with that face, that hair. I felt a sudden urge to pull it, a little girl yanking another's pigtail.

There are no coincidences, Moon's voice whispered in my ear.

And though I was groggy, seeing Thea gave me a hit of adrenaline. This woman looked like me and more than that, she *felt* like something to me. Unlike Grace, who'd never seemed like a sister in any sense of the word.

So I asked Thea about herself, her background—Moon said that siblings from past lifetimes often have similar genetic heritages—and her birthday, just to make sure. And as we spoke, my chest filled with something, a heavy, vibrating certainty that climbed up my throat, threatening to break out into a triumphant, primal scream.

Moon was right. I had a twin. It *was* true.

And if it was true, then I had to play my part. But it wouldn't be too hard; Thea had been waiting her whole life to meet me. The one trick was getting her to follow me in a way where she'd think it was her idea. I knew if I asked her outright to come to the Center, she'd be suspicious. But if she thought I was in trouble, she'd want to help.

My full name was on my hospital bracelet; I knew we had limited time before Moon and Sol showed up. All I had to do was write a note, hide it in a crayon box. And she appeared like clockwork days later.

I had to continuously convince myself—by observing her through the purple door, watching her sleep, searching her things. But even though I knew it was true, a dark dread filled me. If Thea was my sister, then I was going to watch my sister die. Somehow the vortex had spit me out, but if she was the right priestess, then she'd be lost to me forever.

And so I spent the hours in my room or in the cave praying, fervently asking whoever or whatever was out there to get Thea to leave. I even told her to outright. I agreed to leave with her if we could do it the right way, when everyone else was asleep. She said yes, then failed me, getting caught up in Moon and Sol's web.

Now, I lift up the mattress and pull out the diary. Her young handwriting pierces through my numbness. I slam it shut and breathe for a while. And soon I can feel it, that sinking back into the place where nothing exists. Where the horrors I've seen are just a dream.

Here I can acknowledge that I betrayed my sister. I told her to go, but only after I'd summoned her. It felt inevitable to stuff that note into the crayon box when Rachel left the conference room to go to the bathroom, but had it been? I'd known Moon and

Sol would appear shortly—I could feel it. But I could've kept my mouth shut. Thea wasn't even there that morning.

But *could* I have stopped it? Moon would say it's destiny.

Thea's voice comes to me: *They lied to us in that other lifetime, right? Why is everyone trusting them now? They're bad people. We know that.*

It's a good question. I guess it really doesn't sound logical when you look at it like that. All I can say is that Moon explained it to me and it made sense at the time. She has an answer for everything. And now it's too late. Maybe I'd briefly let myself imagine going to New York with Thea, but I'd known even then that it was a fantasy.

I will never leave.

I walk out of my room, pushing Thea's diary down the back of my pants. I need to hide it somewhere, bury it, so Moon or Sol can't touch it and contaminate it. It's the one thing I can do for her. I slow as I near Karen's bedroom. There's a gap between the bottom of the door and the frame, and in the silence, I can hear her talking to someone. I bend down and press my ear to the opening.

"I have to turn the Wi-Fi back off soon." She speaks in a low voice. "When can you get here?" She waits. "I called the police last time. And you know what happened. We waited three days— yes. Just get here."

Her words are a riddle. I close my eyes, leaning my weight on the doorframe. I'm so, so tired.

"This is my fault, Clint. I was their mother. And I'm still supposed to protect . . ." She chokes up.

Clint? Why is she talking to Clint?

"She's acting strange. I guess we all are." Karen sniffles. "I don't know, she might be too far gone. And Moon—no. Absolutely not. I told you, it's a past life takeover. Her former self is now controlling her . . . yeah." She waits. "I know. But this is how it had to happen. Once we get them out, we can leave. It's the only way to end the pattern. Yes. Sedatives—yes. I will."

Karen's footsteps come towards me. I back away, return to my room.

I open the top desk drawer, where I put Clint's scrap of paper. It's gone.

I sit on the bed. I should tell Moon. I'm required to. But if I know, she can probably sense it.

I lie down. There's something else I know. Not in detail, but vague outlines, like a halo.

Whatever I do or don't do, it doesn't matter.

Very few of us are going to make it out of here alive.

53

The hole sucked me in; even as I planned to catch myself, I was hurtling through a tunnel, fast as a water park slide, paralyzed by the freezing-cold water. I hadn't taken a deep enough breath, and now I gasped and water rushed in, filling my mouth and throat and lungs.

I'm drowning. The next few seconds stretched out, my chest on fire, my brain shutting down with panic, and then I was slamming against something and my head broke the water.

For a few seconds, all that mattered was inhaling oxygen and coughing and vomiting out the water. But then in the pitch-black and waist-deep water I noticed things touching me.

Something small and hard bumped against my calf. And something much bigger and softer pressed into my back.

I froze. Silky hair fanned against my palm.

I screamed and struggled in the other direction, back to where I came out, but the tunnel's flow was too much, too strong. I felt around the walls. *I cannot be stuck in this water with—*

There was a ledge. I could feel its bumpy but relatively flat surface. I hoisted myself up, from cold water into cold air. It was barely big enough for me; I tried to sit up and my head hit the ceiling, so I hunched over, then lay down. I could fit on my side.

Grace is dead. She's dead. She's dead.

The knowledge squeezed my chest and my throat with dread.

What happened? Did she hit her head on her way here? Did she drown?

Now that I knew, I could smell it, sweet and sickly. Rotting flesh. I gagged and threw up over the side of the ledge.

But why did she smell if she'd died one day ago? I thought of what had bumped against my leg. There was someone or something else in here too. Something that had been here longer.

Okay. I was on the verge of it—a frenzy, a hysteria, that would hold me in its grip and not let go. I needed to breathe. *Good*. Now I needed to take stock. I moved different body parts. My head ached horribly from when Sol had dropped me in the cave, but otherwise I felt okay. I rubbed my goose-bumped arms. It was freezing. Should I take off my wet clothes? Would that be better or worse? I pulled off my jacket, opening it on the ledge to dry.

Something was pressing into my upper thigh. Karen had slipped something in my pocket right before they'd shoved me in.

It was a tiny key chain flashlight wrapped in plastic.

Oh thank god. I ripped open the plastic and a piece of paper fell out. "Shit!" I lunged but it was too late: the paper was consumed by the churning water.

Another sob lodged in my throat. I had to stay calm. Karen was trying to help me. She'd given me this flashlight because somehow she'd known where I'd end up.

I needed to use the light to take stock. But suddenly I didn't want to, the aversion so strong it took my breath away. I didn't want to see where I was. What was in here with me.

Do it, Thea. I gritted my teeth, clicked it on.

It was worse in the light. Much worse.

I was indeed trapped in a tiny chamber. It was filled with water, rushing from the tunnel to my left and continuing out to my right. But the tunnel out wasn't intact; it broke into smaller holes, all the size of my fist or smaller. The water rushed through but trapped me inside.

No way out. That's why Grace was trapped in here with me. I'd disturbed her body, and now her head bumped against the hole-filled wall. I thought randomly of an exercise I'd been taught in the high school gym unit on swimming—if you were in the middle of the ocean, waiting to be rescued, you'd position yourself like this: arms out, head down. Only Grace couldn't raise her head to take a breath. Her wet neon hair was subdued, a rich copper in the blue-tinged light. And something else floated next to her: a small creature covered in glossy black fur. A dog? A whiff of that rotting scent: it was the animal, further along in death.

They were so close. If I leaned over the ledge, I could touch them.

I shuddered, turning off the light.

I was trapped in this tiny space with two corpses.

I screamed.

I stopped only when my throat felt raw, then curled my head into my arms. My brain felt disconnected; I couldn't comprehend why I was here.

No. I had to think. I had to fucking *think*. Catherine had gotten out of here. I needed to remember that. I just had to figure out how.

I clicked the flashlight again. Had she climbed back out against the current? I plunged my hand beneath the water, but the flow felt too strong. I also couldn't remember how long the tunnel had been. I knew my panic had probably stretched it out, but it hadn't been short.

I played the light all around the cave walls. I even desperately pushed at the ceiling, but the rock was, of course, solid and unyielding.

"Fuck," I whispered. I shoved the flashlight deep in my pocket and rubbed my arms, my legs. This was bad. This was very, very bad.

I forced myself to take deep breaths. Karen had given me this flashlight. Why? If only I hadn't dropped the fucking note. It could've said anything from *Help is on the way* to *I'm sorry, hon.*

I thought of Catherine's bloodied fingertips at the hospital. She'd tried to crawl out of the tunnel. Had she succeeded?

I thought of her blank eyes, staring at Block D's wall. I'd been so curious what had happened to her. What was so horrifying that it had shut her brain down.

Well, now I knew.

54

There was no way to follow the passage of time down here.

I stared into the darkness for what felt like hours, then somehow fell asleep. I woke on the ledge. I felt clear and calm; some part of my psyche had risen from the depths, ready to deal with the situation. The tears had dried up. I knew what I had to do: go back up the tunnel.

I found a little circular hole in the wall to act as a cubby for the flashlight. I couldn't risk it falling into the water, being carried away. I practiced holding my breath, counting the seconds, until I felt dizzy. By the time I dropped into the water, I was certain I'd be out of here soon. I braced myself to touch the bodies, which had resubmerged, but they stayed near the exit holes.

The first time I tried to swim up the tunnel, it felt like pushing into a block of cement. I managed to get a few feet in before the water pummeled me back. Determinedly, I went in again, grasping the edge of the tunnel, trying to launch myself through. But I lost my grip and the water pushed me back once more.

I tried several more times, hardly stopping for breath, until white dots sparkled in my vision. Finally, I pulled myself back onto the ledge. At least my efforts had warmed me up; I was no longer shivering.

I tried to puzzle it out. Grace must've died on her way in here; otherwise she'd be on this ledge, wouldn't she? I could only hope it had been quick.

Eventually, I dropped back into the water, using my hands and feet to feel all around in case there was another tunnel I'd missed. I gently moved the bodies with my foot, holding in a whimper. They were just bodies. Grace was long gone.

Back on the ledge, I cried some more, but I was so exhausted the sobs quickly subsided. A strange thought arose: *What's better to be trapped in, endless sand or constricted rock?* It sounded like a riddle. I closed my eyes and saw the desert stretching out around me. Catherine was beside me — her body, at least. She'd just died and I would soon follow.

Disturbed, I opened my eyes. I was back in the cold, wet darkness. Closed: sun-razed desert.

I forced my eyes to stay open. There were colors, patterns in the darkness. I wondered if I could make myself pass out — by holding my breath or slamming the back of my head onto the rock. I needed oblivion. I needed not to be here. Panic was prickling at my arms and legs. I opened and closed my fists; my fingers had gone numb.

Calm down. You're okay. You're okay.

But that was the funny part: I *wasn't* okay. I was here, and it was my fault. I'd known something was wrong, and I'd stayed anyway. I could be in my bed in New York right now, cozily reading or watching something on my phone. Instead, I was trapped. And unless I could figure out a way to escape, I was going to die.

I slept and woke up in cycles. My teeth chattered. When my feet went numb I started doing clamshells on my side to get my blood flowing. When I was thirsty I lifted palmfuls of water from where it came out. When I was hungry I tried to ignore it.

I puzzled over Catherine's words, trying to find clues.

It must've spit me out. I wasn't the right one.

I was in there, and then suddenly I was with you.

How had it spit her out? Why wasn't she able to fucking remember?

A fiery fury filled me. I screamed and slapped the rock walls and almost fell off the ledge. The anger drained quickly.

I couldn't climb back out. I'd searched; there were no other exits. There was literally nothing I could do. The realization filled me with both bitterness and a strange kind of relief.

I was drifting back into sleep when I heard it: a soft hiss over the burbles of the water. I lifted myself on my elbow, grabbed the flashlight and turned it on. There was nothing there.

After a minute I put the flashlight back. I needed to conserve it.

But then the sound came again.

"What is that?" I said aloud.

A voice answered in my head: *You know who I am.*

The voice was low and resonant. I recognized it immediately.

Oh, okay, I responded mentally. *Sure. You're the snake spirit thing from the desert.*

It was clear what was happening: some part of my psyche was coming up in this form, trying to comfort me. Well, why the hell not. It wasn't like I had any better options. Maybe this tucked-away corner of my brain remembered something I didn't.

Can you help me? I asked it.

Help you?

How did Catherine get out?

She was born.

The vague words frustrated me. Maybe this wouldn't help.

Suddenly, the voice was outside of me, speaking directly into my ear and making me jump. "You are a priestess. You have more power than you know." It paused. "Can you see it?"

"See what?" I responded out loud. Now I was straight-up hallucinating.

"Look."

Lines glowed above me on the ceiling, outlining a square.

"Is that the way out?" I whispered.

"In a sense." Something scaly and cold slid past my arm. "You need to go through if you want to see."

Was I asleep? I shifted, feeling the rough surface underneath me. The door disappeared.

"Not your body," the snake hissed. "Your spirit."

"But how . . ." I went still and the door came back. I closed my eyes, and it remained. It took a while to figure it out, how to get up without moving my body. It was like looking at a magic eye illustration; you had to relax into it. Finally, I was sitting up and pushing the door, my body lying below me like a discarded skin.

A laugh bubbled up deep inside. *Now I'm* really *losing it.*

But I pushed it away. Hallucinatory or not, it was better than lying there, cold and terrified. I pressed upwards, and the door swung up as if on a hinge. I peered into the empty space. Pitch-black here, too, but the air felt different, heavy and viscous. A pressure against my skin, so increasingly intense I cried out.

Then: nothing.

55

Faint beeping noises, hushed voices. I blinked open my eyes. Dom was sitting on the plastic chair near the hospital bed, on her phone.

"Dom?" I croaked.

She lifted her head. "Oh my god, Thea!" She jumped up and paused, hovering above me. "You're awake. Let me get a nurse —"

"No." I sat up, the blue sheets falling to my lap. "Wait. Tell me what's going on."

"Do you remember?" Dom gripped the metal bar of the bed. "Do you remember what happened?"

"Uh . . ." I actually *couldn't* remember. I'd been in a cold, dark, awful space. But where? What had been happening?

"Don't worry about it." Dom waved her hand. "Do you feel okay?"

"I think so." We were in a curtained-off area. Someone on the other side was whispering urgently, presumably into their phone.

We were at the hospital. I felt a pure, sweet relief. I was okay. I was safe.

"Amani called me, and I came as soon as I could. Your parents are flying in." Dom exhaled. "I'm so glad you're okay. I was worried."

"Where's Catherine?" I asked.

She looked at me blankly. "Who?"

The woman in the next room raised her voice. "You don't know what I've been through!"

The back of my neck prickled. Something felt off. I started sliding my legs over the side of the bed.

"Just calm down." Dom leaned over me, hissing into my ear. "Stay there. Don't let them hear you."

"Who?"

Her eyes widened, her mouth stretched into a frightening grimace. "I don't know. But this hospital — it's weird. I tried to talk to a doctor, but . . ." She stared past me, suddenly mute, mouth hanging open. I twisted around to see what she was looking at: a laminated pain assessment scale with cartoon happy faces ranging from ecstatic to anguished.

"They all died." Now the woman in the next bed sounded mournful. "My brother. My boyfriend. Didn't you know that?"

I tried to push Dom backwards so I could stand, but my wrist was bound. Cold fear filled my chest as I saw I was handcuffed to the bed.

"No." I pulled against it.

"Oh, okay." Dom nodded, slipping back into the chair. "The doctor's coming now."

I shrank into the bed, raising my knees, preparing myself.

Someone yanked the curtain back.

"Hi there." The doctor had blue eyes and a sandy beard. I knew him from somewhere. He grinned. "Ready to feel better?" He held up a needle dripping with clear liquid.

I screamed.

"For heaven's sake." Mom shook me. "Just wake up."

I sat up in bed. I'd been dreaming about a hospital, someone coming towards me with a needle . . .

"Let's get this show on the road. You're going to be late." Mom looked tired, her face pale against her teal pantsuit. She dressed up to drive me to school, waving merrily to other parents in the drop-off zone. Then she came home and changed into sweatpants. Then put the nicer clothes back on before Dad got home. Keeping up appearances.

"I don't want to go." My voice was small and whiny. "My stomach hurts."

"Your stomach *always* hurts." She strode out. Daylight streamed in the windows, lighting up the collage of Catherine and Sebastian pictures I'd taped to the wall. Their lives were so colorful and sparkling, whereas mine felt dreary and gray. They could be together at this very moment. My chest ached, even more strongly than my stomach cramps.

"*Hurry up!*" Mom yelled.

I padded into the kitchen. The sadness shifted into anger. Mom didn't care that my stomach hurt every morning before school. She didn't care at all.

In the dining room, she crouched down, scrubbing at the floor with a pink sponge. Her red hair hung in a frizzy braid down her back.

The cereal box was on the counter. I went to the stove and picked up the cast-iron skillet with both hands. It was even heavier than I'd anticipated. I crept behind her and raised it up as high as I could before bringing it down on her skull.

The impact broke my vision into particles like a mirror smashing; when my sight reconfigured I was in a different kitchen. A dark-haired woman slumped at the table, but there was no blood. I was no longer holding a skillet but an empty vodka bottle. It smelled in here: rotting food and unwashed dog. A squeal came from the doorway: a small mutt was whining at me. Ranger. He was hungry. I put the bottle on the table and went to the dog food bag, but it was empty. I got some stale bread from the fridge and put it on the floor, and he tore into it.

"Hey." Steven stood at the entrance of the kitchen. But he was young, sixteen at most, acne sprinkling his cheeks. "You didn't come to school today."

"I couldn't get a ride." I was also sixteen, but Mom had forgotten to sign me up for driver's ed. First she'd had the funeral to take care of. Then she'd fallen into a deep well of depression and now barely spoke. I didn't even know if she'd been fired from her job or if they'd given her leave.

"I told you to call me." Steven took a step forward. "I can pick you up."

"Yeah, the phone's out."

"Oh." His eyes snaked around the room, landed on Mom. "I'll get you tomorrow. I'm just down the street, you know."

Ranger finished eating and went over to Steven, wagging his tail. Steven bent and petted him, distracted.

"Do you ever feel like you want to destroy someone?" I asked.

"Sarah." He focused on the dog, stroking his chin. "You shouldn't say things like that."

Was my name Sarah? I thought I had a different name, but I couldn't remember what it was. Though I was pretty sure it started with an *M*.

"Not, like, random people," I said, brushing the thought aside. "Bad people. Bad people who deserve to be destroyed." Starting with Dr. Miller, the man who'd started my brother Jason on pills he couldn't stop taking.

"I guess so." Steven considered. "Like vigilantism?"

The word impressed me. "Yeah."

"How are you going to do that?"

"I don't know." I sat on the floor, suddenly exhausted. "I was just reading about these shamans in India who can stop their own hearts. And then start them again. Isn't that wild? I wonder if you could do that to someone else. Make their hearts stop."

"Who knows." He shifted. "You know, we should go to India someday."

"Yeah right." I snorted.

He shrugged, clearly wanting to take it back.

"Okay, sure. I'll go with you." Steven's always loved me. He'd do anything for me. It's sweet. But I'm never going to love him back. Maybe before I could've, but now there's a hole inside of me and the sounds coming out of it are so loud I can't hear anything else.

"After Mexico?" he asked.

"After Mexico." That made me smile. Ever since Ella brought photos to school in eighth grade from her trip to Cancún, I'd fantasized about being there. The palm trees, the white sand, the endless blue ocean . . . I could smell the sunscreen, feel the gentle breeze.

Mom let out a snore at the table.

"Is that his?" Steven motioned with his chin. "Was it, I mean? Jason's?"

I was holding a weathered baseball in my hand.

"Yeah." I rolled it towards Ranger, who whimpered and backed away.

"Oh, hey." Steven pulled a camera from his backpack. He trained it on me, smiling faintly. "Say cheese."

The flashes blinded me, though I kept the grin plastered on my face. If I stopped for even a split second, that's the picture they'd use.

Sebastian squeezed my hand. He knew how much I hated premieres. And this would be the worst one of all. I'd have to sit there in a theater filled with hundreds of people, including my parents, and watch myself—well, my body double, Sophia, who looks exactly like me—naked on the screen.

We'd drunk tequila and smoked weed in the limo, and it had softened the panic a little bit, but not enough. I'd had to fight Dad not to take me as his date; that's what he'd wanted. But in a rare show of resistance, Mom told him it wouldn't look right. For once he'd listened to her.

I wondered if anyone would know we were high; we'd used eye drops, but they didn't always work. Nothing to do but let Sebastian lead me. The chaos of journalists and fans was like a hurricane whirling around us. It slowed a little as we paused in front of the backdrop to pose. Sebastian picked up my hand to kiss it, and the clicks increased. He'd cried in the car, but I'd been too numb to do or say much of anything.

This movie had started with my dreams, but it wasn't really about me. Dad had taken it over, controlling it, like he did to everything. I hadn't wanted to be in it. I didn't want to be an actor, period, but when I was eight I'd told Mom and he'd locked me in my room for a full day.

I should've realized back then my life isn't really mine. Maybe if I had a sibling, someone else to take up some of his attention, it wouldn't be this way. But it probably would. I'm his favorite, no matter what. People tell me how lucky I am that he's so invested in me. They don't realize it's actually a curse.

"I've got some coke," Sebastian whispered as we finally walked into the theater.

"Good." It would help me feel more awake; currently I just wanted to lie down on the red carpet and sleep. I closed my eyes, but this time they wouldn't open. Sebastian gripped my arm. "Cath, what are you—" But his hand and voice were suddenly ripped away.

"Time to wake up."

I jerked upright and almost fell off the tiny cot. I was in a small, circular space, the ceiling too low for me to sit up fully. The pitch black softened into the barest amount of light. There was nothing in this space—just me, the cot, and what looked like a chair carved into the floor.

"Would you like to rest longer?" the female voice asked. "I thought you wanted to keep on a regular sleep cycle."

"It's okay." I cleared my throat. Where was I? Whose voice was this? It seemed to be coming from all around me.

"Sit and I'll open the window," she instructed. I slipped out of the cot and dropped into the chair. The blackness in front of me melted into the unmistakable view of space.

Was this a ride? It seemed like something they'd have at Disney . . .

Then I remembered. I was in the cave, and this was a dream. Of *course* I was dreaming of space. It's how *Stargirl* ended, wasn't it? I just had to watch out for that knife.

"No knives on board," the voice said. "Unnecessary for food preparation."

"Great." And I realized that I felt full, comfortably so. It was a relief from the jagged shards of hunger.

It all locked into place: this was a future life. We were sometime far in the future. But why was I alone? The memories were cloudy, trapped behind warped glass. I'd been on a ship with others, but . . .

"Something happened to Catherine." I was suddenly sure of it. I started to stand. "I have to help her."

"You already helped her. She's safe." The speaker's name materialized: Aurora. She was an operating system, and I'd chosen her voice out of five options.

"Oh." I sank back down again. "That's a relief."

"I'm glad you feel comforted."

"Something happened—there was a fight, or an attack, or something?" The knowledge trickled in. "And I'm in an escape pod, but it's damaged. I made Catherine take the one that still works."

"Correct."

"How much time do we have left?"

"Five days." Aurora said it solemnly.

"And we're . . ."

"Eight months from the nearest station."

"Thank you." Strangely, I felt a lack of concern about my imminent demise. It didn't feel quite real. I just had to remember to turn off Aurora towards the end. I didn't want her to be conscious as she drifted in space for thousands of years. That would be cruel.

"You needed time to grieve," Aurora said, apropos of nothing. Maybe she was starting to glitch. "Time to heal. Everyone has their missions, but they need to happen in the right time and the right order. You have to go through the anger first. Why wouldn't you be angry?"

"I don't know." Her words seemed somehow appropriate, though I didn't know what she was referring to. Maybe I was finally losing my mind. It would've happened a lot earlier if I didn't have Aurora. She was programmed to have her own personality, so we'd even had a few fights.

"Would you like me to tell you a story?" she finally asked.

"I actually want to pull up a dream." I'd been having a lot of dreams lately. Some of them were about a colorful castle in the middle of the desert. There was a pool with lounge chairs, where I could smell real flowers and feel the actual warmth of sun on my skin.

"Of course."

"The sunny one, Aurora. Not the one in the cave. Please."

She didn't respond, maybe irritated that I'd called out her mistake. But she'd messed it up on multiple occasions. And I didn't want to be back in that dark, cold space.

"So Catherine's still okay?" I couldn't help but ask. "She's alive?"

"I am no longer in contact with her capsule. But all signs point to yes."

"Good." I exhaled. I hadn't been able to save the others. I imagined their particles dispersing into the void. I opened the map, zoomed in on our solar system, traced the lines.

"Maybe we'll make it back home," I said.

"It's possible." Aurora was programmed to be optimistic.

"Okay, I'm ready."

"Recorded dream ready to play."

I lay back and closed my eyes. "Play."

I was back in the cave.

Damnit, Aurora. I told you I didn't want . . .

I blinked into the darkness. It took a second to settle into reality. I really was in the cave. Aurora and the space capsule had been a dream.

But it had been so realistic. They'd all been. Being in Catherine's body at the premiere, in Moon/Sarah's at her house after her brother had died. Back in my thirteen-year-old bedroom. And all of us experiencing that specific void I'd thought was only within me.

Moon would say the trauma stemmed from a past life pattern. But at a young age, in *this* lifetime, we'd faced neglect, betrayal, even abuse. All of us had longed more than anything for connection, affection, hope. In a word: love.

I shifted and couldn't feel my legs. Desperately, I scrambled for the key chain and clicked it. *There.* My feet were white and wrinkled, but they were there. I slapped and rubbed them, and slowly they began to tingle, coming back to life. Eventually, I clicked off the light and slipped it back into the cubbyhole, pulling my legs up into my chest. I felt sleepy. I realized I was no longer shivering. No longer hungry either.

I'd been down here for some time. Two days? Three? I knew it should take weeks to starve, but with the cold, the exposure, it would probably be much faster. My body already felt like it was starting to shut down.

I closed my eyes, pushing the hideous thoughts away, and suddenly a brilliant kaleidoscope of colors burst into existence, blinking and shifting. I was being shown something significant, but I couldn't quite grasp it. I marveled, taking it in.

There was something special about this place—Moon was right. But like the snake, it wasn't good or evil. Moon was the one who'd imbued it with her own psychic rage. And anger was fine, it was good even, but you couldn't get stuck there.

Easy for me to say. I'd done the same exact thing. And I hadn't even realized the rage was there, buried under the surface. My desire to help covering up my desire to harm. The anger turning in on itself, working to destroy me—with the societally approved poison of alcohol, with self-flagellation and shame. I'd told myself I was broken, when I wasn't, not at all. I might have spent the rest of my life believing these lies.

I heard singing. It sounded like a choir in a Christmas Eve service—one of the very few times I hadn't minded being in church. I pictured my corpse melting into bones. The music got louder, ringing in my ears.

And then: a light. A tiny speck that grew brighter until I had to close my eyes, pressing my palms against them. Was the waiting over already?

It wasn't a cliché. This was really what happened when you died.

56

"Hey. It's all right. You're okay." A male voice with an Australian accent, a heavy hand on my shoulder, warm breath on my face.

"Clint?" It was the faux therapist who'd shown up at the hospital: Mikki's Reddit contact. Former member. Here to save the day?

A ripple of relief, of joy—but I wasn't yet ready to believe this was happening. I'd had enough vivid dreams in here to know I could be ripped into wakefulness at any time.

"Yes, I'm Clint. Good to see you." He paused. "That's Grace, isn't it?"

"Yeah."

Another pause. "All right. Can you open your eyes for me?"

It took a minute or two, but finally I was able to manage the light from the headlamp strapped to his forehead. I had to force myself to pay attention as he handed me a respirator and showed me how to grab onto him with my arms and legs. He explained something about pulling us via small handholds in the tunnel while also being pulled by a rope attached to his harness, but the sound of his voice was like a barrage after the silence of the past few days, and I could barely process it.

"Just keep your eyes closed," he instructed.

And then the respirator was over my mouth, and we were entering the tunnel. It was slow going; we were basically trying to push our way up a waterfall. Clint's wet-suited body moved and shifted below my chest. I couldn't feel my legs, but I was determined to keep them clamped around his hips. I shoved my respirated face against his neck, sure the equipment was going to fly off my head at any second, that the air would be replaced by cold water. I squeezed my eyes tight, my mind blank, not yet ready to accept that this was really happening.

After what felt like hours, but must've been only minutes, the tunnel ended and we broke through the surface. Hands pulled us out, unlatched us, and set us down. On my back, I let my jaw relax and my eyes open. The vastness of the cave stretched above me. I'd never physically felt this much open space.

"Okay, let's get her out of these." Karen was above me, unzipping my sweatshirt. I'd left my damp coat behind. I realized I'd also left the key chain flashlight in its little cubby and felt a small, inexplicable stab of loss.

"Oh my god." Mikki crouched above me, eyes wide. "Thea. Holy shit."

"Let's hurry." Karen pulled at me to sit up and lifted my shirt over my head. "Clint, you ready for round two? How is she?"

"I'm sorry, Karen." He was pulling off his harness. "She didn't make it."

Karen continued to stare at him, perplexed.

"You mean . . ." Mikki trailed off. "Grace—"

"Listen, our first order of business is to get Thea to a hospital." Clint straightened. "We call SOS as soon as we get upstairs. Karen, I'm sorry, we'll have to recover her body later."

Karen nodded, her expression fixed, but tears flowed down her cheeks.

"I'm sorry." My voice sounded scratchy and gruff. I wanted to tell her it had happened quickly, but after the deprivation tank–like time in the cave, all of this—the harsh yet soft words, the two women taking off my clothes and putting dry ones on, the light of the lanterns—felt completely overwhelming.

Mikki was also stoically crying, wiping away tears as she worked sweatpants onto my legs. Karen slipped wool socks over my feet, which were tingling and coming back to life. *Ahh.* Nothing had ever felt so good. The warmth was sensuous, luxurious. Mikki fitted a knit cap over my head. I wanted to thank them but suddenly had to vomit. Nothing but bile came out.

Clint hunched down. "Thea, we're going to go piggyback. Ready?"

Karen and Mikki helped me to my feet. My legs were weak and wobbly, but I remained upright. Clint hefted me up and started swiftly over the rocky terrain. Mikki and Karen followed, lighting our way with lanterns, Mikki hauling a duffel bag.

I glanced back, but the gurgling hole was now in darkness.

Clint didn't stumble once. I had the dazed feeling that I was riding a horse, feeling a strong body's mechanics between my legs. We got to the entry chamber, went straight to the stairs. Clint climbed the steep steps like a machine. His confident physicality felt calming. But I couldn't relax until we were in his car, barreling away from this wretched place.

We reached the top of the stairs, up into the little closet-like room. Clint pushed the door open. The studio was dark, and the familiar scent of paint and ceramic dust reached my nostrils.

Then the light went on. I cried out, pushing my face into Clint's shoulder. He stopped short.

"What a nice surprise." Sol's voice was conversational. "Clint, you didn't want to stop and say hi to us?"

Something broke in my chest, and I yelped. *No.* Not when we were so close to getting out.

"Hi, Sol." Clint let go of my legs, and I slid to the ground, blinking my eyes open. Karen slipped an arm around my waist; she was surprisingly strong too. Mikki was on Clint's other side. Sol and Moon stood in the middle of the room, with Joe and Steven flanking them. Behind, Catherine leaned against the open doorway. She stared at me, her eyes round and blank. The diamond necklace from the cave altar was back on her neck, glittering in the light.

Joe looked uncomfortable, his gaze darting around.

"Hey!" Mikki struggled to hold on to the duffel bag Steven was pulling away from her. With a final yank, he had it, and backed towards the front of the room.

"Shit," Karen muttered, so softly only I could hear.

"So what brings you here, man?" Sol grinned. Moon was silent, staring at Clint, her expression unreadable. "I guess I don't actually need to ask. You must've done this before, huh? It's how you got Cath out. With your scuba gear." He let out a sharp laugh. "The cave diver, of course! I can't believe I didn't think about that. I figured Cath found some kind of aqueduct and crawled back up. *Nope.*" Sol reached into the back of his waistband and pulled out a gun. "Stop right now."

Clint's phone was in his hand. Moon darted forward and snatched it. She turned to Mikki, palm out. Mikki's eyes were trained on the gun. It looked like Joe's—was it the same one? Mikki pulled her phone from her back pocket and gave it to Moon with shaking fingers. Still holding me with one arm, Karen used her free hand to do the same.

"You did it last time, right? You drugged us." Moon shook a playful finger at her, backing away. "The former nurse. I wonder what you used in the wine? I remember waking up feeling groggy. Good thing Steven caught you last night. We were able to swap out the bottle without you realizing."

"This has gone too far, Moon." Karen's wobbly voice strengthened. "Your past life self has taken you over. She's controlling you. She's making you do horrible things. Like—Gracie . . ." The tears started once again.

"Karen, I know this is hard for you to understand." Moon's voice softened. "But this is the way it has to be."

"It's doesn't!"

"It does," Moon said. "You of all people should understand martyrdom."

"Hi, Mikki," Sol said. "I shouldn't be surprised to see you here. The girl with no impulse control."

"What are you planning to do?" Mikki asked quietly. "Shove all of us into that hole, one after the other?"

Don't give them any ideas, I wanted to say.

"Guys," Joe said in a low voice. "Why don't we take a beat? Go discuss?"

"I'm sorry, are you in charge here?" Sol asked over his shoulder. "Or can you just shut the fuck up for a second?"

Joe looked away. "Sorry."

"Listen, mates, we can figure this out." Clint held out his arms. "Grace chose to go in, right? Everyone else is alive and well." He indicated me, leaning on Karen. "So let's just take a breath and de-escalate."

Moon sighed. "You messed it up, Clint."

"I'm trying to help you guys." He pointed at me. "If we hadn't gotten her out—"

"This would all be over. My life's purpose completed. Do you know how different things would be?" She continued to smile, but her eyes hardened.

"It's time to give it up, Moon." Clint raised his voice. "A woman is dead because of all this!"

"I should've known." Moon shook her head. Her accent was gone, her voice flat. "That you're on the side of darkness. I should've felt it the moment I met you."

"For god's sake, just stop! Please!" Clint's voice was both sharp and pleading. "It *isn't real*."

Moon launched off her left foot and flew across the room, so quickly she was a blur. It was only at the last second that I saw the flash of silver in her hand.

If she had just pushed him, he could've held his ground. After all, she was much smaller.

But first she plunged a kitchen knife deep into his belly.

He let out a strangled squawk, looking down, and in that confused moment she pushed his chest with all of her might.

He staggered back through the doorway and fell backwards down the stairs.

57

We stood frozen, listening to Clint's grunts and cries for what felt like an eternity until all returned to silence.

Moon stood at the edge of the hole, peering down. Karen clutched me so hard my ribs hurt. My hand was pressed over my mouth. Was Clint dead? He had to be, didn't he? My heart was pounding so hard I thought it might explode.

"Jesus, babe." Sol continued to point the gun in our direction. "Go get the knife." He sounded weary and unhappy but not in the least surprised.

Moon traipsed down the steps.

Behind Sol, Catherine's and Joe's eyes bulged, their faces pale. Even Steven was looking up, his brown eyes round. I considered trying to catch Catherine's gaze, but there was no point. She was a lost cause.

Moon reappeared a minute later. She held the knife in her right hand, the blade clean. There were large dark marks on the stomach of her gray sweatshirt, where for whatever reason she'd wiped the knife off. She returned to Sol's side, looking calmer, though still perturbed. "He's gone." The accent was back.

"It's okay, hon." Karen raised a shaking hand. "Let's just stop this before anyone else gets hurt."

"He's a bad person, Karen." Moon slipped the knife in her back jeans pocket. Her eyes looked a little too wide. "Let's leave them here for now. I need to go meditate on this."

Once they'd locked us in, Karen eased me to the floor. She and Mikki grabbed their lanterns and disappeared down the stairs.

As much as I didn't want to go back down there, I had to see too. On unsteady legs, I went to the stairs. About a third of the way down I had to sit and rest. If I ducked down, I could see the circles of light at the bottom. Clint lay on his back, his left leg twisted underneath him at an odd angle. His blue shirt was black with blood. Mikki was pressing her fingers to his throat.

"Is he okay?" I called absurdly.

Slowly, Karen rose. "No."

"Fuck!" Mikki cried. She jumped and thundered up the stairs past me into the studio. Maybe it was the exhaustion or the hunger, but I felt completely numb. I climbed back up and settled onto the floor, my back against the wall. Mikki paced around the room like a trapped tiger.

"There has to be a way out of here." She spoke quickly. "Karen? Where the fuck is Karen?"

"I think she's coming back up." I put a hand on my stomach. The hunger pains were coming back, sharp as knitting needles.

"*Shit.*" She rubbed her eyes. "This is bad. We're screwed."

"Did you tell anyone you were coming back here?" I asked.

"Yeah. My editor and my sister. But I told them to call the police if I didn't get back to them in twenty-hour hours. It's been, what, four?" She crouched next to me, studying me. "You okay? You don't look good. What was it—a small cave?"

I nodded.

"How small?"

I shrugged. "I don't know. Eight by eight? But half of it was underwater."

"God. And Grace . . ."

I fixated on a long scratch on the wooden floor. "She was there too."

Mikki shook her head. "That must've been . . ."

"I think she hit her head on the way in. Or drowned. And there was some dead animal in there too. A dog." Maybe that dog Sol kept bringing up—Dionysus?

"Christ." Mikki exhaled. "I never would've come here if . . . I had no idea it would go this far. Karen said Grace went in of her own volition."

"Yeah, because she was brainwashed." I shifted. My hips still ached from lying on the rock ledge. "How long was I down there?"

"I guess this is the third night." Mikki shook her head. "It shouldn't have taken this long. But the first night, Karen waited until late to turn on the Wi-Fi and call Clint, who called me. We were going to try last night, but Karen wasn't able to slip the drug into their wine. So we waited until tonight. It was so horrible . . . I wanted to call the police, but Clint said he tried last time. They took it as a prank call, literally didn't even come out here. So he thought we should get you guys out first and then go to the cops." Mikki rubbed her eyes. "Maybe I should've called them anyway, I don't know. But he and Karen just seemed so confident about what to do. And to be honest, I didn't totally believe it was happening. It just seemed too wild. But then I couldn't get ahold of you . . ."

"You're going to have a hell of an article." I leaned the back of my head against the wall. This still felt surreal, like I'd been pulled into a TV show or movie—the colors too bright, voices too loud.

Karen came through the doorway, her face ashen.

"It's a past life takeover," Karen said again, as if it were obvious. "I should've known after what Moon did to Talia." She settled heavily in the desk chair.

Steven's girlfriend—the one Sol said Moon didn't like.

"What did Moon do to her?" I asked.

"Killed her," Karen replied. "Shoved her off the tower."

"You knew she'd killed people?" Mikki stopped and stared at her.

"She said it was an accident. I—we—believed her. But we shouldn't have."

Mikki resumed her pacing. "We need to come up with a plan. A way out."

Karen crouched next to me and pulled a granola bar from her pocket. I tore it open and scarfed it down.

"Are there any exits through the cave?" Mikki asked. "Like, tunnels or anything?"

"Not that I know of." Karen handed me a second bar, which I also basically swallowed.

"You're the only one of us three who knows anything about this place." Mikki's voice turned businesslike. "So think, Karen. You have to help us figure this out."

Karen didn't respond, just stared into space. She seemed shell-shocked.

"No more food?" I asked, and she shook her head.

"We need to get to Clint's car." Mikki bit at her thumbnail. "He parked about a mile out so they wouldn't hear it. Left the keys inside. I ran track in college, so if I get the chance, I'll make a run for it. Hmm.

Maybe we can hit them with something when they come back . . ." She jumped up and started opening drawers.

Karen watched her. "You want to bonk them on the head? They have guns, hon. All of them. The boys liked to go out into the desert and shoot." She sighed. "They took Clint's too."

"Karen." Mikki stood and flung up her hands. "Instead of shitting all over my plans, let's work together here. *Yes, and.* So: You have any ideas?"

"I don't." Karen gazed at me. "But maybe Thea does."

"Why?" Mikki scoffed. "She got here when I got here. She doesn't know anything."

"But she has powers. Both of them do. It's just that Catherine . . . well, her mind hasn't been right since she was down there."

"Karen, please." Mikki dropped her head into her hands. "Please stop talking like that."

"How long was Catherine in the cave?" I asked.

Karen looked down. "It was too long."

"How long?"

"Nine days." Her eyes were wide as she looked up at me. "I should've called Clint earlier, I know. But . . . I didn't. I think I was in shock for a few days. And then finally it kicked in; I knew I needed his help. But then we wasted more time waiting for the police. They never came. So he flew in with his equipment, drove out here. That night I was able to put liquid diphenhydramine in the wine—it seemed to make everyone pass out early. But even then . . ." Karen shook her head. "I didn't think we'd find her alive, to be honest with you. And we did, but she was . . . not okay. Not speaking. Clint didn't even think he could get her on a plane. So he drove her all the way back to New York. To get help for her. But then at a gas station she just got out of the car. Walked out onto the highway. I don't know why."

Nine days. I couldn't fathom it. No wonder Catherine had burrowed deep inside her psyche, shutting off everything around her. The food twisted in my belly, feeling like chunks of concrete.

"I can't believe I listened to you guys," Mikki muttered, slamming a drawer. "'Oh, they'll be fast asleep. They totally won't hear us all the way down there.' Fucking stupid."

"I didn't think she'd do that to Clint." Karen's eyes filled again with tears.

"*Really?*" I scoffed. "After seeing them tie me up, keep me chained to a bed, and throw me in the hole?" The surprise gave me a boost of energy. "After seeing Talia plummet to her death?"

"I've been blind." Karen shook her head. "She blinded me. All of us. I'm sorry."

Mikki had moved on to another set of cabinets, clutching a pair of what looked like pliers.

"What should we do, Thea?" Karen whispered, a note of hope in her voice. "Use your powers."

But I had nothing. I hadn't figured out how to escape the cave—I'd been rescued by Clint, Karen, and Mikki. And I didn't have any ideas that would help us now.

"I'm sorry." I lay down on my left side, the same position from the ledge. I didn't know if it was the sensory overwhelm or the spiking and sinking chemicals from what had just happened, but I could no longer keep my eyes open.

When I woke, though, I knew exactly what we needed to do.

58

An indeterminate amount of time later, there came the scraping sound of the key in the lock.

"Hi, guys," Sol said in a quiet singsong as he eased it open. "How's everyone doing?"

I thought back to the first day of our retreat. *Great!* After the granola bars and nap, I was feeling stronger. It had to be a hormonal response to the situation, my body pushing out a new round of adrenaline. Mikki and Karen had fetched water with one of the buckets, and we'd designated another bucket in the corner as the bathroom. We'd spent hours going over the plan. I had no idea if it would work, but it was better than nothing.

Sol entered, training the gun ahead of him.

"We want to talk to Moon." Karen said her line immediately.

"Is that so, Karen?" Sol glared at her. "Or should I call you Judas? You know, out of everyone, I really trusted you."

"And I trusted *you.*" She shrugged. "But then again, I am drawn to weak and despicable men."

His glower switched to a smile. "Touché."

Steven stood behind him, holding a tray. Outside in the courtyard, the sun was setting, the light golden. We'd been in here all day.

"We brought you some chow, at least." Sol motioned, and Steven set the tray down just inside the door. The smell of ginger and garlic made my stomach leap. "Thea should probably get first dibs."

"Steven, don't do this," Karen called. I stared at her; this wasn't part of the plan.

He kept his gaze fixed on the ground.

"*Look* at me, goddamnit," Karen yelled. Steven raised his head. "You know this isn't right, Steve. I know you know that. You're a good person."

Sol watched this play out, smiling pleasantly.

"I'm sorry, Karen." Steven's voice was barely audible.

"Grace and Clint are *dead*." She choked up. "Dead!"

"We'll see them again." He sounded like he was trying to be comforting.

"But . . ." She broke down into sobs.

"We want to see Moon," Mikki called, getting us back on track. "Why won't you let us see her, Sol? Scared she'll do something crazy? Again?"

Sol shook his head. "Listen, guys, I never wanted any of this to happen."

"Yeah, fucking right," Mikki muttered.

Sol scoffed. "You think this is good for the Center? *Murder?* Of course not. I want all this in the rearview mirror."

"You're a psychopath," I said. His gaze switched to me. "That's why this doesn't bother you that much. It's an annoyance, but really it's just an obstacle to overcome. You never believed in any of the past life stuff, did you? You just did what you had to do to keep Moon happy. Because your *business* is nothing without her."

I'd hoped to say this in front of Moon, but Steven would have to do. He'd tell her, I knew that. I could tell by the way he watched Sol, his eyes calculating.

"Therapy with Thea, huh?" Sol chuckled. "I love getting analyzed by people who are so unhappy you can smell it. You're pathetic. It's way past time to put you out of your misery. Steven? Let's go." They left, Sol slamming the door behind him.

Moon arrived sometime later.

The three of us were lying on a blanket we'd found, our heads on the scratchy wool, like we were enjoying a nice nap after a picnic lunch. My brain felt clear and quiet. The food was staying down, even though my stomach churned like an ice cream machine. Sol's words vibrated in my mind. *It's way past time to put you out of your misery.* I'd already suspected, but this proved it. Sol was going to kill us. He didn't relish it, but he didn't see an alternative. Maybe if he really did believe in the past life story, we could figure out a way to get him and Moon to let us go. But Sol wasn't about to let us disrupt his business. Much less risk prison.

When the door opened, a cool breeze swept in from the dark courtyard.

"Hi." Moon stood in the doorway, stars visible behind her. This time Joe was by her side, pointing a handgun. "You wanted to talk to me?"

"Yes." I struggled to my feet, and Karen and Mikki rose beside me. No need to waste time. "I know what we need to do."

"What is it?" Moon blinked, waiting politely. Thankfully, she'd changed out of the bloody shirt.

"We need to continue with the sacrifice."

Moon didn't answer, just waited for me to say more.

"I saw things down there," I said. "Past lives. Future lives. And it became clear to me why this sacrifice hasn't worked yet."

Moon took a step forward. "Why?"

"Because we all have to do it together."

Joe frowned. If only he lowered that gun, we could chance rushing him. But Moon might have a gun, too, tucked in her waistband, beneath her flannel jacket.

"Together," she repeated softly.

"There are people here who need to prove their belief." I stared at Joe. "We all incarnated together, we suffered together, and we need to sacrifice ourselves together. That's the only way it will work. Once we do, the world will shift towards the light, just like you said."

Joe glanced at Moon, his mouth downturned. He didn't like this at all.

"This is the way," Karen spoke up. "You can feel it, can't you?"

Moon played with her diamond necklace.

"And let Mikki go," I said. "She's not a part of this. Our group has to finish it together."

"How?" Moon asked.

I pointed up. "We all go to the roof. The tower. It's the best way."

Joe cleared his throat. "I think we should talk to Sol."

Moon ignored him. But after another second, she nodded at us and walked out. Joe followed and shut the door.

"Someone's faith is being put to the test," Mikki said wryly.

"I don't know if it worked." Karen sighed.

But in the same mysterious way that Catherine had known I'd take the bait of her crayoned letter, I knew Moon would do the same now.

"It worked," I said.

59

The three of us curled up on the blanket in the cold room, drifting in and out of dusky sleep, until the door unlocked again.

This time they were all here. Sol, Joe, and Steven all carried guns while Moon and Catherine held lanterns. How gendered. My hands were clammy and I wiped them on my pants. It was go time.

"Hello again." Sol wore a weird smile, and his eyes looked glazed. Was he on something? "So, let's go to the tower." He tossed a pair of my shoes towards me. "I hear you've offered to leap to your deaths. Which sounds unlikely, but stranger things have happened."

Karen nudged my arm as I pulled on my shoes, and I could sense her question: Had Moon not told Sol that we were *all* planning to do so? Was she going to put him on the spot upstairs? It'd make sense—there was no way he was going to agree with it beforehand. Or ever.

"Each of you will get a chaperone." Sol strolled forward. "Thea, I'd love to accompany you." He gestured for me to walk ahead of him. As we exited the room, I caught eyes with Catherine. She, like Steven and Joe, looked deadened and strange.

Though my body was flooded with fear, I felt a stab of pity for her. Moon and Sol would never have been able to seduce her if she'd been happy and healthy. They preyed on people in pain, who just wanted someone to tell them how to feel better. If I'd met Moon, I couldn't say for certain that *I* wouldn't have been pulled into her web of nurturing in the same exact way.

Maybe in different circumstances, Moon's healing could've remained just that. But her longing to help had mutated, devolving into something dark. All because of her fury towards an unfathomably unfair world.

I led the slow procession into the courtyard, up the stairs, down the hall, and up the spiral staircase. The metal staircase shook, and I wondered if it'd detach and fall under our combined weight. Sol shoved the cold, hard muzzle between my shoulder blades, urging me to go faster.

It was a clear night, the stars blazing overhead as I stepped onto the roof. The frigid wind had strengthened, whipping our hair. I thought of when I'd come up here the first time, mere days ago, viewing the rolling hills, the winding gravel drive, the mountains beyond. Now the horizon was black, like a drop cloth, beyond the weak light from the lanterns.

"Stand at the ledge, please," Sol instructed.

I stopped about a foot from the edge, lined with the slightly raised adobe. Below, the SUV and sedan looked like toy cars. This tower roof was the highest part of the castle—at least sixty or seventy feet up. Karen grabbed my hand and squeezed. Mikki stood on my other side. The three of us faced the group.

"Mikki shouldn't be here." I gestured. "She got caught up in this, but she's not one of us. Moon, you know that."

Moon nodded. "Mikki, you can go."

"What?" Sol cried. "Babe, no."

"I *said* she can go." Moon glared at Sol. "That's my final decision."

Sol's mouth worked. After a second he dropped his gun to his side and laughed. "Well, okay, then. I guess it's her word against ours." He smirked at Mikki. "But you know who the cops will believe, right?"

Mikki ignored him, keeping her eyes trained on Moon. Raising her hands, she took a step forward, then two. She then fled past Joe, Steven, and Catherine, racing through the doorway, down the clanging steps.

"Good god," Sol muttered. He waited, watching over the side. "Oh, there she goes."

We could just make out Mikki's small figure below as she sprinted past the vehicles, down the long driveway. Something in my chest loosened. This part of the plan, at least, had worked. Mikki would get to Clint's car, flag the first car she saw, get them to call the police.

"You happy?" Sol faced Moon. "That could really bite us in the ass, babe."

"Don't worry." Moon smiled. "This is all happening as it should."

"Are you a believer, Sol?" I asked.

His mouth was tight with irritation. "What?"

"I don't think you are." I gestured. "Joe either."

Sol squinted at me. "What are you playing at, Thea?" He and Moon were standing closest to us, Joe and Steven behind them, and Catherine by the door. There was not a ton of room to maneuver with this many people up here.

"We all have to go, Sol." I smiled at him. "You realize that, right?"

A slow grin spread across his face. "I see. You're playing chicken, huh? Because I sure as hell don't buy this new believer act."

"She's right." Moon set down her lantern. "It was never just Catherine or Thea. It's supposed to be all of us. We've been blinded by fear, Sol. We have to practice what we preach."

"What the fuck?" Sol whirled towards Moon. "When did this happen? You can't just make unilateral decisions, you know. We're supposed to be a team."

"The three of us came to this decision. Thea, Catherine, and me." She looked back at Catherine, leaning against the door. "Right?"

"Right," Catherine replied, her voice gravelly.

So Moon had talked to Catherine about my plan, and she had agreed. Then again, she would always agree with whatever Moon brought to her. She no longer had a working brain of her own.

"Babe." Sol sighed. "They're messing with you. They're trying to get us to off ourselves so they can go free. It's so obvious. It's so *stupid*."

"None of this is stupid." A note of irritation crept into Moon's voice. Steven came towards them, slowly, slipping his gun into his waistband.

"No, I just mean . . ." Sol puffed out air. "We need to discuss this."

Steven snatched the gun out of Sol's hand.

"Hey!" Sol lunged for it, but Steven backed away, training the gun on him. "Moon!" He turned to her, his eyes wide and desperate. "Honey, what the fuck!"

Steven handed the second gun to Moon. She pointed it at Sol. "We're all going together. You can go by choice, or not. It's up to you."

"Babe, please, stop." He held up his hands. "This isn't right. She tricked you. Thea and Catherine—both of them tricked you."

"Go to the edge." Steven said it in a gruff voice.

"Fuck no. This is ridiculous. I'm leaving."

"Sol," Moon warned. "Stop."

"No, I'm out of here." He strode towards the door. Catherine jumped out of the way.

Sol was in the doorway when Moon pulled the trigger.

The boom was deafening. I crouched down, hiding my face. There came a low groan, then nothing.

I opened my eyes. Sol was splayed out on his stomach, half in the doorway. The back of his jean jacket was soaked with blood, black as oil in the moonlight.

Karen started murmuring, praying, under her breath.

Moon went to him and bent over him, whispering. Catherine stared down at them both, hand pressed over her mouth.

One down!

I looked wildly around; now that the deaths were starting, they wouldn't end. There was no way Moon would have them all die first, leaving us for last. Our plan had extended to shrinking the pool of our captors, but there were still too many of them.

And there was just this small platform, a steep vertical fall over the edge. No way out.

Moon stood up, her eyes sparkling with excitement.

"I can feel it," she cried. "It's working!"

Joe went towards Sol, bent down as if to check his pulse, then stepped over him and took off down the stairs.

"Go!" Moon shouted and Steven ran after him. She scoffed, shook her head. "So many unbelievers. No wonder it didn't work."

Karen and I glanced at each other. Now it was us two against Moon and Catherine. Only one gun.

"They'll come back," I said. "Moon, it's your turn. You, then me, then Catherine." It was worth a shot.

Moon's eyes gleamed. "*Was* this your plan, Thea? Test our faith so that we self-destruct?"

"Of course not." I could hear the desperation in my voice; I tried to force it down. The only way this could work was if I could remain calm and convincing.

"Because I think *you* should go next. Sol has already sacrificed himself. It's your turn." She gestured to the ledge. "Either you or Karen. You get to choose."

"I'll go," Karen said, pausing in her mumblings. "Let me."

"No, Karen." I pushed her away from the edge.

Moon trained her gun on me. She wiped at her face and a smear of blood appeared on her cheek. "Let's do this now before Steven brings Joe back."

Karen tried to take my place, but I shoved her back hard. She stumbled and fell, her head slamming into the raised edge of adobe. She remained still, in a heap.

Fuck. Now it was just me. And if I ran at Moon, she would pull the trigger.

"I'm sorry." I forced myself to take a deep breath. "I'm sorry you went through what you went through. You had a hard time. You lost people."

"I didn't lose them," Moon snarled. "They were *murdered*. By evil people possessed by greed."

"I know. And it ripped a hole in you that never healed. I know."

"But *this* will heal it!" She laughed. "Aren't you ready to end the pattern? Haven't you been waiting your whole life for it?"

"I think we should stay, Moon. We can end the pattern here."

She shook her head. "This is the only way. Come on. We'll go together." She lowered the gun and strode towards me. I envisioned the pushes that had sent Clint down the cave steps, Talia over the tower's edge. I steeled myself, leaning towards her.

But then Moon stopped with a gasp. Catherine was behind her, one arm slipped around her waist. Moon whipped around and I saw it: the same kitchen knife lodged deep in Moon's side. Catherine let go, and Moon raised the gun at her.

"No!" I leapt behind Moon, holding her hand down. The gun went off, shaking the ground beneath our feet. She twisted her wrist, but I held it with all my might.

"Stop!" Moon screamed, struggling. "You have to come with me! You have to come with me!" She tried to wrench from my grip while Catherine, breathing hard, propelled her towards the ledge. Moon stumbled backwards—one step, two, three—until her heels just kissed the adobe edge.

The three of us were connected, and if we weren't careful, Moon's jerks would pull us all over.

"Let go," I shouted at Catherine, whose arm was clamped on Moon's shoulder. She would have to be quick: unlocking and pushing Moon backwards at the same time.

But Catherine didn't let go. As I released Moon's wrist, I saw her other hand snaked around Catherine's waist, grabbing the back of her shirt, her knuckles so white her small hand looked like a skeleton's. They pressed against each other like they were slow dancing.

Moon raised her freed hand, pointing the gun towards me, eyes flashing with rage. I froze in place, watching the barrel's swift ascent.

With a cry, Catherine managed to shove it back down, blocking me with her body in the split second before they jerked over into empty air.

"No!" I cried, but it was too late. They tumbled over the edge.

60

I didn't want to look.

With a gasping sob, I dropped to my hands and knees and crawled to the edge.

There: the small, still pile of limbs, clothes, and hair, silvery in the faint moonlight.

"Fuck," I muttered. I could still sense the scuffle in the air, like a scent. It had all happened so fast. I went to Karen, touching her shoulder. She groaned.

"Karen." I whispered. "We have to hide. Steven and Joe—I don't know where they are. We have to hide until the police get here."

She sat up slowly, looking stunned. "Where—"

"They fell." It hadn't hit me yet, the full force of what had just happened. And in fact I didn't want it to—not until Karen and I were safe.

"Oh no," she wailed.

"Karen, shh. We need to be quiet. Where should we go?"

"Um." She gulped. "Let's go to my room. I can turn on the Wi-Fi on the way."

"Okay." I helped her up. We stepped carefully over Sol's body in the doorway, went down the metal staircase that creaked too loudly.

We started hearing it when we reached the second-floor landing: faint yells. Both of us stopped, clutching each other.

It came again: "Help!"

"It's coming from the cave." Karen hurried down the stairs, through the courtyard and into the room with the purple door. I followed, fear spiraling through my chest.

"Karen, wait!" I paused in the doorway as she approached the top of the stone staircase.

"Joe?" she called.

"Karen!" His voice went up an octave. "He fucking shot me! That motherfucker shot me!"

"Steven?" she said.

"Yes!"

"Where is he?"

"He's down here. I think he's . . . fuck." Joe's voice cracked into a sob. "I didn't want to hurt him, Karen. But he was shooting at me!"

"I know, hon." Karen bobbed her head. "It's okay. We're going to get help."

"It's bleeding a lot, Karen." Now he was fully crying. "It really hurts."

"Just stay put. We'll get help." Face pale, Karen came away from the edge and shut the inner door, hiding the hole from sight. She turned the dead bolt on the outside.

"What should we do?" I hissed. I couldn't imagine helping our captor, but I also didn't want to be the reason he died.

"Nothing." Karen shook her head. "We can't trust him, and he still has a gun. I'm going to get Sol's phone and call an ambulance. It'll take them a while to get here."

I followed her back into the courtyard, but paused as she started back up the stairs. "I need to check on Catherine. I think she's gone, but . . ."

"You do that." Karen gave a brisk nod.

Outside, the indigo sky was just starting to lighten. It felt suddenly difficult to lift my feet, to walk over to the pile.

For a moment I just looked, breathing in the clean, herbal air now tinged with a metallic undertone. Catherine and Moon were still locked in an embrace, facing each other. Catherine's copper hair covered most of her face, except for her mouth, which was open in an unending scream. Beneath her crown, the ground was dark with blood.

I bent down next to her, pressing my fingers to her throat even as I knew she was dead.

She'd saved me. In my mind's eye, I saw the alternative play out: Moon managing to raise the gun, steady herself, shoot me straight in the heart.

A small movement, then a soft moan.

It was Moon. She rolled her head upwards. Her eyes popped open, staring up at the sky.

I went to her side, pulling the gun from her grasp and tossing it away before settling on my knees. Her lips—marked with a small stream of blood—opened and closed. I bent closer.

"I can't move." Her eyes trained on me, wide and frightened.

"Help's coming." My voice shook. "You'll be okay." Why was I comforting her, this woman who'd murdered people in front of my eyes? I could get up right now, turn my back on her and walk away. But for some reason, I stayed.

"I don't want to die." Her eyes filled with tears.

"It's okay," I said. And then, because I couldn't help but console someone imminently meeting death: "You'll come back. Right? You'll come back in the next life."

Her head jerked: involuntary movement or nod?

"Thea!" Karen's crunching steps came towards me. "Ambulances are on their way." She stopped. "Are they . . ."

"Moon's still alive."

Karen exhaled. "I don't think so, hon. She's gone."

I glanced down. Moon's unblinking golden eyes were fixed on the stars.

61

It was Easter weekend and the trees were budding, little verdant sparkles. It felt comforting to be on a train, rushing through the landscape, watching it whip by.

I wondered again about my urge to leave the city for the weekend. Dom had been supremely supportive over the last few weeks, making me soup and bringing me blankets like I had the chicken pox. During the few days I'd been gone, she and Amelia had gotten into a huge blowout and decided to take a break, so we were renewing our lease for another year.

It had been a big relief to be able to stay put during this time. The news of Catherine's strange and horrifying death had blown up, both high- and lowbrow outlets covering the cult massacre. Six people had died—including Joe and Steven, who were both gone by the time the ambulance arrived. Seven, if you counted Grace.

Somehow multiple journalists had gotten my name and number, and I now had a dozen voicemails I was ignoring. A photographer had even shown up at my apartment, shocking me with the *click-click-click* of his camera as I unlocked my door. A week later, a scandal with a much more famous actress broke, and the public eye turned away.

I'd started back at work last week, and luckily the patients had totally missed the story. Amani and Rachel had dug for details, and Diane had called me into her office to confirm I was receiving "support." That plus Dom's concern had caused me to start scanning the therapist listings.

I realized now that my old therapist Cynthia had handled our termination badly. She should've made sure I was in an okay place before cutting off our sessions, and/or supported me in transitioning to someone new. And even though we hadn't been working together anymore, she could've responded to my desperate text.

In my eyes, she'd messed up. But she was human. And even if I started with the Perfect Therapist, someone with incredible attunement skills, it didn't mean that we wouldn't have disagreements and misunderstandings. This time, though, I wanted the chance to work through them. This process was so inevitable that there was even a therapy term for it: "rupture and repair."

I'd met twice with a woman named Toni. I hadn't yet told her what had happened at the Center: it was too fresh, and there would be weeks, months, and years to fully process what I'd experienced. For now we were talking about my alcohol use (which I'd curtailed since being back), my family of origin, and everything that had happened with Pastor John and Adam. They were all so connected, so intertwined: the early emotional neglect and the later abuse, both creating pain that only alcohol—a coping mechanism that was often sanctioned and even encouraged—had been able to soften.

I'd also forced myself to tell her about the orgasm situation. I hadn't felt at all sexual since the Center, but I knew that would eventually change. Regardless of whether or not I still needed to imagine the shed, there was a lot of excavating and healing I wanted to do in this area. It felt time to integrate those deep threads of dominance and submission, light and dark, that would probably always be with me.

Another thing to eventually discuss: The lingering sense that there had been something inexplicable going on out in the desert. That while Moon had been destructive, using her beliefs to justify horrible things, she'd known things about me—my dreams, details of my current life trauma—that she shouldn't have.

Maybe it'd be helpful to talk to Karen about it—when she was no longer under investigation and could be in contact with me again. The one time we'd texted, she'd mentioned starting to "deprogram" with specialists and also attending grief counseling. I wondered how long it would take to unravel what she'd believed and what she'd done.

Because I myself felt confused by what I'd seen and experienced. If Catherine and I weren't deeply connected, if she was someone I'd just met just for a short time, then why was my grief for her so intense that I couldn't look at it directly? There was guilt too—because if Catherine and I had left at 4:00 a.m., maybe Joe would've let us go. Maybe she'd still be alive.

There was no way to know.

To ease this, sometimes I let myself imagine that all of it was true:

That Catherine and I had been sisters in a past life. That we'd been given the opportunity to save not the world but each other. She'd clearly sacrificed herself for me on the roof. Maybe I'd do the same for her, in a life far into the future. I remembered the kaleidoscope I'd envisioned in the cave, and for some reason it made me think about all those lives, happening simultaneously. Moon had said it to me first: *Time is a construct, right? So these lives are all happening at the same time.* Was that the reason Catherine and I couldn't remember saying yes to the snake spirit? Because we hadn't decided until we were on the roof, or in the spaceship?

I knew that these far-out musings were just me trying to help myself feel better, less culpable. But they usually left me feeling unmoored and wistful. There may be larger mysteries about death I'd never know the answers to. But the truth about Catherine, at least, was concrete: she was gone.

A text dinged from Mikki: Hey! Still on for lunch next week?

I responded with an Of course! Mikki was finishing up her major outlet story, an essay-like piece about her experience and about how she'd initially been pulled in to investigate Moon's impersonation of a Mexican woman. I'd told her more about Moon and Sol's belief in reincarnation, but not the visions I'd seen in the sweat lodge and cave. I didn't want to give their philosophy more credence, nor prompt any more anonymous hate messages from their unhinged virtual followers.

A new text from Dom: Did you see this???? A link to an hour-long documentary on a streaming service: *Sex Cult Love.* I squinted at the description. *They looked for love in the unlikeliest of places—and found each other.*

"Wait, what?" I murmured. I grabbed my headphones and clicked play.

Dawne and Ramit filled the screen. They were sitting on stools, in front of a background of a tidy, blank living room.

"My name is Dawne." Her makeup, so flashy in real life, looked perfect on-screen. "I was at the Center for Relational Healing and left about a week before the massacre." She turned to look at Ramit.

"I'm Ramit." He seemed much more uncomfortable, his eyes wide and darting. "I was also at the Center before the massacre."

"It's actually really ironic." Dawne squeezed Ramit's arm. "We went to the Center to find love, but we found only hate. When Ramit and I reconnected in LA to process what we'd been through, we realized the answer was right in front of us." A grin overtaking her face, she held up her left hand. "We each found our soulmate." The camera panned in on the enormous diamond, glittering merrily in the studio lights.

I'd sent my parents an article (the least garish one) so they knew what had happened, but Mom didn't ask about it beyond "Are you okay?" when picking me up from the station. Her lip curled with unconscious distaste: my suffering still made her acutely uncomfortable. Dad gave me a slightly longer hug than normal when I saw him at the house but didn't bring it up.

That night—like every night—I hoped to dream about Catherine. But I woke without remembering anything. I took a long walk around the property on Saturday, taking pictures of the flowers springing up. The daffodils were so cheerful-looking.

Mom and Dad were surprised when I said I wanted to go to church with them on Sunday morning. We drove there in silence, my dress hanging on me because of the cave-induced weight loss I was still recovering from. The brick building came into view with the familiar sign out front: OUR SAVIOR CHURCH AND SCHOOL.

Decades later, my parents still went faithfully to the hybrid church/school that had so affected me. In college I'd finally refused to go—a bold move for me—so it had been many years since I'd been back. It looked exactly the same as I remembered. I glanced at the jungle gym on the way in; the rubber surface of the ground looked new. I pictured my younger self standing by the slide, posing for the class picture.

It smelled the same too. A mixture of cleaning products and sweaty children and mustiness. We passed the gym and several classrooms on the way in. Up the stairs, past the enormous picture of a blond, pretty Jesus standing over his flock.

I felt strangely calm. At least until I saw her, standing in a group of people talking in the narthex. My old best friend Melissa, jiggling a baby in her arms.

My chest tightened as she glanced at me, sensing my gaze. She looked shockingly like her mom two decades before. I remembered my last message to her: Maybe ask your amazing husband how he took advantage of me on our eighth-grade trip while calling me horrible things (fat, ugly, etc). Unless you knew already?

But as if nothing had happened, she grinned. "Oh my gosh! Thea!" She hurried over and pulled me in for a half hug. "Hi, Mr. and Mrs. Meyer! Oh yes, this is my youngest, Luke."

The surprise quickly melted away. Of course she wasn't going to bring up my message. She and I had both been raised in an environment where people constantly pretended not to see the upsetting things going on around them. I thought suddenly of Mrs. Iona, our eighth-grade teacher, who had placidly ignored the daily bullying happening right under her nose.

I pasted a smile on my face as she chatted with my parents, who excused themselves to get their preferred seats. I scanned behind her for Adam. That old fear reared up, but as Melissa watched me, swaying with her baby, a wave of calm washed over me.

I'd gone through more than either of them could imagine. This was nothing.

"Is Adam here too?" I'd go right up to him, stare him in the face, and shake his hand, if only to let him know that I was here, that I existed.

"He's on a boys' trip this weekend." She smiled less brightly, her lips pressed together. "Anyway, how are you? I haven't seen you here in forever. What brings you back?"

"Oh, you know. Just wanted to get out of the city."

She nodded sagely as Luke burbled at me. "I've heard it can be a lot." She grinned. "Please tell me you're staying for the reunion next weekend?"

"I'm thinking about it," I lied.

"Great!" She seemed satisfied. "We can catch up more then."

"Mommy!" A toddler ran up to Melissa and grabbed her leg, staring up at me.

"This is Catherine." Melissa put a protective hand on her head.

The name startled me. "Catherine?"

"Say hi, honey," Melissa directed.

"Hi," she said shyly. While Luke had his mom's blue eyes and wide mouth, Catherine's dark curls and dimple were pure Adam.

"Hi there." I smiled at her. Just a coincidence. Nothing more.

"Let's go find Mrs. Becker." Melissa took her hand. "We'll chat more next weekend, okay?"

"Sounds good." I squared my shoulders and went into the church.

Thirty minutes later, I studied Pastor John at the pulpit, expounding on Jesus's miraculous return. The sickly-sweet scent from the Easter lilies filled the sanctuary.

He looked older, though I knew that from his Facebook profile: sandy hair receding, beard patched with white, crinkles around his nose and mouth. He must be in his mid-forties now. It struck me, for the first time, that I couldn't have been the only teen he'd had an inappropriate relationship with. Who knew—it was possible that he'd felt bad about it, vowed to change his ways. But the way he'd responded to my Facebook message . . .

You fucked up my life.
I'm sorry you feel that way.

He still had that smirking overconfidence, maybe even more so now, similar to a certain cult leader I'd known.

I'd been waiting for his eyes to meet mine, pulled in by my laser gaze. But there were hundreds in the crowd, and so far it hadn't happened.

What if I stood up and yelled the truth of what he'd done to me?

I already knew the answer: he would smile sadly, call for security, say that he hoped that poor woman got help.

I was sitting on the edge of the row, and even though it was the middle of the sermon, I got up and headed up the aisle, towards the exit.

In the narthex, I took a deep breath. Mom and Dad would be embarrassed that I'd walked out, but their judgment no longer affected me. I wandered down the hall to get a sip of water from the fountain (how many times had I drunk from it?). One of the nearby classrooms was full of kids, their laughs and exclamations spilling into the hall.

Sunday school. I took a few steps closer, and a familiar woman inside smiled at me.

I approached the doorway. "Holly, hi." *Mrs. Becker*—it was Holly

Becker, who'd been in our class. "How are you? You're teaching Sunday school?"

"Yep." She looked disturbingly similar to her eighth-grade self, her long blond hair still in a high ponytail. She seemed somehow unsurprised to see me. "How are you? Haven't seen you in a long time."

"Yeah, I know, it's been a while. I'm good." I noticed she was standing above Melissa's daughter, Catherine, who was scribbling away at a piece of paper. "How many of these kids are from people in our grade?"

"A couple." She surveyed the room. She'd been another nerdy kid, and I remembered with shame that at some point, I'd stood silently by while Ashley and Adam had made fun of her acne. "How long you back?"

"Just the weekend."

"I saw what happened." Holly's bright eyes found mine. "In New Mexico. Wow. Are you okay?"

"Yeah, I'm fine." I said the words automatically.

She looked like she wanted to ask more, but suddenly Catherine jumped up and ran over to me. She pushed a piece of paper at my thigh.

"Read!" she yelled.

I laughed at her insistence. "Okay. Thank you."

I turned the paper over. It was messy but discernable: a triangle surrounded by a spiral. The triangle had a door and windows: it was a house.

"Why . . ." I looked up, but Catherine had already scuttled back to her seat and was violently crayoning a new piece of paper.

"She's really into tornadoes these days." Holly pointed to the spiral.

Little Catherine looked nothing like Big Catherine. She was too old to be the reincarnated version of her, anyway.

But it was something. A small reaching out. A sign.

As much as I wanted to keep it, I handed the paper back to Holly. It would look weird for me to hold on to it.

"Hunter!" Holly cried out, swooping back into the room as another toddler started to hit and scream at his neighbor.

I backed away, into the hall. I could hear voices from the church in a rousing call and response with Pastor John.

"He is risen!"

"He is risen indeed!"

I continued away from the noise, down the stairs and outside where the sun shone pale overhead. I sat on a bench, suddenly looking forward to taking the train back to the city that night. To going to work tomorrow. I'd begged Diane, and she'd finally relented, maybe because she was still concerned about me: we were going to start using watercolors in art therapy group, not just crayons. There was a new patient named Jessa who'd reacted with an actual squeal to this news.

I'd also ordered an easel and some canvases for myself, and they were set to arrive in the next few days. I'd already pulled out sketch pads, oil paints, and charcoal pencils from the back of my closet. They sat ready and waiting in the corner of my room.

The playground was empty. I smiled at the ghost of my young self near the slide. All this time, she'd been stuck here. But I'd take her with me when I left. She'd be reunited with her diary, which now sat on my nightstand. And neither of us would have to come back here again.

I'd finally done it: I'd broken the pattern.

Acknowledgments

First and foremost, thanks to you, dear reader, for picking up this book. It's been one of the great joys of my life to connect with readers like you, being an avid reader myself. I'm especially appreciative because you have so many options of what to do with your time these days—it means more than I can express that you would choose to spend some of it within these pages.

Thank you to the readers, booksellers, librarians, reviewers, event organizers, and bookstagrammers who championed *The Writing Retreat*—you completely changed my life. I have so much gratitude for you, and I can only hope you connect with *The Last Session* too.

One of the reasons I wrote this book was to explore the ongoing draw of cults. I credit two main books (along with countless other books, documentaries, and articles) for helping me understand the intricacies of cult psychology: *Combating Cult Mind Control*, by Steven Hassan, and *Slonim Woods 9*, a virtuosic and haunting memoir by Daniel Barban Levin, who survived the Larry Ray/Sarah Lawrence cult.

In this book, I also wanted to explore the throughline of white supremacy within past and modern-day spiritual communities, especially with regard to appropriation. I want to thank some of the writers who have informed my ever-evolving understanding of this topic: adrienne maree brown, Prentis Hemphill, Tricia Hersey, Robin DiAngelo, bell hooks, Isabel Wilkerson, and Resmaa Menakem. Thank you also to Sky Koltun and Rebecca Liebmann-Smith for our anti-racist therapist group, which has helped me better understand the psychology of white supremacy.

I have unending gratitude to the incredible team at Emily Bestler Books/Atria; I am so lucky to work with you all. Thank you to Emily for your unflagging enthusiasm and deep wisdom. Thank you to Hydia Scott-Riley for going above and beyond in your assistance and support for this book. Thank you to my publicist Alison Hinchcliffe and marketing manager Maudee Genao—you are both the best of the best. Thank you also to publisher Libby McGuire, associate publisher Dana Trocker, cover designer and art director Jimmy Iacobelli, interior designer Esther Paradelo, managing editor Paige Lytle, and assistant managing editor Shelby Pumphrey. I truly can't convey how much I appreciate you.

Thank you to my agent, the brilliant Alexandra Machinist—it is such a dream to work with you—and to Xanthe Coffman for your helpful assistance. Thank you to Sarah Harvey and Cathryn Summerhayes for your invaluable work on foreign rights. Thank you also to Josie Freedman, film agent extraordinaire.

Thank you to those who read early drafts of this novel: Stephanie Wrobel, Donna Freitas, Rebecca Liebmann-Smith, Andrea Bartz, Amanda Leipold, Ana Reyes, Meghan Felice, and Saumya Dave. Your feedback was crucial, and I'm so lucky to know you all!

Thank you to those I spoke with for research purposes: Pat Feghali, Erin McSherry, and Patrick Gendron, thank you for helping me better understand New Mexico, particularly its remotest areas. Thank you to Robert Laird, cofounder of IUCRR, for offering feedback on underwater cave rescue and recovery, as well as the fascinating anecdote about seeing "the light" that you kindly allowed me to use. Thank you to Florrie Barron and Annie Wendland for offering important feedback about working in a psychiatric unit. Thank you to Western New Mexico University Museum for providing helpful information about Mimbres pottery and practices. Thank you to Rebecca Liebmann-Smith, for coming on my research road trip and making it so much more than that!

Thank you to my mentors, therapists, and healers: Britton Williams, Erika Ackerman, Meghana Sawant, Pam Arm, and all the meditation/yoga teachers at HealHaus.

Thank you to my family and chosen family for your ongoing encouragement and support. I love you guys. And thank you to Rey González, a source of my own relational healing. *Te amo.*